ASCENSION

KELAHYA UNBOUND

ASCENSION

KELAHYA UNBOUND

V. & D. POVALL

This book is a work of fiction. The names, characters and events in this book are the products of the author's imagination or are used fictitiously. Any similarity to real persons living or dead is coincidental and not intended by the author.

Ascension – Kelahya Unbound

Published by Dragonfly Media
Oceanside, CA

ISBN (paperback): 9781662900389
eISBN: 9781662900396
Library of Congress Control Number: 2020935393

Writing never happens in a vacuum.
Many are those who help in different ways.

Thanks

To
Ray Bradbury and Isaac Asimov for igniting our imagination,
and to J.K. Rowling for inspiring us in the creation of an
imaginary world.

To
J.D. Barker, our mentor, who inspired, encouraged, and
reinvigorated us. His guidance enabled us to expand the
narrative and discover new paths.

To
Bob and Jim, for their willingness to jump into this world
and find the areas that didn't sing for them and
needed our attention. Their advice was invaluable.

Contents

Introduction: Talderon Era — ix

Chapter 1 Kelahya Devona — 1

Chapter 2 Dionysus — 12

Chapter 3 Intelligence Gathering — 30

Chapter 4 Minders — 46

Chapter 5 Warfare Tactics — 59

Chapter 6 The Alliance of Stars — 73

Chapter 7 The Endow — 82

Chapter 8 The Olympus — 95

Chapter 9 Nastrius Astronomy — 111

Chapter 10 The Endow's Event Horizon — 125

Chapter 11 Cybernetic Organisms — 142

Chapter 12 Commodore Zenubus Priaminian — 159

Chapter 13 Subterfuge — 169

Chapter 14 Torture — 184

Chapter 15 Procreation — 192

Chapter 16 The Continuum — 203

Chapter 17 Gambit — 216

Chapter 18 Talderon Ideals — 228

Chapter 19 Humanoid Experimentation — 242

Chapter 20 Inexorable Attraction   256

Chapter 21 Lies   265

Chapter 22 Dissociative Trauma   273

Chapter 23 The Zontirius   287

Chapter 24 Prophecy   299

Chapter 25 Mind Fusion Techniques   311

Chapter 26 Spiritual Teachings   321

Chapter 27 Subversion   337

Chapter 28 Good and Evil   348

Chapter 29 Revenge   362

Chapter 30 Superstitions   377

Chapter 31 IWE   395

Biography   407

Introduction
Talderon Era

———◆———

*Excerpt from the **Corpus Galacticum**, 137th Edition*

*In the centuries that followed the **Ethnopecuniary Wars** in the 9th millennium, violence and chaos ruled most civilizations in the galaxies. The extensive displacement of the various inhabitants of the known civilizations became identified as the age of **Anarchic Disarray**. As humanoids expanded through the universe, mutations began to occur. Some changes resulted in diseases that wiped out entire planets, others produced physical transformations, and a few resulted in the evolution of superior mental development. That is when **Minders** (beings capable of reading and influencing the minds of most species in the universe) emerged, and with them the struggle for power took center stage.*

*During the 1st Century TE (Talderon Era), the **Incorporeal Fellowship** arose in an effort to establish universal order through the issuance of the **Talderon Ideals**. Its stated objective was the establishment of rules of behavior and spirituality, intended to enable civilizations across the known universe to have a common* *ground for bringing about spiritual, social, and political balance.*

*The universal order required that the **Incorporeal Fellowship** originate patterns in the mental mutations to maintain stability. As a result, each mutation was categorized into varying levels of proficiency, and specific universal tasks were ordained accordingly.*

*Two Minders, **Nestor** (the creator of the Talderon Ideals) and **Poliate** (the founder of the Alliance of Stars, were ordained to lead in their respective domains.*

Nestor, and his direct descendants, were destined to become the spiritual leaders and assume the mantle and name of Nestor, Supreme Pontiff of the Galactic Sanctuary, and Scribe for the Incorporeal Fellowship.

Poliate, and all his direct descendants, were to inherit secular command and the mantle of Poliate with the titles Director of the League of One and Supreme Commander of the Alliance of Stars.

The balance of power shared between two leaders of equal rank, brought about spiritual, social, and political stability for over five centuries.

*The Fellowship's succession remained unbroken until the mysterious disappearance of the last known Nestor during the insurrectionist rebellion of 684 (TE). This unexpected calamity forced **Kronos Deucarrion**, descendent of Poliate, Director of the League of One and Supreme Commander of the Alliance of Stars, to assume the mantle of spiritual leader. Thus, he became Supreme Pontiff of the Galactic Sanctuary, and Scribe for the Incorporeal Fellowship as well. In a gesture of humility, he declared himself unworthy of bearing the names of both Poliate and Nestor, and chose to rule under his birth name Kronos Deucarrion.*

*Kronos' rule has imposed peace and stability throughout the galaxies, and he is credited with numerous victories over rebel insurrections that have threatened his dominance. He is particularly celebrated for his unyielding commitment to suppress the **Rebellion**—the underground uprising created to destroy the universal order—which named its leader 'Nestor' in a flagrant affront to the Talderon Ideals ordained by the Incorporeal Fellowship.*

*One of his most powerful weapons in the fight against the insurrectionists is **Kelahya Devona**.*

CHAPTER 1

Kelahya Devona

—◆—

Kelahya Devona, *born in the 680th cycle TE (Talderon Era) to Terrian mother, Felicia Loran and Dyonisian father, Modyor Devon. She became ward of Kronos Deucarrion after their sudden deaths.*

An exceptional warrior, she ascended in rank with unprecedented speed and currently holds the coveted position of General of the Alliance of Stars and Commander of the XXVII Confinement Brigade.

As the right hand of Kronos Deucarrion, she has brought about innumerable victories in the pursuit of peace throughout the Universe. Her dexterity, intellect, and acuity are legendary, as is her fluency in countless dialects and languages.

She is believed to have assumed numerous identities to penetrate the ranks of various cells within the Rebellion brining about their demise.

Murderer!

"No!" Kelahya shrieked. "Not me!"

She glanced with alarm about the cabin. She was alone. No one on the space freighter could hear her. A cold sweat sent a shiver down her entire body.

Images of blood and death flooded her consciousness—Kronos, throat open ear to ear, collapsed to the floor, eyes fixed on hers.

Murderer!

She clamped her hands over her ears. "Not me. Never. It's a lie. He's not dead. How could I? He's everything to me."

And yet, he made you what you are. A spy, a killer, the nightmare behind her eyelids asserted. *He forced you to sacrifice it all for him. The powerful Kronos Deucarrion, omnipotent ruler, charmer, politician, and...*

"And?"

...master of genocide. Have you forgotten?

She squeezed her eyes shut. "No...I refuse to believe it."

Then, why run? Why escape?

"To find the truth."

That's a contradiction.

"Stop! The only thing that matters is the truth."

Then, why lie to yourself? Where is your laser knife?

"I don't remember. Lost."

Not lost, the voice inside her head insisted. *We both know the truth.*

"You're determined we do, but we don't. We're hurt, we're dissociating, we—"

Kelahya, enough! Find your courage. We need it. Now!

She fought back tears as she peered out the large porthole and stared into space. For the first time since boarding the freighter she noticed the hum of the ionic thrusters.

We must regain composure...Focus on the past...

"Why the past?"

Because the past is where the truth lives. Dive into a memory of a time when you were invincible...Altonia.

She shook her head. "Pure luck."

No. You were indomitable. Courage and ingenuity never failed you. They brought about your rise to Commander and, more importantly, won you the respect and admiration of the all-powerful Kronos.

After a few deep breaths, she leaned back in her seat. Her pulse slowed and the pounding in her head subsided. With eyes closed, she willed herself to a different time.

"Cuetzalan must be destroyed, Kelahya." Kronos himself had selected her to command this crucial battle, despite her fledgling military career. "He and his followers must be executed without clemency. Do you understand?"

"Perfectly, my Lord."

Kronos always dealt firmly but fairly with insurrectionists and terrorists. The unequivocal order to terminate Cuetzalan and his allies had been more extreme than usual, but so were the crimes for which they were responsible.

This mission represented the most important command he had ever entrusted to her. A test that would define her military future.

"Ulasti, change of plans. Have Blue Squadron drop to sector two," Kelahya spoke the words with unquestionable confidence. "Cuetzalan's forces must be destroyed before we land. He won't expect you to come from that sector. Do it now."

"Acknowledged," came the quick reply.

Captain Mathiah intruded into her private comm. "Major, permission to speak freely."

"Talk."

"Our actions contradict the orders of Commodore Priaminian. Are you authorized to go against the Minister of Defense and Control?"

"He may be the Prime Strategist of the Alliance, but he isn't here, and I am. This tactical decision represents the best, if not the only chance for victory with minimum loss under current circumstances."

"There will be hell to pay."

"I'll take my chances. Follow my orders, Captain."

"Understood, Major."

You've gone against the Commodore's instructions before, and always managed to come away victorious. As usual, her consciousness stepped in to scrutinize her decision.

Conversations with her inner self, were the time-tested way in which Kelahya had learned to analyze every event in her life. A habit from her formative years which she had learned to rely on without question.

"Indecision leads to defeat. I learned that lesson the hard way."

And you never repeat past mistakes. Determination, quick wit, and perspicacity have set you apart.

"That's why many resent and fear me."

They also admire and respect you.

"If you say so."

"Cuetzalan's forces at twelve clicks west of our present position," Ulasti reported. "A unit of the League of One troopers is half a click behind them and gaining."

"Understood," she said with a smirk of satisfaction.

To the ordinary observer, it appeared that Cuetzalan's attack plan spelled doom for the troopers.

"Captain Mathiah, let's give the Emperor a little surprise. Deploy your forces at Halfmoon Pass on my command."

"It will be so, Major," came the response.

She checked the monitor array. "Gold Squadron, on my command, Oblivion Mode."

The screen showed Cuetzalan's men rushing the troopers as they advanced through the gorge with the obvious intent of trapping them.

Kelahya smiled. As she expected, moments later, Cuetzalan's hidden divisions emerged from their concealed positions and surrounded the troopers in a vice-like grip.

"Mathiah, deploy. Ulasti, attack. Gold Squadron, follow me, fire at will. Happy hunting everyone." She squeezed the throttle and her Raptor shot through the canyon toward Halfmoon Pass, the Gold Squadron fighters aligned behind her like a ribbon of fire.

Mathiah's men spilled from the transporters and rushed in behind Cuetzalan himself. His entire division, taken by surprise, scrambled desperately to encircle their leader.

Kelahya's squadron strafed the hapless soldiers as they scrambled to reform a line of defense. Ulasti's Blue Squadron mowed down their quarry like sorghum under a harvester, then rushed to join Gold Squadron.

In less than thirty hexicons, the previously undefeated armies of Emperor Cuetzalan, the most feared in the quadrant, were reduced to a few dozen encircling the tyrannical leader. Their comrades' bodies lay strewn by the thousands, blanketing the hillsides and ravines of Altonia, while the armies of the League of One suffered less than two hundred casualties. It constituted a monumental victory by any standard.

Kronos himself couldn't have done better.

"All units cover me. I'm going to pay a visit to our defeated tyrant," Kelahya ordered. "Containment Mode at your discretion."

"Major," it was Captain Mathiah's voice on the communicator, "let one of us handle his capture. Director Kronos will have our heads if anything happens to you, and—"

"You have my orders, Captain."

"Aye, Major," came the meek reply.

Kelahya guided her attack Raptor down to the surface with deliberate slowness. By the time her craft settled and the side hatch opened, a protective squad of troopers surrounded the vessel.

Kelahya stepped forward and paused to take in the scene of her triumph. She towered above the troopers, and the beauty and power that emanated from this Amazon warrior intimidated even her closest allies. She read in the faces of her soldiers a clear admiration for having led them to such an overwhelming success.

Captain Mathiah stepped before her, a scowl clouding his face. "Kelahya, I implore you to return to your ship and let us handle this. It's far too dangerous."

She smiled at him. Five cycles together at the academy had earned him the license to address her with such familiarity. "Do you recall that history lesson in, what was it, level three? The one where Professor Gaugh told us how Kronos dealt with tyrants and traitors before he became Scribe, and the satisfaction his victories gave him?"

Mathiah nodded.

"Well, instead of coming himself, Kronos entrusted me with this mission."

"That is precisely why—"

"Would you deprive me of the satisfaction of seeing the look on this murderer's face when he realizes that it is I, not Kronos, who has brought him to this well-deserved end?"

Mathiah stepped close enough to avoid being heard by his soldiers. "Kelahya, this situation is far too volatile. You may be able to read and control the minds of many species, but if anything should go wrong, Kronos will execute us all."

She placed her hands on his shoulders in a gesture of understanding. "Nothing will happen, Mathiah. Trust me," she whispered.

The Captain dropped his head and nodded, then stepped back and resumed military decorum. "At the ready!" he commanded.

The platoon snapped to attention and swiftly formed a protective box that moved to engulf Kelahya and lead her off to meet Cuetzalan.

She arrived before the Emperor's tent and looked inquisitively at her squadron leader who stood with his men facing Cuetzalan's Imperial Guard.

"He refuses to come out."

"Does he, now?" Kelahya grinned. "Let's persuade him." She stepped toward the tent with the clear objective of going in.

The sound of scraping metal cut the air, and before anyone could react, three of Cuetzalan's Imperial Guards lunged at Kelahya, daggers in hand. She spun around to face her attackers. A flurry of motion followed, and a moment later, the three men lay dead at her feet, each stabbed in the neck with his own knife. The splatter of their blood mottled Kelahya's uniform.

"Anyone else?" she said with a look of disdain.

Alliance officers and soldiers stood silent, mouths agape in stunned amazement. The remaining Imperial Guards dropped to their knees. Kelahya had struck with deadly precision. No one present had ever witnessed such prowess.

"You knew they would attack," Mathiah whispered behind her. "You let them do it."

"A Minder's advantage, my friend." A spot of blood appeared through a gash on Kelahya's left sleeve. She glanced at the wound. "I underestimated their speed. A mistake I'll never make again." She eyed the tent. "Now, bring that pig out here." She turned to her troops and bellowed, "Let's teach him what fate befalls those who dare attack an emissary of Kronos, and an officer of the League of One."

The roar of approval echoed through the hills.

"They recognize a leader when they see one," Mathiah said.

The troopers plunged unopposed into the tent and emerged moments later dragging the hapless Emperor. They dropped him sniveling at Kelahya's feet.

She looked down at him, and what she saw—grotesque crisscrossing marks upon his face—caused an unwelcome tremor to rush through her. Every time she saw such marks, the memory of the creatures who had kidnapped her as a child erupted within her, producing a cold, irrepressible rage.

The marks meant that Cuetzalan was Kayroan, one of only a few races whose psyche Minders couldn't penetrate, and his lineage added to her disdain.

"I am Emperor Cuetzalan of the Mardakish, I demand to be treated with respect," he managed to mumble between sobs. "The League of One has no jurisdiction here."

"Really?" She produced a digiscroll from her side pocket and pressed it into action.

"I demand to be taken to the Galactic Sanctuary," the Emperor went on with obvious difficulty. "I am a person of rank and must be treated as such. I recognize no other authority. Only Kronos himself can judge me."

She leaned close enough so that only he could hear her voice. "I may be unable to penetrate your mind, vermin, but I am going to crush your life."

"No, you can't! You have no authority."

She stood and addressed the troops on both sides, "Listen, one and all, for this is the will of the Galactic Sanctuary." Kelahya turned to the scroll and read: "For crimes of the most vicious nature committed against the Penorat Klan, I, Kronos Deucarrion, Scribe of the Legislature and Supreme Pontiff of the Galactic Sanctuary, find the man who calls himself Emperor Cuetzalan, guilty as charged. The penalty is death."

"No! No, no, I can explain if you'll only give me a chance. This is all a misunderstanding."

She went on, "For crimes of the most vicious nature committed against the people of the Zefrenian System and for the murder of their Queen, Lady Allaroon, I, Kronos Deucarrion, Scribe of the Legislature and Supreme Pontiff of the Galactic Sanctuary, find the man who calls himself Emperor Cuetzalan, guilty as charged. The penalty is death."

"No, no, you are making a grave mistake. This is treachery. Kronos would never allow it."

She glanced down at the sniveling lump of Kayroan humanity that groveled at her feet. "There are twelve more such charges," she yelled to her forces. "Twelve more such verdicts. Must I read them all?"

"No!" came the massive response. "Let the verdict be carried out."

"Mercy, please," Cuetzalan pleaded. "Have mercy. It was for the glory of Kronos. I can prove it if you give me a chance. Please."

"Did he show mercy to the Penorats?" she called out.

"No!" came the massive reaction.

"The Zefrenians?"

"No!"

"The Haladites, the Moscovians, and all the others?"

"No, no, no!"

Cuetzalan's only response came in the form of convulsive sobs.

She turned to Mathiah. "The entire family of this parasite participated in the atrocities carried out in his name. Where are they?" she asked.

"We have them all. Most are dead, but three live."

"Drag this Kayroan rubbish and his kin to the Valley of Flames. Keep them alive for the next three turns. Don't let them die before that. They must slowly disintegrate. Kronos wishes them to suffer fully for what they've done. Understood?"

"It's unlikely they can live that long."

"Do not help them die. Let them rot. Kronos commands it."

"It will be done," Mathiah said, and bowed his head.

"We're finished here." Kelahya marched back to her vessel. The roars of the troopers soon drowned Cuetzalan's screams of terror.

She boarded her Raptor and sat in the cockpit contemplating what had just happened. She'd attained an historic victory, ordered the execution of a vicious killer and his family, yet she ached with sorrow. Why?

Soon the familiar warmth came over her and she knew what would happen next. Kronos' thoughts would take shape within her and reverberate like a loud whisper in her ears, every word crystal clear, and every emotion a deep-felt pleasure.

"Major Devona, all is well?" Kronos asked.

"Yes, all is well."

"I feel you're in pain. Why?"

"I'll never get used to it. The killing."

"Let me help you."

"No. I need to feel this. I need to find my own way."

"Kelahya, tread with caution. Minders like us must keep our emotions in check, especially painful emotions. They lead to a schism that can, in turn, bring about our demise. It's the Minder's greatest weakness. Never forget that."

"I am well aware. I can handle it."

"As you wish." He paused. *"I must say I'm displeased with you."*

"Oh?"

"You disobeyed orders. You can expect the wrath of Commodore Priaminian. The risks you took were unnecessary."

"They were necessary to succeed. And succeed we did."

"Indeed. Promise me never to do it again."

"I can only promise to try."

"So be it. You will be rewarded for this victory."

"I have no wish for rewards. My fighters deserve them, not I."

His tone hardened with evident impatience. *"Honorable sentiment, Kelahya, but unnecessary. Your team will be generously compensated."*

"Thank you, my Lord. I meant no offense."

"You're tired." Kronos voice softened. *"Don't punish yourself for what was necessary. Cuetzalan is an animal, a fiend who needed to be stopped. Not an iota of your being should be wasted on such as he."*

"True. But his warriors only followed orders. They did not—"

"They should have left him and refused to obey!"

"Yes, of course, My Lord."

"Enough is enough Kelahya, no more sorrow." He eased into her soul, caressing its core.

"Stop," she whispered.

"As you wish." He withdrew, leaving behind the echo of his presence.

She sighed.

"Your mission is complete and you are triumphant. You shall return to us with full honors." He paused to emphasize his next statement. *"Today, you have earned your ascent to Commander. Congratulations, Commander Kelahya Devona."*

CHAPTER 2

Dionysus

———◆———

*Excerpt from the **Corpus Galacticum**, 137th Edition*

Dawnzehya Gleva, *known as the burning planet, and its inhabited moon **Dionysus**, hurtle around the Preena sun 9,000 times faster than any other inhabited planet in the cosmos.*

In turn, the Preena system races along at the outer limits of the small galaxy named Khamet F'Ha in honor of the messenger of the gods.

*As a result, time on Dionysus is distorted—a cycle on Dionysus is roughly equivalent to five cycles on planets like **Terra** and **Palkaviel**.*

Travel to and from this world is an experience like no other in the universe. The Dyonisian race is credited with the invention of the particle transporter now in use throughout the known galaxies.

A tenuous ding jolted Kelahya away from the memories, back to the freighter and the urgency of escape.

Ding…Ding…

The sound, antiquated, annoying, and impossible to ignore, always prefaced ship-wide announcements.

"Uh, all hands prepare for docking procedures and the…uh, all passengers prepare for transfer," a high-pitched male voice intruded into her cabin over the comm. "Passengers need to go to level four and find the particle transporter. That's in the, uh, aft section of the ship next to the cargo bays which are also aft. And…uhm, what?" He paused to listen to someone. "Oh, if you're interested in seeing how…uh, viewing, yes, viewing the docking…uhm, procedures, we have that on the viewscapes in the messlounge. That would be on level four. Forward of the transporter and the cargo bays."

There was an awkward pause during which Kelahya could hear voices chattering some distance from the man on the comm.

"That's all for the moment," he said at last.

She had arrived. The sudden realization produced a blend of anticipation and anxiety. In a matter of hexicons, she'd be stepping onto the most complex and remote inhabited world in the cosmos—Dionysus. A safe haven, she hoped, and the start of her desperate and inexplicable search for answers.

Kelahya looked around the grimy freighter cabin to collect her belongings, and scowled.

"Nothing like the immaculate Alliance transports I've traveled on most of my life."

It was the only ship headed for Dionysus. Best of all, they required no identification to book passage, and the price was more than reasonable. Now comes the fun part, the particle transporter.

"By all appearances, maintenance ranks at the bottom of this rusty old tub's list of priorities. On the other hand, doing business with this moon requires a transporter in perfect working order, so it may not be so bad."

Whoever handles maneuvers on this lumbering hunk of metal shows considerable expertise.

"And freighters are clumsy even in the best of circumstances."

Not for you. Kronos taught you docking procedures at the helm of battlestar cruisers the size of cities.

"Why mention him? If the images you portray are truthful, my actions on his behalf are unforgivable."

Yet, you acted with unquestionable obedience.

"How could I have been deceived for so long?"

Love justifies everything. He won your trust and—

"Used me…my strength, my Minding power, my entire being, everything to serve him and him alone. How then could I have murdered him? Don't you understand how devastating that is?"

Tears rolled down her cheeks.

"If that were true, if I killed him, every inhabited planet, moon and way station would be crawling with troopers and centurions with orders to kill me on sight."

That's why survival is our only hope. You've streamed on termination vessels and laser ships to every inhabited body in the galaxies. You've learned how to blend into new societies overnight. Use that knowledge now.

"Impossible."

To escape from Kronos' personal guards was impossible, but you managed it. Even if we don't remember how.

Fleeting images of her escape erupted into her head, but none of them made sense. Her first clear recollection consisted of boarding the freight vessel she now prepared to disembark.

After a final glance about the cabin, she gathered her overcoat and haversack. "Let's find the truth."

She made her way through the maze of corridors and gangways to the messlounge on level four. During the entire trip she had taken refuge in the solitude of her cabin—the fewer people who saw her, the better. Therefore, this was her first sojourn through the bowels of the freighter. It came as no surprise to find half the viewscapes out of order and the lounge packed with cargo, which obstructed most of the view. Still, it was better than nothing.

The observation lounge faced away from her destination with only the Preena sun visible far out in space. She turned her attention to the viewscapes and found one that produced a reasonably clear image of the docking process.

It pained her to admit that, aside from her jumbled thoughts, her weapons and two changes of clothes were all that was left of a life that felt as distant as the edge of the cosmos.

The now familiar voice cut into the comm once more. "Attention all hands, docking procedures have been initiated. Uh, lock down anything that isn't locked down already. And you passengers, once the cargo is transferred, you'll be…notified to go to the transporter. We'll tell you when to do that. Uh, in the meantime…we hope…"

"Yes, we must have hope."

Hope for what? That you didn't kill him? That your mind is not disintegrating?

A cavernous male voice reverberated within her, and an unexpected reply took shape. *"Nestor. Find Nestor."*

She'd heard that same voice before at the precise moment her mind began to unravel. *"Dionysus. Find Nestor,"* it had said then. Try as she may to silence it, it had locked in and refused to release her.

Now, as she stood motionless in the messlounge, something in her very core insisted that the voice was right. Somehow, the notion that this moon at the edge of space was her only hope for survival felt indisputable and absolute.

Find Nestor? Find the enemy?

She shook her head.

The viewscape focused on the flickering lights outlining the transport module hangar that orbited Dionysus.

For the tenth time in as many hexicons, she patted the haversack and checked the weapon clamps, then brushed her hand along the side of the bag. Everything was in place. It reassured her to have the weapons there, invisible to the uninitiated, but accessible if needed.

The vessel's attitude shifted and the transport module revolved to the right, but experience told her that the freighter was the one actually turning. They were close enough for her to notice the dock lights flash in alternating yellow and purple strobes. Behind them, the edge of Dionysus floated into view. *Remote and deadly Dionysus.* The words from a lecture spoken by a tutor in her distant childhood emerged from some hidden corner of her memory.

The freighter glided into the gaping hangar, then floated down to touch the hangar floor. A solid jolt and loud thump confirmed contact, the artificial gravity doing its job with absolute efficiency. The order to disembark echoed over the comm.

After a deep breath to gather herself, Kelahya exited the messlounge and followed the faded indicators that directed passengers to the transporter.

She arrived first at the designated area. Four additional passengers, all Terrians, formed a short line behind her. A discreet perusal suggested that none of them was fit enough to be a League of One Trooper.

"Step into the transporter and place the security straps around shoulders and waist," said an obese man who stood at the transporter entrance behind a metallic bar.

The access bar across the gate slid back, and Kelahya, mouth dry, heart pounding, sauntered down to the transporter where another man stood waiting. He tilted his head toward the module as she arrived.

Why do they all look like coffins?

She shuddered with anticipation as she stepped resolutely into the cylinder and dropped her bag onto the magneto cart to her right. The straps were tight, and the buckle required some effort to make it lock. The rigid body brace clamped her into immobility, which made breathing difficult. It came as no surprise—she'd been in particle transporter modules countless times before—but the experience never ceased to be unpleasant.

"Keep your eyes closed until instructed to open them," said the man. "At the sound of the third tone, take a deep breath and remain motionless for fifteen milicons," he instructed. "Pleasant travels."

A polialloy door slid across to seal the cylinder. The endless silence was unnerving. Then three short "bongs" rang inside the cylinder.

Kelahya knew the drill.

Less than fifteen milicons later, she heard a different door slide open followed by the rumbling voice of a Dionysian male. "Breathe on the norm and bare the eyes," he instructed in Eniat. The language of Dionysus was an irregular version of Terrian uttered with an esophageal sound that resonated as if from some deep cavern.

Specks of light danced across her eyes. The Dionysian official's enormous hands tapped the body brace then released the straps. Kelahya gasped, sucking in as much air as her lungs would hold. She focused on the Dionysian's huge arms as her legs twitched in an effort to regain coordination. Civilian Particle transporters always left the muscles limp and caused momentary disorientation. Especially the newer, faster models, and this was the fastest she'd ever experienced. She realized her contempt for the grungy freighter had been misguided.

Very clever. Making the freighter look like an outdated relic avoids detection by the League of One patrols.

As her eyes regained focus, she realized that the Dionysian was typical of his race. This particular male had not yet reached eight feet in height and, though quite young, his natural strength was already evident through the uniform.

"To the clear," he said with a motioned of his head.

As soon as she stepped out of the cylinder, it closed automatically. She spotted her gear on the magneto cart but saw no other passengers.

"To wait now it is. Orbit to adjust."

Kelahya smiled. *Welcome to Dionysus. Welcome to Hell.*

That's what the original prisoners had called it. For hundreds of cycles the convicts of the numerous inhabited planets and moons of the Preena system had been sent here, on the assumption that no one could survive in hell.

But survive they had. And over the centuries they had fused into a new race, superior in both physical strength and mental capability.

Later, during the Cosmic Ethnopecuniary Wars, and the endless cycles of chaos that followed, countless refugees fleeing racial purges, political reprisals, starvation, slavery, or the law, had come in search of a new life.

By the time the migrations ended, Dionysus had swelled to ten times the population it had prior to the wars. Its ethnic diversity became a microcosm of the humanoid inhabitants of the Preena system and beyond. Derelicts and geniuses, terrorists and philosophers, individuals who had been persecuted for one reason or another came to find a safe haven in the red hills and dunes of Dawnzehya Gleva's moon. The mere remoteness of Dionysus almost guaranteed protection against bounty hunters and political assassins.

If Kelahya's visions were true, then she'd become the same type of refugee, and gone from hunter to hunted in the blink of an eye, for a crime no one within the boundaries of civilization, including herself, would ever have dreamed possible. True, or not, instinct dictated that hiding represented her only hope. No place offered absolute safety. Not even this impossible land, Dionysus. Her birthplace. For it was on Dionysus that she'd been taken from her parents at the age of four.

"Inspect on red door, out by right." Again, the head motion. "Bag kit will lag."

She followed the Dionysian through a red door where he directed her into the inspection chamber. Her belongings were already there. The door closed behind her and scanner rays flooded the chamber. Moments later, the doors opened and she stepped out. The Dionysian stood at his terminal scrutinizing the information scrolling before him.

"Progressive weapon concealment." He looked at her and tilted his head inquisitively. "Illegal. State endeavor on Dionysus."

The effort to probe his psyche for any signs of danger produced a searing pain in her head, the inevitable symptom of her mind's dissociation. She stopped her probe in milicons, but saw enough to convince her the Dionysian represented no threat, and that Kronos' troopers had not yet appeared. The probe also yielded the answer to his question.

"Escape," she whispered.

He hesitated for an instant, then glanced back at his terminal and studied it. Satisfied with what he found, he entered new data into the console. He looked at her again. "Identity revision?"

She nodded. *Can it really be this easy?*

He stared at her for a moment then entered another series of codes on the terminal pad. A blue card popped out. After inspecting it, he handed it to her. The card displayed her image and a series of codes and letters in Eniat. "Cost, two thousand stipends, adopt Quaytra Playaar identity for remain Dionysus." He then added, "Five thousand stipends, to include weapons keep, Quaytra Playaar identity with history, stable dwell, one thousand journals credit."

Kelahya gritted her teeth and probed again. She saw in his mind that the Quaytra Playaar persona was more than satisfactory. She took a deep breath as she ceased her probe and paid the five thousand.

The Dionysian smiled and turned to his console. His fingers danced deftly on the entry pad and, moments later, two magcards emanated from a slot at his left. He looked them over and nodded with approval, then handed them to Kelahya.

"Welcome return Dionysus Quaytra Playaar. Safe journeys." He motioned toward a blue door to her right.

Kelahya picked up her bag and headed through the door, confident that her cover would never be revealed. The longstanding Dionysian code of secrecy was inviolable—their continued success as a lucrative refuge for the hunted depended on it.

She stepped into a large indoor conveyer station and paused to assess her surroundings.

Under an enormous translucent protective dome, which permitted the bright reddish hue emanating from Dawnzehya Gleva to safely illuminate all areas, countless transport units, jitneys, and trams traveled expediently in every direction. Commercial establishments and eateries crowded the edges of the bustling station.

It was morning. Thanks to an eccentric orbit, day here meant that Dionysus was, on the one hand, moving farther from Dawnzehya Gleva, the burning planet, and on the other, that it was emerging from behind the planet into the white light of Preena, the sun.

The result was twofold—temperatures grew cooler as the moon moved farther from the planet, and the light from Preena made the day far more radiant than the night.

Night on Dionysus was a reddish twilight, the result of permanent combustion on Dawnzehya Gleva, which was also much closer during those hours, making the night an oven tolerable only inside temperature-controlled domes. It was common knowledge that Dionysians often lost their minds when forced to live on planets where nights were dark and cold.

Kelahya knew that the huge moon and its giant mother planet hurtled around the Preena sun at speeds that were several times that of even the fastest inhabited planets. As a result, time on Dionysus was a different type of cosmic beast, which made travel to and from this remote world an experience like no other in the universe.

To resolve this dilemma, the Dionysians had created the particle transporter, and she now realized how that invention had led to unparalleled prosperity through a multitude of products and services available nowhere else. But Dionysus never forgot its roots, and one of its most profitable enterprises remained the business of providing asylum for the hunted and disenfranchised.

Escape, however, came at a heavy cost. Not only in terms of the stipends required for payment, but in the final price as well. Dawnzehya Gleva emanated radiation particles that lodged in the tissues of the visitors to Dionysus, and to which only native Dionysians were immune. Particles that remained stable and harmless in the moon's atmosphere, but which, when exposed to other atmospheres, produced severe tissue deterioration in those who had lived on moon for more than five Dionysian cycles. Limited exposure of two to three cycles had, so far, proved survivable. But to most, even in freedom, Dionysus was a prison.

Kelahya activated the locator on her travel magcard and it instantly displayed the route parameters and specific transporters needed to reach Quaytra Playaar's dwell. For reasons she could not begin to fathom, she felt unexpectedly light and optimistic.

Spotting a matching transporter access gate, she sprinted toward it, then stopped abruptly, realizing that her exuberance might attract unwanted attention. She knelt to give the appearance of checking her haversack while she scanned her surroundings. It amazed her to realize that no one cared. She was not watched, or even noticed. A sea of Dionysians and humanoids of every description surrounded her, dashing to transports or along walk ramps, and not one seemed aware of her presence. Her height and color, the biggest challenges when attempting to blend into other societies, were not even a consideration here. She was as tall and strong as anyone. The Dionysians were her race.

She took a deep breath and permitted herself a subtle smile of relief. She'd arrived and was alive. At least for now.

With each step she eased into a strange comfort unfamiliar to her until that very moment, a wonderful sense of belonging.

The mood carried her along as she hopped onto a transport unit and inserted the travel card.

"Dwell 1543, Caledonian Complex, arrival in fifteen hexicons. Transport in progress," said the lifeless voice. The card popped out and a soft melody of crystalline chimes began to play in the background. Kelahya retrieved the card, took a deep breath, and closed her eyes.

Welcome home, she thought as the jitney started to move.

Without warning, an abrupt, scorching pain shot through her, as images gushed forth like a bursting dam.

＊ ＊ ＊ ＊ ＊ ＊

"Kelahya." Modyor's voice sounded gentle as a breeze when he spoke his daughter's name, even though it seemed to emanate from the very core of Dionysus. "Come to me."

His arms stretched toward the four-year-old as she skipped across the dwell floor. He clamped his huge hands about her and whisked her into the air, spinning across the room like a huge tornado.

Kelahya giggled, eliciting the usual thundering guffaw from her father, who found her giggles amusing beyond reason. Dionysians didn't giggle and it had taken months for him to control his reaction even to the melodic Terrian voice of Kelahya's mother, Tenecia.

"Be careful, Mody. She's not that strong yet." Tenecia's concern carried with it a warning. In his exuberance, he'd hurt the child once before, and she was not quite recovered even now.

"Sweepings! She strong like me, this one. No worry. Modyor for remember too clear and not forget. This one, she be Modyor's heart."

"Please, Mody." Tenecia touched his elbow. The giant melted and handed Kelahya to her mother then smiled that gentle smile that had warmed his wife's heart from the beginning.

Modyor Devon was one of those remarkable beings that creatures in other systems referred to as asynchronous, out of context for their own race. Even the largest Dionysians were several units shorter than he, and none were as strong.

"More!" the little voice squealed, triggering her father's laugh once again.

"Tenecia sees? This my child is wanting for Da," Modyor pleaded through his chuckles. "I careful to her." He winked at his daughter and smiled. Then he looked into Tenecia's eyes, and his huge hand brushed her cheek with incongruent softness.

"Tenecia Modyor's heart, too." He leaned down to kiss her.

"Modyor speak Eniat for make heart softer in Tenecia," she responded in the Dionysian dialect. "I worry you hurting child in happy play." She caressed his face and smiled. "Modyor, Eniat speak not change Tenecia wishes now. Modyor stop happy play. Us ready for dine."

He peered down with resignation into his wife's lovely eyes and nodded. "As you wish, my love," he said in perfect Terrian. "Can't blame me for trying. After all it's always worked before. Kelahya, help Ma bring dinner. We'll play some more when you're fully recovered."

"Ma...Da...I not stop. Kelahya strong. I happy play Da."

"Eniat won't do the trick with Ma tonight, Kelahya," he said. "Let's get ready for dinner. Time to help Ma. I'll go to the cellar and get some ale." He kissed the tip of Kelahya's nose then leaned over to kiss his wife, before heading for the cellar.

"Come on darling, help me set the table," Tenecia said as she set Kelahya down.

Hand-in-hand they danced toward the kitchen across the sandstone loungeroom. Tenecia handed Kelahya the smaller dishes to carry, and soon an array of vegetables in a colorful arrangement brought a touch of art to the limestone whiteness of the dineroom.

The food displayed, the table set and ready, Tenecia propped Kelahya on her chair and crossed the dineroom toward the cellar door. She smiled at the child as she shook her head. "Where's that husband of mi—"

The explosion demolished the window and sent Tenecia's body flying into the limestone wall across the room covering it in blood. Lifeless, she dropped to the floor like a heap of soiled rags.

Kelahya, eyes wide, uncomprehending, sat motionless and afraid. Then a scream of terror burst from her throat.

A second explosion followed, and the front door slammed to the floor.

Kelahya screamed repeatedly as seven assault troopers, creatures unlike any she had encountered before, stormed into the room brandishing long black metal objects.

The heads of the creatures turned for an instant toward Tenecia. Then, the troopers' heads flashed around and the metal objects were pointed at the child.

Kelahya saw her reflection in the face shield of the trooper nearest her as he reached toward her.

"No!" It was the thunder of Modyor as he emerged from the cellar and thrust himself upon the troopers. The two he seized were dead almost instantly. Those beyond his grip turned and pointed their metal at the enraged father. There was a silent flash. Modyor, and the two troopers in his grasp, collapsed to the floor. The shooters reset their weapons and approached the massive body.

"Stop!" a graveled voice outside the door commanded the troopers. "I will dispose of him."

Another trooper entered, then another and another. In moments, the room was filled with black uniforms, all with metal sticks in their hands, all giving passing glances at the child. They gathered around Modyor's motionless body.

"The child, bring her to me," said the voice again.

* * * * * *

An unrelenting buzzer snatched Commander Kelahya back to the transport unit. Her heart pounded, her lungs struggled for air, her upper lip was damp with perspiration, and droplets trickled down her ribs. She was shaking.

She saw a smiling woman reflected on the window who lovingly looked down at her. A huge explosion erupted, and the woman's body flew against a wall and dropped to the floor in a haze of red. A child's face emerged through the smolder of the wreckage. In a flash, the image transformed into a trooper's visor. She spun around in horror, expecting an assailant to pounce upon her, but she was alone. The conveyer jitney had come to a stop and the only visible activity was a blinking light on the instruction array.

"Dissociating into my past and reliving my life can be the end of me." She inhaled deeply, and then let the air slowly escape. After a moment, she pressed the button with the flashing light. The buzzer stopped.

"Dwell 1543, Caledonian Complex. Two journals will be charged to your central account. Disembark now," the monotone voice informed her.

The door opened onto an enclosed walkway.

Kelahya glanced at the magcard in her hand. Her image stared back from the card with the name Quaytra Playaar emblazoned next to it.

"Disembark now. For alternate destination state parameters," said the jitney's voice.

"This will do," she said as she picked up her bag and dragged herself onto the walkway. The jitney sped away behind her.

Moments later, Kelahya stood in the entrance of the complex that housed her new stable dwell, or rather, the stable dwell of one Quaytra Playaar.

It looked far better than anticipated. The entrance nave shot up to a dizzying height. The decor reflected the noncommittal design of communal housing, but at least some attention had been paid to esthetics. The setup made it clear that security received the greatest consideration. Access to the lift area appeared virtually impossible except from the transporter, and access to any lift other than her own remained cut off by a translucent barrier. She spotted an array of other security measures and felt certain there were even more devices beyond identification even to her trained eye.

How many other exiles live here, I wonder?

Kelahya made her way to the lift and dropped her haversack onto the floor.

She placed the magcard against a small screen. The lift closed and began its ascent.

The lift cylinder slowed and rotated forty-five degrees as it came to a stop. She slipped her card into the access groove. The doors to her dwell slid open and the lights glowed into life as she stepped in.

The spacious entry hall offered a combination of Terrian and Dionysian furnishings, a pleasant surprise that belied the utilitarian exterior.

"Welcome home, Quaytra Playaar," the soothing female voice announced in perfect Terrian.

"I couldn't have said it better myself," she responded with an attempt at humor. She dropped her bag onto the floor. "Indirect light only, Gaelic Terrian music and…Daltic ale." *Might as well put it to the test.* The lighting changed and the Terrian tunes began to play.

She lumbered into the loungeroom. It was a large chamber, also furnished with a comfortable blend of Dionysian and Terrian fixtures. She paused in the center of the room and heaved a heartfelt sigh.

The dwell sat on the one hundred and twentieth level, and the floor-to-ceiling windows of the chamber offered a spectacular panoramic view of Esroal. The capital city of Dionysus was a thriving metropolis. The indirect lighting along with the vanishing rays of Dawnzehya Gleva created an ethereal atmosphere that filled Kelahya with a much-needed sense of relief and comfort. The tension in her muscles eased ever so slightly as her eyes scanned the domed skyline.

"Privacy window protocol."

"Privacy in place," responded the female voice.

Strange. Time doesn't feel any different.

If she hadn't been abducted from Dionysus, she would be a young girl, the flame of passion still far from igniting. The irony of it elicited a sardonic chuckle.

She took the glass of Daltic ale from the duplicator unit and, after sipping it, ambled into the sleeproom. A large bed lay at the center of a hexagonal room, and a sophisticated communications console covered one entire wall. Two other walls held three-dimensional reproductions of Dionysian landscapes and another opened into the hygiene unit. The remaining two walls formed full-length windows.

"Two messages have been retained for Quaytra Playaar," said the female voice again. Kelahya glared at the console with apprehension.

"Oh?" she said. "Play."

The viewscape flickered on and the image of a Terrian woman appeared. The name Doriah Miltron Playaar scrolled across the screen. "Quaytra, my precious, so sorry we didn't get to visit with you. But Klantay hates the heat. Old age, I suppose. Next trip I promise to make time. Safe travels." She was gone.

The screen flickered again. This time it was a Dionysian male, well past his prime. The scroll read Cool Restore Service. "Apologies, Fellow Playaar. Repairs in delay for this morrow. All in order now to your satisfy. Until soon."

Kelahya smiled, pleased with her investment of five thousand stipends. The Dionysian's sophisticated means of providing for the safety and concealment of their clients had always thwarted the League's most efficient agents. For the moment, at least, it made her feel safe.

Quaytra Playaar's dwell offered a dazzling mixture of comforts from Kelahya's combined ancestries. Assumptions regarding her habitat preferences had been made with astonishing accuracy, presumably by the officer who welcomed her at the transporter station.

The touch of the messages was so elementary as to be almost comical, but their very simplicity placed them beyond suspicion. They also underscored the pervasive element of danger. Kelahya shuddered.

She retrieved her bag and tossed it onto the bed. As the ale began to work its magic, the days of accumulated tension relinquished their hold on her muscles, her exhausted body moved with increasing slowness. She downed the remainder of her drink and slid out of her clothes.

As she turned toward the hygiene unit her eye caught the mirror and she froze, stunned by the image it reflected.

The light of Dawnzehya Gleva that filtered through the windows of the chamber, made her emerald green eyes even deeper, her cinnamon skin, a chocolate brown, her long wavy black hair, a deep blue. The statuesque body glowed with strength and self-confidence, its only imperfections, the almost invisible hints of fading where the scar-regenerator had done its work. It was a body that had served her well.

She stood there, staring at the reflection in the Glevan light. It reminded her of an image she'd seen before. But where? When? A cold shudder fluttered along her skin, and the torrent of memories swept through her with such force that it made her breath catch.

With a jolt, the tension took hold of her once more and her mind reeled. For a moment, everything but the reflection in the mirror spun out of focus.

Then, she recognized it. It was the image of her mother. The skin and hair were darker and Kelahya was much taller, but otherwise the resemblance was almost perfect. An image she had not recalled in all the cycles away from Dionysus.

"Find Nestor."

She whirled around looking for the source of the deep male voice, instinctively ready to repel any attack. But as before, there was no one, except inside her head.

A sharp pain shot through her brain.

The voice, always the voice! Make it stop!

She squeezed her head between her hands in a futile attempt to force the pain away.

Kelahya now accepted with absolute certainty that her mind was dissociating, which invariably led to a Minder's death. Unable to distinguish reality from illusion, dissociation resembled existing in a time-freeze populated with incongruous images where past and present amalgamated into a frenzied nightmare. Preventing dissociation was vital. Survival depended on her ability to keep her judgement intact and under control, but the extraneous visions that now assaulted her, came with increasing frequency and ever-greater intensity.

She stumbled to the bed, collapsed onto her back, and pounded her head in a futile attempt to force her psyche to re-associate. As the pain intensified, her legs kicked and pedaled in an involuntary motion to escape. Tears streamed from her eyes. Deep convulsions caused her to shake without control.

Once again, in what was now a daily struggle to fight off fatigue and emotional distress, she forced herself to evoke the Minder's Mindstill stratagem. She would never know how long it took to regain control, but at long last she succeeded, and drifted off into a restless sleep.

Chapter 3

Intelligence Gathering

———◆———

*Excerpt from the **Corpus Galacticum**, 137th Edition*

Intelligence networks form and integral part of the League of One's system by which information is collected utilizing more than one inter-related source.

The League of One utilizes distributive intelligence protocols, operating a massive network of reliable informants and sources. The basic strategies are usually infiltration and penetration, although a manifold of unrevealed tactics is also employed.

The evidence gathered is then processed by highly specialized Science Minders and turned into an intelligence product.

Information is then conveyed in a variety of secure, clandestine means through a conglomerate of networks.

"Ma! Da!" Kelahya screamed.

A trooper stomped over to the child, gathered her under his arm, and carried her through the smoke and dust into the reddish night of Dionysus.

"Bring her here. Then stand guard by the giant's body. No one is to touch it." The gruff voice emanated from a tall lanky figure now approaching.

The trooper shoved the child toward him and returned to Modyor's body.

The figure reached down a green-gloved hand and lifted the child's face. His own face was almost invisible behind the amber helmet shield, but Kelahya could see the distortions, though she couldn't understand them.

"So, Modyor does indeed have a daughter. Good. We shall use her well." He lifted her into the vehicle and pushed her in.

"Maccabeus." This time it was a female voice, coming from another figure that rushed toward the tall man with an air of urgency. She was dressed in red from her helmet to her boots. "Nothing was said of this infant. Kill it and leave it with its mother."

Kelahya's eyes grew wide as Maccabeus' hand shot toward the red figure's throat and locked in place.

"Never presume to tell me what is best, Tzalina." The voice was shockingly calm in contrast to the action. "This time shall be the last. Clear?"

As best she could, Tzalina nodded.

"Into the rig," Maccabeus commanded.

When the hand released Tzalina, her knees buckled for an instant. She recovered quickly and clambered into the transport, giving Kelahya a violent shove toward the back. The child fell over and began to cry.

Maccabeus slammed his hand on the door, and it slid shut. There was a faint buzz, and Kelahya could tell the transport was moving.

"Ma! Da!"

Tzalina's red glove produced a smacking sound as it made contact with the girl's cheek. Kelahya was stunned into silence. No one had ever struck her before. The stinging in her cheek was bewildering. Her weeping shriveled and she cowered into the corner.

Tzalina removed one glove, then the other. She tucked them into a pocket around her waist then gave the red helmet a small snap to the right and pulled it over her head.

Kelahya gasped audibly at the sight of her captor's face. She showed the same deformities that Kelahya had guessed through Maccabeus' shield, but there was something else that frightened the child—red eyes—made all the more startling by the unexpected grayness of the skin. Unable to help herself, Kelahya stared at the face above her.

The deformities were disturbing. Symmetric crisscrossing lines that covered most of the surface of cheeks and forehead, but nothing on the chin. The long green hair was slicked back on the front and sides into a ponytail of sorts that draped almost to Tzalina's waist once it was free of the helmet. The thick eyebrows ran the entire width of her face, thinning only slightly above the bridge of the nose and the temples. The lips were the pale blue of death.

Tzalina turned her terrifying eyes toward the child and frowned. "You anger me," she barked. And with that, she reached over and pressed behind the child's right ear. Within milicons Kelahya lay unconscious.

She awoke to the sensation of an abrupt stop and a door sliding open. Tzalina hoisted her to her feet and flung her toward the door. "Out!"

Kelahya fell through the door and, as the ground grew closer, an arm locked around her with a jolt.

"What is?" a husky voice asked.

When Kelahya's feet were on the ground, she looked up at her rescuer and found a smiling face. It had the familiar Dionysian cinnamon color, although the eyes were an almost white blue.

"Slow and caution, small one. Falling brings the pain."

"Lock her in Maccabeus' quarters. Place a guard," Tzalina barked as she stomped off across a huge courtyard, toward a large door.

The man took Kelahya's hand and, with a gentle tug, led her in the opposite direction, toward another door guarded by several armed men. It slid open as they approached and closed behind them.

Her tiny eyes grew wide at the astonishing sight that welcomed her—an outdoor area surrounded by a wall, the surface covered in miniscule green stems that looked like very short hair, the edges festooned with…she had no name for them. They were like…feathers. That was it. Her Ma had a feather with a rainbow of colors. *The feather must be from here*, Kelahya concluded.

But this place was awash with colors, in such vast numbers and hues that the child froze, mesmerized.

Vegetation was scarce outside the protected agricultural domes of Dionysus, and Kelahya had never encountered such wonders. Only the tempered regions at the poles permitted the rich soil to bear anything other than the oil-filled bushes, which sprouted here and there in the shaded patches below the ridges of the canyons or the sheds beside the houses. And their color was nothing like this. Most shrubs were only slightly darker than the red-brown soil in which they grew.

The gentle tug on her hand made her turn back to her captor. Or could he be her savior?

The man smiled. "Pretty flowers of this garden, or no?" She smiled back. He allowed her to remain a few minutes contemplating the beauty of her surroundings, smelling the perfume in the air and enjoying the crisp cool breeze.

"Air here feel good to have. To breathe it full, young one," he advised as he inhaled. Kelahya did the same, letting out the air in a big puff.

The man chuckled and tugged her hand again, leading her around the flowers and into an endless series of corridors along which, at regular intervals, were smaller doors, all closed.

A chilled air filled the halls. She'd never felt this cold before and the new sensation frightened her. She tightened her grip on his finger.

There was a whitish light, not unlike the daylight of Preena, which seemed to be everywhere and come from nowhere. The man stopped at one of the closed doors and removed a small box from his breast pocket. A minute light from the box shone on a square high on the door, and it slid open.

For an instant there was darkness inside, then something flickered and the room was filled with white light. A faint, musty odor came and went.

"Enter to stay."

Kelahya went in.

"Wait in room. Call for needs, to you will come the aid." There was a kindness to his gruff voice, a friendly twinkle in his eye, and a touch of sadness in his smile.

The door slid shut and she was alone.

A platform with a soft surface protruded from the wall. She stood in the center of the room and brought both her tiny hands to her lips.

"Ma? Da?" She shivered.

* * * * * *

The bright light of Preena blasted through Quaytra Playaar's dwell window. Startled, she bolted up.

Another dream…another glimpse into my past…

She sat on the edge of the bed, stretched, and took stock of her condition. She had managed only a few hours of restless sleep but felt sufficiently invigorated and energized to concentrate on her survival.

"All right." She stood up and shook every muscle awake. "Listen to me, Mind, we have no time for you to drift away. I must focus. If I fail in my search, and dissociation continues, we'll be sucked into the void."

Depending on the speed of her decline, she estimated, or rather, hoped, that she had twenty days or so at the outside.

"But even if we find Nestor, and even if he turns out to be the powerful Minder portrayed in legend—"

And we harbor serious doubts about that.

"The question remains as to whether he will help me or not."

He had no reason to. She had hunted him endlessly, coming ever so close time and again, only to have him vanish without a hint of the how or where.

Despite the urgency, she allowed herself the luxury of a long, relaxing cleaning treatment. Four days on the freighter had made it a necessity as well.

The Dionysian had guessed right again, she did prefer the older cleaning units with their abrupt, gruff handling. The newer ones were of such subtlety that many used them as surrogate sex partners or meditation chambers. She wasn't in the mood for subtleties. Every inch of her felt tight with strain and she needed the relief this more vigorous unit provided.

The soothing blue water sprayed her with warmth as the washers jostled her about, relaxing every muscle in her body. When she felt the time was right, the flick of a lever switched to the cold jet streams for thirty milicons. Then the blowers did the rest and she emerged alert and refreshed. Even her head felt untroubled.

The nutrition chamber was fully stocked. Her appetite satisfied, she donned her recon suit then removed her weapons from the bag and checked them. She was pleased that her equipment hadn't been confiscated. Dionysians understood all too well their clients' need for protection and their willingness to pay for it.

She found the data pad in a side pocket and removed it. All the information she had on Nestor was in that small unit, making it almost as vital as her weapons.

The data pad would also give her information on where to get the transportation she needed for her quest. After all, it contained intelligence gathered by the best in the League of One, and precious little eluded them.

She connected the pad to the dwell's viewscape and examined the area of her search. The prospect was intimidating at best. According to the data, she was headed into the most inhospitable mountain range on Dionysus, named the Talothia Hage.

No one in his right mind would go there.

"That makes me the perfect candidate."

After snapping her saber into place, she holstered her weapons and tested the thermal unit in her recon suit.

As her gaze fell on the mirror, she felt a shiver crawl across her spine. An all too familiar response. Fear.

"You have no choice, Kela— Quaytra Playaar —keep yourself together and do it." She took a deep breath, pressed her lips together, gave herself a reassuring nod. Equipment in hand, she exited the dwell and made her way to the building's transport hub. She summoned a jitney and loaded the destination data. Seconds later, she was on route to the slums of Esroal.

Aside from the endless climate domes that covered the entire city, Esroal offered the same social and economic zones of any other large city. Those who could afford it had the best, those who couldn't, didn't.

The better areas were around the center while the periphery claimed the more unsavory sections. Beyond the agricultural zones, the dives, brothels, and other buildings of dubious purpose existed in areas under the oldest domes, some of which appeared on the brink of collapse.

The jitney pulled up and opened its door in front of a dilapidated building that appeared vacant.

"1771 Kandalho, twenty-four journals will be charged to your central account. Disembark with caution," said the jitney's voice.

Kelahya got out, and the transport rolled away. A moment later, two Dionysian males appeared out of nowhere.

"Sweet tidings, maiden. Is fun time, or no?" chuckled the larger of the two, who also looked the oldest. "Look you for wowdust? Best exchange to such favored maid. You give, we give, yes?"

Kelahya slid her hand onto the blaster concealed in her recon suit.

"Not a mind to play, go peaceful like," was her terse reply.

The younger one slapped his hands together while producing an exaggerated and utterly insincere laugh. "Question not for answer, filth. We tell, you do."

They separated, trying to outflank her on both sides, but before they could take a second step the blaster appeared in her hand, and in quick succession, they dropped to the ground stunned into unconsciousness.

"I did warn you."

Her satisfaction was snatched away as the arms of a third man locked around her from behind squeezing so tightly that she could scarcely breathe. He smelled like a refuse heap.

He whispered in her ear, "We do nice now, yes?"

"Yes, we do nice."

He released her just enough to allow her to catch her breath. It was all she needed. She raised the blaster gun to his elbow and blew it off along with the rest of his arm. He staggered back in pain.

She raised the blaster again and blew a hole in the center of his chest. He dropped like lead.

Kelahya glanced around the street seeking out any others waiting in the wings. She spotted a couple of faces peering around a corner, but they quickly turned away and vanished.

Satisfied that no one would be coming at her again any time soon, she leaned against the wall of an abandoned building and consulted the data pad. She was definitely in the right place. The coded words on the pad indicated that the entrance was around the side. She was stunned to see the password that would get her admitted. It gave her pause.

It has to be coincidence.

After another reconnoitering glance at the street and its buildings, she sauntered around to the side door and kicked it, making almost no sound at all.

From the feel of it, she concluded that it was covered in metal but filled with some type of mortar. There was no visible lock and the hinges were safely hidden on the inside.

She was about to kick it again when a rumbling voice spoke through some invisible source at the base of the door.

"To vanish or to perish."

Hesitation spelled disaster, so she uttered the words, despite her doubts. "Cuetzalan," she voiced the password.

"Back."

She tried to spot the source of the voice on the assumption that some means of visual control would be there as well, but she could find nothing. The League's intelligence turned out to be accurate—she was dealing with a professional.

She was about to kick the door again when it produced a hum. A second later it started to move. When there was enough room for her to squeeze through, it stopped.

"Inside," the voice said.

It was even tighter than it appeared, but she managed to force herself through the opening. As soon as she was in, the door closed, leaving her in utter darkness.

"Bad treating for guest," she said.

Silence.

An orange ray shot from somewhere above her and started a scan. She could tell she stood behind a translucent barrier not unlike the material that domed the city. The scan stopped and the darkness returned.

"Business?" the voice asked.

"Mine only to know," she replied.

Silence.

"You breedmix, yes?"

"Yes. Is no matter."

"Weapons are League of One."

"I to steal off League Trooper. Do on Tsaltos III. I say no more."

Behind the barrier the light grew slowly until she could make out the figure of an older Dionysian standing only feet away, a snipershot held firmly in his left hand.

"Have you stipends for spend?"

"Only for buy what need."

He nodded. "Leave weapons in seal," he said.

"No."

He raised an eyebrow at this.

"We are not knowing you to me, not me to you," she said with aplomb.

He nodded again then turned to speak to some hidden companion. "Keep shot to her."

The barrier slid away and an endless array of lights flashed on.

She stepped forward and extended an upturned palm. He slapped it with a crippled hand and smiled. The greeting was now complete.

She declined to do a mental check on her host. Not only for fear of the ensuing pain, but also mistrust of the stability of her Endow. She'd have to rely on mere experience and skill.

"What need is yours?" he said, turning toward his inventory.

She glanced around the small warehouse structure filled mostly with junk.

"Kronos demand finer to this," she snarled.

He was clearly shocked to hear Kronos' name, and the picture became clearer. She had the weapons because she was either a centurion or a trooper. Either spelled trouble.

"To pardon, maid, all this is I have," the old man apologized only half-heartedly concealing his cynicism. "Prime this is for what there are." His mutilated fingers pulled a scooter upright and with a mighty huff he blew the dust away.

Kelahya fanned her hand across her face to deflect the cloud and stepped back. "Trash! What more?" There was impatience in her voice.

The old man took notice and looked around at the heap of junked scooters. He mumbled to himself as he appraised the remaining machines. He turned and moved close enough for Kelahya to catch a whiff of the pustules that covered his body. "Might be to have some better."

"To see. Now," she said as she recoiled.

"To pardon. For more stipends only." He shrugged an apology, as if the mere mention of more money was an insult.

"Stipends no concern. Time is all for me. To waste will bring the wrath." She slid her hand to her side and produced the handle of her saber.

He recognized the emblem at once. The mangled hand gestured for her to stop, and the wrinkled face twisted into a forced smile.

Kelahya's hand moved to her belt and slid a stipend from underneath. She gave it to him, and he bowed obsequiously.

"New I have. More good than to find from maker. Trail me." He tilted his head in the direction of a low door and slithered off toward it.

Kelahya followed and smiled to herself. She'd dealt with enough black marketeers to recognize a good one when she saw one. She would get what she needed.

Once at the door, the old man pulled out his key, a black card covered with small squares. With one gnarled finger he entered a code and slid the key into a slot. He pressed two buttons next to the slot and the door slid open without a sound. He rushed her through and closed the door.

His merchandise proved even better than she'd hoped for. She gave the man a sly glance with a hint of admiration.

"Look, see." His pride was uncontrollable. The man knew he had something not easily available, and a client who could recognize that fact. "Look, see," he said again.

Kelahya took a long, slow look around the room. It boasted four vehicles in impeccable condition. Two cruisers, which, as far as she could tell were fully equipped, and two surveyors, one standard, the other a highly customized ready-for-anything adaptation, complete with shifter camouflage. The walls of the room were lined with standard issue desert survival stocks. Top quality.

Kelahya circled the vehicles with an appraising eye. She heard the man chuckle under his breath. When she finished the circle, she snapped her fingers and pointed at the customized vehicle. "Fetch to me the one there."

The old man hesitated. He forced a smile to his lips and was about to encourage her to turn her attention toward one of the other vehicles when Kelahya yanked the collar of his coat and yelled.

"Fetch to me." She felt his body quiver through his thick coat. She gave him a shove in the right direction, and he stumbled off trying to catch his breath.

It was exactly what she needed and at the price she planned to pay. He would not haggle with her. The saber ensured that. So, he settled for moaning throughout the transaction, and cursed her under his breath.

She sped away in her surveyor toward Dionysus' Talothia Hage.

* * * * * *

Am I the only one like me in this world? Kelahya wondered. She sat on the walkway playing with some pebbles removed from a nearby flowerbed.

Trying to play, really. It was a game her mother had taught her before the big explosion. Before the ugly man had peered at her through yellow glass. Before the horrible woman in red had slapped her across the face for no reason at all. Before the endless trips from garrison to garrison in transport after sweltering transport.

She tried to evoke how the game went. There was a circle, of that she was almost certain. It had some funny shaped things that ended in points at the center. Ma had used some shiny stones to place in each space, and they had to be moved along. Somehow.

And there was a song. How did it go? She hummed what sounded like a familiar tune.

"Hmmm, hm…skippy-skip…and hmm…and skip…"

It was no use. Only Ma knew the game. Only Ma knew the song. Only Ma. Tears welled in her eyes. One trickled down her cheek.

She gathered as many pebbles as her tiny hand could hold and flung them across the walk.

BOOM!

She looked around in a panic.

BOOM!

It was happening again.

BOOM!

A wall behind her cracked and part of it collapsed to the ground.

She leapt to her feet, unsure which way to run.

"Ma! Da? Ma!" she cried.

BOOM! BOOM!

One of the huge doors that led to the small garden burst open and a platoon of the now familiar League of One Troopers burst through and headed straight for her.

"Maaaa!" she screamed as she ran toward the grass, trampling the delicate flowers as she went.

The troopers dashed by and swung open the door at the other end of the enclosure. Explosions echoed far and near, making the ground shudder.

Kelahya slumped to the grass. Crying in terror she covered her face.

More troopers stormed by. A cacophony of voices and explosions increased outside the garden.

Looking for a place to hide she peeked between her little fingers. Through her tears she saw troopers running in every direction.

Three of them fell in a heap outside the door to the garden. Two lay motionless. The third writhed in pain.

A handful of men dressed in garb the color of the Dionysian sand came into view. One of them walked to the wounded trooper and pointed something at him. A silent light flashed. A moment later, he stopped moving.

Kelahya's crying swelled to hysterical screaming.

The man with the light spun around and spotted her. He moved toward her, but when the chaos of battle grew louder, he headed off with the others in the opposite direction.

"Come, child."

It was Maccabeus. He had materialized out of nowhere as far as she could tell. Yet there he was, blaster in hand. He scooped her up with his free hand and rushed off with her into the building as another blast hit the wall and more of it disintegrated into rubble.

"Althenion," he yelled as they entered a hallway. "Where the blazes are you?"

A young trooper came running down the hall. "Here, Excellency. A million pardons. The—"

"Take the child to my quarters and protect her with your life. Do you understand?"

"Yes, Excellency," the nervous trooper sputtered.

"With your life." Maccabeus glared into the young man's eyes and the effect was obvious and immediate.

The trooper's lip trembled as Maccabeus handed the girl to him.

"Be off."

The trooper nodded, then spun on his heels and rushed down the labyrinth of corridors with perfect awareness of his destination.

After an endless succession of twists and turns, he stopped at a huge door and removed a metal card from his pocket. He slid it across a matching plate on the door and it swung open.

As soon as the door was safely closed behind them, he set Kelahya down.

"Are you well?" he asked, gasping for breath.

She nodded.

"Good. Good." He noticed the tear tracks down her cheeks and glanced around the room. Finding what he was looking for, he moved toward it. "Come."

Kelahya hesitated then did as he requested.

From a shelf he removed a small napkin and turned to the child. He knelt before her and wiped the tears from her face.

"Who are you?" he asked.

"Kelahya," she replied in a tiny voice. "Who are you?"

"Trooper Third Class Althenion Saller, at your service, Miss Kelahya." He gave her a practiced smile.

"What happened?"

"We were attacked."

"What's that?"

"Attacked? Uh, well, those people who were wearing the brown hamott cloth are rebels. We try to keep them under control, but they are very good at eluding us. Sometimes they sneak up to fight our garrisons." He rose to his feet and tossed the napkin in the refuse unit.

"What's 'eduding'?" she asked.

He looked down at her and pondered over it for a moment. "Eluding…it means…hiding where we can't find them. Probably in the caves out in the desert. Nestor is very good at finding places to hide his men."

"What's 'Nestor'?"

"Nestor is a man. A very evil man. You needn't worry about him, though. We'll track him down and kill him."

"Evil? Maccabeus evil?" Kelahya asked.

The Trooper was taken aback by her comment and struggled to regroup before he found the words to respond, "Well, Maccabeus is a soldier. He follows orders." He searched for understanding on the child's face. He found none. "He saved you, just now. He brought you out of the battle."

"He hurt Ma and Da. He took me away."

Chapter 4

Minders

———◆———

*Excerpt from the **Corpus Galacticum**, 137th Edition*

*Through the ages, some mutations resulted in the evolution of superior mental development. At the highest level are **Minders**, beings capable of invading and influencing the minds of most species in the universe.*

The universal order required that the establishment of protocols in the mental mutations to maintain stability. As a result, each mutation was categorized in varying levels of proficiency, and specific universal tasks were ordained.

***Level One Minders** are at the lowest level of telepathic mental proficiency in the overall order, and are usually technicians, or planners.*

***Level Two Minders** have a significantly higher level of telepathic proficiency so their tasks are usually those of scientists, officers, or medics.*

***Level Three Minders** are highly sophisticated, so their tasks are more complex and they serve as healers of the mind and spirit, or scribes of our sanctuaries.*

> *Level Four Minders have the highest telepathic mental proficiency and are rarest of all, as such their tasks are ordained in the service of the Incorporeal Fellowship.*

In less than one hexicon, Commander Devona reached red desert sands of Dionysus.

This arid terrain is familiar.

The moon of her birth was a tortured dominion. Nature had been unkind to this distant world, subjected as it was to the heat from which rained from above, as well as the heat from the furnace that burned incessantly in its interior.

But the desperate need for survival had forced the early Dionysians to make areas of the planet habitable. And, if Dionysus possessed one redeeming factor, it had turned out to be the abundance of metals and relentless heat.

Even water, undrinkable until filtered, had been available from the start. It was deep underground, in the caverns, under the mountains and deserts, but it was there. Huge lakes of gas-emitting boiling water that shot to the surface here and there. In short, Dionysus was a huge, hot rock, full of metal and water, and covered with dust.

In her mind's eye, on those rare occasions when she had allowed herself the pain of reliving her childhood, the reddish landscape conveyed a romantic image in its beauty. Now she saw it as it really was, and the stark, abrupt mountains jutting up to either side of the road grew more intimidating with each passing moment. Dionysus screamed its ferocity from every stone and crevice.

Small wonder that the Dionysians are a strong, indomitable race.

At length, the surveyor skidded to a stop in a cloud of dust. Kelahya had programmed the precise coordinates into the guidance console of the surveyor and had now reached her destination. But as far as she could tell, she was nowhere in particular.

The coordinates were based on the intelligence reports of the latest alleged sightings of the desert giant. For many cycles now, she had followed such reports hoping that in time the truth about the giant would be established. But time had run out. She could no longer wait for his confirmation. Now, it was vital that she find him—if there was anyone to find.

Propping herself up on the seat of the surveyor, and without taking her eyes off the desert ahead, Kelahya reached over and extracted a site scope from one of the compartments.

With the approaching sundown, the temperature rose accordingly. In a couple of hours, she'd be forced to go back. The desert was not the place to be at night. Legend had it that only one man had survived the deadly furnace of night, but she feared it was only that…a legend.

With the help of the site scope, Kelahya scanned the horizon looking for anything out of the ordinary. Something that stated *this is the way.* She found nothing. She scanned in a slow, circular movement that included the desert behind the surveyor. Beads of perspiration formed on her scalp and face.

Abruptly, she stopped. *Could that be it?* Several hundred feet off the road, at the base of a bread-loaf shaped hill, a bush. Something, someone, she hoped, had snapped the brittle stem just above the ground. Whatever, or whomever, had done it needed to be carrying considerable weight. This wasn't an environment that bred weak flora.

She took note of two landmarks to help her triangulate the bush's location, tossed the site scope back into the compartment and, with a turn of the wheel, sped off in a shower of pebbles and dust.

Close to the spot, she slammed on the brakes and rushed to the bush. She hadn't been deceived. The branch was broken and the earth around it leveled by something flat and heavy. And the sap was sticky.

She ran to the surveyor and took out the site scope. She scanned again. Nothing. The rocky soil was perfect for hiding tracks. There was, however, enough dust to allow for an occasional imprint, if one was not careful. And careful he would have to be indeed, if he was still alive after all this time.

Her eyes scoured the ground. The light was shifting to red as the temperature increased. *How long would his steps be?* She tried it. *My longest step is about four feet. His might be as much as six, more if he tried to extend his stride.* She took several long steps, first in one direction, then another, adding the two or three extra feet that she assumed his stride could measure. Nothing.

She stood by the broken branch and pondered. Her eyes scanned the ground ahead of her. *Which way would I go?*

The hot breezes began to stir. As far as she could observe, there were no clues to indicate a preference. Behind her lay the sloping valley she had just traversed. On either side the steep crevices of the eroded cliffs. Ahead, the valley swelled toward a mountain that marked its end.

The valley. Why not?

She trotted back to the surveyor and sped off toward the end of the valley, between two escarpments. She stopped. The reddish light made distances a flat, two-dimensional deception. She'd have to search on foot.

At the base of a hillock to her left stood a large boulder, big enough to hide a surveyor. The vehicle whirred into action and, moments later, was completely concealed.

She double-checked the hydropods and nutrition pellets, hung the site scope around her neck, slung the pack across her shoulder, and secured the surveyor. From beneath the rear seat she removed a case and tapped the bolts. The lid rose. From the case, she took her black Squall Blasting Gun and the Hermit Phase Beam. The former fit neatly into her belt, the latter snapped onto it hanging under her hand for easy access. The weapons had served her well throughout countless encounters in the past and they would be at her side again now. The last item was a Gemno Field Searcher, a souvenir from her days on Kronos' secret service. She slid on the goggles and, with a deep breath and a glance toward the cliffs, marched into the furnace night of Dionysus.

* * * * * *

"Wake up, little one, you have arrived," a mellow voice cut into the child's nightmare of her mother's body being flung across the room. "Wake up, it's time to come home."

Kelahya stretched involuntarily, blinking and yawning herself into consciousness.

"Ma?"

A slender woman with light skin and tightly curled red hair sat beside her, smiling down at her.

"Hello. I'm Chantall."

Only once before had Kelahya heard anyone, other than her mother, speak with a Terrian voice, and he'd been a trooper. She blinked again and glanced about the compartment, then began to shake. This reality was a part of her nightmare. She recoiled as tears gushed into her eyes.

"Now, now, it's going to be all right." Chantall's soothing arms wrapped about the girl and pulled her close. "Hush," she whispered, as she rocked Kelahya in her arms. "Come. I'll show you your new home."

Chantall led the exhausted and bewildered little girl out of the transport. Kelahya had no idea how many different ships she'd been on. Every time she awoke, she found herself in another ship being taken by another stranger to yet another empty chamber flanked by another group of soldiers. In a daze, Kelahya followed Chantall through yet another labyrinth of corridors, a detachment of guards only steps behind them.

At length, they arrived at another guarded door. It opened silently. The soldiers and transport station remained behind as the doors closed. The sudden silence startled Kelahya. Only their footfalls echoed along the unending hall. Moments later, another door slid open and they entered an enormous open space filled with wondrous sights, but Kelahya was too tired to care.

"This is your new home, Kelahya." Chantall smiled with pride. "This planet is called Uxiel. It's very similar to my home planet, Terra." Reassuringly, Chantall patted the little girl's hand before continuing.

"This is your garden. Come." Chantall led the girl out among the flowers and stopped. She knelt in front of Kelahya and smiled. "Look. The ground is covered with what is called grass. Here, let us run our hands over it." Kelahya obeyed automatically and knelt to touch the grass. It made her smile.

Chantall fought back a tear and stroked the little girl's cheek. "It tickles a little, does it not?"

Kelahya nodded as she glanced about. She pointed to the flowers as she stood. "What are those?" she asked.

"Those are all called roses, and there are many different kinds of flowers. Each one has its own name, just as you and I? Do you remember my name?"

Kelahya nodded but did not speak the name. Instead she was pulling Chantall toward a much larger object.

"What's that?" she questioned.

"It's called a tree, and as with the flowers there are many kinds of trees. In time I will teach you the names of all the flowers and trees. Would you like that?"

Kelahya stared at Chantall, her eyes sad and tired. "I'm not going on another ship?"

"No, child, you are to remain with me." Kelahya turned away from Chantall and looked at the garden. She noticed a bird in one of the trees and ran to it. Startled, the bird flew away.

"What's that?" Kelahya's eyes were wide with wonder.

"A bird. There are many birds in the garden. You'll also learn about the birds and their feathers."

"Feathers?"

"Yes, the colors on the birds are feathers."

"I saw a feather," Kelahya bragged. "Ma has one."

Chantall picked up the little girl and embraced her warmly.

Chantall is good to me, Kelahya thought. She was not her Ma, but she was soft and kind.

"Where's Ma?" Kelahya finally ventured.

Chantall stroked the child's arm and forced a smile. "Where I come from, we speak of a place where all good people go when they can no longer be with us. It's a nice place. That's where your Ma is."

"Can I visit her there?"

"You cannot actually go there, no. But if you close your eyes and visualize her, she'll be there, inside you, and you can even talk with her if you wish."

"Where is that place? How did Ma get there?"

Chantall's smile faded. Her lips tightened and a tear rolled down her cheek. She squeezed Kelahya's hand ever so gently. "Well, sweet child." There was a thickness in her voice that caused her to clear her throat. "I changed places with her."

Kelahya tilted her head inquisitively. Another tear trickled down Chantall's face and found its way to the corner of her mouth. Kelahya's little fingers followed the path of the tear and wiped it.

"My little girl had to go to that special place as well, and your Ma agreed to look after my little Muyulu if I would look after you." Chantall's voice trailed into muted sobs as she pulled Kelahya to her, her teardrops falling into the girl's soft hair.

Kelahya reached her little arms around Chantall and hugged her.

* * * * * *

"Okay, I can't stop you from reliving the past. What do you hope to achieve? You wish us dead?"

No.

"Then be present!"

Every promising crevice and ravine had led to a dead end. With each step she took, the nighttime inferno of Dionysus increased. The Talothia Hage proved to be far more inhospitable than anticipated. Perspiration soaked her clothes and her energy waned.

We must rest.

An outcrop of rock provided only minimum relief, but she welcomed it. She folded her legs into the limited space and opened a hydropod.

With practiced discipline she slowed her breathing and heartbeat, and in no time her body cooled. Only her eyes labored, relentlessly scouring every inch of the valley.

This resting place offered a superior view, not only of the valley below, but also of the escarpment to either side. A myriad of details shifted into focus.

There was more vegetation here than down the slope. Not enough to merit the delight of the farming community, but certainly enough to indicate a significant difference in the feasibility of life.

The man she sought would look for such a place if he expected to survive. With renewed interest she peered through the site scope, examining every feature with critical keenness. It was useless.

"If he's out here, and that's a crucial 'if' indeed, he certainly has mastered the art of concealment beyond any I've ever come across. If he's hiding in these heat-battered hills, I must find a way to understand his mind and be one with him."

In the past, you'd concealed yourself in dangerous deserts, jungles, and mountains throughout the galaxies with astonishing success.

"This shouldn't be any different. If I were hiding in these hills what would I do? What precautions would I take to ensure myself against the unexpected visit of undesirable guests?"

Kelahya smiled mischievously as perspiration dropped from her chin. She downed the remaining contents of the hydropod in a single gulp and patted the two remaining ones on her belt.

An instant later she leaped to her feet, took two deep satisfying breaths, and trotted out into the most visible area of the gorge. A familiar song came to her lips.

"This is my hand. Take it.

Grasp it when the going gets too rough.

Hold it when the moon begins to rise.

Use it when your own begins to shake

And you need a little help

To dust the clouds out of the sky."

She sang the lines over and over, enabling her to focus on the task at hand. She made her way in the deadly heat following an arc that led from rim to center to rim, then along the edge at the foot of the cliffs.

After running the circuit four times, it became clear that she'd deluded herself. No one lived here.

The rumors of her enemy living in the Dionysian desert were nothing more than sterile desires of a fantasizing civilization on a hot, eventless planet. There were other deserts on Dionysus, but they were host to mining operations that clustered large groups of workers. Not a safe place for a myth to hide.

Then, she heard falling pebbles hit a boulder a few feet ahead. Without hesitation, she pivoted and headed back the way she had come.

More pebbles fell a few feet ahead. She'd made the right decision. *Someone is in this valley.*

Her hand groped automatically toward her weapon. She turned away from the falling pebbles once more. After some sixty yards she stopped. There were no more pebbles. She listened. Silence.

I did hear it. It's not an illusion. It's real.

Is it?

She glanced around the barren landscape until she recognized the large rock that had been at her left upon ending her march about the rim. The surveyor was there.

As she took a step in that direction, there was a faint hissing sound.

A shield shot up around her, its electric discharge making her muscles twitch spasmodically. Her feet were pulled from under her, and she hit the ground hard. The breath burst from her lungs. She felt immense pressure on her forehead and the blazing heat yielded to the cold of unconsciousness.

* * * * * *

"Kelahya, my little one, come," Chantall beckoned.

But Kelahya did not intend to obey. She enjoyed the garden too much and was tired of the dwell. She preferred the outdoors.

She liked the breeze, the warm rays of the two suns of Uxiel, the singing birds, the feel of the grass on her bare feet and back, and the flowers in her hands. She loved her garden.

So, she ignored Chantall and remained lying on the grass with her eyes closed, listening. She could hear the light footsteps on the soft grass, the rustling of Chantall's robes.

And something else.

At the edge of sound, she could hear something she'd never noticed. A distant whisper— a conversation, not in words but in feelings. No, in vibrations. Moments later, she felt Chantall's presence next to her.

"I notice that you're not asleep and that you've heard me, but I'll pretend to not be aware of these facts, so you won't have to be punished for disobeying me. We shall begin again."

Chantall walked away a few feet. She turned and cleared her throat. "Kelahya, my little one, come."

Kelahya rolled onto her stomach, her wide eyes pleading with Chantall. "Must I? It's so pretty here. May I stay a little longer? We could do the lessons here."

Chantall smiled. She held out her arms and walked toward the girl.

"That's a much better response. But we cannot, sweet child. Today we must learn about the different foods there are in the galaxy, and for that we need the duplicator units. Come." She pulled Kelahya up into her arms.

The girl wrapped her legs about Chantall's waist.

"You're getting heavy, little one. One of these days I'll no longer be able to carry you."

Kelahya threw her arms around Chantall's neck and hugged her. "Yes, you will. You'll carry me always. I like it very much, and so do you."

"Yes, I do, but you're growing very fast and very tall."

"You can carry me all right. You'll carry me even when I am too big. I know it."

Chantall leaned her head back and peered down her nose at the girl. "And how are you so certain, my child?"

Kelahya paused for a moment. "I can see it."

Chantall stared at her ward and smiled. Her fingers danced along Kelahya's ribs and the tickling made her squirm and giggle. As they headed toward the dwell, they hugged, and their laughter echoed about the walls of the enclosure.

Once inside the dwell, Chantall put Kelahya down. "You must change your tunic, it's wet."

"Oh, very well." Kelahya turned and burst into song as she skipped down the corridor.

"This is my hand. Take it.

Grasp it when the going gets too rough.

Hold it when the moon begins to rise.

Use it when your own begins to shake

And you need a little help

To dust the clouds out of the sky."

Chantall smiled and followed her. It had been only two cycles since Kelahya's arrival, and the bond between them had undoubtedly saved both their lives.

She entered Kelahya's chamber and found her standing, naked, watching the carousel of tunics wander past. Chantall shook her head. She stopped the rotation and picked a pink and blue tunic. She handed it to Kelahya.

"This one will do well enough. Put it on along with the undergarment."

Without hesitation, Kelahya slipped both on.

"Chantall, can we visit Uxiel City today?"

"No, darling. There is no need to do so. Everything you need is right here."

"But I want to see the city."

"You have seen it in the vidlog."

"It's not the same."

"Maybe when you're a bit older you'll be allowed to leave."

Kelahya frowned. "You always say that."

Chantall took her hands between her own and patted them. "You want for nothing here, Kelahya. What is this frown for? Look around you. You have a beautiful garden, a most attractive chamber to sleep in, and many delightful rooms for playing and for learning. And there's the Grand Salon where we pretend that we're great ladies. Let's not forget the vidlogs, the viewscapes, and the virtuofiles where we learn about the universe, and even create our own worlds. You lack nothing, my child. So, don't frown. You're indeed a very lucky little girl."

Kelahya shook her head, a scowl evident on her brow.

"What is it? You don't like your quarters? Is there anything else you desire?" Kelahya nodded. "Speak up. What is it?"

Kelahya looked Chantall squarely in the eyes. "I wish to be like the birds and fly out of here."

Chantall embraced the girl and stroked her hair.

Freedom is the one thing you cannot have, Chantall thought, and Kelahya heard the vibrations of these musings in her own mind. Somehow, she was inside Chantall's head.

In a flash, she witnessed the death of Chantall's husband and child at the hands of the dark troopers, and the nightmare weeks of uncontrollable grief that followed.

She observed how, before Chantall could carry out her plans for her own death, Kronos had commanded her to travel far from Terra to mentor an orphan girl on a distant planet called Uxiel.

Kelahya understood that Chantall had no choice. She couldn't disobey Kronos.

She realized how Chantall had gathered her shattered life and transported it across the cosmos in a daze of non-reality.

She saw Chantall enter a military transport surrounded by the machinery of war to gather the sleeping child named Kelahya.

In an instant, Kelahya grasped how she, a girl of four, so little, so frightened, so very fragile, had made life bearable again for Chantall who, in turn, freely showered her with all the love stored within her trampled heart. Their need for each other created an instant bond, and both had embraced it without hesitation.

It was at that moment that Kelahya perceived her Minder's Endow.

She understood that this gift was hers alone. A gift, she imagined, which had been bestowed upon her by the birds she loved so—those beautiful creatures that had the freedom to come and go as they pleased from this opulent cage.

She took Chantall's hand and whispered, "I understand now."

Chapter 5

Warfare Tactics

———◆———

*Excerpt from the **Corpus Galacticum**, 137th Edition*

Supreme Commander Kronos Deucarrion is credited with establishing a training regime designed to prevent League of One Forces from capitulating or revealing classified information. He also created complex strategies designed to stimulate unconditional surrender by the enemy.

Historian Lourenus has recorded numerous such successful encounters in the 13th Edition of the Cosmic Combat Anthology, used by the League of One's Military Academy. Two examples, summarized here, are permitted for public dispersal.

In 659 TE, a cell of elite League of One Troopers who had been captured and imprisoned by EntAir, withstood excruciating torture for many moons. The troopers, trained to mask their pain appeared unfazed, and never capitulated. Unable to break their captives, the usurper and his followers failed to withstand the assault by the League of One troops who came to their aide. Kronos credits the success of the mission to the resilience displayed by the captive troopers. The Director later stated, "The troopers honored their training and showed that not one single being in our known universe can breach a warrior trained by the League of One."

In the winter of 673 TE, Director Kronos launched Operation Array to overthrow and arrest the tyrant Nurdiwes, who had captured and tortured innocent youths in an effort to force their families into submission. Three platoons of specially trained League of One Troopers tracked down and surrounded Nurdiwes in his hidden fortress beneath the waters of Rori. Still, the tyrant refused to liberate his prey.

The Rori river tributaries were damned and the lake itself was drained. Isolated and deprived of water, Nurdiwes was unable to withstand the seclusion, freed the children, and surrendered.

When Commander Kelahya Devona regained consciousness, it seemed at first as if she were watching a laser concert like the one she'd attended with Kronos on Menar.

As her ability to focus returned, she realized that what her mind had perceived was the flickering of flames reflected on crystalline stone.

Where am I?

Knocked unconscious. Trapped.

She moved her hands, surprised to find them free. But that revelation paled in comparison to the shock of finding herself naked. A thick, tattered blanket lay atop her nude body. The unexpected vulnerability made her cling to the smelly cloth like a lifeboat.

There was a crackling of fire and she recognized the scent of burning stonewood. She strained to hear any other sounds that might provide a clue to her surroundings. Except for ballot moths that fluttered about what could only be a cave, no other sound could be heard.

Stiffness and pain assaulted every muscle and joint. Her ears rang, and her head throbbed on the left side. She snaked a hand up to touch it. A sizable knot protruded above her ear.

As quietly as possible she sat up and looked around. A large boulder to her left separated her from the fire. She tightened the blanket about her.

"Greetings." Her voice, deepened by the smoke, reverberated throughout the cave. When there was no reply, she tried again. "Salvos and health," she yelled. It was the common salutation among the natives. Again, nothing.

Pulling her aching legs up to her chest, she rocked onto her toes. Without relinquishing the blanket, she groaned to a standing position, and limped around the boulder.

A fire burned at the center of the huge cavern, but there was no one in sight. Nor did she notice any visible exit.

She sat down and pulled the blanket tighter. Kelahya Devona, soldier, diplomat, spy, and now prisoner, sat by the fire, legs pulled to her chest beneath the coarse blanket, and stared into the flames, fighting off fear.

Is this real, or am I imagining it all?

"How could I have allowed the trap?"

You're not yourself. You must regroup. You can't succumb to fear. Your captors would capitalize on that. Focus on escape. Only escape. Focus…focus!

She closed her eyes and concentrated on the Mindstill stratagem in a desperate fight to regain control of her thoughts. The whirlwind of images flashed through her brain with dizzying speed. Slowing mental chaos to a standstill was the stratagem's paramount tenet, and she strove to reach it. It would provide the necessary resistor to bring the turmoil under control, at least for a time.

At length, she succeeded. The pain in her head subsided, her breathing returned to normal, and the need for a plan of action slowly came into focus. The first priority must be to become familiar with the battlefield.

She fashioned a torch from a piece of stonewood and a swatch from the blanket. Even if she found a way out, it was unlikely she could get far, especially with no clothes. She needed to learn more about her surroundings.

Holding the torch above her head, she set out to explore the cave.

Despite the considerable heat from the flames, a moist coolness lay heavy in the air. She noticed the shimmering walls of the cave.

Pure water. The most elusive commodity on Dionysus. I must be close to a great abundance of the vital liquid.

A hexicon later, she'd completed the arduous task of examining the cave walls in as much detail as the poor lighting could accommodate. Five tunnels led off in as many directions.

Ballot moths clustered at the mouths of the passageways, but none ventured into the larger chamber where the fire was.

Unusual behavior for a moth.

She selected the leftmost tunnel of a group of three and headed in. It slanted uphill in a gentle climb and turned abruptly to the left, where it shot upward at an impossible angle into absolute darkness. After checking for any possible offspring tunnels, and finding none, she labored back down the rocks to the central cavern.

Her feet, unaccustomed to the roughness of the ground, were sore from the abrasions and frequent stubbing. She stopped a short distance from the fire to remove a tiny stone embedded in her right heel. The blanket slipped off her shoulders. She left the blanket behind and limped closer to the fire to check her feet.

"You strong, wench."

Kelahya spun around and reached instinctively for her weapons, her hand slapping against a naked thigh. She lunged for the blanket and pulled it over her breasts. Her heart pounded in her chest, her breath a rapid series of puffs.

"Be of no fear…presently." The deep voice conveyed no threat as such, but the word "presently" had a clear touch of warning.

The man before her was covered from head to toe in the same cloth her blanket was woven from, and the angle of the fire lit only the tip of his nose. He glided along the ground. He chose the opposite side of the fire so that it stood between them. Two gloved hands emerged from his flowing sleeves and rose to remove the hood that concealed the face and head.

He was a Terrian. He'd spoken in Eniat, the broken language of Dionysus, but his features were undeniably Terrian.

With great caution, she attempted to enter his mind. Nothing. She was peering into a void. To her surprise, this penetration produced no pain.

Has my mind weakened to where I can no longer penetrate others? Or is this the effect of advancing dissociation and descent into oblivion?

Either prospect was terrifying.

Focus on the enemy.

His hood was attached to a robe, or coat, that brushed the ground at his feet.

"Identity?" His voice echoed off the rocks around them. The face showed no expression. He was tall for a Terrian and wore no visible weapons.

"To speak your presence here," he insisted.

Kelahya searched for a reply that would place her captor at the answering end of the dialogue.

"Is this how Dionysians treat visitors? By stealing their belongings and taking them prisoner?" She spoke with a touch of indignation but avoided any hint of threat or superiority. "I have done nothing to you."

"You are who?"

"Well, who are you?"

He walked around the fire until he stood a breath away from Kelahya.

She towered over him.

He stared into her eyes, but it was more like looking behind them, as if attempting to peer through a hole that led directly into her soul.

She invaded his mind. But found only darkness.

"To rejoin you for answers." He turned away. "Upon readiness, inquiries will have answers." He took several steps toward the group of three tunnels.

Kelahya had to act fast. "Wait!"

He stopped without turning.

"You startled me. I need a moment to recover. I will answer your inquiries…be patient with me."

The man remained immobile.

"I come from far away. From Terra. I'm originally from this planet, but I left with my parents when I was a child of four. I've only recently returned and am not yet familiar with your customs. If I offended you, please tell me what I can do to prove I have no intention of harming anyone. I was examining the unusual rock formations in the valley. I'm a mineralogist."

He turned to her. "Identity?"

Kelahya took her time. "My name is Quaytra Playaar."

He turned and stared deep into her eyes then, without a word, he turned away and glided toward the farthest tunnel to the right disappearing as fast as he'd appeared.

"Wait! Why are you holding me here?" Her voice echoed about the cavern.

Gathering the blanket around her, she picked up the torch and followed him. The cave divided immediately into four more passageways. She took the one on the right. It split again. There was no one. Only silence. To continue was useless, she couldn't find her way out of this labyrinth.

* * * * * *

"But, who's Kronos, Chantall? Why does he keep me here?" Kelahya stomped the water about her feet as Chantall rinsed the soft young body.

"I've told you, he's the Director of the League of One. He's the most powerful man in the recognized galaxies, and your protector." With a smile she watched the water trickle in small rivulets along the girl's skin. Kelahya was her child now. For five cycles, they had found comfort together and filled each other's emptiness and replaced each other's loss. Chantall was proud of "her girl".

"You've told me that part many times. I must learn about him. How does he look? How old is he? Does he live here? Why have I never met him?"

Chantall reached for the towel and wrapped the girl inside it. "I can tell you only what I'm permitted to say. It's forbidden to speak of him. You're well aware of that."

"Why? Why is he my protector? I need to understand," she pleaded, her vivid green eyes filled with wonder.

Chantall could never resist. She embraced her and whispered almost inaudibly, "I'm proud that you respect my thoughts. You've learned well to master your gift."

Tenderly, she brushed her long, wet hair.

"Very well, I'll tell you what I can. He's never been here. He receives vidlogs of you every day, and orders only the best for you. He's dictated your education and care, step by step. He's the most powerful man in the universe, and he's chosen to care for you."

"Why?"

"Mostly, I believe, because he's of your same species."

The child's brow furrowed inquisitively.

"Your mother was Terrian, as I am, and your father was Dionysian. Am I correct?"

Kelahya nodded.

"Well, so it was with the Director's parents."

Kelahya's eyes widened with amazement. "My parents are the same as his?"

Chantall smiled, kissing Kelahya on the tip of her little nose. "No, child, no. He had different parents, but like you, he's half Terrian and half Dionysian. You and he are the only two remaining."

Kelahya pondered her guardian's words. "So, we're the only two in all the universe? Why?"

Chantall picked a new tunic; there were always new tunics for her to wear, and this one was so beautiful that Kelahya gasped with pleasure.

"Terrian and Dionysian is an unusual match. Your father was big, and your mother was like me, much smaller. Is that right?"

Kelahya nodded, her emerald eyes sparkling with wonder.

"Only two Terrian women are known to have birthed children of Dionysian men. At least, that is what the vidlogs of the League of One tell. Your Ma was very special."

Kelahya deliberated for a moment, then proudly added, "And so was Kronos' ma."

Chantall smiled with a deep sense of relief. "You're a very clever little girl. Indeed, so was the Director's ma."

Chantall gathered colorful ribbons and braided the child's long hair while Kelahya admired her reflection with a satisfied smile.

"Is that why he's so powerful, because he's the only one in the universe?"

"So it is said. And you're a very lucky little girl to have the protection of such a mighty man. Everyone follows his commands."

Kelahya turned to Chantall with a mischievous little smile.

"Not everyone."

But Chantall didn't smile. She cupped Kelahya's little face in her hands and looked sternly into her child's eyes and whispered, "Everyone...everyone."

"You don't."

Chantall's face clouded as she hugged her ward. "That's our most important and deepest secret," she whispered.

"Our lives depend on it." She tightened her embrace. "Do you understand?"

The girl nodded.

Chantall relaxed the embrace and held Kelahya at arm's length. "Enough of this. Our lessons await. Today we learn more of the creatures that inhabit our universe."

"You said today we'd practice the imperial stride and astral dance. I have a pretty tunic for that."

"We will indeed, but first to the viewscapes. What if you encounter one of these creatures in the future? If you can't understand them, how would you greet them?"

Kelahya's eyes widened with excitement. "I'm going to encounter others?"

"Of course. In due time."

"When?" she queried with anticipation.

"When the Director decides."

Kelahya felt a pain that emanated from the deepest core of her being and she heard her mind scream.

So, I am a prisoner.

Sensing something was wrong, Chantall knelt before her ward.

"What is it? Are you not well?"

Kelahya shook her head and smiled. "I'm all right. Let's go prepare for this future you speak of."

The future that Kronos has planned for me.

* * * * * *

Well, at least remembering distracts me. Is that why we're traveling to my childhood? Do you guide me to find a parallel that will help?

Commander Devona guessed she'd been alone in the cave for more than one Dionysian day, but it could easily have been four. The true sense of time eluded her. Often, she'd believed someone was approaching, only to discover it was the fluttering of ballot moths in the tunnels.

Three times she'd rekindled the fire and added stonewood. She'd paced the cavern, hummed, cursed, and called out to whomever might hear her, yet not once had she pleaded for help.

She waited quietly, staring into the flames while her mind wandered to images of a youth populated by long forgotten memories.

Kronos had always kept her waiting, as well. She'd learned from him that it was a common, and very effective tactic in interrogation.

"Give me the strongest will and endless time, and time will break the will," he'd told her. "There's no antidote for boredom and despair. The harder they resist, the more violently they crumble. Indifference breeds insanity. Nothing is more devastating to a prisoner than being locked up alone with himself. He'll convince himself of anything. All it takes is time." And she'd witnessed how he'd used this technique over and over.

Stripping the victims naked was a refinement. The sense of vulnerability accelerated the descent into madness, an effective tactic. Kelahya wondered if her captors realized that her mind had begun to unravel before she'd even reached Dawnzehya Gleva.

"I bring you food." He appeared without a sound, as if by magic, and his voice echoed in the damp air of the cavern.

She grasped the blanket and pulled it tightly around her. Her eyes followed as he placed a container near her feet.

"Are you cold?"

"No, but I'd like to have my clothes back."

He flicked the lid of the container open. "When you have answered my questions without playing games, you may have them back. Not until then." He was speaking Terrian now.

"I've told you who I am." She tried to sound bewildered. It didn't work.

He gazed into her eyes without emotion then turned away. She had to give it a shot.

"All right. Don't go. Ask me anything."

"Give me the information I seek. Speak." In one fluid, effortless motion, he sank to the ground, his coat sliding from his shoulders, surrounding him. There was an ethereal quality about him. "Why don't you eat?"

Trying to reveal as little of her body as possible, Kelahya reached for the container and pulled it toward her. There were two smaller containers inside. By the shape, she could tell that one probably contained liquid, the other some sort of solid food.

It was a clumsy and uncomfortable operation to remove the containers without losing the blanket, especially with her hands shaking from hunger and thirst. His leaden eyes did not facilitate matters. Twice she lost control of the blanket, and twice his eyes roamed about her body with indifference.

Quickly, she scanned the food. As with the fire, the offering of food meant her captors planned to keep her alive. The food, a vegetable combination she'd never tasted before, was invigorating, and her body responded to it instantly. She scarfed several bites before beginning. "Very well. What should I call you?"

"Speak, Kelahya Devona, or I shall go."

They know who I am.

There was only one way he could have discovered her name, a retinal scan. A glimmer of understanding began to take form.

"What do you wish of me?"

"Why are you here?"

"Well, if you have my name, you must also be aware that I'm Modyor Devon's daughter."

The man nodded.

"After he died, I was taken elsewhere. I was a soldier for the League of One. Now, I'm coming home. I arrived here..." she realized she was not sure how long ago that had been, "... the day before you brought me here. That's it. If there's anything specific you wish to learn, then ask."

His expression didn't change. He stared into her eyes and appeared not to breathe.

She hoped the bit about the League of One would remove any doubts he had regarding the veracity of her statements. Since no one in their right mind would reveal such information, he should take it to mean that she was speaking the truth. If it worked, the rest would be easy.

"State your purpose in this valley."

I'm still in the valley. "I seek my father's grave."

He stared at her for what seemed a lifetime. Not once did he waver in his intensity. He didn't even blink. She had to push him. This was the moment.

"Well?" Kelahya raised her eyebrows and tilted her head to emphasize the question.

With the same effortless flowing motion with which he had sat, he now picked up his coat, rose to his feet, and turned to leave. Kelahya leaped to her feet.

"Wait." Her voice carried the undeniable authority of someone used to being in command. He stopped without facing her. "Who are you? Why are you tormenting me? If you asked me specific questions, I could give you specific answers. But I don't imagine you really seek answers. It's clear that your only intention is to torment me. And eventually kill me."

She moved around the fire to face her captor head on.

"If you don't give me my clothes, and tell me what your orders are right now, I'll have no choice but to assume that I'm correct. And, when you return, I will no longer be alive."

She moved so close, she almost touched him.

"As I perceive it, I have nothing to lose. Either I kill myself, or let you destroy me little by little. And if you know who I am, you understand what I'll do."

He stood there, motionless, looking but not seeing her. He was stunned. Kelahya held the gaze.

"Decide. My life or my death." Her voice was a raspy whisper.

Without warning his whole body shuddered. Then, he was immobile. His eyelids dropped closed. He appeared to be dead.

She smiled in triumph. His behavior had been perfectly human, but without humanity. Too obvious for the trained eye—her eye.

She glanced around at the tunnels. Someone would come for the robot sooner or later. She chuckled, unable to contain her satisfaction with this significant, if only minor, victory.

She undressed the robot, tossing its nude synthetic body against the boulder at the side of the cavern. Kelahya donned his clothes and smiled remembering how she used to make Chantall laugh on those occasions when she would try to elicit conflicting reactions from the robots that cared for them.

She loved to show Chantall how she could make them shake, shudder and disconnect by providing them with conflicting orders that clashed with their programming. The fun was in finding out what their programming was. And she'd become a master at such sleuthing.

Look at this robot. Disarmed by one of the oldest tricks in the book—a command impossible to obey. This robot though, is quite sophisticated, excellent movements and voice. The Dionysians have made some outstanding improvements, hard to detect as robotic, superb assembly. Programming somewhat basic.

The robot had been ordered to make sure that no harm came to her. He would feed her, ensure her wellbeing, and return with information. No variations. The possibility of Kelahya harming herself if he left her was not anticipated. Unable to reconcile protecting her from herself without hurting her in the process, his program shut down, and he ceased to function. Overload automatically triggered a shutdown to protect the internal components from damage or destruction.

She tried his belt, but it was too tight. The coat, however, had a tie belt, so she removed it from its original garment and tied it around her waist. *Not high fashion,* she reasoned, *but certainly functional.* Then she tossed another stonewood on the fire, perched on the boulder where she could watch all the tunnels, and prepared to wait.

CHAPTER **6**

The Alliance of Stars

—————◆—————

*Excerpt from the **Corpus Galacticum**, 137th Edition*

*During the 1st Century TE, after the Incorporeal Fellowship issued the Talderon Ideals, **Poliate**, a level four Minder, was ordained by birthright to assume secular command of the universe. He was known for his intolerance of social injustice and assumed control of what was then known as the Planetary Union. He was charged with bringing to an end the period historians now call the Age of Anarchic Disarray.*

His first order of business was to gain control of the planets and systems that for centuries had been victims of tyrannical dictatorships, and kingdoms where widespread corruption had fostered slavery, unlawful conquest, and generalized crime. Thus, began a new era of peace and prosperity.

He instituted a new code of secular laws based on the Talderon Ideals, known as the Poliate Code. The first laws were inscribed on twelve bronze plaques which became venerated as the Twelve Tablets. These laws include

73

rules of legal procedure, civil and property rights, and a constitutional basis for all future laws.

Countless despots and dictators were brought to justice and continue to be prosecuted to this day. New systems of government created by the populations themselves, gradually brought justice and equality to the vast majority of systems.

Among the many legacies from that era, are the constant stream of technical inventions, scientific discoveries, and socially organized realms that have flourished throughout the cosmos.

Having succeeded in system-wide reforms, Poliate founded a universal government under the banner of **The Alliance of Stars**, *and a central government named* **The League of One**.

Kronos Deucarrion, direct descendant of Poliate, is the current secular leader and Supreme Commander of the Alliance.

The cubicle door slid open and Chantall flew into the room, her eyes wide, and a nervous hand over her mouth.

"He's here. By all the heavens, he's here. Hurry, hurry. Get dressed."

Kelahya set her vidlog aside and turned to her guardian, as the light about the room grew bright. "Who's here, Chantall? What are you talking about?"

"I'll explain as we go. Come along." Her hand clamped onto Kelahya's wrist and she pulled the girl out of the cubicle and along the corridor that led to her room.

"Ow, you're hurting me."

"Stop whining and hurry. By all the stars, why didn't they warn me?"

"What are you talking about?"

"I always feared this day would come. But I had hoped…" Chantall's pace quickened even more, and Kelahya recognized the look on her face. It was the look of fear. "That's why we were barred from entering that side of the compound. They've known about it all along and told me nothing," she growled with a resentment she would never be able to express out loud.

"Chantall, stop pulling me."

They reached Kelahya's bedchamber and Chantall slapped the panel that opened the door. She flung the girl into the room, closed the door and rushed to the dressroom.

"If I hadn't gone to fetch your meal…thank goodness the mealmasters were forewarned, otherwise there would be hell to pay." She turned to her ward, a look of despair clouding her face. "And now you don't even have time for dinner." Her fear was reaching the panic stage and Kelahya's impatience toward her grew by the moment.

Chantall touched the dresser panel and it slid open. "And now, today, this night, he's coming here." She reached inside the dressroom, touched the wall, and the carousel of dresses initiated its rotation. She selected a floor-length, bright red dress with holographic ruffles around the bottom, neck, and cuffs that reproduced a faint image of Kelahya from various angles. She tossed it onto the bed.

"I don't like that one," the girl whined. "It's strange to have my own face staring back at me as I move. And I'm not putting on a special dress. I don't like it."

"Do as I say." Chantall's tone was the harshest Kelahya had ever heard. The shock caused her eyes and mouth open wide with surprise. Then she saw the tears.

"Why are you crying?"

"Listen to me, child," the woman said, fighting the anguish in her voice.

"I'm not a child anymore."

"Yes, you are. You are blossoming, but a child, nonetheless. Never mind that. It is Director Kronos. He's arriving any minute. He's coming for you. If you're not ready—" she couldn't finish.

Kelahya rushed to her dear companion and hugged her. Chantall's body shook as she threw her arms around the girl and sobbed.

Abruptly, she pushed Kelahya away and shook her head.

"There's no time for this now. You must get dressed." She held her at arm's length and tried to muster a smile. "Wear that dress and the matching jewelry. It's his command."

Kelahya started to object.

"If you disobey, I suffer. Do as I say. Please."

His power was boundless, and his will was law. She'd also been told that the day would arrive when he would come, or summon her to him, but Kelahya never considered it a real possibility. She felt the reality of it now and found it utterly terrifying. Tears welled in the young emerald eyes. "I'm afraid, Chantall."

A tiny smile tried to take shape on the older woman's lips as she sniffled and wiped her own tears. "Remember me, as I'll remember you. Think of me from time to time."

"Remember you? Why do you sa—"

The soft chime played its musical notes indicating someone was at the door. Kelahya picked up the red dress and rushed into the dressroom as the door to the hall slid open. She left the dressroom open and pressed herself against the wall to hear the exchange in the room.

"The Director's transport arrives in twelve hexicons. The girl is ready?"

Kelahya relaxed. It was a robot. The flat inflection was subtle, but Kelahya had easily learned to distinguish it from that of humanoids many cycles ago—a skill Chantall had been unable to master no matter how hard Kelahya tried to teach it to her.

Robots were designed so that their speech reflected a subtle version of emotion or intention, which was very effective in disguising their true nature. And they did fool almost everyone—but not Kelahya.

"She will be there," Chantall said impatiently. "Your interruption shall be the cause of her tardiness."

"It's a robot, Chantall. It doesn't fear you."

Chantall examined the robot with her usual mixture of awe and confusion, and then added, "Leave." In an instant, the robot was gone.

Kelahya poked her head out of the dressroom door. "I refuse to go."

Chantall let out a startled squeal as she spun toward her ward. "Universe of galaxies. Get dressed silly girl. Now."

She rushed over and pulled the dress down over the blossoming young body. Her expert hands had Kelahya bejeweled, combed, and ready in minutes. When every detail was in place, she took the girl by the wrist and pulled her toward the door.

"Listen to me for the last time, sweet girl. You're only thirteen, but you must become a woman before we reach the Grand Salon. You will not speak to me once we leave this room. From now on, I shall exist no more."

Kelahya wrenched her wrist out of Chantall's grasp. "Then, I won't go."

Chantall shook her. "We have no time for this. Listen and conform. You'll obey Kronos in everything, without hesitation. If you don't, he'll have you killed, or worse. He'll have me killed as well. In time, you'll find your path. I can't tell you what that path will be. But whatever comes, you must remain true to yourself, your feelings, and your mind. Promise me this." The tone and intensity of Chantall's voice left no room for argument.

"I promise."

The woman placed her hands on either side of the girl's face, kissed her forehead, and took one last long look at her ward… her daughter. As the tears flooded her eyes, she became rigid and stepped back.

"Chantall, does my future hold my freedom?"

"It will, if you wish it." She opened the door and bowed obsequiously to Kelahya.

The girl hesitated.

"Go," came the whispered command, and Kelahya stepped into the hallway.

Her breath caught in her throat.

A guard of rigid soldiers, in greater number than she'd ever beheld before, lined each side of the corridor for as far as her eyes could see. They wore the green and black uniforms of the elite guard of the Alliance of Stars. Chantall's careful schooling had taught the girl that the green and black was a ceremonial uniform, used only by those who had proven their loyalty to the League of One, specifically to Kronos.

Alternate corridors were blocked off, leaving her only one route. With a deep breath, she regained her composure and commenced the slow imperial walk she had so often practiced. Learning it had been amusing, although quite ridiculous. Now, it felt almost natural.

Chantall followed, several steps behind, glowing with inner pride. She'd spent long tormented hours with this rebellious girl teaching her how to walk, sit, listen, and look. Today, this day of days, she did it all to perfection. Her child was becoming a woman with each advancing step.

The carpet along the hall that led to the Grand Salon stretched like an endless path of gold and white, bordered by black and green. It was the only floor in the complex that had this material down its center.

"It's supposed to make the room important," Chantall had explained long ago. It certainly looked important now.

Kelahya felt like she'd been traveling the corridor for hours. Cold droplets trickled down her back. The temptation to look at the soldiers standing so motionless had almost made her giggle on more than one occasion. When she unconsciously sped up her pace, Chantall's instructions came to mind and slowed her down.

Through it all, she'd maintained her head high, her eyes focused, her step firm.

Let all of this be over with quickly. Kronos should leave me here with Chantall. Maybe he's not aware that that's what I desire. I will tell him.

The corridor gradually curved to the left, and she knew the salon would soon come into view. She felt dampness in her freezing hands, and noticed the silence. Only the rustling of her gown made a rhythmic swish. Her mouth was so dry she couldn't swallow.

The turn in the corridor ended. The doors to the Grand Salon opened and a strange noise flooded into the corridor. Even at this great distance, Kelahya could tell the room was bursting with humanoids.

The entire galaxy must be here.

As the strange noise subsided, she became aware of a musical beat emanating from the salon that matched her steps. She noticed that, as she passed, each soldier unsheathed and raised his or her saber in salute to her. She felt wetness above her lip and wanted desperately to wipe it dry, but she dared not.

Chantall's words echoed in her mind. "*You're untouchable, you're sublime, perfect. You're his creation. You're never nervous, never uncomfortable, never rude, never loud. Never anything but perfect. Your life depends on it. Kronos will protect you more fiercely than the Alliance itself. But, if you let him down, if you fail him, he'll destroy you more fiercely than the planets he's annihilated.*"

The huge doors to the salon loomed ever larger with each step. The strange noise resumed. It was a hum of a sort she couldn't recognize. The unsheathing of the sabers slashed the air before her.

A few feet from the doors, the unusual noise faded, and she realized it was the din of hundreds of voices that abruptly ceased as she arrived at the Grand Salon.

She walked through the doorway, and into the silence of the crowd. A sea of creatures stood shoulder to shoulder, forming a wall of galactic specimens. She gasped.

They slowly parted, forming a living corridor that stretched farther and farther across the huge room. When the motion ceased, she could make out four steps leading up to an enormous empty translucent throne she'd never seen before.

Did they bring this for him?

The gold and white carpet ended at the throne, which stood surrounded by holomatic standards of the members of the Alliance that formed the League of One. The insignia of the League itself emanated from the throne and filled the room with a whimsical light.

Why is it empty?

An odd creature emerged from the crowd on the left in front of the throne. His face caused her to bite her lip. It was a face that had haunted her childhood nightmares with the symmetrical scars crisscrossing the cheeks and forehead.

Her mind spun into a frantic whirlwind, the sharp pain making her wince. *This is Kronos? It cannot be. I met this creature before, long, long ago. This is Maccabeus the one who took me away,* her mind screamed. *My parents' killer!*

Fire exploded inside her. *Run! No! Better to scream my pain and share my hatred with the hundreds about me!*

No, do not do that.

Something, or someone, deep within her coaxed her to remain calm and quiet. She didn't understand why, but she obeyed.

The doors closed behind her and the steady music that had followed her steps went silent. She heard the rustling of clothes as the hundreds of strangers pressed against each other to get a better look. She took a few steps toward Maccabeus and stopped.

He moved toward her, and she felt an instinctive tightening in her stomach. Her hands became two fists ready to protect her. He continued forward then, all of a sudden, his left knee went down on the carpet. The back of his right fist came up to his forehead and rested there.

She was petrified. *What now?*

A fanfare of music exploded. The crowd on her right moved away as the man before her, still on his knee, turned and faced toward her right.

Whatever is going to happen will come from that direction. She turned toward the parting crowd. Everyone dropped to one knee and bowed.

Kelahya remained standing. Then she saw him.

Is this a man or an apparition?

He towered over all those present and wore a white body sheath that glowed and sparkled as he moved. A long, black and green cape with golden borders hung from his shoulders, barely touching the floor around him.

The body sheath fit him like a second skin, as if painted to his body. His hair was silver gray, his eyes a deep blue, his skin a luminous brown. He was not a young man, she could tell that, but he emanated a strength and power that permeated the vast room.

She watched in awe as this most beautiful and electrifying being walked toward her, a warm smile across his face, a twinkle of mischief in his eye.

He stopped just out of reach and let his eyes scan the young girl in the red holosilk gown.

She could feel a tingle that excited her through and through. Little bumps formed all over her body and a slight shiver shook her from head to toe.

As she did, one of his eyebrows raised almost imperceptibly. He'd understood her reaction, and an uncomfortable warmth invaded her cheeks.

His right hand came up, exactly as Chantall had said it would, and he spoke, "Kelahya Devona, you are more beautiful by far than images or words ever described. Come."

She took his hand and allowed herself to be led by this vision in white that represented the utmost power in the universe— Kronos Deucarrion, Director of the League of One, Scribe of the Legislature, Supreme Commander of the Alliance of Stars.

Chapter 7

The Endow

————◆————

*Excerpt from the **Corpus Galacticum**, 137th Edition*

*The fundamental attribute of Minders is the **Endow**, an invisible synapse where nerve impulses are transmitted and received throughout the vibrations of the dimensional strings within the time space continuum.*

Their cells have access to supreme intelligence and can arrange, at the atomic level, hadrons, protons, neutrons, molecules, electrons and the like, in the correct order to achieve diffusion.

What are you trying to show me? Is the answer to our riddle in my past?

Yes, the answer is in our past.

"It's been a long wait," a voice reverberated about the cave. "But in this makeshift facility our infrastructure is…outdated, let's say."

A Terrian.

The man's long, angular face carried the creases of age with dignity. Deep brown eyes peered from hollows beneath a forest of eyebrows. The thick mustache drooped like black and gray threads around his mouth to the edge of his chin. The nose was large and curved. A strong perplexing face, with a combination of wisdom, kindness and intensity, and a dash of cruelty tossed in for good measure.

She attempted to penetrate his mind, but he was impossible to read… something around the man protected him from any type of telepathic invasion.

A shield? How?

"We missed Canelo over there." He nodded toward the naked robot.

"I demand to be released." She emphasized the command by bolting to her feet.

"I understand your outrage, certainly, but we're somewhat outraged ourselves." He turned with a gesture toward the jagged wall opposite the tunnels. "Shall we?"

"After you." She detected no exit in that direction, despite visually examining every inch of the cavern several times.

"By the way." The old man stopped after the first step and brought his wrinkled face very close to hers. "My name is Jofan Valsin. You may call me Jofan." He smiled and headed off again.

Kelahya took one skeptical step after another. *I don't trust this kind-looking old prune.*

As he arrived at the rock wall, Kelahya found herself stopping in expectation of what the man would do when his face hit the rock.

He disappointed her by disappearing into it. Vanished. Her face tightened.

"Hologram," she mumbled.

"You disappointed us when you didn't even consider the possibility," said the withering voice from somewhere directly in front of her.

She plunged ahead with such anger she almost knocked the old man down.

Jofan stood in a tunnel, illuminated just enough to indicate the correct route. "An antiquated, but effective device. The opening can be sealed with a force field, if necessary." He smiled again, then turned and headed down the tunnel. "This way."

After a sudden turn, they came upon a large door of some metallic alloy, which Kelahya couldn't readily identify, that slid open without a sound as Jofan approached. The whirring of machines and the bleeping of electronic devices gushed into the tunnel.

Kelahya stood in the doorway of a small control room. It appeared to be somewhat primitive, but she'd encountered enough intelligence centers throughout her career to recognize an efficient set-up when she saw one.

"What is it?" she asked, feigning ignorance.

"Now, now, Commander Devona. We must not play games."

Kelahya glared into the old man's eyes with contempt. "I rather imagine that games are very popular with you."

She stormed imperiously into the room, using her anger to veil her appraisal of the details.

Three females and two males operated the room. Of the females, Kelahya recognized one as being of the Trianon species with a voice-activated communication device on her collar. Another, a Glenarian, was preoccupied with discharging energy into a faserdeck.

Outdated indeed.

The third, a petite Terrian brunette, had no obvious purpose other than to keep an eye on the prisoner. Kelahya immediately pegged the males as androids of even less sophistication than Canelo and probably task specific.

She took her time examining one set of displays after another. Her tour finally brought her face to face with Jofan. He smiled.

"Satisfied?"

Without waiting for an answer, he glanced at the small brunette and waved her over. "Caveat, take the Commander to her quarters. Make sure she has everything she needs." Caveat nodded. He turned to Kelahya. "When you are more...comfortable, we shall talk." He turned away.

"We will talk now," Kelahya's thundering voice commanded.

Jofan stopped. He remained motionless. Caveat reached for her weapon. All the others were unarmed.

"I need answers, Jofan. Now!"

After a few milicons, Jofan issued a huge sigh followed by drooping shoulders and head, then came the tired voice. "So be it. Come." He waved Caveat away then headed into the corridor in front of him.

Kelahya, disarmed by the lack of a fight, felt the adrenalin pump through her body. His indifference to her indignation was infuriating and unsettling. She rushed after the old man.

He led her down a corridor carved, as they all were, from the rock inside a mountain. He walked in silence, his brisk pace belying his ancient appearance.

They turned into a second corridor. The ceiling was stone, but the walls were covered in a luminous synthetic, a common lighting device. Closed doors lined one side of the corridor, and each displayed a small plaque by the door with a symbol, letters perhaps, common to barracks everywhere.

Living quarters.

Jofan stopped before one of the doors and it slid open. He stepped back and ushered her in, then followed as the door closed behind them.

The chamber was everything that the rest of the installations were not. Spotlights in the ceiling accentuated the various wall hangings, paintings and sculptures spread about the room. The furniture was Terrian, inviting, and cozy.

Kelahya stood in the center of the room surprised by how much at ease it made her feel.

"Sit wherever you like, Commander Devona. Or do you prefer General given your recent appointment?"

Kelahya remained impassive.

"As you wish, Commander. Would you care for something cold to drink?"

Jofan swung open a large cabinet that displayed assorted colored bottles and carafes, glasses in varying sizes, and mirrors that reflected in all directions, catching the subtle light from about the room.

"Or food, perhaps?"

Jofan's politeness unnerved her. "Something to drink."

Jofan smiled. "Very well."

A particular piece of artwork across the room caught her eye. A dimensional painting covered the entire wall and gave the impression one could actually disappear inside it. The subject was the Talothia Hage, where she'd been captured. The depiction of the valley had achieved an ethereal quality that almost felt inviting. The real thing was anything but.

"Try this, Commander, it'll appeal to you." Jofan held a long-stemmed glass containing a lavender liquid that bubbled with a slow effervescence.

She took the glass and stared at him, attempting to penetrate his mind.

Much to her surprise, his mind remained beyond her reach.

He looked at her with a raised eyebrow.

Old prune, how can you resist with such ease? Unless… Are you a Minder? The notion shocked her. *Impossible. Oh! Celestial Heavens! Have I lost the ability to enter other minds? Is that why I now feel no pain?* The notion terrified her. Her hand trembled slightly.

The old man offered his non-committal smile again and sipped his glass as he headed toward a large chair across the room. He'd obviously placed his lounger in that exact position so that he might fully appreciate the painting's wonderful effect.

He pulled over a large stool and patted it invitingly.

"Let's enjoy it together."

Kelahya gave him a curt nod as she crossed the room and sat beside him.

"Interesting place, the Talothia Hage. It even has some vegetation, a rarity in the area." He took a sip of his drink. "Care to tell me what brought you to my valley?"

"Are you in the habit of capturing every traveler who ventures into 'your' valley?"

Jofan chuckled and the liquid caught in his throat, inducing a coughing fit that the old man appeared to be ill equipped to handle.

Kelahya watched him with a smile, implying more satisfaction than she really felt. Her merciless gesture was lost on Jofan.

The unrelenting cough was too much for the old man.

Kelahya hesitated, but his face was turning a deep crimson.

Finally, she leaned him forward, placing his elbows on his knees, and slapped the middle of his back with her hand. The cough gave immediate signs of relenting.

He sputtered, like an old machine, until the fluid moved on, enabling him to catch his breath. With subdued enthusiasm, he managed a couple of coughing chuckles.

"So, Commander, you have a heart. A dangerous quality for someone in your line of work." He cleared his throat and took a deep breath before speaking again. His eyes watered and his face was flushed. "I suppose I now owe you an answer to your question." He continued to clear his throat. "As for venturing into my valley, the answer is quite simple. Aside from the occasional military training expedition, which Garrison commanders feel obligated to carry out to reassure the League of One that they can clamp down on hostility, only two humanoids have ventured into the valley in the last five cycles."

He took a sip of his drink before going on. It cleared his air passages further. "One came to commit suicide. He was from Tasadia, probably a refugee. The radiation had damaged his tissues beyond survivability. Probably could no longer tolerate the pain. Blasted his head right off. The other became lost, we assume. He died of exposure. Different purpose, same result."

He waited for her reaction but saw none.

"In any case, they were 'travelers', as you so quaintly put it. Unlike you, however, they were not Commanders under Kronos

Deucarrion. To the best of my knowledge, they weren't even soldiers." His expression grew stern. "Or spies."

The cold tone carried unmistakable meaning. This was not to be the beginning of a beautiful friendship.

He waited for her to comment. When she didn't, he went on.

"Commander Devona, I must emphasize that my position here doesn't allow for endless chit-chat, so let me come to the point. We're clear about who you are, but not why you're here. If you choose to give me no answers, your life here won't be enjoyable. To put it succinctly, your wellbeing depends on your cooperation. That little outburst in the..." He stopped to consider the right word. "Control room," he continued, with a forced smile, "is not acceptable. If you're disagreeable, we will restrain you, if you cooperate, you will earn a certain degree of freedom. In short, you have no rights here, Commander, other than what we determine you should have. And provocation doesn't have a positive impact on our disposition."

Kelahya felt an icy moisture form in the palms of her hands. Jofan's speech had been direct and unemotional. Experience dictated that he wasn't bluffing. *If I could only enter his mind.* She needed time to decipher him, therefore, cooperation became the only alternative.

"I'm at a serious disadvantage, Jofan. No matter what I tell you, my life is at risk. You have a great deal on me, but should I gamble telling you more?"

"That is your decision," the old man said plainly.

Kelahya stared into her drink for a moment seeking a satisfactory game plan. Too many things needed sorting out. Appearing to collaborate, at least for now, was clearly the wiser choice. She turned to face him. "If we have the same objective, my information will serve our common cause and you'll be in my debt for providing it. If we aren't, I'm as good as dead. And others will die, as well." She held his gaze for a moment, then stared back into the lavender liquid and downed the content without effort.

"I'm a soldier first and foremost, Jofan. If I must die to protect my own, then that is my fate. But if by chance you and I seek the same things, then my death would be a devastating blow to those I mean to help. Do you understand my dilemma?"

The old man's penetrating gaze bore down on her with an intensity difficult to resist. But she held firm. She must, if she was to have any success.

"I'm afraid," the old voice said tiredly, "that we're at an impasse, Commander. For the safety of my people, I must eliminate any threat you may pose."

Jofan had aged perceptibly in the past few moments. He rose with stiffness from his chair and went to the desk beside the refreshment center. He pushed a button on the terminal then turned to Kelahya.

"I can wait for you to change your mind. No matter how long it takes."

A patrol android stood outside as the door slid open

"This is not a persuasion robot. He has specific orders regarding you, and termination is not a problem for him. Your wellbeing is not his primary concern, either. I suggest you do as he says."

Kelahya gave the android an instantaneous and expert evaluation. She noticed no weapons, which meant they were built into his anatomy so they could not be wrested from him by force. This robot could be destroyed, but not disarmed, and whatever vulnerable spots it might have, they were surely well protected.

"Come with me, Commander," the unemotional voice said. When she didn't move, the robot took a step inside the room and repeated the command, "Come with me, Commander."

Jofan ambled over to Kelahya.

"He won't repeat the order. His next action will be forceful. Possibly fatal."

"All right." She rushed out of Jofan's quarters.

* * * * * *

Young Kelahya sat next to Kronos in enraptured amazement as the hundreds of delegations from the infinity of planetary systems were presented to her. She had no idea how long she'd been there, smiling and nodding at this endless sea of races. It thrilled her to be in the presence of that many different species, speaking such a variety of languages, and expressing themselves in so wide a diversity of manners.

Regardless of external appearances, or strange sounding utterances, one thing was clear, they all venerated Kronos. He embodied, without question, the center of their adoration. Some knelt before him and kissed the edge of his cape, others bowed their heads, and extended their arms toward him, others clicked their heels, or fell to one knee. Males and females alike, all rendered homage to Kronos.

And there she was, Kelahya Devona, sitting beside this god-like man in the Grand Salon. Treated by him as…she knew not what, but far differently than he treated the others. He hadn't asked her to bow nor had he made her follow behind him.

Instead, he'd led her toward the throne at the end of the salon, and when they reached it, he had eased her into it. A second chair had quickly been brought for him and he'd sat down next to her, his firm hand clasping hers.

With a reassuring smile, he'd turned toward the gathering and nodded. Only then had the interminable procession of delegates begun to present their respects to him.

And to her.

At first a knot of anxiety had gripped her stomach, but as the delegations bowed before them, the tension had eased, and the sheer joy of surveying this promenade of unusual and fascinating creatures had taken over. It was the most exciting feeling she'd ever experienced.

Now she was almost relaxed. She felt safe. And with that inner calm came the courage to look at her protector, to gaze upon this enigma of a man called Kronos Deucarrion, the power that ruled the universe.

He's magnificent. The embodiment of power and intelligence. She noticed a brightness emanating from his muscular, disciplined body. *But how could this be, how could light surround him?*

Yet there was an aura about him that she could detect with increasing clarity. *The skin on his face and hands is smooth, light brown, like mine, but lighter. His hands look so strong and hairy. I wonder how it would feel to touch the hairs. Are they soft? Do they tickle?* She chuckled at the thought.

The muscles on his arms and thighs were taut. His chest was wide, and she could clearly feel his vitality with every breath he took. As she examined the details of his face, he turned to her and his eyes met hers. She felt a sudden tingle underneath her skin. She sensed the blood rushing to her cheeks, and wanted to turn away from his gaze, but she couldn't.

"You don't have to turn away from me." She heard his voice inside her head.

He winked and smiled, then rose to his feet, reaching for her hand. The room plunged into silence. Without a word to the congregation he led her out of the salon, and down one of the huge familiar corridors she'd so often played in growing up.

He guided her with imperceptible authority, like a dancer.

They said nothing.

When he finally brought her to a halt, they stood at the center of a corridor that extended forever in either direction.

She glanced both ways and then at Kronos. He smiled that warm, irresistible smile.

He placed his hand on a wall and, out of nowhere, a double door appeared, opening into a chamber. With a nod, he invited her in.

She stood there, motionless, her young brain searching fervently for a logical explanation as to where this chamber would take her. She could find none.

Noting her reluctance, he entered first. She followed, not half a step behind. The doors slid closed behind them.

She entered a room she'd never been in before. Its mere existence came as a surprise. It was larger than any other in the compound, with the exception of the Grand Salon of course. It featured walls covered in moving holomatic illustrations of magnificent planetary landscapes, all in shades of blue. The room itself glowed in a bluish tinge with indirect lighting from an undetermined source that resulted in an absence of shadow. The furniture was translucent, and the fabric on the large bed glistened like the waves of the ocean under a faint moonlight.

"It's like being—"

"Underwater," interrupted his voice inside her head.

"Yes," she responded, and the sound of her own voice startled her.

"So, you're a Minder. You have the Endow," Kronos said as he took off his cape, and tossed it onto one of the chairs.

"Minder? Endow?"

"You're endowed with the knowledge, the talent to hear my mind."

"I can't do that."

"You just did. Did you not respond 'yes' to my statement?" Kelahya's eyes widened as he approached her and cupped her face in his hands. "You're truly magnificent, Kelahya Devona. More than I ever imagined."

Her young body trembled. *Why do I feel this tremor when he comes close to me? What is this feeling?*

"It's your awakening. Don't worry, little one, it's early yet. You'll understand as you grow older."

He released her and went to a table at the corner of the room. Kelahya stood in a frozen stupor. Kronos signaled for her to join him. He handed her a drink. "Eat and drink, Kelahya. You must be hungry."

She was at a loss as to how to act. Chantall had described Kronos in such untouchable terms that she feared it was improper to sit beside him. But his demeanor appeared so relaxed and familiar that it felt as if she'd known him forever.

She sat across the table from him.

"That looks very good, your Excellency. I must admit I am hungry and thirsty. Thank you," she managed to respond. She gulped down her drink and reached for the food. She handed him her empty glass.

"May I have more, Excellency?"

"You may, indeed."

As he poured it, he chuckled. *I can imagine how my subjects would react if they could peek at the omnipotent Kronos playing nursemaid to a child of thirteen...But oh, Mighty Perseus, what a child she is.*

"Who's Perseus, my Lord?"

"Never mind that."

Kelahya sensed that somewhere a door had been closed.

He watched, captivated, as she continued to eat and drink with the healthy voraciousness of a teenager.

"Aren't you going to eat?" she asked between bites. "These little ones and the blue ones are delicious."

"I am eating," he responded.

A broad smile formed on her blushing face. "You are not. You're sitting there, looking at me."

"Looking at you is all the nourishment I need."

Kelahya laughed her beautiful, deep, satisfying laugh. "That makes no sense."

"Tell me, Kelahya," Kronos reached over and softly touched the back of her hand with his fingertips, "are you happy?"

"You mean, right now?"

He nodded.

She considered it for a moment. "I believe I am. Are you?"

The question caught him off guard. "I..." He paused.

"Well, yes or no?" she insisted.

He sighed. "I never asked myself that."

"Then why do you ask it of me?"

He gazed into her eyes. "Because there's nothing more important to me than your happiness."

She smiled then looked away, unable to sustain his gaze.

"Does that surprise you, Kelahya?"

She shot him a shy glance. "Yes. Well, no. Because I believe that you care about the happiness of all your subjects."

"You obviously never met my subjects."

"No matter who they are, you should care about them."

"You are too young to have any idea what I should or should not do."

"I'm old enough to have learned what's right and what's wrong. Of that much I'm certain."

Kronos bolted to his feet, his chair crashing behind him, and stared at Kelahya. She stood her ground.

"Aren't you afraid of me?"

"Should I be?"

"Most are."

"Why?"

"Because their lives are in my hands to do with as I wish. So is yours."

"You told me you care for my happiness. I believe you."

"Do you, now?" He laughed, picked up his chair, and sat down again.

"And can you guess what else?"

He raised his brow and grinned.

"I like you best when you smile, and even more when you laugh."

Chapter 8

The Olympus

———◆———

*Excerpt from the **Corpus Galacticum**, 137th Edition*

The Olympus *is home to the seat of power of the Alliance of Stars and the League of One. A spacecraft designed as a functional city capable of constant stealth space flight. As such, its location in the cosmos is unknown.*

The Olympus is a spacecraft designed as a functional city with capabilities for constant stealth space flight by manipulating the dimensional strings with astral energy.

The Olympus is home to the seat of power of the Alliance of Stars and the League of One, as such, its location in the cosmos is unknown.

The guidance systems of the Olympus overtake the control of any vessel sanctioned to dock or launch, and automatically deletes all locator data from the processors of those ships.

The unique modular design of the Olympus enables entire self-sustaining sectors to be added, detached, or modified. Each sector is capable of independent flight, and when separated, can rejoin the Olympus as needed.

This method allows for greater flexibility in operation and overall speed of flight.

The Olympus is impregnable and is not affected by solar flares, magnetic fields, radiation, orbital pulls, or lack of outer gravity.

Commander Kelahya Devona lay on her bed, peering at the ceiling of her new prison.

Every time I close my eyes you yank me to the past.

It's the way out of our dissociation.

The door glided open and the android stepped into the room.

"Clothes and food." He dropped the bag of clothes on the floor and placed the tray on the table.

"How long are they going to keep me here?" Not programmed to respond, the android couldn't answer, but she assumed her question had been transmitted to someone who could.

The android left the room without a word.

Kelahya opened the bag and spread the clothes on her cot. She examined them inside and out, searching for anything that could indicate where she was or who her captors were. Nothing. She tossed the old robot's clothes into a corner and put on the clean uniform. It fit like a glove.

They know everything about me. Or so they claim. Except my reason for being on Dionysus, if I'm to believe them. The hurdle is that I can't discern what true and what's not. Does Jofan have the Endow? Could he be a Minder? Can he read my thoughts?

She shook her head.

I haven't felt him probe my mind. Yet, I've been unable to pick up anything from him. In some, that's a sign of learned strength. And without question the old man is strong. Perhaps... Why not put him to the test?

She focused inward and prepared to feel the excruciating agony that followed the use of her Endow ever since its fissure. However, she felt no pain when she reached Jofan's mind. Instead, she transmitted her demands with ease. *I grow tired of your games. You can hear me, Jofan and you're watching. Let's talk. Better yet, let's share a meal.*

Nothing. Not even a flicker.

She'd finished dressing when the door opened. The android remained outside.

"Follow me, General."

This time she was happy to comply with the android's orders. At least, she'd be out of confinement.

She followed him through the corridors back to Jofan's quarters, stopping twice to test the android's response. His reactions were instantaneous. She expected that. But it was fun to play with him.

When she entered the old man's quarters, they were empty. She turned to the android.

"Wait inside." The door closed.

To find herself alone in Jofan's quarters surprised her. After all, she'd come prepared to spar with him.

Alone...well...let's explore.

She found nothing in the room that could be used as a weapon against him or the android, and nothing to indicate where she was or how long it had been since her capture. She touched several data pads on the console. No response.

With a shrug and a sigh, she looked around. She spotted the bar and poured herself a drink from the bottle Jofan had used before. It tasted even better than she remembered.

She paced about the small chamber, running her fingers along the furnishings, taking in every detail. Jofan was Terrian, no doubt of that. His possessions were all designed for the senses. The indirect lighting on the various pieces of artwork, the variety of textures, and the chair facing the painting of the valley, were all quirks typical of his race.

She needed to get a handle on Jofan. On the one hand, she couldn't reach into his mind, and on the other, here she was, alone in his quarters.

Why? He must realize that by allowing me in here my ability to access his brain will increase. Is this a trap or a trick of my mind? Am I imagining that I'm here?

She sat in the old man's chair and leaned back to look at the painting. It seemed as if she could escape simply by walking into it. It gave her an idea. She stared into the painting and concentrated. To her relief, the pain in her mind remained absent. As she probed the image of the Talothia Hage, it enveloped her senses. She closed her eyes. Then, slowly, very slowly, piece by tiny piece, the images jelled and shifted into focus. Once again, without the searing pain, she had released her Endow and had entered Jofan's mind.

He was in the control room studying a monitor. A series of symbols danced across the display. There was someone near him… no, it was a shadow…a very large shadow.

Kelahya concentrated. *Who is that?*

With remarkable dexterity, Jofan's hands entered a series of codes into the computer console. A white aura surrounded him, and she sensed warmth and fulfillment. Jofan was a satisfied man, content with himself. Loyal.

Loyal to whom?

To the shadow.

And to…me?

Abruptly, Jofan turned away from the monitor as a burst of white light blinded Kelahya's mind.

* * * * * *

Young Kelahya woke to the sound of her door sliding open. "Chantall?"

Kronos stood in the doorway, smiling. "Fine morrow, Kelahya."

Startled, the girl sat up.

"Fear not your friends, Kelahya. I've protected you always and shall forever do so."

Fear? Was this fear she felt? If so, this was a different from any she'd experienced before. Her captors had caused her fear…no, it was terror she'd felt then. If this was fear, then it was a fear she enjoyed. Her heart beat furiously, her breath came in little puffing sounds as she exhaled, her palms were wet and cold, her cheeks afire.

Kronos smiled again. "You're all that your supervisor said you'd be, and a galaxy of stars more. Chantall shall prepare you for the mealtime. Until then, sweet girl."

And he was gone. Only the sliding of the door gave testimony that he'd been there at all.

A deep disappointment came over Kelahya when he vanished. For an instant, she was overcome with a feeling of emptiness, and the awful idea that she might never be with him again.

That's silly. He'll be back.

As she relaxed, her breathing slowed along with her heartbeat, and her hands regained their natural heat.

"Oh, child. My dear, dear child," Chantall whimpered as she tiptoed into the room, one hand over her mouth as if such action could conceal the fear in her voice. A tear rolled down the woman's cheek. "Are you well?"

"Chantall, where have you been? You left me alone all night and when I woke, he was there. Standing in the doorway, looking at me. Why?"

In an instant, the woman reached her ward, held her hands, her dark eyes scrutinizing every inch of the child's flesh.

"Did he hurt you?" Chantall's deep voice cracked.

Kelahya was bewildered. "Hurt me? No. Why would he hurt me? He stood there, in the doorway."

Chantall stiffened. "Standing in the doorway? All night?"

Kelahya's chuckle was like the tingling crystals of Thelonia. "Constellations, no. This morning when I woke up, a few moments ago, before you came in, silly."

Chantall's eyes dropped and her deep voice became a whisper. "What of last night?"

"After meal, you mean?"

Chantall nodded. Kelahya crossed her legs into a lotus, puckered her lips, and squinted as if to squeeze the memories from her mind in succulent detail.

"Well…he took me from the ballroom and led me here. Had you ever been in this room before? Isn't it magnificent?"

In a reflex gesture, Kelahya took Chantall's hand in hers and gave a deep sigh in an effort to extract more memories from her speeding mind. "We talked, and talked, and talked."

"Is that all?" Chantall whispered.

"Of course, silly. What else would we do? Mostly, he talked to me about how well I'd handled myself in the ballroom and how nice my dress looked. Oh, and what good work my 'supervisor' had done with me. Who is this 'supervisor'?"

Chantall couldn't contain a certain pride as an almost invisible smile forced its way onto her lips. "I'm your supervisor."

The girl's face shifted from smile to perplexity as she straightened her back, tilting her head a little to the right. "Explain 'supervisor', then."

Chantall blurted out an uncomfortable nervous chuckle. "It's…a person who…well, who's in charge of someone's…care I suppose, of their development and well-being. Kronos' orders were to educate you in the things he believes will make you perfect. To turn you into someone the whole Alliance will look up to when…you leave."

"Leave? What does that mean? You said a similar thing yesterday. You said, 'Listen to me for the last time'. What does that mean?"

"It means nothing. Not anymore. Kronos has seen fit to grant me a boon. I shall continue in your service."

Kelahya pushed the older woman away and stomped across the room. "Boon? What's a boon? What are you saying? You speak to me in riddles. Say what you mean."

Chantall rose slowly and approached her ward with a tender smile on her fleshy lips. "They told me that after the ball, he'd take you away and I wouldn't be near you ever again. But last night Maccabeus came to my shelters and said that…" her tears drowned her words, "…that I am to be with you henceforth. Kronos approves of my teachings and has ordered me to be with you, always."

Her sobs mingled with her joy, producing a convulsive weeping laughter, as she enveloped Kelahya in her long arms and squeezed the girl with all her strength.

The thirteen-year-old stood dumbfounded. A trickle of mortality rolled aggressively down her spine. She shuddered.

"Taken away? From here? From you? Where?"

Chantall's weeping subsided and she released the youngster who had become such a vital part of her very soul.

"With Kronos."

Kelahya's hand clamped onto the woman's wrist so tightly it made her wince.

"Where is Kronos taking me? Why would he separate me from you?" Kelahya's voice wilted into a plea. "I'm afraid, Chantall. You're the only person I trust. You've been my friend… my mother. Where's he going to take me?"

A silence that screamed with terror whirled about the room.

Kelahya stood motionless, her eyes locked into Chantall's, her mouth agape, her energy gone. Chantall felt a tear roll down one cheek and then the other.

"I don't know where. You are his, and he'll do with you as he wishes." She threw her arms around the girl and held her tight. "But don't fret. We will not be separated. We'll always be together."

Kelahya stood rigid, staring at nothing. "For as long as he wills it."

* * * * * *

When Commander Devona regained consciousness, she'd been moved from Jofan's quarters back to her chamber.

Her temples pounded to the beat of her heart. The pain across her forehead made her squint under the light, and she emitted a weak groan with every breath.

She tried to sit up only to collapse back onto her side. She placed her palms against her eyes in an attempt to sooth the pain. The pounding intensified, so she removed them. She rolled her knees over the side of the bed and pushed herself into a sitting position, placing a hand on either side to stabilize herself.

Mighty Constellations, my head burns! What happened?

A rumbling that sounded like distant thunder reached her ears.

As her breathing normalized, she looked around the room again. She had to squint, but at least things were almost in focus.

Again, the rumble. It didn't come from inside her head. She concentrated and listened. With a heartfelt groan she rolled back onto the bed and sucked in a few more deep breaths.

Another rumble. Then came the sound of her door gliding open. She closed her eyes and feigned sleep.

Jofan burst into the room and gave Kelahya a violent shake. "Get up! Come. There's no time to lose."

With lightning speed, Kelahya yanked Jofan's arm down, spun to her feet behind him, and pinned the aging man onto the bed, his face buried in the cushions. The harder he fought, the more she leaned on him.

The android gave no warning as he sneaked up behind her. He held her firmly and pressed in the hollow behind her skull. Kelahya knew what would follow. She had learned the application of the Athanaan Press early in her military training. Her vision narrowed to a concentric circle, her knees buckled beneath her, her arms dropped to her sides.

They need me conscious, but helpless.

She felt her head hit the floor and heard Jofan roll over gasping for air.

An explosion, distant but unmistakable, reverberated along the corridor outside the chamber.

We are under attack. The recognition was accompanied by the indifference brought on by her condition.

Jofan, recovering, motioned to the android and said, "Help me up."

The obedient machine complied and lifted him up to a standing position.

"Carry this stupid female to the hydrotube." Jofan's normally vibrant voice was breathy and weak.

"You are my primary concern, Jofan," came the flat-toned response.

"I'll be fine. Get her out of here, quickly."

Another blast, closer than the previous one, rocked the walls.

Kelahya felt the sturdy arm of the android lock under her armpits and lift her upper body. A second later, the other arm lifted her legs. She felt a change in the air.

The corridor.

Jofan ordered another robot into action. "Krind, take me to the hydrotube."

With each pounding stride the robot took, her head bobbed up and down, her arms dangled rhythmically, her legs swayed. She tried to force her eyes to see. They were open, she was sure of that. She blinked several times, but to no avail.

She closed her eyes and pushed her mind. *I am Kelahya. General Kelahya Devona, Commander of the XXVII Confinement Brigade. I am...*

Little by little, muscle control crept back into her arms and legs. She experimented by opening and closing her mouth on command. It worked. She strained her eyes again. Light. Figures were undistinguishable, but at least she saw light.

Another explosion, this one beyond the wall, echoed with deafening power along the corridor. The wall cracked, but the synthetic reinforcement held it together. The android staggered for an instant, breaking into a sprint as soon as he recovered.

Dust from the ceiling fell into Kelahya's eyes, making her blink. Instinctively, she lifted her hand to remove the debris, but stopped and let it drop to the side again. She must resist the temptation to rub her eyes clean. She felt certain the android was unaware of her recovery. Surprise represented the only possible advantage against him.

Other footsteps mingled with the android's. She tried to decipher how many there might be. Tears were welling in her stinging eyes. *Good. That'll wash them out.*

"Move!" It was Jofan's voice. "They're targeting the infrared sensors. The hydrotube is our only chance." The robot turned to the left into what sounded like a river of bodies that flowed in frantic motion toward some forward destination.

"Where's Nestor?" Jofan's voice came from somewhere behind the android.

An unfamiliar female answered, "He's already in Central. He's been told you're on your way."

Kelahya's mind reeled. *Nestor. The rumors were true. Nestor has been on Dionysus all along.* She could hardly contain her excitement.

The lights in the corridor walls flickered then shut down as a piercing siren began to shriek in intermittent waves.

Controlled reactions of dread penetrated her ears from everywhere.

If I could only see.

A moment later, a bluish hue emanated from the ceiling producing enough light for safe visibility by the escapees.

Another explosion rocked their surroundings.

The distorted pitch of an electronic communicator brought a momentary a hush to the melee. "Level three is sealed. Four minutes."

She heard the river of bodies slow to a trickle. Most were panting with anxiety. Only the android, incapable of emotion, remained eerily calm.

"All Protocol droids take the chutes," ordered another female somewhere ahead.

"Guardians and Containments, use the lifts only if you have cargo. Otherwise, use the chutes. Hurry," said a third female.

Terrians, Kelahya mused. *Mostly females. Does Nestor command an army of female Terrians?*

Somewhere ahead, a synthetic voice issued commands with repetitive monotony. "Down…down…down…"

The robot spotted her subtle movement to look around and promptly knocked her unconscious.

* * * * * *

Kronos turned and smiled as Kelahya entered the room. The sentry bowed and withdrew into the corridor from which he and the girl had emerged. The door closed behind her. Kronos stood at the far end of a magnificent room next to a vibrant light that emanated from a rectangle on a long console. Similar rectangles on either side were dark, as was the huge screen that covered an entire wall from floor to ceiling.

"Come in, sweet Kelahya."

"What is this place? Why are you taking me away?" She couldn't conceal her fear.

Kronos chuckled as he crossed toward her and held out his hand.

"I understand your concern, Kelahya. But I hope you believe me when I say there's no safer place for you than by my side. Come."

She placed her hand in his and followed him.

"From now on this will be the center of your life," he said, nodding at the array of technology around the room. "All your questions shall find answers here."

Puzzled, she studied her surroundings. "Why do I have to leave my dwellings on Uxiel?"

Kronos closed his hand on hers.

"First, because I need you by my side. Second, because your education must continue and that can only happen here, near me. No need to be afraid. It'll be an adventure. One that will outshine even your wildest imaginings."

As he guided her to the consoles, he put his arm around her waist. He intended an affectionate gesture. However, his body betrayed him. Her female essence, her warm skin, the fullness of her young breasts against his side, produced a reaction that couldn't be concealed.

He jerked his arm away and turned his back to her.

His sudden evasive move startled Kelahya. *What have I done wrong? Why did you pull away from me with such anger?* She shuddered with the remembered sensation of his arm around her waist.

He moved back to the console as he struggled to compose himself.

Feeling bewildered and rejected, Kelahya remained rooted where she stood.

"You're young," he said, as much to himself as to her. "There's much for you to learn."

He pressed his fingers to the console. Images of the Preena system appeared on the monitors around the room and filled the huge screen. He pointed to one of the spheres, a small moon, located near a huge smoldering planet.

"That's Dionysus, the moon of Dawnzehya Gleva, where you were born. In this room, you'll further your knowledge of your motherland, and many other wonders in the cosmos. You'll learn even more about the universe and the galaxies." He turned to her, a solemn look upon his face. "Most importantly, you'll learn of my role, and yours, within the Alliance. You'll also learn to interpret what is written in the Scripture."

"Will I learn why I was taken from my home? Why I am your prisoner?" There was more than a little defiance in her voice.

"Your questions are not a complete surprise. I expected they would come sooner or later, only not so quickly. You're special, very special, young Minder, my incomparable Kelahya Devona."

He returned to her side and was about to take her hand in his, but instead, he placed his hands behind his back.

"You're not my prisoner, Kelahya. You're my ward. My protégé."

The girl shook her head in a gesture of incomprehension.

"I knew your father and mother. We shared the same ideals. No one lamented their… death more than I. It took some time to apprehend and punish their killers. But I made sure that it was done."

She felt a lump build in her throat. She swallowed hard and squeezed her lips together. A chill ran down her back and she felt her hair bristle.

"If that is so, what's Maccabeus doing at your side? He murdered my parents. He's my captor. And you're my jailor."

Kronos stared into the beautiful eyes and a somber shadow of despair enveloped him. Unable to sustain her gaze, he looked down as if some unbearable burden had been laid upon his shoulders.

The interminable silence sank into Kelahya as well. *What have I done?* She swallowed hard as she searched for some way to end his agony, some way to take back what she'd said.

His silence encompassed anger and sadness, and he appeared to shrink with the weight of whatever memory played through his mind. He stood motionless, staring at the floor, disintegrating before Kelahya's very eyes.

"Your memories are understandably confused," he said at last. "Maccabeus saved you. But he arrived too late to save your mother and father." His face contorted as if he might weep, fire burned in his eyes. His was a pain she couldn't fully grasp. "There was a traitor in my ranks. Tzalina. She murdered them. And she would have killed you if Maccabeus hadn't stopped her."

She felt an eerie shock wave under her skin as the memory of Maccabeus' hand around Tzalina's neck swept through her.

"I personally disposed of Tzalina. She exists no more. Her death, however, is of little consequence, it will not replace your parents and for that I am truly sorry." His tightly controlled voice was barely audible.

He closed his eyes and dropped his head in dejection. A heaviness descended upon him, crushing him. He lost stature, strength, power, vitality.

Kelahya was mesmerized by his transformation. *Kronos must have loved my parents very much for the memory of their death to overcome him like this.*

At length, Kronos turned away and crossed to the lights flickering on the long console. He placed his fists upon the synthetic surface and let his weight shift forward. The lights went out, the images on the screens disappeared. Darkness engulfed the chamber. Only a faint purple glow emanated from the cornices of the ceiling. When Kronos spoke again, the voice came across as if disconnected from the body.

"We'll talk of this again. Be patient with me. I cared for your parents more than anyone. I've suppressed these memories for a long time, and they're difficult for me."

Kelahya glanced about, unsure what to do next. Her impulse was to somehow comfort this man, but she remained apprehensive about the newness of her situation.

"Should I leave now?" she ventured with a whisper.

Kronos cleared his throat and straightened up. He had regained complete control.

"No, stay. There are some things I should show you. Indeed, must show you." The Director touched the console and a rose-colored light bathed the chamber. He motioned her toward him, and his fingers danced across the data pads. The screens burst to life again.

"If anything is unclear to you, please stop me, and I'll do my best to explain. Agreed?" The sparkle had returned to his eyes.

Kelahya nodded, stunned by this sudden recovery.

A rotating image of a huge ship floated in the center of the screens.

"We are now aboard my command vessel. The *Olympus*. This is where I live most of the time. And now, so will you."

He tapped the data pads again and the various monitors displayed an assortment of images that included sections of the ship as well as maps, animals, plants, and vast areas of the galaxy.

"This particular chamber has been designed specifically for you. It's here that you'll learn about the wonders of this vast universe. Here you'll discover all that has led to the creation of the League of One and the Alliance of Stars. Their history and their purpose."

Kelahya stood in awe as the images scrolled along showing planets, cities, faces, dizzying beyond comprehension. Kronos' satisfaction reflected in his smile.

"The hall you traversed is also a part of your private quarters, which in fact, comprise this entire level of the ship. They're quite large, as you'll soon discover, and offer great variety. However, should you find anything lacking, simply tell Chantall and she'll make sure that you get it. You shall want for nothing. Only you, your supervisor, and I will have unrestricted access. Anyone else will need my approval…and, of course, yours." He waited for her reaction to this.

He'd captivated her beyond words, and she could only smile.

He tapped a pad and the image of the *Olympus* filled the larger screen once more while the rest went dark.

"Keep in mind that this is a battleship." There appeared to be a tone of regret in his voice. "Therefore, it has areas that are restricted even to you. For this, I apologize. But I can't govern efficiently from any other place. Mobility is essential to keep peace. You'll learn about that at the proper time. Any questions?"

The girl shook her head. He smiled.

"Go to that console over there, and place you hand on it." He pointed toward a particular station in the long counter with the embedded monitors.

She did as he said. The instant she touched it many other monitors and displays came back to life.

"Those displays are information monitors, vidscapes, viewscapes, and vidlogs for your amusement and, most importantly, your education. The one on the far left will permanently display any information you seek regarding our next destination as we travel about space. All information under military restriction will be excluded, of course. Do you understand this?"

She nodded, more out of reflex than real understanding. He crossed to a set of lounge chairs at one end of the huge room.

"Come, sit by me." He patted the seat next to him.

She did as he asked, then looked up at him, smiling. The green in her eyes captivated him. He clutched her hands.

"By Centaur's Mane, you are truly beautiful," he blurted out with a gasp.

His outburst startled her, and she pulled back.

Kronos smiled, producing great kindness in his eyes. "I meant that to be a compliment, and instead I've frightened you. I apologize. Please believe that I'm your friend." He chuckled under his breath. "That will no doubt seem meaningless to you at present. You have no reason to trust me or believe me. But, in time…perhaps."

He gave her a smile that begged for understanding as he rose and hovered above her. "Enough for now. I'll come to visit with you as often as I can. As often as you'll allow me the joy. Chantall will be here shortly."

He turned and walked at a slow confident pace out the door and was gone.

Chapter 9

Nastrius Astronomy

*Excerpt from the **Corpus Galacticum**, 137th Edition*

Nastrius Astronomy, *an archaic science solidified in the 3rd millennium, states that energy is not continuous, but comes in small but discrete units. It shows that the atomic world is made of basic elements that randomly behave both as particles and waves, and that their position and momentum cannot be measured—atomic particles simultaneously exist in more than one location at a time.*

Nastrius Astronomy describes the nature of the universe as being fundamentally different from the world that is seen and experienced.

Through the millennia, it has demonstrated the accuracy of one of the most essential lessons known to science—an observation is only valid in the context of the experiment in which it is performed.

To ascertain that something behaves a certain way or even exists, one must first observe and detect the real context of this behavior or existence, since in another context it may behave differently, or not exist at all.

The principle derived from this astronomical reality is that what at one given point in time is experienced, may or may not be what it appears to be.

This principle is taught to children at an early age through the use of the electron experiments. It is commonly accepted that an electron is not a particle. Yet, that is not the case under certain situations—an electron can be a particle when it behaves like a particle. To determine its true nature, one needs to see how electrons behave under differing conditions.

Once this concept is understood, subsequent training focuses on how this principle can be applied to dissect deceitful actions by shifting the conditions of a given event.

Nastrius Astronomy termed the teaching of this principle **Deciphering the Paradox**.

"Level four is sealed. Three minutes. Decoy liftoff in forty-two clicks," the communicator announced, snapping Kelahya awake.

Did I fall asleep?

As the android carried her along, Kelahya detected a swooshing sound that came between the monotonous synthetic voice commands.

As gently as she could, she let her head tilt to the right and cracked an eye open. The lingering irritation from the debris made it difficult to focus, but between blinks she managed to assess the situation.

An evacuation station…That noise must be the hydrotubes.

The android moved forward one step at a time.

She could hear four doors opening and closing sequentially about every fifteen clicks. Her best estimate was ten passengers per trip. She and the robot would probably be on one of the next five.

"Levels five and six are sealed. Two hexicons. Decoy liftoff in ten clicks …nine…eight… seven…six…Ignition…four…"

The entire structure rumbled.

Thrusters.

The vibration increased to deafening levels as the thrusters, somewhere beyond the walls and corridors, lifted the decoy into space.

"Pray it works," whispered a female, inches from Kelahya's shoulder. She could almost picture the Terrians raising their eyes to the ceiling, as if to follow the fireball climbing into the skies above Dionysus, with a twinge of fear and nostalgia.

In moments, a leaden silence spread about the structure and its inhabitants. Even the attack seemed to have ceased. The stillness only interrupted by the repetitive, computer-generated toneless command "down," followed by the predictable swoosh.

"Down…"

Swoosh.

"Down…"

She imagined the escapees in introspective stillness and paralyzing fear. The type that grips humanoids at the most inner core of their being and holds them immobile, unable to either fight or flee.

"Move! We're not out of it yet!" The thundering command of Jofan erupted, its abruptness electrifying the flow of real and artificial flesh back into the urgency of the moment.

Kelahya's captor moved into the hydrotube.

Swoosh.

She could feel gravity cease for an instant as the hydrotube dropped. There was a musky scent in the enclosure. It slowed and stopped.

The doors opened and a cooler air swept in. New sounds echoed as the robot carried her out.

The android stopped for no apparent reason.

To the experienced soldier, the odor of lubricants and fuels was unmistakable. The clanging of heavy equipment, the urgent orders echoing off the metal alloys and flat walls, the pools of light, the whirring of mini-transports and weapons conveyers, were the undeniable earmarks of military installations.

Kelahya let her head dangle around to peek in front of her, but it wasn't enough, and to push for more would reveal her state of alertness to her host.

"Yes," the robot said to no one.

Kelahya strained a little more, but all she could glance at was the wall and a minute section of floor. Clearly, they were alone.

"It is across the pad," the robot answered.

Kelahya raised her head slightly and looked at the android. Instantly, his eyes met hers.

"She has regained mobility…I will take her there directly."

Well done, Kelahya. So much for the element of surprise.

Without ceremony, he dropped her to her feet, spun her around, placed a blindfold across her eyes, and pulled her at a brisk pace across the installations.

"Step up," the android commanded.

She did as he said and felt the metal step beneath her boot. Twelve metal steps later the android pushed her head down, and she felt the change of sound as they entered some sort of craft.

The robot dragged her along a narrow corridor into a larger compartment and shoved her into a flight seat where he buckled her flight restraints. He removed the blindfold and Kelahya opened her eyes. The android stood behind her seat.

"Where am I?"

"You will be silent."

She felt his mechanical hand clamp onto her shoulder, tight enough to reassure her that he wasn't there for conversation.

Kelahya nodded and eased her body left in a futile attempt to peer down the aisle.

"Is he here?" Jofan's voice came from somewhere beyond her view.

"He's in place," a male voice down the aisle answered.

"When do we leave?" Jofan barked.

"With the next launch."

The old leader groaned as he made his way to the seat next to Kelahya and buckled his restraint.

"Prepare for departure," the male voice commanded. Two uniformed androids joined the one behind Kelahya and Jofan and snapped their restraints into place.

"Who's attacking you?" Kelahya ventured to intrude on the old man's silence, but his only response was a cold stare.

The craft vibrated with a gentle hum and a chart of the Preena System, showing their projected flight path, flickered onto the monitor ports.

The hum rose in pitch and Kelahya sank slightly into the cushioned seat. In a matter of milicons, however, her body registered the uniformity of speed between all components on the craft.

"Remain at departure stations until further notice." The command came across the audio in a language not unfamiliar to Kelahya. It was, however, the first time she'd heard it spoken here. She'd encountered it briefly during her sojourn on Tanta Kantut and been amused by the popping sound given to the equivalent of "T". Later she learned that it was Tul, one of the most obscure languages in the Arguille cluster of galaxies, the most widespread being Terrian and Xiabush, and their assorted variations.

The unexpectedness of it, however, made her shoot an inquisitive glance at her companion. All conversations with Jofan, thus far, had been conducted in Terrian. He'd even addressed his subordinates in Terrian. But this had been an important command, and, to her ever-increasing dismay, it had been delivered in Tul. She remembered the symbols in the corridor outside Jofan's quarters. The implications were staggering. Dionysians, after all, spoke almost exclusively in Eniat.

Jofan felt her inquisitive stare and tilted his head enough to allow her to register his subtle smile of control. But his satisfaction was short-lived as the entire ship lurched to one side under the impact of an explosion on the exterior of the craft.

Kelahya watched as the color vanished from the old man's face. Without hesitation he raised his left hand and tapped his ear with his middle finger.

"Status?" he said in perfect Tul.

Kelahya searched Jofan's face for the response to his command. Intensity was all he showed. She assumed he had a transmitter installed subcutaneously, on which he heard the response to his request. Smaller impacts jolted the ship two more times. He tapped his ear again then relaxed back into his seat.

"Well?" Kelahya demanded.

This time he didn't smile. "Do you follow any religion?"

"What?"

"No, I suppose not. Your religion would be your devotion to that murdering Kronos of yours. At any rate, Commander, barring a miracle, you'll remain my prisoner for the foreseeable future." With no further indication of emotion, he leaned back and stared at the overhead light.

"By the moons of Bronteion! You are an exasperating old leech!" Kelahya pounded the armrests of her seat as an alternative to pounding Jofan.

The last thing she felt was the android's grip on her neck.

* * * * * *

Practicing filled young Kelahya's days. The vidlog created a paradox early every morning and her response needed to be rendered by that same evening. It hadn't been easy at first. In fact, it took her several days of arduous work to unravel the first paradox and find the correct answer. But with time and constant practice, the speed and accuracy of her responses improved at a steady rate.

And then there were the endless physical workouts, the self-defense classes, the weight training, running, survival sessions, wrestling, and hand-to-hand combat.

All of this, along with the growth that was natural to the Dionysian race, had transformed her into a stunning specimen of beauty, stamina, and power. She stood almost as tall as Kronos already, and her strength was superior to most male humanoids.

Two cycles had lapsed since her first meeting with Kronos, and with each day her adoration for him increased. She looked forward with eagerness to their meetings during which, while teasing her about her response time on the paradox, he would play along, infusing her with techniques to understand and master the riddles of the universe.

It was all too easy for Kronos. His response time to the paradoxes was instantaneous. He grasped the core of the propositions without the need to peel away the layers that covered them.

Today's visit was special, however. After not seeing him for several days, she missed him, but there was more. He'd promised that today he would take her on a shuttle flight to the periphery of the Varailian system. To that end, Kronos' guard had escorted her to the foredeck outside the transport bay.

But he was late. He was always late. He did it on purpose, so that her level of anticipation would rise. He liked for her to be anxious.

By now, she could not only read his mind, she also learned his little tricks. At least, those he allowed her to sense. She couldn't invade his mind totally, but neither could he completely invade hers. Their secret silent communication had become a delightful game for her. However, Kronos didn't take it as a game, and continually admonished her in stern tones.

"You're powerful, and your Endow is strong. Stronger than mine, I believe. But the Endow is not a toy and being a Minder isn't a game. It's a gift. One that must be guarded with the greatest of care, or it can destroy you. The Endow is a Minder's greatest strength and most vulnerable weakness. It's vital that you understand this. I'll guide you in its proper use."

She could use it now to locate him and discover the reason for his tardiness, but she dared not. It would spoil everything.

At last, the doors opened, and he appeared. In one swift move, he took her hand and brought it to his lips.

How can a man so tall, so strong, be so gentle?

She liked his impressive musculature under the various skin-tight body sheaths he wore. Most importantly she enjoyed the feeling of Kronos' power when he comforted her. This mighty man was not ashamed to show how much he cared about others, or to express sorrow, or embarrassment, or even pain.

How can you be so perfect?

He flashed her a warm broad smile, a twinge of malice in his eyes.

"Are you ready to explore the outer worlds?"

Kelahya bolted past him. "You're late as usual. It's getting tiresome, Kronos."

As she rushed through the third set of double doors, a guard appeared and blocked her way. At moments such as this she realized how much of a prisoner she actually was, and it always sent a chill down her spine. She hated it.

"Stand aside," she growled.

The guard stood his ground.

Kelahya spun to challenge Kronos.

He stared her down with a long angry glare. With his authority reaffirmed, Kronos nodded to the guard. He stepped away and let her through, but she didn't move. She waited for Kronos to reach her.

No sense in being stopped at every door.

"I like your fire, Kelahya," Kronos whispered.

"It's mostly ice, Excellency," came her sharp reply.

"You must control your anger, my beauty. Never let it get the best of you. Dominance of your temper will disarm your enemies."

You are not my enemy.

He chuckled as they continued toward the shuttle port.

As they entered, the soldiers parted and Maccabeus appeared, as usual, out of nowhere.

"Everything is ready, Excellency." He bowed to Kronos, then turned to Kelahya with a bow that was more like a nod. "My Lady."

She nodded back, curtly. She didn't like this creature, no matter what Kronos said. She sensed ambivalence in him.

Like all Kayroans, he possessed a natural inner core that protected his mind, preventing her from invading it. Not even Kronos could enter his mind. In spite of that, or perhaps because of it, Kelahya couldn't bring herself to trust him.

But today, Maccabeus didn't matter. Her adventure with Kronos was her one and only concern. She rushed to her seat in the small shuttlecraft and strapped herself in. Her companion, the Director of the League of One sat next to her. No one else entered and the hatch closed.

Kronos reached to touch her hand and smiled, his winning, warm, delicious smile. "Are you ready, my Lady of fire and ice?"

She nodded with anticipation, unable to conceal her excitement.

"Well, then proceed. Take us out." He tapped a pad at his left and the controls on Kelahya's console sprung to life. Lights flickered, screens flashed.

"What?"

"You heard me, take us out."

During the countless hours spent in the simulator, it never crossed her mind that she would be allowed to pilot a craft so soon, with the Director himself as a passenger to boot.

Excitement shot through her like a bolt of lightning. Heart pounding, hands sweating, she readied herself, and initiated flight procedures.

Kronos observed in silence as, with the dexterity of an experienced pilot, she maneuvered the craft out of the hangar and into the vastness of space.

She tingled with exhilaration at finding herself at the controls of a real spaceship in the middle of the galaxy, with the most powerful man in the universe at her side. It mattered not one iota that it was a mere transport shuttle.

She turned to Kronos, seeking to share her emotions with him. He didn't have to say a word—she beheld the pride in his eyes.

"Where do we go now?"

"Wherever you wish, my beautiful Kelahya. Let's explore this system together."

She searched the displays for the most distant planet in the system. Then, with the confidence of a veteran pilot, she locked the heading into the craft's computer, checked the fuel supply, and engaged the guidance system.

It was clear that Kronos enjoyed watching her operate with such aplomb, and her competent maneuvering and sophisticated skills impressed him.

"Kronos," she whispered. "This is…I have no words to describe my feelings, my opinions, the images my eyes and mind perceive."

He smiled, and she felt him enter her consciousness and revel in the emotions that were sweeping through her. In the silent universe of their mental union, she told him, *"It's beyond compare. I never dreamed it could be so wondrous."*

"This is but a small solar system in an unremarkable galaxy. I'll show you more. Much, much more," he replied.

The next instant Kelahya was flooded with sensations she'd never encountered before. Warmth permeated her head and swiftly flowed through every inch, every atom of her body, to the tip of each extremity. Her reaction was so wonderfully pervasive, the ecstasy caught her breath in her throat.

He'd entered her mind and she'd penetrated his, as he shared his own experiences, visions, and recollections. He led her through the memories, impressions, and images collected from all the planetary systems, stars and galaxies he'd explored. With surprising ease, she followed him. He didn't have to pull at her or help her through the moment. She traveled at his side marveling at all he shared with her.

He turned to meet her gaze. Her adoring eyes rested upon his.

"Kelahya," he muttered.

Unable to withstand the intensity of his power, her body shuddered.

He blinked, and withdrew from her mind, then turned away.

"Thank you," she whispered.

"I shouldn't do that," he snapped. The unexpected harshness of his voice startled her.

"Why not? It was mag—"

His glare stopped her. It was no use discussing the matter. He never permitted himself, or her, to invade someone else's mind to such a degree. He had told her time and time again to avoid it, given that the risk of losing one's id in another's reality was too high.

However, she'd come to believe that such a danger could not be real. She'd convinced herself that his admonition was intended to shield himself. He didn't intend for her to learn what he really felt, what he really thought. His reluctance, and her analysis for its reasons, had taught her to also lock the inner sanctum of her own thoughts. She'd rationalized that if he chose to close himself for protection, so could she.

Yet, moments ago, he'd taken her with him on a wondrous journey. Without the slightest hesitation he'd guided her on a breathtaking trek through his emotions, his reality, and back again.

Why?

The locator beacon frequency indicated they had arrived at their destination, and the computer was commencing its planetary search and analysis activities.

"It's called Learmes. It has breathable oxygen air and is completely devoid of humanoid inhabitants. There's vegetation and a few lower forms of life," she reported with an air of self-accomplishment.

She studied the planetary charts. "It looks inviting. Can we disembark?" She checked the console. "The temperature is warm, quite warm, in fact, but tolerable. Can we?"

He nodded.

She disengaged the computer controls and manually guided the shuttle toward Learmes. She cruised above the tiny planet looking for a good place to land. The mountainous terrain was covered with plush vegetation. Finally, she spotted a valley with a small body of multi-colored liquid. With expert dexterity, she piloted the craft to a safe landing.

After a quick scan for predators, they grabbed weapons and quadrucators, and prepared to exit the ship.

The shuttle door opened, letting in a burst of hot, humid air. She scanned their immediate radius with her quadrucator. "Nothing harmful here. We can go."

Kronos gave her a reassuring smile.

She advanced into the foliage without hesitation, consulting her quadrucator at regular intervals, and performing with the confidence of a veteran soldier.

He watched her every move with pride.

She didn't miss a thing. She observed, studied, learned with every step. They reached the edge of the multicolored liquid. With expert touch, she handled the quadrucator as she analyzed, calculated, and measured the content and depth of the liquid.

"It's mineral water, only ten metrics deep."

Smiling, he nodded. His calm demeanor told her something.

She smiled. "You've been here before."

"I have," he said almost apologetically.

"Why didn't you tell me?"

"Learning is more effective in the experiencing than in the telling."

"Why have you been here?"

"To bathe in the waters," he said matter-of-factly.

"How did you guess I would come here?"

"You chose our destination. Not I."

She turned toward the water. "Can we bathe?"

"If you wish."

She dropped her weapons and the quadrucator and stripped off her suit. She stepped cautiously into the water. It felt warm. As different parts of her body made contact with the liquid, she felt a tingly sensation as if millions of tiny needles were softly prickling her skin.

"It's wonderful. Come bathe with me."

"Not today. We shouldn't stay too long. The temperature is rising."

He watched her dive beneath the water, enjoying her delight in the discovery of the new sensation these waters gave her. At length she came out. Her wet golden skin flowed as her sinewy muscles moved beneath it. Her legs were perfectly molded. He relished her rounded firm buttocks, the dark fuzz of pubic hair, the slight curve of her abdomen. Her breasts were firm, ample, and well-shaped, with dark pink aureoles and rising nipples. Her arms were long and graceful, their strength easily apparent. Her beautifully sculptured body was, in a word, magnificent.

But more striking than her body, was her face, with its full mouth, straight narrow nose, high cheekbones, emerald green eyes with long lashes, and narrow arching eyebrows. Her finely chiseled features combined into an elegant harmony that was hers alone. And, above all, there was her razor-sharp intelligence.

Kelahya noticed Kronos watching her and felt that as he saw her naked body in the light of day, he considered her exceptional, stunning, and unique. She smiled, savoring his admiration.

"By the Mane of Centaur," he muttered, "never have I set eyes on a woman of such breathtaking beauty." His arousal was apparent and immediate.

She finished dressing and came toward him, radiant, and invigorated from the bath and his adulation.

"It was delicious, Kronos. You should ha—" She stopped, paralyzed by the animalistic power of his gaze. She stared into his deep blue eyes and felt them pulling her in. Her heart pounded. Her knees weakened. Her face grew red and her body shuddered. Ashamed, she tore her eyes from his.

Her childish embarrassment jolted him, and he regained control. He caught his breath and jumped to his feet.

"Come, we must return."

Chapter **10**

The Endow's Event Horizon

———◆———

*Excerpt from the **Corpus Galacticum**, 137th Edition*

A *Minders Endow is conceived as an invisible synapse where nerve impulses are transmitted and received throughout the vibrations of the dimensional strings within the time space continuum. At the atomic level, they can arrange hadrons, protons, neutrons, molecules, and electrons, in the correct order to achieve diffusion.*

*When injured, Minders have been known to succumb to the **Endow's Event Horizon**—a boundary at the cellular level of space and time from which there is no return. Best described as a Minder's internal black hole.*

The descent into their black hole is triggered by a fissure in the synapse—the site where all signals pass. This fracture cuts the signal to the axon thus inhibiting the release of neurotransmitters into the synapse.

The result is dissociation—a break in how their brain handles information. Minder's feel disconnected from their thoughts, emotions, memories, and surroundings. Dissociation can affect their sense of identity and perception of time.

125

As their minds dissociate, the black hole gains in mass and nothing can escape its gravitational pull. Often, this is described as the boundary within which the warped elements of a Minder's mind are absorbed by the black hole. Once an element is inside the horizon, the black hole sucks it deeper and deeper, thus making it impossible to travel backwards and regain control.

Death usually follows complete dissociation and full penetration into the event horizon.

"Sorry to wake you," Jofan said. "We've arrived. And we're in one piece."

"I was not sleeping," she retorted, somewhat surprised by Jofan's conciliatory tone.

The attitude of the craft shifted indicating that docking procedures had begun.

"Indeed," he responded, a sardonic smile briefly crossing his lips.

Without ceremony, the android replaced the blindfold and marched Kelahya out of the craft and into a disembarkation chamber. The doors to the craft slid closed behind them as they squeezed into a narrow corridor, then another door slid open and they entered a chamber that immediately accelerated upward.

"The situation has changed since we last conversed," Jofan said as he removed her blindfold.

"That's certainly an understatement." Kelahya rubbed her eyes. *Odd...we're in a rather rudimentary lift.*

Jofan chuckled. "No, no. I'm not referring to this incident. A trifle, an inconvenience, nothing more." He shifted positions and looked straight at her. "Your actions have unleashed a string of violence throughout the League of One, and beyond. The enemies of the Director are being arrested and executed everywhere. Forces are on alert in every quadrant of the Galactic Triangle." He stated the facts without passing judgment.

"A simple trip into the desert could hardly—"

His voice dropped to a growling whisper. "Kronos, General Devona. You are being sought for killing Kronos."

He is dead! Her mind bellowed. *Stop! This could be a ruse on their part.* Caution stepped in. *If he's indeed dead, that explains the attack. They're after Nestor, not me. The League has no clue where I am.* "What?" The question sounded more like denial than surprise. She chose to remain silent to avoid worsening the situation.

"Unaware of this event, General?" The question emanated from the audioscope. She raised an eyebrow and let her head tilt to one side.

"And, who are you, Faceless Wonder?"

"Let's say, for now," Jofan cut in, "that he's one of your captors, and your life may depend on him."

The lift chamber stopped, and the doors opened. An attractive young officer stood before her. The genuine warmth of his smile dissolved her anxiety. A sense of peace washed over her. His eyes entranced her—deep, alluring, gray eyes that released a charge difficult to resist.

"General," he said, nodding a greeting. Then, to Jofan, "Welcome."

Kelahya recognized the voice as being the same she'd heard moments earlier over the audioscope.

Behind Kelahya's back, Jofan gestured in her direction. "Any news?"

"Command suggests that we bring the General to the situation room with us," the young man replied.

Kelahya noticed Jofan's amusement at the officer's reply. She might have challenged Jofan, but for the moment, her senses were completely entranced with this irresistible specimen.

What power does he have? What is it that pulls me in?

"If you'll follow me, General," he said, "I'll escort you there."

She nodded as she struggled to regain her composure—but to no avail. Not since her first meeting with Kronos had she been so overcome.

She eased into his mind, only to discover that he'd invaded hers, and now guided her sensations.

A Terrian Minder? The possibility was unnerving. *Whoever he is, his power is strong.* She fought to release her thoughts from him, but his hold was unrelenting, and far too invasive. At the same time, the penetration was restrained as if she'd agreed to it. Yet, she hadn't. At least, she didn't believe she had.

"Please follow me, General," he said, and headed down the passageway.

Another android materialized. The realization that first her body and now her mind were held prisoner swept over her with a chill. That reality hit at the core of her being. With a burst of fury, she snapped her thoughts free of his grip.

Stay out of my mind!

The young officer halted momentarily. Then, without a word, continued down the corridor.

Kelahya smiled in triumph. *Guard against him. Any chance of survival depends on it.*

She moved into the corridor, and despite the proximity of Jofan and the androids, she assessed her surroundings. *A battleship.* The shuttlecraft they used to escape from Dionysus must have docked with this new ship. She'd estimated the size of the shuttlecraft and concluded it was designed, at least in passenger logistics, unlike any other she'd boarded before. It was obviously adequate for short-distance travel, however, a solid hit from anti-spacecraft artillery had failed to cause any damage. It couldn't be a cruiser, because anything that size required great distances to acquire planetary exit speed, yet the craft had entered hyperspace in no time.

Nothing made sense. Try as she may, the pieces refused to come together. The clutter of events had unfolded too fast, and her weakened awareness failed to grasp the logical thread to it all. *Why did Jofan bring up Kronos' death so matter-of-factly? What do they hope to achieve?*

A double door slid open and one of the androids nudged her into a small vestibule a step behind the young officer. An instant later another double door slid open, and they stepped onto a conveyor encased in glass that ran alongside the Situation room.

It resembled all other situation rooms and command centers that General Devona had experienced, with one difference—it had a staff of no more than six crewmembers.

Dimensional projectors and holoscanners stood at the center of the room, surrounded by consoles and emergency communications stations. To the right side, behind transparent walls, she noticed a conference chamber large enough to accommodate twenty, while the left displayed a simulator array and a hyperspace computer empathizer.

"Let's use the Talkutkeh room." The young officer's command sounded more like a logical suggestion. No one contradicted him.

The six officers running operations stopped for an instant as they spotted the group crossing behind them.

The conveyor came to a halt, and a door slid open.

The Talkutkeh was a small room by comparison, with seats for no more than ten. Jofan indicated the seat on his right as he turned to Kelahya. "Sit there." His old voice betraying the exhaustion of the obstacles they had left behind.

She did as instructed.

Jofan and the young officer stepped out. "We shall return." The doors closed behind them.

The confinement and isolation triggered tension and rage throughout Kelahya's entire body. *Calm down…Calm down!*

She felt the room close in around her, the lights flicker, and the air dwindle. *Stop!* She clasped her head between her hands and shut her eyes. *Fight this! We can't dissociate!*

Still laboring to catch her breath, she rested her forehead on her arms, and evoked the Mindstill stratagem.

* * * * * *

"Never allow your enemies a glimpse of your emotions," Kronos said. "The minute they discover what's inside you, they'll have the advantage."

His advice meant little to Kelahya, who continued to play with the water in the fountain. "I have no enemies, Kronos. No one would dare. They're terrified of your wrath."

He smiled as his eyes drifted along her beautiful hair, loosely cascading about her bare shoulders. She spun around unexpectedly, and her eyes met his.

"How can this world exist inside a ship? It reminds me of my garden on Uxiel, only bigger." She nodded in one direction, then the other. "Look at the mountains in the distance, the trees, the flowers. It's spectacular."

"It exists inside you. The virtuoscope stimulates your senses and makes it feel real."

"But I've never experienced marble. This fountain is made of marble."

"Indeed. But I'm here with you, and I am familiar with marble. Besides, you've learned about marble through the vidlog." He stood next to her, one foot planted on the side of the fountain, his elbow resting upon his knee.

She looked up at him and smiled.

She possessed a yielding gentleness that drew him to her with a force difficult to resist. Only four cycles had passed since he'd first beheld her, and much remained for her to learn.

"You're pulling away from me again," she whispered.

"Stay out of my head," was the stern reply.

"I sensed you drifting away. Don't be angry with me."

"Kelahya, be careful with your power. Your Endow grows ever stronger. I've told you hundreds of times the dangers hidden in the misuse of it. Minding is not a game. You find it far too easy to penetrate others. In this, you are mighty. Most can't even feel you within them, and therein lies the danger. You can become lost inside their heads. Each time you invade someone you absorb the core of their experience. It's a talent you must respect and handle with extreme care or it'll destroy you."

"I'm careful. Sometimes it simply happens, and before I can stop, I'm inside someone."

"I understand. But control it you must. Else it can—"

She reached for his face and caressed the smoothness of his cheek. Her touch held him spellbound. Though she intended no erotic implications, his involuntary response came from a deeper source, and caught her by surprise. He was about to walk away, when she closed her hand on his.

"*Don't leave me,*" she pleaded.

"You were inside me and I didn't even feel it. Your power is increasing at an astonishing rate."

A cold, furious wave swept through him and into her.

"*Now, experience my full power!*" he bellowed. "*It is the only way that you'll learn!*"

She shuddered as the breath exploded from her lungs. Kelahya felt herself wrenched into an obscure corner of his mind, flung toward an abyss.

She hurtled through unrecognizable space with Kronos. Unable to free herself, she could only feel his rage at the core of her being.

A vortex of mayhem erupted around her as if every atom in the universe were shooting past her in all directions.

He drew her into a place beyond words, beyond rationalization, where she perceived only raw sensations. She understood that he'd pulled her in, both to instruct and protect her, yet the emotions were so tortuous she begged for him to stop.

But he didn't. He wouldn't.

Nausea overcame her, then a dizzying sense of vertigo. Her brain strained within her skull as if it demanded to expand.

Abruptly, everything stopped.

She entered a void, pitch black, dark and cold. A place with no beginning and no end from which she had no hope of escape.

As terror crept in, she sensed that something…no, *someone*, reached for her, and yanked her back from the abyss.

Then Kronos stood by her again and, for a brief moment, a warm feeling of reassurance swept through her.

But it was short-lived. He no longer guided her. He simply stood there.

Why?

There was no answer. Instead, they were moving again. Her surroundings turned gray, then became luminous, and finally iridescent. Their speed increased. They were flung through a tube of some sort, the sides like the walls of a bubble, and moved faster and faster toward…toward…

Nowhere! She screamed but made no sound.

She felt herself falling into the deep, cold, black void again. Only vaguely did she sense that Kronos remained with her. They continued hurtling downward, deeper and deeper into the darkness. She attempted to go back but knew not how. There were no visions, no true light, only absence—a terrifying absence.

The void engulfed her. She no longer felt Kronos. She was alone.

Dread filled the empty space. Her lungs strained with every breath. *Where am I? Am I dead?* From deep within, she screamed for help, and desperately fought to get out.

Motion again. The blackness faded. She was back in the gray luminous passage of iridescent light. Clear landscapes appeared. Planets. Star systems. Galaxies. They transformed into unfamiliar shapes and structures of brilliant and unnatural colors. *Where am I?*

She fought to escape from this voyage, to return home. But the more she struggled, the more she slipped into the empty darkness.

There it is again. The iridescent light...the tunnel...the darkness. No!

As the horror of death swept through her, someone called her name and cradled her along into a sensation of intense speed and complete safety—a beam of light riding inside an impenetrable shield.

Kronos. Inside the shield. Or was he the shield? He reached out to her, grabbed her arms, and pulled her toward him. A blinding flash exploded behind her eyes.

Kelahya regained control of her body, her breathing. Her eyes flickered open, and Kronos stood looking down at her as he held her in his arms. The intense fear in his vibrant blue eyes changed to immense relief. She tried to speak but the words wouldn't come.

He smiled. *"We are one. No need to speak."*

"What happened?"

"You rode the event horizon of your mind."

"A black hole?"

"You experienced the end your mind will meet if you don't learn to control your power."

"How could that happen?"

"In invading others their experiences become one with yours. That's why you must always be in control of the actions of your mind. If not, in time it can lose its ability to separate what is theirs from what is yours. You'll dissociate. When it reaches overload your mind will snap. It'll cease to distinguish the real from the unreal. In the end, unable to establish rational thought, it'll destroy itself. And you."

The realization struck her with such force that she shuddered.

He held her reassuringly against him. Her arms reached up to embrace him.

The shudder of fear gave way to the familiar pulsations of restrained desire. Her mouth was so close that he could feel their breath joining as one. His entire body screamed for her. His mouth came to hers. As his lips touched hers, they parted. Slowly, gently, carefully. His tongue caressed the inside of her lips.

Her heart beat so fiercely she expected it to explode.

Then, jerked away by an invisible force, he broke their mental link, and the kiss vanished.

"Forgive me, Kelahya."

He released her and raced away without looking back.

* * * * * *

If Kronos is dead, it can't be by my hand. Do you comprehend how I could never, ever, under any circumstances kill him? she told herself.

Yes, you were smitten with the great man, no doubt about it.

"Kronos' death will not be lamented by any of us," Jofan said.

She snapped around. They had returned to the meeting room and she had not heard them enter.

"It does, however, bring about certain complications that could have a...detrimental effect on us."

"Explain," Kelahya demanded in an attempt to conceal her disorientation.

"Turning you in will not solve our dilemma, General. It might even complicate matters. You've learned far more about our true capabilities than we care to make public. So, if we decide to get rid of you, it'll not be through exchanging you for our freedom or any such nonsense."

Kelahya glared into Jofan's eyes. "At least, you found the courage to provide me with the first direct answer since my detention began." She let the comment dangle for a moment. When the effect had struck home, she continued, "But make no mistake. The attack against you on Dionysus was not due to me. No one followed me. Of that, I'm sure."

The young officer had remained standing behind Jofan. He pushed off the wall and leaned across the table facing Kelahya, his eyes piercing through her.

"So, your sole purpose on Dionysus was to escape and hide?"

"I told Jofan—"

"I'm aware of what you told Jofan. You seek a dead man you claim to be your father."

Kelahya's eyes became embers, but her tone was cool and threatening. "He was my father."

The young officer seemed unimpressed. "According to our information, you said the same thing on your trip to Kyu, during the Application."

"That…was different."

"Was it also different on Artienda, or Grantza? Or perhaps you don't know who your father really is."

The young officer's iron grip clamped around Kelahya's fist before it reached his face.

"Commander Hathan!" Jofan blurted out.

Unable to conceal her surprise, she felt her lips whisper the name, "Nestor Hathan?"

She struggled to twist her hand free, but Nestor kept her motionless.

I can't believe this is Nestor. Nestor Hathan has been a legend for as long as I've been alive. He should be at least as old as Jofan, and a giant.

"Let me go," she finally said, mustering as much indifference as she could.

"With pleasure, General." His grip loosened without haste. Nestor straightened up and came around the table toward her. "For what it's worth, General, Modyor Devon was, in fact, your father. I've learned a great deal about you, and your family. And your activities." He pulled a chair away from the table and sat next to her with his hands across his lap. "Why did you kill Kronos?"

"Who says I did?"

"Come, come General, no more games," Jofan interjected.

"I told you before that I couldn't reveal certain information to you without risking my life. That decision has been made for me, however. So why not deal with reality, Jofan? If you're a pawn of the League, then do what you must. I'm not part of some galactic plot, I merely traveled to Dionysus for reasons that have nothing to do with politics." She paused and glanced at Nestor. "Satisfied?"

"I expected you to be an idealist. Not one I sympathize with, but an idealist, nonetheless. Am I to understand that you murdered Kronos out of vanity, General Devona?" Nestor made no effort to conceal a hint of sarcasm.

She held his gaze for an instant. The pain seared through her head and she felt the flash of dissociation shoot through her. *The pain is back. Stay present!* She fought it with every ounce of mental strength she could muster. "If there have been political repercussions," she forced herself to say, "they're not of my making. The Director's reasons for the attacks are known only to him. Unless they were ordered by someone else."

Jofan's eyes drifted toward Nestor. The young commander stared intensely at Kelahya, and the old man understood what that meant.

Kelahya did as well and held firm. She wouldn't allow him to invade her again. She would out-maneuver them both. If they tried to destroy her, it would cost them their lives. First in line, Jofan.

"You expect me to believe..." Jofan started his question, then for some reason paused, "that you didn't contemplate the consequences of such an act?" he finally concluded.

Kelahya had penetrated the old man's mental shield and couldn't refrain from a faint smile. He was hers. Even the pain had waned. She saw his military prowess, his ability to close himself to Minders, his devotion to his leader—Nestor she assumed—his loyalty to the Rebellion and...his concern for her wellbeing. *Why would he care about me? He certainly means me no harm. Why?*

Everything about him is confusing, unacceptable. What's real and what's an implant?

She needed time. "I am very tired, Jofan. Frankly, I expect you'll believe whatever suits your political and military needs. Then, you'll dispose of me one way or another. I don't care anymore. You've played games with me for… how many days? Three? Four? Perhaps, even five. I'm drained. I'm empty."

When Jofan hesitated, she understood what had happened, he'd weakened under her spell, and now looked to Nestor for direction.

Nestor is indeed his leader. Maybe, his teacher. Did he school Jofan in the Minder's Endow? How could this simple Terrian be aware of the Endow?

The young officer squinted with the effort of penetrating her mind, but she had locked it firmly. When he felt Jofan's stare, he relented. Then, he blinked and drew a deep breath.

"Leave us please, Jofan," Nestor whispered.

Jofan nodded and left the room in silence.

Kelahya's face twisted into an impatient smirk as she turned toward the mesmerizing man called Nestor. "Look… Nestor…I refuse to play your games anymore. Kill me, lock me—"

"Save it, General." He smiled as he studied her.

She held his gaze. His face was relaxed and beautiful.

"Betrayal," he said at last. There was bewilderment in Nestor's voice as he placed his elbow on the table and leaned toward her. "That's why you killed him. Betrayal. Emotional betrayal, at that. You killed the most powerful man civilization has ever known, because you were…" he chuckled, "jealous. Amazing."

She couldn't sense him inside her thoughts, and he wasn't letting her in, either. However, there was a definite link between them, a sensation she'd never experienced, except with Kronos. *Is this link the key to my survival, or my demise? He's strong, unbelievably strong.* Unsure of the impact this connection might have on her safety, she attempted to break it. But Nestor was immovable.

"I would say more than simple jealousy. I would say he betrayed…" he raised an eyebrow, "…your love for him."

She leaned as close as she could to Nestor's face and slammed her hand on the table. "No use. I have nothing to say."

His eyes locked into hers, and she could feel him probing the recesses deep behind them. She fought back.

Despite the searing pain, she reached for his mind, forcing his probe to reverse itself so she could look into him.

Understanding her wishes, he released her, and did nothing to resist her probe any further. He allowed her in.

Once inside, she encountered his knowledge of her and with it, his longing, his desire, his yearning for her.

What are these emotions? She didn't expect this. She certainly wasn't ready for this. *What is he doing? Why does he have these feelings for me?*

She saw his need, and her own surfaced—an uncontrollable urge to reach over and touch that noble face, caress that brow, that mouth.

"No!" she yelled.

Nestor blinked. The link snapped.

They both sat there catching their breath, two gladiators, exhausted without defining a victor.

He stared at her with admiration and a tiny smile crept onto his lips.

"As you wish," he finally said. "We shall speak again." He rose and walked to the door. As it hissed open, he stopped and turned to Kelahya. "For what it's worth, you're no longer a prisoner on this vessel. You're free to go anywhere on this level of the ship, with the exception, of course, of restricted military areas." He began to form another word but stopped.

As Nestor left the room, she felt the burden of anxiety go with him. He'd reached into her very soul and she'd reached into his. They were now left to sift through the images and impressions in search of reality.

Bit by bit, an uncomfortable awareness of her new, yet thoroughly familiar situation, took hold. She was, yet again, a free captive.

An android escorted Kelahya to her new quarters, a tiny military cubicle with the standard amenities, including a vidscreen console for communication and entertainment purposes imbedded in the wall opposite the bed. Except for that, and the fact that she could open the door whenever she wished, it amounted to little more than a prison cell.

She sat on the bed with her face in her hands, motionless. After several minutes, she rubbed her eyes, drawing deep breaths as the pressure caused her to experience colorful patterns of light shooting in all directions.

She was tired. But not the fatigue that wanes with a few hours of sleep or the expectation of pleasure. No, this type of exhaustion came from disillusion, the tiredness that creeps into every fiber of the body as fear recedes, the bone-weary painful fatigue that is accessory to the emptiness and loneliness born from captivity.

No telling how long this trip might last and escaping from the ship would be difficult to impossible. She now resided in a very safe trap. Not the place she'd planned to be.

Insufferable irony. For the second time in her life, she'd been taken from her home planet against her will. Once more, she hurtled through space on a battlecruiser, at the mercy of strangers, toward a fate she couldn't foresee. Her destiny continued to impose a will of its own unyielding to her desires.

And, what about Nestor, the so-called legendary hero of the Liberation? She hadn't expected to find him. But she had. Or rather he'd found her, and the outcome promised to be exciting at best, deadly at worst. His Minding powers were extraordinary, but how could that be possible? She'd come across Minders in the past, some quite weak with very limited ability, others more sophisticated, yet not a single one had come close to her capabilities, let alone the power of Kronos. Nestor dominated his Endow with effortless supremacy, able to enter her mind undetected.

I must be on guard every moment. If he senses me dissociating, he could destroy me. On the other hand, he might help me.

It was tempting to romanticize the images and feelings she'd found inside him, but she must fight to prevent him from invading her without her consent. Although everything she'd perceived within him inspired trust. However, in her current state, the thread between truth and deception could be stretched to the snapping point, and she must ensure that deception didn't win.

She took a deep breath and released it in a heart-felt moan that brought a sarcastic smile to her face.

Perhaps, there is some hidden meaning to this repetitive cycle of capture. Can this be the beginning of a new life? It certainly was so when I was taken from my parent's home so long ago. Could this in fact be the future I seek and I'm simply unable to recognize it?

Her tired eyes strayed to the cylindrical pillow and, in spite of herself, she surrendered to its invitation. She stared at the ceiling, the nape of her neck embracing the softness of the pillow.

The idea of succumbing to sleep frightened her. The floodgates would open, and images would gush into her mind with no means to control them. Clearly, discerning reality from fiction became increasing difficulty with the passage of time. Sleep would unlock the door to her subconscious, her past, and thus increase the possibility of dissociating even further. And yet, her need for rest had reached the crucial stage. Experience dictated that exhaustion impeded proper function. There was no choice. If sleep meant allowing her mind to wander, so be it.

She stared at the blank ceiling for a moment before closing her eyes. As expected, the dreams flowed from her subconscious in a rapid succession of images. There was Kronos in all his splendor, conducting the Assembly. Her fleet following her charge against the enemy. Explosions of destroyed ships flashing everywhere. Her father's gentle face. Kronos' loving looks. Explosions of surface battles as she stormed fortifications. Maccabeus' grotesque laughter. Kronos solving the paradox. Her father with open arms, beckoning her. Kronos' inert body lying in a pool of blood. Kelahya with a bloody laser knife in her hand. The incessant images came in endless repetitive floods, her restless sleep persisting through the night.

CHAPTER **11**

Cybernetic Organisms

———•———

*Excerpt from the **Corpus Galacticum**, 137th Edition*

A Cybernetic organism *is a self-regulating being comprised of both biological and robotic systems. They can be created from any type of living creature and survive even when they retain mere traces of the biological and cognitive elements of the original being. Usually they possess enhanced aptitudes due to the technology that regulates their subsystems. Severe pain, however, continues to burden these creatures.*

*The proficiency to alter living beings emerged from the study of **Cybernetics** in the 2nd millennium. On or about the 5th millennium, historian Lorenus recounts, that the transdisciplinarity of Cybernetics produced unprecedented success in the design of technological, physical, biological, and cognitive closed signal loops. These closed loops proficiently enabled cybernetic organisms to transmit information throughout their subsystems as if the robotic elements did not exist.*

This circular causal relationship, vital for survival, continues to evolve, and as of the 6th Century TE (Talderon

Era), this science has been perfected to the point of being able to create Cybernetic Organisms that retain only minute biological and cognitive elements of the original being, yet remain alive.

"Do you trust me, Kelahya?" Kronos begged as his eyes scanned her face.

Tightness gripped her throat.

During her time with the Director, she'd learned that he didn't ask her serious or deep questions about himself very often, but on the rare occasions when he did, his motivation turned out not to be as innocent as he'd inferred. This time, his question carried an edge that made her even more apprehensive than usual.

Over the past cycle and a half, he'd arranged for her to witness his official activities with increasing frequency. She'd been at his side during such historical events as the commuting of sentences for the Insurrectionists of Daladion, the interminable hearings on the groundbreaking Legislative Chamber Amendments, and even routine inquiries into the loyalty and ideology of key military personnel.

Through it all, two things became crystal clear—Kronos was shrewd beyond compare, and his probing always carried a purpose more profound and far-reaching than the politicians and the military advisors that surrounded him could ever grasp.

This inquiry, however, appeared to be the most threatening question he'd ever asked her. Mostly because, for the first time, he'd asked a question directly linked to him. But worst of all, it related to trust. Trust meant loyalty, and loyalty meant the utmost truthfulness.

"Yes. I trust you." Her voice was almost inaudible as she wrestled with the tightening around her vocal cords. "Why do you ask?"

He smiled. "Oh, my dear Kelahya, I startled you. I apologize." He paused to await a smile from her in return.

When she obliged, he continued, "My real question is whether you trust me as your friend, not as your leader."

She hoped for control to return to her voice and swallowed to verify it. "I trust you in either case."

"Good." He took her hand and led her out of her quarters. "Come along, there's someone I want you to meet."

In silence, they traversed several corridors and up several levels. They entered at last into a darker narrow hallway, which led, as she knew only too well, to the Command Center of the League of One—the most restricted area on Kronos' command vessel, the *Olympus.*

Kelahya felt a knot of anxiety tighten in her stomach.

"Have I done something wrong, Excellency?" she asked showing a palpable fear in her voice.

Kronos stopped in his tracks. "Wrong? No, by the galaxies." He acted confused for an instant, then he smiled. "I'm truly sorry, Kelahya. I fear I'm not handling this well. Please be patient. All will become clear in a moment."

He led her down a final section of the corridor, which slanted off to the left and ended at a double door. He placed his thumb and middle finger on the identification sensors and the doors slid open.

"Come," he said.

She followed him in and heard the doors close behind her. Her heart pounded and her mouth felt as dry as desert sand.

Until that moment, entrance to the Command Center had been strictly forbidden to her, as it was to everyone, except top-level military officers and advisors.

Her imaginings raced in a thousand different directions. *Why has he brought me here? Who am I to meet that requires Kronos to bring me to this chamber of all places?*

As they entered the circular room, a dizzying array of consoles, displays, keypads and monitors came to life in instantaneous succession from left to right, presenting screens full of information that glanced by at varying speeds. Some she recognized as maps or blueprints of some sort, others rolled endlessly as words and numbers in various languages scrolled across them.

It took less than fifteen clicks for all the stations to be lit and fully operational. To the left of the room, a large oval table projected a holopattern of red lines that intersected at right angles several inches above the surface, forming a series of interlocking grids. Two complicated sets of keypads and lights delineated workstations on each side of the table.

To her right, where Kronos now took a seat, stood a semi-circular lounge sofa surrounding a table of reddish stone.

At the center of the room stood a large ergochair encircled by four floating control panels. Emblazoned upon its back were the symbols that identified the Directorship of the League of One, the Seat of the Legislature, the Throne of the Galactic Sanctuary, and the Commander in Chief of the Alliance of Stars—the offices embodied by one man, Kronos Deucarrion. The same symbols were repeated on the wall around the entire circumference of the room.

Kelahya felt an anxious awe as she internalized the true scope of the power that emanated from this imposing fortress in space, controlled by this imposing a man. The impact of it all shot through her like a shock wave.

"Sit beside me." Kronos patted the sofa on his right.

Mesmerized, Kelahya obeyed. As she sat, the touch of his hand brushing against hers yanked her out of her befuddled state.

His voice was almost breathless. "I realize that I'm somewhat clumsy when it comes to talking to you. I tend to startle you with the directness of my questions."

He glanced about the room. "I live surrounded by war and politics, so delicacy is antithetical to me." He patted her hand, and she gasped. "I assure you I didn't mean to frighten you. Will you forgive me?" Again, that unexpected tone that appeared almost as a plea.

"Excellency," her voice failed her once more as she shook her head in confusion, "I don't understand." She could feel moisture welling in her eyes. She'd never seen him like this. Clearly, he was troubled by something far deeper than she could comprehend.

"You have nothing to fear, my dear, I promise you that." His hands tightened around hers. "During the past two cycles we've become quite close. You've entered my mind as I have entered yours. We understand...no, we sense each other. Even our bodies are—"

The apprehension in her gaze was so intense and her fear so emphatic that it pulled him toward her.

"We have become too close, perhaps. It is dangerous," he whispered.

"Dangerous?" Her voice was little more than a breath.

For a moment he disappeared within her eyes. Her gaze enveloped him so completely that in spite of himself he quivered. He slid aside and rose from the sofa in an effort to stem his physical reaction to her. "You're a child."

He crossed the room and leaned on one of the consoles, then shook his head to rid himself of her spell. After a few milicons, he straightened to his full stature and cleared his throat. When he finally spoke, there was a strained effort in his voice. "I've endeavored to show you much of what I do. You've witnessed the complex variety of people I must contend with." He turned just enough to signal that this non-question required a response.

She nodded.

"What are your impressions?"

"I...well...they . . ." She hesitated, unsure of what to say.

"I'm going to tell you the truth about something the official records and history logs do not mention." He paused. "I am hated, Kelahya. It is no more complicated than that. But do you understand why?" A dark scowl clouded his face.

"No."

"They resent the fact that I rule." He paced aimlessly about, a controlled anger simmering beneath the surface.

"They choose to forget that before I established control," he finally went on, "there was chaos in what we laughingly called the civilized universe. The history books have conveniently neglected the importance of this very critical detail. They speak of general disarray, but somehow, they have omitted the fact that entire star systems were being destroyed, annihilated by petty warlords hungry for universal power and determined to exterminate each other at any cost. The invaluable resources of this vast region of space were being squandered and destroyed. Wasted. I alone had the vision to consolidate power and bring order to that disorganized mess. But the official records recount history only since I assumed power so as to whitewash the horrid truth and foster the notion that all was well with the universe until I came along."

He halted, his eyes lost in the memories of his life's actions.

She stared at him in disbelief. All she knew about him, she had learned from the Corpus Galacticum, and there was no reason to doubt it, since it expressed reality, and nothing but reality.

Never before had Kronos shared how he came to be the most powerful man in the universe. Never before had he shown her the pain that accompanied his duties as supreme leader. Never before had he appeared so fragile.

"It was my destiny then," he continued, "as it is now, to consolidate the Alliance of Stars and protect it through the League of One, in order to prevent universal chaos from reoccurring. That is why they hate me."

He paused to make sure Kelahya understood the full meaning of his words. "My one and only purpose is to safeguard harmony and peace throughout the galaxies. I was born to bring about and ensure peace in our universe so that future generations can coexist in accord with each other. Without me, civilization as it now stands, would cease to be. And the barbaric chaos would return."

Once again, he paused. He tilted his head back as a wry grin came to his face. "You'd surmise that such an ideal would make me beloved or venerated. Instead, I'm reviled."

Kelahya sat motionless. The impact, not only of his words, but also of his sadness and indignation, cast a spell over her. She'd sensed the hatred, as well as the fear in the eyes of many who came to pay homage to Kronos, but she'd never realized how deeply it affected him.

"Fools. But it is to be expected. They take notice of my power and they covet it for themselves. Not to maintain order as I do, but to satisfy their own ambition and hunger for control. They do not, and never will share my vision because they cannot understand it, and they were not ordained to do so."

He looked at her and paused, his eyes filled with anguish. "Ponder this Kelahya, each decision I make has a direct effect on someone somewhere, often on entire systems or even quadrants of the universe. But they don't grasp that my every action is directed toward the realization of that single mission, that single dream. A universe without war."

Kelahya noticed a tear trailing down his left cheek as his eyes scanned the air.

"They desire my power. But the power I wield comes from forces beyond the living. This power comes from the universal need for peace."

He turned to the young woman with a sudden look of resolve, his voice growing in intensity with each succeeding word. "Most importantly, it is not my power. It is our power, yours, mine, everyone's. It's the power that created the universe, the power that refuses to let it be destroyed. I'm only the vehicle, the messenger. My strength comes from my understanding of what the universe needs to survive, to fulfill its ordained purpose." He slammed his hand down onto one of the consoles, causing it to shudder.

Kelahya realized that she'd been holding her breath and released it as silently as she could. She watched as the great man took several deep breaths of his own, then glanced at the output scanners.

"Look around you. These screens and terminals reflect but a miniscule sample of the information I must sift through each and every day. Problems screaming for my attention week after week, and in spite of this treasure-trove, this constant flow of information, I know almost nothing!"

Kronos spun around as his fist swung at an invisible adversary. Beads of perspiration glistened on his forehead, and his breathing was audible across the room.

"Most of the delegates you've observed attending the hearings and the Legislature, would like nothing better than to take my place. Not because of any inherent desire to do better, but because they covet the power. Greed and envy, pure and simple."

Kelahya looked at the flickering displays and discretely dried her icy palms on her lap. She looked to him as he continued.

"They do their best to undermine me. They feed their people lies about me. They do terrible things to them in my name, in the hope of turning them against me. They support violent rebellions throughout the galaxies, they encourage mayhem and chaos." His eyes were fixed in space as if he might be glimpsing a terrifying future.

"The universe would inevitably self-destruct if I left it in the hands of these power-hungry cretins. But it will not come to pass as long as I draw breath. My vision has strengthened the League, and it is my will alone that maintains galactic control. My will. Only I can keep order in the universe."

He paused, to make sure his words had the desired effect.

When he spoke again, his voice sounded old and tired. "For all these reasons, Kelahya, I can trust no one." He sounded like a man condemned. He dropped his head in dejection and an overwhelming silence descended upon the Command Center.

Kelahya remained silent, having no idea what to do or say. Nothing in her experience had prepared her for such a moment. In spite of the endless battle training, the intense holographic combat, the continuous study, hers was a life of privilege. She was used to the hypothetical, not the cruel ugliness of reality.

She watched him as he stood in the middle of this center of power like a wounded bird and, she understood. The mightiest ruler in the history of the universe was alone. Something deep inside her shattered. Instinctively, she went to him and placed her gentle hand in his.

He turned and looked into her eyes. "I trust only you, Kelahya. I need your help."

Her breath caught in her throat for an instant. "How… how can I help? I don't even unders—"

"Your parents trusted me as I trusted them. They helped me. And were killed for it. I can never redeem myself for that." He closed his eyes in an effort to force away the pain the memories brought on. When at last he opened his eyes, two glowing emeralds full of love and concern stared back at him.

"I have fostered the hope these many cycles," his voice wavered, "that someday…you might wish to take their place. To stand at my side, as they did, and help me ensure that their sacrifice was not a futile one." He shook his head. "But now, I look at you, and I'm not sure. There are… too many risks."

He allowed the silence to stretch between them to the snapping point before continuing. "But I have no choice. The time has come for me to find out if this… is your choice."

He recognized the fear reflected on her beautiful eyes. He slid his hand away from hers and dragged himself back to the sofa. He crumbled onto it and let his head fall back, sighing as if being freed from a great burden.

Kelahya's heart produced a rhythmic thud in her ears. She clenched her fists and felt a cold dampness in her palms. Her breath felt heavy. She swallowed hard then took one leaden step after another until she stood before him. "I'll do whatever you say," she managed at last.

The Director looked up at her for a moment, then shook his head and sighed again. "No, my dear. I can't force my wishes upon you. This time it must be what you choose. My politics have cost you far too much already. You've sacrificed more than I would dare ask. No, this time I can't command your loyalty, you must give it freely. I already ask too much of you. It hurts me to do so and I'll understand if you refuse." He leaned forward and buried his face in his hands. He looked lost and defeated.

His tone of disappointment sliced through her body. This man was her savior, her guardian. He'd given her everything. She couldn't repay him with indecision. She hated herself for being afraid. She felt petty and insignificant.

Without warning, from somewhere in the recesses of her memory, the image of her mother being flung against a wall in a splattering of blood, and the flashes of light killing her loving father exploded into her mind's eye, then the hate engendered by these images surged into anger, and the anger into resolve. The fear in her face transformed into hardness as a stern coldness came over her.

When at long last she spoke, the weakness had disappeared from her voice. Instead, it carried the resonance of determination. "I trust you with my life, Kronos. You and my parents shall not be disappointed. My destiny is yours to command. I am yours to command." The words emanated from the very core of her being, and she hoped that he sensed it.

Any doubt was swept away in an instant.

As he raised his eyes, his face radiated with a smile, a combination of triumph and pride.

Her heart soared with a pride of her own. She'd done the right thing and his satisfaction was her reward.

"I was right about you." He sprung to his feet and clamped his strong hands onto her shoulders. "You're indeed the daughter of the great Modyor Devon, and you'll be every bit as great as your father ever was."

As Kronos leaned forward to kiss her forehead, she felt an overwhelming urge to embrace him and bring his lips to hers.

"No, my child," he whispered to her. "I must guard against that. You're young. So very young."

Without warning, he released her and went to the intercom security lock and uttered several commands composed of words and numerals. He then turned to her with a broad smile across his face.

"Now that that is settled, we must begin your military education in earnest. I brought you here to meet Commodore Zenubus Priaminian."

Kronos delighted in Kelahya's reactions, and this time she didn't disappoint him.

She was stunned. Her eyes opened wide and the will to speak deserted her. She coughed a couple of times then took in a deep breath. "I'm to meet Commodore Zenubus Priaminian?"

Kronos chuckled at her reaction. "He's not as terrible as all that. However, he knows more than anyone alive about military tactics and the power and strategies of intergalactic politics. That's what you'll learn from him."

The words of the vidlog's Academic Policies educator flashed before her—*Commodore Zenubus Priaminian, Minister of Defense and Control is the most brilliant strategist in the service of the League of One.*

Kelahya had spent hours at a time with the vidlog's educator in long dissertations on the political strategies of blockades and insurrections conceived by the legendary Zenubus Priaminian. It was rumored that entire armies had surrendered at the mere mention of his name and negotiators had capitulated the moment he entered the room.

"Zenubus," she whispered, regaining some measure of control.

Kronos was silent for a moment as he moved closer to her. With his hands clamped onto her shoulders he glared into her eyes. "Yes, you'll meet him, and he'll school you. But pay attention, you'll discuss his teachings with no one but me. Your life and mine depend on it. Do you understand?"

Again, she sensed his fear, coupled with it his desire for her. She gave a feeble nod. "I understand, but—"

He released his grip on her. "What is it?"

"Why can't you be my military educator?"

"Ah, dear girl, if only I could. It's no longer possible for me to spend so much time in close proximity to you. I can't control my—" he shook his head. "No matter. Do not dwell on that. In time you'll understand." Kronos smiled. "Let's meet your destiny together." He offered his hand and led her to the command chair. "Sit," he ordered, as he pushed her into the seat.

"I can't sit here," she gasped.

She tried to rise, but he pressed her down with a firm but gentle hand and smiled.

The announcement tone informed them of the presence of someone at the door. Kronos stood beside her and she felt him straighten to the full height of his commanding splendor. Her need to turn toward him almost got the best of her, but the sound of the opening door stopped her. She noticed she was wringing her hands and stopped, then dried her palms on her thighs.

Commodore Zenubus Priaminian crossed the threshold and the door closed behind him.

"Come in, Commodore. There's someone for you to meet."

With painful slowness, the man advanced. It looked as if he might cease to exist before her eyes. Like a disintegrating cloud, he floated across the room without raising his gaze from the floor.

This is the terrifying master of interplanetary secrecy and terror, espionage, and intrigue? He must be extremely old.

When he arrived before the young woman, Kronos continued, "This is Kelahya Devona, my ward. It is she whom you will instruct."

The decrepit body raised its head and the eyes looked into Kelahya's. The face was young and fresh. But the violet eyes carried the weight of wisdom. The skin was pale and smooth, and white wavy hair covered the head. Two small black tubes entered the neck on either side.

Kelahya felt her heart skip a beat. With a start, she noticed the almost imperceptible sound of exoskeleton whir each time the man moved and realized what he wore under his garments. The vidlog's Artificial Life lectures had presented a detailed diagram of such an artifact, illustrating the interdependence of robotics, android sciences, and survival rehabilitation techniques.

A cold shudder skimmed along her skin. *"Is this a living example of artificial life? Kronos, does this creature live inside a synthetic shell that keeps his organs functioning? How does he move about?"*

"It is indeed artificial life, my dear girl. Notice how the move commands feed into the shell by means of electrical impulses implanted in the spine and cerebellum, which in turn connect to miniscule motors inside the casing. You have read how individuals who survive in cybernetic devices of one kind or another carry out some of the most technically difficult and dangerous assignments throughout the universe."

Now, much to her consternation, she stood face to face with such an individual, the terrifying Zenubus Priaminian. However, her deeper apprehension grew from the gradual realization that she would spend her future, hour after hour, alone with this humanoid cybernetic organism, whose every appalling characteristic clashed with the world of beauty and perfection she'd become accustomed to.

Why did you not prepare me for this? Are you testing me?

"She is beautiful, my Lord." The floating man's voice emanated from a microfilament located in a hydraulic resonance box somewhere on his chest.

Even his voice is not his own.

"She'll be a splendid student, I'm sure."

Kelahya experienced increased difficulty in maintaining her composure in the presence of this veritable symphony of electronic gadgetry, whizzing and whirring as it made him breathe, forced his heart to beat, his vital functions to perform. She felt cold, afraid, and sad…very sad.

"I'm sorry, Kelahya," the resonance box said. "You've never seen my kind before, have you?" A mechanical whisper emanated from somewhere and he floated several feet back. "I should've been more considerate."

"You'll address her as my Lady, Zenubus. Is that clear?" Kronos ordered.

The eyes shifted toward Kronos and, for an instant, Kelahya glimpsed at one corner of the thin mouth as it curled into an awkward smile.

"Of course, my Lord."

"Go, now," Kronos commanded. "You have my instructions. You'll begin tomorrow."

"With pleasure, my Lord." The eyes shifted back to her and the lust they reflected made Kelahya shudder. "Tomorrow… my Lady."

* * * * * *

Kelahya opened her eyes with a jolt. It took her a moment to realize where she was. And then she noticed that she lay on the bed in her new non-prison. An annoying bell kept ringing and a tiny blue diode blinked in the upper right-hand corner of the monitor block. She glared at it, wishing the ringing would stop. It didn't.

"Yes?" she managed to utter, her voice sounding as if her mouth were full of cotton.

"I apologize, General. We didn't realize you were sleeping." It was a female voice. "But the rotation for lavatory and hygiene services is now in our sector of the ship's quarters, and we wondered if…"

Kelahya shook the drowsiness from her mind. "What?"

"Would you like to freshen up?"

Kelahya yawned.

"You'd rather sleep. Sorry."

"No. You're right. I'd very much like to…freshen up, as you say."

"Good. I'll arrive at your quarters in a few minutes to escort you."

Kelahya rubbed her eyes and dragged herself back to the land of the living. She reached into the small sink and water poured into her hands. She splashed her face and rubbed vigorously. She pulled a disposable and dried her face, then turned to the tiny mirror.

It was a comfort to find she didn't look as bad as she felt. It almost lifted her spirits. She rolled her head and heard several vertebrae pop into position. Then, she stretched every painful muscle in her body and groaned with each one. *Why does my body ache? I didn't suffer any physical violence.*

She rinsed her mouth then stood there, motionless.

Her mind was numb, and she realized with relief, that despite dreaming of her past, it had held together, and she had actually slept. No new violent images meant she only needed to contend with available information, regardless of its veracity. Especially now that she harbored more doubts than ever regarding her captors and the possibility of freedom.

The door chimes interrupted Kelahya's introspection and she opened the door.

"Lyndsor Caveat, Captain Third Class."

Petite and charming, the antithesis of everything Kelahya classified as military stood outside. Her tiny Terrian figure burst with sensuality, and her face had an alluring, almost childish beauty. Kelahya remembered her from the operations room when Jofan had first removed her from the cave.

"How about starting with a Terrian massage?" Caveat asked, nodding down a hallway to the right. She moved a step closer to Kelahya and whispered, "I prefer real hands. They are far more invigorating than cleaning units, in my opinion."

Her charm was irresistible, so was her irreverence for protocol.

Kelahya smiled for the first time in days and shrugged. "Of course, why not?"

"Follow the leader," commanded the diminutive dynamo as she headed down the maze of corridors.

Kelahya chuckled to herself as she pictured the incongruent image they must cut trotting through the ship, with Caveat, small even by Terrian standards, and Kelahya, lofty even by Dionysian standards.

We're like characters in a humor pix.

While entertained with the behavior of her companion, Kelahya realized she had failed to examine her surroundings. They had entered a decahedron shaped reception area with doors in every wall. She noticed the Eniat signs on the doors then hurried to catch Caveat as she disappeared through one of them.

What did the sign say? I didn't retain its meaning.

They made a quick series of left and right turns, finally stopping at a narrow counter. The Captain removed the insignia from her left sleeve and slid it into the wall plate behind the counter, then turned to Kelahya.

"Now yours," she said, pointing to the small blue circle on the Commander's left sleeve.

Kelahya removed it and followed suit.

"Twenty-two and twenty-three," came the faceless response as a set of doors opened on their right.

They stepped into a small vestibule that led to a large chamber, filled with a light mist. At the far end of the chamber were two rows of loungers totaling some eight in all, four of which were occupied at the moment by both males and females of varying species, relaxing, enjoying each other's company, or sleeping. The fact that they all were without a stitch of clothing was clearly irrelevant. The walls of the room were lined with cabinets, each with numerals. Translucent doors led to the steam rooms.

Rather small hygiene quarters for such a large vessel.

"Here we are," came Caveat's cheerful revelation. "I am twenty-two and you are twenty-three." She pointed to two cabinets on the wall.

The Captain's voice prompted a reaction from the males, who looked in her direction and smiled with satisfaction when they confirmed who it was. But, when they noticed Kelahya, their attitude changed.

The Captain Third Class undressed in no time, and Kelahya understood immediately why she aroused such interest. The tiny woman possessed a most enticing body. Every curve, every sinew, every muscle was a work of art. A glance at the entranced males confirmed that this was a woman they desired unabashedly. And the delicious little lady was oblivious to it all.

"When you're finished, go through that door over there," Caveat said, pointing to the opposite end of the room, "I'll get things started."

Kelahya removed her clothes and followed her new acquaintance's directions into the massage chamber without so much as a glance at the male contingency.

Caveat was waiting and pointed toward a small chamber to her left.

"Duriat is ready for you. He's one of the best. Enjoy."

"You certainly have this well-organized. It's almost too good to be true. Seems unreal. Thank you, anyway."

"It's what I'm here for. Have fun." With that, Caveat skipped off through another door and disappeared.

"Welcome," whispered Duriat. "Please relax on the recliner face down."

Kelahya willingly complied.

He placed two fingers on the nape of her neck, and Kelahya's consciousness floated away.

CHAPTER **12**

Commodore Zenubus Priaminian

———◆———

*Excerpt from the **Corpus Galacticum**, 137th Edition*

Zenubus Priaminian, Minister of Defense and Control *is recognized as most brilliant strategist in the service of the League of One.*

Credited for being the father of prevailing strategic designs, Commodore Priaminian has defined military strategy as the "art of distributing and applying military means to fulfill the ends of galactic policies".

The Commodore gives pre-eminence to political aims over military goals as he directs martial planning, the conduct of campaigns, movement and disposition of forces, and of course, what he is renowned for—deceptive maneuvers.

Historian Lorenus, has written that for Commodore Priaminian galactic policy is the principal tool to secure universal peace. It is written that the Commodore professes strategic design as far superior in perspective than military tactics, which simply involve the disposition and operation of units on the battlefields. Galactic strategy on the other hand, takes into account what is

*deem to be best for the Alliance of Stars, and therefore
utilizes a myriad of intelligence to craft proficient, agile,
and original tactics.*

"Open your eyes, my Lady."

The artificial voice made young Kelahya flinch. Despite her best efforts, it made her self-conscious to have this floating voice box with his whirring organs hovering about. During the last cycle, her discomfort had metamorphosed into pity. The incongruity of seeing the moving lips while the sound emanated elsewhere clashed with her sense of normalcy.

One undeniable fact remained, however, Zenubus Priaminian was kind, at least to her. Maybe his gentleness emanated from his fear of Kronos if he mistreated her, but she doubted that. She sensed no fear in the Minster of Defense and Control when Kronos was present during her lessons. On the contrary, he displayed an attitude of defiant humility, as if taunting the great man.

Zenubus was hard to read, even for a Minder as skilled as Kronos, let alone for Kelahya. He had mastered control of his mind to such a degree that only what he wished you to sense or perceive was available for the taking. Kelahya surmised that the Minster had learned to create a mental shield, not only to avoid intrusions from the Supreme Commander when designing strategic battle tactics, but also as protection from the lesser Minders that served Kronos as officers, soldiers, or medics. A virtuoso, Zenubus had created an indomitable fortress around his mind, and Kelahya admired his mighty will.

Early in her training, she'd come to accept that attempting to outguess her teacher by invading his mind was a complete waste of time. Repeatedly, she'd extracted the right answer, only to discover he'd intentionally provided the incorrect outcome, and had easily manipulated her. So, she abandoned that tact, and focused on her training without any telepathic intrusion. In the end she'd enjoyed this process more, pleased that her wits had carried the day without the use of her unique gift.

However, when they were alone, she needed to maintain a physical distance from her floating teacher to keep his lustful emanations in check. Zenubus would sneak up behind her sometimes, but she was learning to sense his miniature motors buzzing away long before he could get close enough to intimidate her. In a way, it was flattering. No other man dared insinuate himself upon her. At least, none had dared so far. Flirting, therefore, was limited to this small encasement of electronics and viscera, in a game she enjoyed all the better now that she understood it, and at which she was quickly becoming a master.

"Open your eyes, my Lady," the Commodore insisted.

"I'm not asleep, Zenubus," Kelahya snapped. "I'm pondering." She took a deep breath and leaned back. "I detect no discernible reason for it. Frankly, Zenubus, I don't believe it would work. The entire plan makes no sense to me."

She stood and moved around the desk in a feigned manifestation of frustration, but she was, in fact, avoiding him.

Zenubus halted, aware that he couldn't catch her.

"It's a ruse, my Lady. A trick."

"Then, it's a stupid trick. Thousands of military personnel would be killed with this 'trick'. It would be a pathetic waste of forces." She waved her arms at him to emphasize her indignation. "If the Aant-tahal decided to fire, he would be annihilated along with his entire fleet, correct?"

The young face with the decaying body became stern. Zenubus rolled his eyes. "Repeat the scenario for me. Perhaps you've not understood it."

She took a deep, exasperated breath, and stomped about the room in rhythm with her explanation.

"In this 'scenario' the League's fleet consisted of eight destruction cruisers, fully armed, twenty sonic destroyers, sixty-four—"

"Five."

"Sixty-five attack fighters and over three hundred missile launchers, unarmed, and unmanned, except for the pilots.

Correct?" She placed her hands on her hips in a gesture of defiance. She could sense him mustering patience, and she loved it.

"Yes," the box said, as the lips moved.

"Against two hundred armed interceptors, and countless numbers of ground-based anti-spacecraft arrays, all of which had the power to destroy the League's vessels as they floated around Aanttahalia. If they chose to fire, as well they might, then—"

"Stop," he ordered as he floated toward her. "Why would they consider firing? The cruisers and missile launchers alone could've destroyed their defenses and their cities instantly."

"At a very heavy price, Minster."

"That's beside the point, my Lady. The point is that they were well aware of the inevitable outcome and, rather than sacrifice their people, indeed the entire planet, they chose to capitulate. The holoscape display of the battle illustrates graphically the futility of resisting. It's very clear."

Zenubus was really worked up this time. She could hear his motors whizzing and whirring as they worked at a frenzied pace to keep his vital signs below the danger level. Time to deliver the final blow.

"That's precisely the flaw. Had their leaders been more interested in freedom than self-preservation, or if they had a healthy dose of pride, they would've sacrificed all to avoid submission. Better to die than to lose one's freedom. Especially, when nothing guaranteed that surrender meant survival. Correct, Commodore?" She paused for effect. "Consider this, one massive volley at the bulk of Kronos' fleet and their civilization would now be acknowledged as the most heroic in the annals of the League of One. Not to mention that it would've been a first step in the possible annihilation of the League of One. They could've dealt a devastating blow to Kronos' forces that would've carved a weakness and allowed his other enemies to finish him off." Another strategic pause. "My dear Commodore, you're fully aware that no such fate awaited them in surrender. No guarantees. Correct? That's the key… and the flaw." She'd taken her tone from a defiant growl to a soft, humiliating whisper, and the effect had been even better than she'd hoped for.

Zenubus was angry, belittled, and speechless—for now, anyway. His tired, violet eyes fluttered like the wings of a Deno moth as he struggled to calm himself to deliver his response.

When he floated toward her, she held her ground.

When he finally spoke, in that synthetic voice, he did so with a heavy slowness that drifted down like ash after an eruption.

"No planetary leader would sacrifice his entire population and allow another civilization to reap the benefit. No such idealism exists at that level of command. Self-preservation overcomes idealism every time. That's why the plan is a masterpiece, my Lady. Because it's infallible."

"Even the weakest of beasts will attack when it's cornered without hope. To ignore this, is to risk extinction."

Water upon ash. They glared into each other's eyes for what seemed an eternity.

Then, she saw it, a microscopic twitch at the corner of the mouth. The subtle indication that, once again, Zenubus found her arguments compelling and, she was sure he'd say, also amusing. As he let the smile broaden, the two of them chuckled.

"Your point, my Lady, is valid… Amusing, I must add, if also impractical." And there it was…the lust.

She twittered across the room with a playful skip.

"Then I deserve a reward. Can we stop, please?" she asked, in that pitiful childlike voice that he could never refuse.

He chortled with even more joy than before. "Go, my Lady. Go."

* * * * * *

General Kelahya Devona, Commander of the XXVII Confinement Brigade, reclined onto the lounger and shook her long hair over the headrest. After inhaling as deeply as her lungs could expand, she exhaled with a grunt of relief that caused Captain Third Class, Lyndsor Caveat, to burst into laughter.

"By Takultkeh's Staff! That was the most…heartfelt sigh I've ever heard."

Kelahya sighed again. They were in a small room filled with a soothing aromatic steam, their naked bodies glistening with moisture.

Kelahya filled her lungs again, exhaling very slowly. She smiled before sitting upright and staring at her small companion across the round table that separated them.

"Captain—"

"—Caveat," interrupted the young woman.

Kelahya smiled then went on. "I realize I'm only your… assignment. Nevertheless, I appreciate the company and the relaxation you've provided me. Thank you."

The Captain glanced at Kelahya, then her eyes dropped toward a glass on the table, which she caressed, as the smile left her lovely face. She raised the glass and sipped the amber liquid, then ran her tongue along her lips. Finally, she looked back at Kelahya and shrugged.

"Let me be honest with you, General. I requested the duty. You wouldn't have noticed, of course, but when you were first released from the cave, after you so expertly disabled our android, I was one of the…observers in the control room you saw. It was I who first spotted you in the valley. It was I who programmed the events during your captivity in the cave." Without taking her eyes off Kelahya, the dainty bundle of sex appeal took another sip from her glass.

Kelahya felt tightness in her stomach. *You are my captor? I can't believe that.* She sensed she should wait for the rest of the Caveat's admission before responding.

"I must confess." Caveat smiled. "That I've become an admirer. I find myself fascinated by you. And, for what it's worth,

I like you." She leaned forward, resting an elbow on the arm of the lounger, her piercing brown eyes never leaving Kelahya. "To be perfectly honest, my first reaction was to hate you. I took your clothes. Introductory breakdown is my specialty, and I've studied the techniques developed by the League of One, plus I've inserted some refinements of my own. I created the entire scenario of your captivity. I wanted to watch you crumble and suffer the way people in every corner of the universe have been made to agonize by your soldiers. I dream of someday having the satisfaction of standing face to face with Kronos, assuming we can ever take him alive, and paying him back with a little of what he's done to us. I practiced on you."

Kelahya bolted up. "What did you say?"

The captain gave an ironic snicker. "Yes, a foolish notion. It was insensitive of me to say such a thing. I apologize."

"You said, 'assuming we can take him alive'?"

"Well," the captain chuckled, "let's face it. The likelihood that Kronos will ever be captured alive is extremely remote, at best. The likelihood of me being there to address him…an impossibility. Then again, I believed it equally impossible to ever meet you face to face. But here we are."

Kelahya drifted back onto the lounger, weighing the implications of what she'd just heard.

Is it possible that the news of Kronos' death hasn't been imparted through the ranks of the Rebellion? Why? The news would be cause for celebration on every planet within the Alliance. What could be the purpose of keeping this information secret?

Unless…Kronos is not dead.

Can it be that the images in my mind are similes? Implants?

It's possible… Someone with strong mental power could've suggested the images to make me give Kronos up for dead. Nestor— if that's who he is—could be capable of it.

Perhaps this is another plot to destroy Kronos.

A very subtle and dangerous plot, but…why not?

It certainly makes more sense than the idea of me killing him.

Separating me from Kronos is the most efficient way to destroy us.

"Yes, here we are," Kelahya whispered at last. Her mind raced in an attempt to quickly piece together all the information offered so freely.

Caveat laughed. "I assumed I'd bored you with my chatter and you'd gone back to sleep."

"Far from it, I was reflecting. Tell me something, Caveat. How long have you served Nestor?"

"Oh, Nestor," she said with a meaningful chuckle. "He's attractive, is he not?"

Kelahya smiled stiffly. "I've met worse."

Caveat leaned closer across the table. "Just between us, every female on this ship has attempted to lure him in. No success stories yet. He's interested in nothing but his mission. Pity." She finished with a tone that matched her gesture of disappointment.

"What do you know about him?" Kelahya persisted.

"Quite frankly, I know far more about you." Caveat chuckled as she leaned back, glass in hand. "Nestor, like the others, bears the name of the legendary leader of the Rebellion, which lends him an air of mystery and superiority. Very effective, I might add."

"The others?"

Absentmindedly, Caveat nodded before proceeding, "Jofan pretends to be in command here, but I've caught Nestor giving subtle signs of approval or disapproval. Considering the sessions you've had with both of them, you're probably better informed than I am."

"How many other Nestors are there?" Kelahya asked.

"I'm not sure. Five or six, at least," Caveat offered freely. "I've served with four."

"How long have your served with this one?"

"Not long. He's rather special, though. And, as far as I can tell, he has far more power than any of the others. It's to be expected.

He's the one who orchestrated your capture, with my help of course." Her cheeks flushed. "I'm sorry General, I didn't mean to gloat and—"

"It's of no importance, Caveat. You were only doing your duty. Tell me more about these many Nestors."

Caveat squinted as she searched her memory. "Let me count. Four cycles ago, I served with two of them at the same time. They overlapped for a while." She paused. "Hmmm…I served with another for one mission a cycle ago."

"I'd venture it's hard to keep up, especially if you're ignorant of the real one's whereabouts. Assuming there is a real Nestor," Kelahya offered.

A bewildered smile appeared on Caveat's face. "Of course, there's a real one."

"Have you ever met him?"

She laughed. "Oh, no. Only the Nestors and Jofan have ever met him, so they say."

Kelahya felt a sense of ease flowing into her stiff joints and muscles. The massage had helped, but mostly it was the sense of trust that emanated from this tiny bundle of energy—a welcome feeling. Despite fearing the excruciating pain in her head, she had to confirm Caveat's honesty. She eased into Caveat's mind.

"What will they do with me, Caveat?" she asked to distract her.

The Captain pursed her lips as she stared into Kelahya's eyes and considered her response. "I'm out of the circle, General, where those decisions are made. I can guess, but that's all," she said, with a hint of regret.

Kelahya finished her drink and leaned forward. "Then give me your best guess."

She now was in full control of Caveat's mind with none of the pain associated with the previous release of her Endow. Kelahya's spirits lifted.

Caveat considered the question for a second, then nodded and leaned closer to keep the conversation as private as possible.

"I know Jofan as well as anyone, maybe better. I've worked with him for six cycles now. He appears frail, but he's as tough as they come. He hates Kronos more than anyone, and as far as he's concerned you represent Kronos. I then interpret, that for him to have let you off as easily as he has, someone far higher in command has ordered it. Nestor, if you ask me."

She winked at Kelahya, before continuing, "Why, you may ask? Search me. You may have information they could use. Or they hope they can use you as a bargaining chip with Kronos. You can fill in the blanks far more effectively than I. But, if they intended to kill you, you'd be dead. Have no doubt of that." Caveat tilted her head and held out her arms with a shrug that indicated she was as much at a loss as Kelahya, then relaxed back into the chair. "Just between us, I never would have asked for this 'assignment', as you call it, if I believed you were to be executed."

Kelahya's mouth stretched into a smile as she leaned against her chair and released Caveat's mind. *She is sincere.* "Thank you, Caveat. I appreciate and welcome your honesty." She sighed and closed her eyes.

CHAPTER **13**

Subterfuge

———◆———

Subterfuge *is a key technique perfected by Supreme Commander Kronos Deucarrion to prepare Centurions and Senior Officers to resist interrogation by enemies that utilize psychological means to obtain information.*

The trainees not only acquire knowledge as to how to withstand said interrogations but gain vital expertise on the application of these techniques.

The training includes recognizing deception practices such as the propagation of beliefs that are not true, or appear as half-truths, or simply as omissions. The training includes dissimulation techniques such as the utilization of doctrine, allurement, distraction, camouflage, and concealment. Centurions and Senior Officers are methodically trained on self-deception procedures and learn how to avoid being double-minded with conflicts of spirituality, ethics, or loyalty.

"They are heading for the south side of the Oversyus Canyon," Zenubus pointed out with some urgency.

Kelahya and the Commodore were in a battle pod, followed by a small fleet of fifty.

"What do you say, my Lady?"

"They're likely to move in that direction erroneously expecting it'll lead them out of the canyon. The topomaps show an exit."

"What makes you think there's no exit?"

"I don't think, Zenubus, I know," she answered with aplomb.

"You're leading a team of fifty. Their lives are in your hands."

Kelahya glared at her instructor. "Do you believe me to be stupid?"

He shook his head. She shot him a sardonic smile and addressed her fleet. "They're proceeding as anticipated. Disregard the topos. There is no exit from Oversyus Canyon. Units twenty-one through thirty, remain at the entrance. All other units follow me." With mechanical precision she maneuvered her ship into the canyon and smiled at her instructor. "By the way, Zenubus, your life is also in my hands."

"I'm painfully aware of that, my Lady."

She closed on the enemy at breathtaking speed, then spoke into her comm and addressed the fleet. "Follow their ships into the narrow tributary on the north quadrant. I'll signal when we're there. It's tight, so stay sharp. Units thirty-one through forty, maneuver HH-4 and establish the trap. Units forty through fifty, stay at the mouth and block the exit. The rest, follow me."

"A highly unorthodox maneuver, my Lady, with high risk to our fleet."

"Do not distract me with useless chatter, Zenubus. If you have a constructive comment to offer, I'd love to hear it. Otherwise, be silent," she snapped.

"You're outgunned. How will you compensate for that?" Zenubus retorted.

"Patience, Excellency, and you shall be rewarded."

With effortless dexterity, she maneuvered the battle pod through the narrow canyon, her remaining fleet behind her.

"On my mark, exit the canyon in vertical formation and level off in five tarsecs. Two…one…mark."

She yanked the controls back and the battle pod shot upward, zoomed out of the canyon, and over the surrounding peaks. Her fleet followed at close range. With astonishing quickness, she entered a series of codes into the computer, calculating speed and distance.

Zenubus, thankful to be strapped in, observed in silence, except for his ectomotors, which were working at full throttle.

"Coordinates, 55 by 12, speed 3.18. Set directionals. We'll enter the Canyon at its deepest, one tarsec ahead of the enemy. Start full array discharge in ten clicks. Stay alert. We can't allow them time to discharge weapons. On my mark. Three…two… one…mark."

Zenubus bit his lip as she plunged straight down at breathtaking speed. His hands clamped onto the armrests, the straps straining to hold him in place, the whizzing and whirring of his motors intensifying as they struggled to maintain his vital signs below the danger level.

Kelahya loved to get him worked up like this. He liked it as well, though he would never admit it. Her battle strategies always surprised him, and she reveled in it.

She was different from anyone he'd ever dealt with, and her ability to always do the unexpected made her a fearsome adversary. The mighty Commodore Zenubus Priaminian, Minister of Defense and Control for the League of One, knew he could claim no superiority to this brilliant twenty-year-old strategist.

To his great delight, she'd immersed herself in his teachings and absorbed every nuance with a hunger he'd never experienced in anyone before. Now, in practice, she deftly applied that knowledge with clarity and creativity, enhanced by her own uncanny intuition, creating a mixture that was lethal beyond his wildest expectations.

She sliced into the canyon and breathed a secret sigh of relief. Her calculations had been accurate. The enemy was nowhere in sight. Her devoted fleet had followed her without hesitation and remained right behind her.

"Full throttle hover," she commanded.

Their current position provided visual confirmation that there was no exit from the canyon.

"My Lad—"

Her hand shot up to silence him. Out of the corner of her eye, Kelahya saw the enemy's lead attack pod, followed by several others. All her strategy would be for nothing unless she acted without delay.

"Full discharge! Two…one…mark!"

Without hesitation, she charged at the enemy, her fleet right on her tail.

Zenubus feared his oxygen regulator could be reaching the breaking point.

The enemy froze in their cockpits at the unexpected sight of Kelahya's battle pods charging at full speed. There was no room for them to maneuver and fire their weapons without self-destruction.

As she anticipated, in their confusion, the enemy ships swerved and tried to reverse course.

She followed in close pursuit, the enemy no more than a few metrics away.

"All units," she commanded, "disable enemy vessels."

In a matter of milicons, it was over.

"Suspend discharge, Lady Devona. We're yours," came the breathless request from the enemy.

"Thank you, Captain Mathiah. The exercise was great fun," Kelahya said, masking her pride with terse professionalism.

"Fun?" Zenubus exploded. "This was a battle exercise. Battles are not fun."

Kelahya turned to him with a smile that warmed his heart. "My dear Zenubus, I apologize for my poor choice of words."

He nodded, reluctantly accepting her apology.

"But, admit it. You had fun, too," she added, with a mischievous smile.

"Take us back to base," he commanded.

"Return to base," she instructed her troops. The battle pods left the canyon and headed back to the *Olympus*.

"How did you ascertain there was no exit from that canyon?"

"I made sure there was none."

"How?"

"I came down two days ago and…rearranged the geography. I used a refractor to project an image that makes the canyon appear closed. Unit One is retrieving it as we speak."

"You what?" His motors threatened to overload.

"Calm down, Commodore. The important thing is that I was victorious."

"That's…unethical."

"A certain Commodore Zenubus Priaminian writes in his *Tactics for Victory*, and I quote, 'There are no ethics in war'."

* * * * * *

"There are no ethics in war," mumbled Kelahya.

"Is that so?" asked Caveat.

"What?"

"You said, 'there are no ethics in war' and I wondered why you said that?"

Snapped back to the present, Kelahya's eyes narrowed as she quickly assessed her current location—a bar. *How did I get here?*

"So?" insisted Caveat.

"Nothing, really. Remembering something I'd read some time back."

"You seem…detached."

"Do I? How?"

"At times, even when you are looking right at me, your eyes go inward. They're open, but not present in our surroundings. It's odd."

"Really? Did I do that?"

Caveat nodded.

"How long did I look like that?"

"Oh, not long. A moment or so."

Kelahya inhaled deeply, then slowly exhaled. *Given the circumstances, that's a relief. But how come I can't trace my journey? How did I get here?* "Well, I'm not surprised." She smiled at Caveat. "The relaxation offerings I've experienced today, coupled with this drink you've ordered for me, have worked their magic. I'm tranquil. That is all."

"Caveat!" a young officer called out as he stretched his arms out.

"Sorry, General, I promised him this dance."

"Enjoy." Kelahya smiled and nodded.

The charming Caveat marched off to the dance salon, leaving Kelahya alone to enjoy her drink in the private alcove that overlooked the bar. The barkeep approached her table and, with an indifference that brought a smirk to Kelahya's lips, plopped down another round and left.

Robots like this one are too predictable. Why not alter their mechanism to offer a variety of behavior? A bit of a surprise in places like these would go a long way.

Kelahya had visited bars and similar establishments on countless ships, planets and outposts, both for fun and on assignment. The decor varied, the names of the drinks and tidbits changed, the faces and species were somewhat different, but the atmosphere was, with precious few exceptions, identical. Some peddled unconventional substances and services, others, especially on fleet vessels, served the social function of attenuating inhibitions and promoting companionship.

However, bars on military vessels were, in a subtle way, more threatening than those found on planetary establishments.

On military vessels, one was usually shackled to the same group of companions for long periods of time, often several cycles. The possibility of slipping off into the night to thwart unwanted advances was difficult at best. The same crews worked the same shifts, only rotating every two cycles. Day in and day out one was stranded, in effect, on a miniscule island from which there was no escape. Familiarity bred audacity.

For the patrons bent on intoxication, bars in vessels offered as safe an environment as they could ever expect to find. If they lost control, or consciousness, either their comrades or the Control Troops would always get them back to their quarters. If they were lucky, and boredom had a way of providing such luck, they would end up in the quarters of a member of whichever sex they found most enticing. Promiscuity in this environment was a way of life, and the alcoves that surrounded the bar were designed to offer seclusion for personnel to engage in pleasures in comfortable anonymity.

As Kelahya savored the concoction Caveat had ordered, she noticed that no eyes roamed in her direction, but she was far from comfortable. Caveat's comments earlier in the day had bewildered her. She had sifted through her words seeking a loose end. Why was she unaware of Kronos' death? Why did she offer information so freely? Kelahya searched for a string she could pull that might unravel the web of confusing information, or at least undo it a little. But nothing surfaced.

She took another sip from the glass and realized that she'd almost downed two drinks. She chuckled to herself. The flavor wasn't unpleasant at all. It struck her that it tasted like a berry derivative, but what type eluded her. The effect was pleasing, however, and she could already feel warmth spreading through her. She took another sip, allowing the savory liquid to linger in her mouth then trickle down her throat leaving behind a sweet aftertaste.

The image of a dead Kronos materialized right in front of her as a distant reflection on one of the vessel's mirrors. It immobilized her, and she stared at it unable to look away. At long last she blinked, and the reflection disappeared. She glanced around her to scan if anyone had noticed her or the image. With relief she realized that no one had. The private alcove where she sat provided enough seclusion, and the handful of patrons at the bar tables were unaware of her presence as they laughed, chatted, and went about their business.

This is not the time or the place to break apart. Seek a memory that is useful.

* * * * * *

Trudging the green sand dunes of Vlatzeba Tendor, Commander Kelahya scanned the area around her with painstaking care before each step. She struggled to keep her anger in check, well aware that her life depended on making no mistakes.

She'd insisted on pursuing the runaway transport unit on her own, ordering her troops and even her own attack ship to wait in orbit. Her panic-stricken officers had argued vigorously against it, and even made a feeble attempt to stop her, but their efforts merely succeeded in egging her on. This was a matter of honor. Her honor.

Over the protestations of his advisors, Kronos had commissioned her to the extermination of nearby Jobiah Dah Tendor, an insignificant planet that had chosen to rebel against the League of One, threatening the fragile peace within the Tendor System. The Jobiahite sneak attacks and terrorist activities had been directed at the planets in the Tendor System that had aligned themselves with Kronos seeking his protection. In addition to their open rebellion against the League of One, the underlining objectives of the Jobiahite attacks centered around their need to annihilate then plunder these weaker planets.

Kronos and the Legislature had warned the leaders on Jobiah Dah time and again of their eminent destruction if their criminal activities did not cease. They not only ignored the warnings, but also mobilized the population on neighboring planets outside the Tendor System, forcing Kronos' hand. Now, their extermination would be a warning to others with similar ideas of rebellion. If political or military leaders chose anarchy and violence over the peace and stability offered by the League of One, they could count on suffering the same fate as Jobiah Dah.

But what should've been a routine extermination, had transformed unexpectedly into a troublesome one.

Moments before the neutronic bombardment of Jobiah Dah, a transport unit had managed to escape. Kelahya had not anticipated such action on the part of any of the inhabitants of Jobiah Dah, since all spacecraft on the small planet had been incapacitated. The fact that the reports were obviously wrong made little difference to her now, and the reason for such a failure would be investigated later. What mattered to her was the capture of the transport unit.

Kelahya took personal responsibility for the failures of her personnel and, in this particular case, for not verifying the reports herself. More importantly, her lack of verification was a violation of the basic Priaminian rule of military maneuvers. A mistake she would not forgive in others and was not about to forgive in herself. Therefore, the destruction of the runaway transport had to be hers.

After tracking the transport unit to Vlatzeba Tendor, she had now reached the coordinates where the runaway had last been detected. She activated the particle transporter in her vessel and materialized on the surface of the planet. The Jobiahite transport unit was nowhere to be found.

It must've penetrated the dunes and is hiding underground.

She focused her holoscanner and systematically scrutinized the area. Her scrutiny halted, as she focused on a sight that brought a smile to her face. She stepped with caution as she searched in her pouch for a luring module. She placed it on the ground in front of her, then backed away.

Two tiny lumps moved sinuously toward the luring module. They raced with surprising speed under the green sand, popping up to reconnoiter from time to time. They were two young cubines, a rare treat indeed.

Cubines were beautiful, white, furry little creatures, native to the green dunes of Vlatzeba Tendor, cherished as pets and highly valued throughout the galaxies. Kelahya watched them in rapt fascination, thrilled at the prospect of capturing the tiny creatures and bringing them to the ship. Chantall would be delighted.

The cubines were drawn to the luring module and without hesitation they examined it and attempted to consume it, their tiny teeth clicking against the hard surface of the lure.

An explosion of sand accompanied by a loud roar shattered the silence of the green desert. Out of nowhere, a keliotrops emerged from the bowels of Vlatzeba Tendor, propelling the runaway transport unit like a child's toy into the air.

Instinctively, Kelahya aimed her nullifier and fired. The transport unit exploded in midair.

Kelahya caught her breath as her attention focused on the new threat. She had studied keliotrops on vidlog and knew everything about them—in theory. But seeing the gigantic creature face to face was different, entirely different.

This one was an enormous male, his scaly bulk reeking of his mating stench. The keliotrops glanced at the explosion, but it didn't hold his interest very long. The luring module was far more attractive and, as he turned toward it, his single eye focused on Kelahya, who remained crouched near it.

Kelahya held his gaze, while out of the corner of her eye she saw that the little cubines continued to be captivated by the luring module.

The beast's tongue hissed through the air searching for her scent, attempting to ascertain what variety of creature she was. A yellowish liquid oozed from between his scales to remove the sand. It leaned back on its tail, the diminutive claws dangling in the air.

Kelahya watched in complete amazement. Never had she been in the presence of a creature so ghastly or had smelled a more repulsive odor.

The luring module's pulses finally dominated the beast's attention and he went at it. Surprised by the presence of the tiny cubines, he backed off for a moment. The keliotrops made up his mind, decided to take the small creatures along with the luring module, and wrapped his slithery tongue around them all.

Kelahya wasn't about to let this foul monster deprive her of her priceless cubines, so, as the keliotrops lurched forward with his prey wrapped in his long tongue, she followed. She'd studied their habits and knew their weaknesses. The nauseating scent meant it was mating season and food was one of the bribes used in courtship, so he would keep the cubines alive until they were delivered to his prospective mate. To do that, he'd have to stay above the surface of the sand.

She also understood its strengths, which outweighed its weaknesses by far. Keliotrops moved through the sand the way creatures on other worlds moved through water, the only sign of their presence being a vibration that permeated the surrounding areas. Keliotrops were powerful and merciless when it came to killing their prey. They were also fearless. Nothing on Vlatzeba Tendor could threaten them.

Kelahya's adventure into the desert of Vlatzeba Tendor had resulted in the destruction of her target—the runaway transport unit—and not proved to be a stimulating challenge. The success of her new goal rested on killing the keliotrops before he reached his mate, otherwise she'd become dinner along with the cubines. She might have a chance of defeating one, but never two.

The cubines were biting away at his tongue and an idea formed in her mind. If she openly attacked the beast, he might be persuaded to drop the cubines. If he did drop them, she could rush to catch them while initiating the transmission sequence for transport to her ship.

She aimed at his tail and discharged her weapon. It worked. The keliotrops, although not injured, was startled enough to drop the cubines, and with a mean and ugly snarl he sprang straight at her.

Constellations! This isn't good! The vidlog outlined their attack mode. Keliotrops are not supposed to attack above ground and they never charge without first assessing their pray. This one must have missed those chapters.

Her instant reaction was to discharge her weapon again, but the setting was on "stun" and there was no time to reset it. If she discharged with this setting, it would do nothing to stop his charge and was likely to infuriate him even more.

Instinctively, she yelled at the keliotrops at the top of her lungs and flapped her arms vigorously.

The keliotrops stopped, wondering what this strange creature was doing.

Behind the beast, she spotted her cubines as they scurried to safety. Although she'd lost them, she was glad they had escaped this smelly fiend.

The keliotrops burrowed into the green sand.

He's preparing to attack.

She reset her weapon and stood her ground.

"My Lady…" echoed her communicator, "I'm transport—"

"Don't dare move me without my command," she directed.

The keliotrops was gone. An eerie silence spread across the green sands of Vlatzeba Tendor. Kelahya waited, motionless.

The ground shook with such force that she lost her balance and dropped to her knees. She sprang to her feet and spread them apart in an attempt to keep her balance. Stillness again.

There was no sign of the keliotrops. He'd buried himself deep into the ground and was ready to attack. When the sands shuddered again, Kelahya aimed her weapon in front of her and waited. When she felt she might lose her balance, she discharged it at full power into the green sand.

The explosion sent her flying, along with the stinking body parts of the keliotrops and clouds of green sand.

In midair, Kelahya dematerialized.

She materialized on the floor of her vessel. "That was intense."

"Are you all right, my Lady?" came the voice on comm.

"Yes," she answered, as she rose and headed for the cockpit. "All is well. Let's head back to the Olympus. The Jobiah Dah transport has been destroyed."

"As has the keliotrops."

"Indeed." She laughed.

Shortly after she docked on the Olympus, she reported to the Control Room only to be welcomed by Zenubus' angry glare.

Before he could utter a word, Kronos appeared before them. Kelahya gasped. Zenubus shrunk away.

"Is this how you care for my ward, Commodore Priaminian?" Kronos growled.

"Excelen—"

Kronos' hand shot toward Zenubus, a threatening finger pointed directly between his eyes.

Kelahya jumped to her feet and rushed to Zenubus' side.

"Kronos, it was my fault, he had nothing—"

Kronos' furious glance silenced her. He glared into Kelahya's eyes, or rather, into her soul, and let his fury smolder there for a moment. Then his eyes shifted back toward his Minister.

"Zenubus, you shall never endanger her life again. Is that understood?" His voice was shockingly quiet in contrast with the action. The pointing finger remained in place until Kronos was satisfied that his meaning was clear.

Kelahya turned toward Zenubus, but Kronos grabbed her arm and yanked her to him.

"To my chambers. Now," he growled.

He dragged her through the corridors in silence until they reached his private chambers. As soon as the doors slid shut, she yanked her arm free from his grasp, rubbing it in an attempt to return some of the circulation.

"Your grip has caused me more pain than the keliotrops," she yelled.

Kronos didn't move. He didn't breathe. Didn't even blink.

Kelahya sought a new approach and tried to sound more conciliatory. "You shouldn't have done that to Zenubus. It wasn't his doing. I insisted on going." She forced herself to look at Kronos. His frozen stare made her shudder. "What's the matter?"

He remained motionless as stone. She waited.

After a frigid silence that lasted an eternity, he whispered, "I feared I'd lost you."

Her heart skipped a beat. Her throat tightened. She cuddled up to him, wrapping her arms around his waist, resting her head on his shoulder.

His arms tightened around her, and he clenched her to him with such force that she whimpered in pain. Immediately, he released her.

"Forgive me," he muttered as he walked away from her. "I'll call for Chantall, she'll care for you."

She followed him, placing her hand in his.

"Don't send me away yet. Please. It's so long since we've been alone. I miss our time together. We no longer speak as we used to. We are always surrounded by endless throngs of ministers, officers, and ambassadors…"

He wrapped her hand in both of his and looked into her eyes, but he didn't smile. "So be it," he nodded.

When she looked into his vivid blue eyes, she saw they were filled with fire and pain. "What is it? What troubles you?"

"It is difficult for me when you endanger your life."

"But you have no choice. I have no choice. As you've told me many times, our lives are not our own. We serve the many. It's our destiny."

His lips touched hers and parted them gently. Her body trembled under his embrace. She was so earnest, so fervent.

Kronos became rigid as stone again and stepped away. Holding her at arm's length, he stared into her eyes, and for a moment Kelahya noticed a tear. Then, without a word, he turned and exited the room, leaving her baffled and more alone than ever.

Chapter **14**

Torture

————◆————

*Excerpt from the **Corpus Galacticum**, 137th Edition*

*Vast numbers of **torture** techniques are currently utilized. The most common include isolation, enclosure in unconventional spaces, environmental manipulations, inferred fear, slow mutilation, and religious sexual, racial, and ethical degradation.*

Mind probing, manipulation of implants, insertion of slithergores, and scan burning are preeminent within the most sophisticated galaxies. The less advanced planets tend to resource to cruder means of torture often resulting in premature death and the inability to obtain the necessary information.

Open your eyes.

She obeyed.

I'm still in the bar.

Kelahya inhaled a couple of times to settle herself down and took a slow and deliberate sip of her drink.

As she perused her surroundings, she spotted the Stardate Standard Chronometer and the Median Time Code box hanging from the ceiling above the bar.

Thirteen days? No, that can't be right.

The warmth from the drink quickly drained away as she attempted to account for the lost time. It had taken four days to reach Dawnzehya Gleva, and she'd been captured on the fifth. Of that much she was certain. By her reckoning, she'd spent two days—day six and seven—in the cave, taken onto the evacuation craft on the eighth, boarded this ship on the ninth, and spent the tenth day relaxing. The time distortion of Dionysus could possibly eat up one day, but certainly not cause the rest to disappear.

Unless my subconscious has been probed and…that's it! Nestor, or whoever he is, delved into my mind while I slept!

This unwelcomed exploration, she surmised, must've happened in the cave after her capture and during the phase when her mind drifted between alertness and unconsciousness.

But how could they have kept me in a state of semi consciousness for three days? Unconscious yes, but semi unconscious, no. And for what purpose? It makes no sense. And what about Caveat? She's definitely ignorant of Kronos' death, and yet is convinced that she controlled the entire process in the cave. And Jofan? Why did he tell me he knew I'd killed Kronos? Whether it's true or not, it would be an unforgivable breach to provide a prisoner with such information. An officer of his rank and experience would never make that mistake. What in Hades is going on?

"May I join you?"

Kelahya snapped around so abruptly that Nestor stepped back with a chuckle.

"Perhaps this is a bad time." He glanced at her drink and smiled. "Or maybe you should stay away from whatever it is you're drinking."

She peered into the deep gray eyes filled with subtle humor… and desire. They reached deep inside her. Her body responded with an unexpected tingle that brought a faint gasp to her lips. Disconcerted, she broke eye contact. "I'm sick of being pried into," she countered.

"Well, hello to you, too. Maybe another drink would mellow you out." He waved at the barkeep. "What are you having?"

"Something brown," she said, making it sound more like an insult than a color. "And I don't care for any more." She rose to leave.

"Wait." He grabbed her arm, sending an electrical shock through her body.

She stopped.

"Please," he begged.

Kelahya remained motionless, staring at nothing in particular.

"Hear me out," he said, "and if you're not interested in what I have to say, leave."

She wrenched free and glared at him with a combination of contempt and curiosity that brought a smile to his lips.

The barkeep arrived and Nestor said, "Trellian ale for me and another...brown drink for my guest."

The robot spotted the two empty glasses and removed them. Nestor sat down and leaned forward placing his elbows on the table.

"I'm sure that if our situation were reversed, I'd feel the same... hmm..." he searched for the word, "...disdain you feel toward us, General. But will you do me the honor of listening for a moment?"

She sat and faced him, with her arms crossed in a gesture of undeniably defiance. "On one condition."

Nestor raised an inquisitive eyebrow.

"You'll stay out of my mind."

His luminous eyes calmly locked onto hers. "And you?"

"I'll stay out of yours," she said coldly.

Nestor's eyes remained fixed on Kelahya, then he smiled. "Fair enough."

"I'm listening."

"Officially, no one in the League of One or the Alliance of Stars, has acknowledged the death of..." he glanced about him, "... your lover. Not one word has been uttered in that regard."

"But you told me that we were under attack because of what I did."

"Did I?"

"Either you or Jofan."

"Well...interesting...I don't recall that. Maybe you misunderstood us. What has occurred is a massive mobilization of the Regulator Forces and Containment Brigades in virtually every quadrant under the control of the League. I would surmise they are looking for you. The largest contingent that we've been informed of landed on Dionysus shortly after we captured you, and you have now lived through our swift escape."

"But we were under attack."

"Where we?"

The barkeep brought their drinks and ambled away.

Nestor poked his finger into the drink and rubbed the rim of the glass. In a matter of moments, it produced a faint ringing sound. Nestor looked at Kelahya and smiled. "I enjoy primitive sounds." His eyes sparkled and his face was radiant. He stopped the ringing and leaned into her. "I would like to be your friend, Commander."

A sarcastic smile colored her reply, "You can dispense with the social warmth. My friends don't lie. Kronos' defenses are impregnable, and no one could accomplish what you suggest."

"You mean kill him?"

"Your words. Not mine. You've used every means you could imagine to pry out whatever information you believe I possess. Now, you lure me into...what? Trusting you? I'll walk through an Ionian eruption before I fall for that little charade."

Nestor smiled and nodded in a gesture of understanding. "With Kronos dead, the Rebellion is in a perfect position to eliminate his tyranny once and for all, and there may never be a better time than now. However—and as a strategist you'll appreciate this—our exuberance over the situation shouldn't blind us to the reality. Maccabeus, Zenubus, Parkathan, Rentiustan, and every spurious leader in the universe who covets the Directorship is salivating as we speak. As much as these so-called leaders hate each other, they will unite to prevent a threat by the Rebellion… unless we offer none, and they believe there is no threat. In that case, they will ignore us, go after each other, and chaos will ensue. So, we are forced to play the game to its conclusion. However, you possess intelligence that could make a difference. I'm sure you recognize that if you're to be useful to anyone, it must be us."

His gaze met hers without passion or hesitation as he continued, "I understand why you killed Kronos. Jealousy, or it could be betrayal… If I'm wrong with either one, I'll correct my mistake."

Kelahya felt tightness in her throat. She sipped her drink to buy time. "If no official word has emerged regarding Kronos, how can you be sure that what you claim is true?"

"You mean, did we extract it from you?"

Kelahya nodded.

"We extracted a confirmation."

"In the cave?"

It was his turn to nod.

"There are three days I can't account for. What happened?"

Nestor shrugged matter-of-factly. "Dionysian time disturbance accounts for almost two. As for the third, we had to neutralize any implants you might have had. You were scanned while you were unconscious. We were surprised, to say the least, when we found that you had already neutralized them yourself. That's the only reason you're alive today. On the other hand, you have a reputation for being resourceful to the extent of sacrificing your own safety, so…" Nestor shrugged.

"So, you can't trust me, no matter what I say. And, I have no reason to trust you. We have a stand-off."

Nestor sipped his drink, savoring it as he licked his lips. He leaned forward with a doleful look.

"Not quite. As I said, you have a reputation for your wit and brains, so you're useful to us. Not indispensable, but useful. We control you, or rather, your destiny, so your cooperation will make your life a bit more tolerable. Plus, I suppose you'll choose us rather than Maccabeus and company."

He remained silent for a moment. When she offered no reaction, he continued. "Let me be blunt, General Devona. I happen to believe that you're interested in fighting for the same things we are."

"From your probe of my mind."

He smiled and nodded. "Yes. But there are those here who disagree with me and believe you have tricked me. Your mind is… confused, let's say, so it's hard to distinguish what's true and what's a clever ruse on your part or someone else's. But that's beside the point. What matters is the choice *you* must make now."

"What choice."

"To trust me or not. I can't help you with that one, other than to say that, even if you decide to trust me, things will not be easy for you. We also have power-hungry politicians and officers who would stop at nothing to consolidate their own supremacy, just as the Alliance does."

"You, for example."

He shrugged with a noncommittal smile. "Perhaps."

Her mind grasped his. He jerked forward glaring at her. They were locked in the grip of each other's gaze as she stared into his soul. He didn't reject her. He permitted her to wander the hallways of his mind and peer through the doors he allowed her to open. All others he kept tightly closed. Finally, she released him.

"We had an agreement," he said.

"I lied," then took her glass and toasted to him.

"There are indeed traitors in your organization."

He nodded.

If he was deceiving her, then he was expert at appearing as honest as she was. He almost begged her to confide in him. Given the situation, the choice was becoming inevitable.

"What can you tell me of Caveat?" she inquired.

"She's argued very strongly on your behalf, and she can be trusted."

"She gives information very freely. She told me interesting things about you."

His answer was simple and conveyed no detectable reaction. "She's cleared to tell you whatever she likes. Accordingly, her information is limited. General, I can offer you no tangible proof regarding my intentions, or those of my superiors. Your choice isn't easy, I'm aware of that. But time is crucial. Can I count on you, or not?"

Kelahya tilted her head and squinted. "Count on me for what?"

"Does your hate for Kronos the man, extend to the government he created?"

The word *hate* stirred unexpected feelings of long held rage and betrayal, along with the need for self-preservation. The emotions welled into her eyes. "I've...been shown what he purportedly created," she managed to say, "and what he destroyed... what I destroyed on his behalf. If what my mind tells me is true, then yes, I reject it." She paused. "What do you offer?"

"I offer you more war, more pain, more bloodshed. And, if we succeed, at long last, freedom, and with any luck, peace."

"You know as well as I that I must accept. At least, I must say that I do."

He reached for her hand. A tremor overtook him as he felt her shudder as well. Every time they made contact it was like touching a live wire.

"I'm tired," she announced, liberating her hand. "I must go."

"Please allow me to escort you to your quarters."

She nodded and they both rose.

An uncomfortable silence chaperoned them as they traversed the ship's narrow corridor. In no time, they reached her quarters. The door opened as she pronounced her name. She stepped inside and turned to Nestor.

"You're sure—"

Before she could finish, his hand covered her lips. Another shockwave traveled through them. He laughed with exaggeration as he spoke. "Yes, General. I'm sure." Nestor made an almost imperceptible nod in the direction over her right shoulder, then his eyes shifted slowly, and focused on the panel that included the intercom. When she spotted the transmitter, he touched his left ear as if to scratch it. "We're not completely devoid of humor, even in these conditions. In fact, I'm sorry you have chosen to retire so early. Many of my fellow officers would welcome the chance to meet you. Are you sure you will not change your mind?" His head shook indicating she should answer negatively.

"No, thank you again. Please don't insist. Those drinks and the massage have drained me. Perhaps another time."

"I look forward to our next meeting, Commander. Good night again, and sleep well." He bowed slightly and winked, then marched unceremoniously down the hall as the door closed.

Kelahya remained motionless for a moment then let out a deep-felt sigh of relief. She engaged the security button on the doorframe, then collapsed upon the bed, and stretched with an audible groan of exhaustion. She fluffed the pillow and lay back. *What is this energy between us? How can this man provoke emotions I believed were forever lost to me?*

CHAPTER **15**

Procreation

———◆———

*Excerpt from the **Corpus Galacticum**, 137th Edition*

Procreation *is a biological process by which a new organism is produced. Reproduction is a fundamental component of what is known as "life" in the known universe.*

*Through the millennia species mutations have occurred. Some mutations resulted in diseases that consumed entire planets while others produced physical transformations that have spread throughout the cosmos. To avoid planetary infestation of ill-fated mutations, **The Fortrum Treaty** was issued in the 1st Century of the Talderon Era. The Treaty establishes approved methods of procreation and categorizes them in two methodologies—asexual and sexual.*

Asexual reproduction is defined as procreation without the involvement of another being. It occurs by the split of a cell into two, yet it is not limited to single-celled organisms. The Treaty enumerates the specific species and organisms sanctioned for procreation. If a species, other than those listed in the Treaty, gives life, the offspring is considered an abomination, and both are exterminated.

Sexual reproduction is defined as procreation that requires the involvement of two beings. With sexual procreation, organisms create descendants that have a combination of genetic material contributed from members of the species of each being. Sexually reproducing organisms offer differing groups of genes for every inherited trait. The Treaty enumerates the species allowed to join and thus procreate. If a species, other than those listed in the Treaty, gives life, the offspring is considered an abomination, and all are exterminated.

Kelahya had seen little of Kronos over the last cycle. He was avoiding her—of that she was sure. They saw each other only at crowded receptions, or when Zenubus, Chantall, or the detestable Maccabeus were present.

Try as she may, she failed to understand what she'd done to alienate him so. She needed him. She missed his laughter, his teasing, his touch, his kisses.

Oh, scarlet moons of Zanubi, how I miss his kisses.

As for her military education, she excelled at every task and commission assigned to her and had long since surpassed Zenubus at strategic planning and political analysis. She now solved paradoxes as quickly and easily as Kronos.

And yet, Kronos didn't commend her, didn't come to her or call for her. And, on the rare occasions when she did see him, he remained remote and impersonal.

His mind had been closed to her for some time, and he'd not entered hers either. She'd grown accustomed to his gentle intrusions, quietly watching all, knowing all, protecting her, guiding her. His absence had left a frightening emptiness.

She was morose this night, as had often been the case of late. The opening of the Legislative Hearings tried her patience, as did Chantall in her endeavor to make Kelahya look her best.

Chantall's expertise with her hair and wardrobe readied Kelahya to be in the presence of Kronos and the Legislators, but only Kelahya could force her mind ready. She found it more and more difficult to be near him in the presence of others, impossible to concentrate on the proceedings, or respond to his queries and those of the ministers and legislators. Every cell in her body cried out for him and would not be appeased. And that, she was certain, had to be the problem. Kronos could sense her struggle for control, and it upset him.

"You're very quiet, my darling," Chantall said, interrupting her musings.

"Why does he avoid me?"

"Why do you believe it is avoidance? Perhaps, he's preoccupied with matters of the Alliance."

"No, I sense it's avoidance, but I can't be sure. He's closed his mind to me."

"Avoidance is usually a sign of fear," Chantall said absently.

"Fear?" Kelahya guffawed sarcastically. "Kronos fears nothing."

"Precisely. He's a man of almost infinite power. He fears nothing and no one. Except, well…"

Kelahya held her breath waiting for Chantall to finish. When the pause became unbearable, she exploded, "Except, what?"

"Except perhaps, himself."

"Don't speak in riddles."

"It's no riddle. Not even a puzzle. Look there…" she nodded toward the huge mirror that reflected the beauty and splendor of the woman Kelahya had become. "You're no longer a child. What you see there is what he sees, and that's what he fears."

"What nonsense. Why would he fear that?"

Chantall didn't respond. She gazed into her ward's eyes with a familiar look that told Kelahya she would have to unravel this one on her own.

"Surely, he understands that I love him? I haven't closed my mind to him."

"But he may be unsure as to your readiness to…"

Kelahya understood. Her brow furrowed. "Receive him as man? Is that it? Why have you not spoken of this any sooner? Why let me yearn for him all this time, and not mention this to me?"

Smiling, Chantall clasped her hands. "Obviously you were not ready to understand. My mind is always open to you, yet you have not pried. Now you are ready to understand. Kronos could've taken you the first time he met you. I was so worried about you, so frightened of the pain. But he didn't take you. He waited. Only great men behave as he has. He gave you the highest gift a man like him can bestow upon a woman. He allowed you to grow. To make up your own mind about him."

Exasperated, Kelahya yanked her hands free. "I loved him since the first time I saw him. You knew that. And so did he. Why wait?"

"First, you were a child. It could have been mere infatuation. And you didn't know him then. You saw his power, his strength, but not the man. Now you are a woman. You have learned how he thinks, what he feels, what he believes. You've come close to the man, not the legend, not the reflection. If you love him, if you desire him, your decision carries the weight of knowledge. That's what he intended. That's what he needs. That's why he waits."

"How do I tell him I'm ready?"

"You'll find a way."

Kelahya embraced Chantall. "I do miss our times together… those simple times back on Uxiel. Now everything is so complicated, I hardly ever spend time with you. I crave your counsel."

Chantall took Kelahya's face in her hands and kissed her cheeks. "It is, nonetheless, our reality. Destiny has made you what you are today, an unrivaled warrior, a caring leader, and a revered commander. I'm proud of who you are and of the small part I've played."

"But I miss you."

"Your focus is to bring peace to the Alliance of Stars. Mine is to ensure that all your needs are taken care of so that you can fulfill your destiny. But, for the moment, you must go to the Assembly and perform your duties." Chantall nudged Kelahya out of her chambers and into the corridor.

Kelahya heard the door close behind her and she felt like a child again as she walked with tentative steps along the endless corridors toward the Legislative Assembly. Everything Chantall had said replayed inside her head. As her resolve increased, her tentative steps became more decisive, and soon she marched along, back straight, head held high, eyes steady, and the tiniest of smiles etched across her lips.

When she reached the Assembly Chamber, the doors opened, and the woman known to all as Counselor Kelahya Devona, made her grand entrance.

She spotted Kronos in a corner of the huge chamber talking with two of his most trusted Senators.

Maccabeus, as usual, appeared from nowhere and bowed. "My Lady, you look radiant, as always."

"Thank you," she responded with impatience.

Kronos saw her and came toward her. She felt the warmth rise inside her body. He held out his hand.

"Counselor Kelahya Devona, welcome. We've been waiting for you." He smiled warmly and led her to her chair, next to his.

The Assembly was convened, and the order of business began.

But she wasn't concentrating on the proceedings. She watched him as he stood beside her addressing the Legislators. He appeared more magnificent than ever, and it reminded her of the day she'd first met him—how she'd looked at him, and how he'd perceived her innermost thoughts. A mischievous smile illuminated her face.

"I love you Kronos Deucarrion, and I need to be yours," her mind screamed to him.

Kronos stopped mid-sentence. He turned toward Kelahya with an angry glare.

She answered his glare with a naughty smile.

He turned back to the Assembly. "If the Assembly would excuse us, a matter of utmost urgency requires my immediate attention. Lady Devona and I shall return momentarily." He turned to Kelahya, and she sensed his fury under tight control. "Counselor, follow me."

He pulled aside the curtain behind the dais and stormed through it. Kelahya trailed him as a cold hush permeated the Assembly.

They trod down the corridor. Kronos' gait increased with every step and Kelahya kept pace right behind him. Moments later he pivoted toward her, yanked her arm, and dragged her into an anteroom. He slammed his fist on the door controls and it closed behind them.

Once alone, he released her arm and glared at her.

"Never invade my mind. I warned you of—"

"I understand all about your warnings."

He spun away and paced the room in an effort to suppress his anger. "Your power is strong. You must learn to control it."

"I do control it."

"No, you don't. To you, it's a game. You can't even control your childish fantasies."

"They're not childish fantasies, Kronos. Not anymore. And I knew exactly what I was doing. I called to you… and to you alone."

In one menacing bound, he stood face to face with her, his eyes searching for the truth in hers. She stood her ground with undiminished resolve.

Time stood still.

And then, it happened. She felt the softness of his mind spread through hers like a velvet fog. The joy of feeling him inside her mind so overwhelmed her, that tears welled in her eyes and she smiled. *"Search, my love. Everything I am is yours. Find the truth in me."*

He did. The sea of repressed desire surged within him like a storm, wave after exploding wave washed through with such force that, unable to restrain it, he succumbed. He pulled her to him and kissed her with ravenous abandon.

She threw her arms around his neck and surrendered herself completely, then felt his breath come with increasing speed as it mixed with her own. She felt his arms wrap around her with such force that their bodies melded as their minds had.

Unexpectedly, she felt him ease out of her mind, and regain control.

"Don't leave me," she said. "I can't be away from you, anymore."

She heard his breathing slow as his hands pulled hers away from his neck.

His eyes poured love into hers. At length, he muttered, "We must finish the work of the Assembly. I'll speed it up. When it is done, go to your quarters. I must attend to something before I come to you."

Kelahya did as she was told, and they returned to the Assembly. Their demeanor showed no signs of impending doom, nor any other looming catastrophe, on the contrary, they looked quite at ease. The members of the Assembly relaxed, relieved to notice that their Supreme Commander was calm. The proceedings resumed, and they were rewarded with a pleasant and speedy session.

As instructed, Kelahya left immediately for her quarters. The minute she entered she called out, "Chantall, I told him, and he understands. He'll be here any moment. Help me be ready for him."

Chantall told Kelahya exactly what to expect but left her with the admonition that every man was different, and that Kronos, the most powerful man in the universe, was likely to demand more than any other.

Then, she waited for him, alone on her bed, intoxicated with angst and wonder. *What's taking him so long? Why does he always make me wait?*

She wanted to escape her chambers and run to him. This wait, if it continued much longer, could weaken her resolve, and she feared that the long-repressed hunger would implode.

Finally, the doors opened, and he stepped in. Her heart raced.

He approached her bed and looked down upon her. The gossamer gown Chantall had chosen revealed every detail of her strong, sensual body.

The sight of her made him gasp. "By the stars of Uribe, you are a splendid creature," he whispered. He moved around the bed and settled next to her, stretching out and resting on one elbow. He stared down, filling his eyes with her beauty, her innocence, her yearning.

His arm slid around her waist, and with the softness of a butterfly, placed his mouth on hers, parted his lips and let his tongue travel along hers. He then let the pressure of his kiss increase.

"I'll be careful. This is, after all, your first time, and it should be perfect. Our future together depends on it."

He kissed her again and again, tracing her cheeks, jaw, eyes, forehead, and neck. He reached her ear and breathed his warm breath into it, his tongue tracing the contours. He nudged aside the gown and covered her skin with fervent kisses, tasting every corner of her body.

"Why does my body shiver so?" she asked.

He moved back to her mouth and answered, "Your body calls out to mine. Don't resist it. Allow it to flow through you and into me. Feel it, savor it." He kissed her while his hand labored to remove the rest of the robe.

"Let me," she whispered. She arched her back and pulled the robe away.

Kronos sighed, "Oh, Kelahya." His voice was a growl of desire. He kissed her opened mouth fiercely then buried his face in her breasts. With an abrupt jolt, he backed away.

"Is anything wrong?" she asked.

"No. Oh, no, never. I long for you to such a degree, that I find it difficult to keep my self-control. I wish to make it right for you. You're so breathtaking Kelahya, that I fear—"

"Anything you do will be right," she whispered, and pulled him back.

He kissed her again, caressing the smooth body, his hands traveling the fullness of her breasts, the dip of her waist, the smooth curve of her buttocks.

Trembling, she closed her eyes and reveled in the sensations.

"Kelahya. My Kelahya," he murmured.

She felt him move away and opened her eyes. He stood by the bed and removed his clothes, and for the first time she gazed upon his naked body. It mesmerized her. He was all that she had dreamed, all that she'd imagined, and more. Her eyes took in every detail of the splendid physique, making her desire rise to new heights. At length, she reached up and pulled him back.

They rolled onto the bed and her hands explored his body, finding the tickle of hair on the chest, the taut muscles of the legs, the softness of the stomach…she hesitated…then seized his groin.

He gasped and closed his eyes as her hands toyed, caressed, and felt the fullness of him. She tasted it, smelled it, her lips and breath causing an irresistible mixture of warmth and cold. She discovered the joy of taking the hairs around his groin between her lips and gently pulling on them. Each time she did so he grew larger and harder.

After a few moments, writhing from the stimulation, he pulled her to him. He found the tender nerves of her neck and throat, licked them, then blew a soft breeze, his lips barely touching the soft skin. She exploded with desire. His leg nestled between hers and pushed upward; the warmth there inflamed him even more. He pressed with his knee and her body undulated to the sensations with rhythmic surges.

His mouth followed the path between her breasts. He heard her breathe hard, and moan with every kiss. He ran his hands over her entire body, a combination of gentle caress and possessive groping. His hands glided along her while his mouth explored every inch of the woman he so desired.

With a whimper she flowed along with the waves of exquisite sensations traveling through her. "Kronos," she cried, her fingers digging into his shoulders, pulling him to her.

"I'm trying to be careful not to hurt you. My size…it can—"

"It won't hurt. We're alike you and I. Come to me." Her legs moved apart, and she arched back to receive him.

With the gentlest of care, he entered. Softly, he pressed a bit more. The rupture was sudden.

She gasped and wrenched him into her. "Give yourself to me, my love." Her warmth embraced him fully. He drew back, and cautiously plunged deeply into her. She wrapped her legs around him, pulling harder and harder each time.

"Kronos…let go…give yourself to me. Love me," she pleaded.

With complete abandon, he finally surrendered to his own need without restraint. "Kelahya," he cried out.

She rose up to him as he surged into her, reveling in the sheer sensual pleasure of complete penetration. His deep, throaty cries rose in harmony with her breathless moans. Their spasmodic release came simultaneously.

They shuddered without control, locked in each other's grasp, their frantic breath gradually slowing to a whisper. Finally, spent to exquisite exhaustion, he collapsed on top of her, his face buried in her hair.

They'd given all to each other; every fiber of their being had shared the experience. Neither of them moved.

"I don't want it to end. Ever," she whispered.

"My love…" he managed to say.

Kelahya's awakening revealed not only the pleasures he could provide her, but also the ecstasy she could provide him.

"Lovemaking has never been…satisfying," Kronos whispered. "Never had I found a compatible mate. Dionysian females have the depth but lack the sensuality of Terrian women, who in turn are too small for me. All other species have proven a great disappointment."

"We're the last of our kind. We're meant to be."

"Yes. Never had I imagined the unique and splendid sensual connection we just experienced. Oh, I'm sorry, I must be getting heavy."

"No. Don't leave me yet." She held him tighter, her arms a loving prison.

"I'll never leave you, Kelahya. Never."

CHAPTER **16**

The Continuum

———◆———

*Excerpt from the **Corpus Galacticum**, 137th Edition*

*Fellowship Cleric **Rindahlton,** writes that an archaic science in existence prior to the 1st millennium described space-time as an equation that joins space and time into a single concept termed continuum. Initially space-time was conceived as a four-dimensional manifold, with three dimensions of space and one dimension of time. However, the discovery of curved spacetime and how gravity and accelerated motion affect it, opened a new window into understanding the universe. By uniting these concepts scientists understood how the universe works at the galactic, atomic, and subatomic levels.*

Therefore, the narrow interpretation of a four-dimensional principle evolved during the millennia into what is now generally accepted as multi-spatial dimensions in the known universe.

Cleric Rindahlton posits that the most intuitive way to conceive of multiple dimensions, is to think of them as variations of time and space within the space-time continuum.

Kelahya Devona, dressed in standard gladiator combat attire, raised her left arm, and tapped the deflector shield disc to protect herself from an incoming laser beam. The instant she touched it, a force field formed around her, and the laser was deflected. She released the force field as she darted for cover behind one of the polished metal partitions that formed the maze at the center of the crowded stadium.

Her narrow escape elicited roars of approval and frustration from the vociferous crowd, their clamorous din flooding the arena below where Kelahya and Caveat endeavored to defeat two gladiators.

The weapons of the two women were simple—each had one laser speeder and one shield disc. Their opponents, Zontam and Krat, two ominous Argol males, were not only formidable in size, bulk, and strength, but also carried laser blasters, boomerang vacators, and nullifiers. The four shared only one thing in common, the characteristic gladiator combat attire.

The cacophony of thousands of spectators, as they each bellowed in their native tongues, was oppressive.

At every turn, Kelahya fired her speeder at the ground. The crystallized sand would serve to mark it. Sooner or later, she would find a way out of the maze. Of that she was sure…well as sure as she could be, as long as her mind didn't decide to dissociate.

Caveat, on the other hand, was oblivious to the direction she traveled, darting from one corner to the next with increasing speed. Both were drenched in perspiration, every muscle taut and ready, their minds fixed on survival.

As Caveat made a turn, she came face to face with Krat who fired his blaster in a knee-jerk reaction. With the blazing speed typical of the tiny woman, she dropped into a rolling crouch and activated her force field at the same time, projecting the laser from her speeder. She missed Krat and grimaced with frustration as he darted for cover around a corner of the maze. She released the force field and sprinted off in pursuit of her prey as the crowd roared with excitement.

Krat, recovering from his close call, edged toward the periphery of the maze, while Caveat, having taken a wrong turn, headed at blinding speed down a lane that would carry her back to the center and in Zontam and Kelahya's direction.

Kelahya, in the meantime, methodically ran and turned, establishing a pattern of escape.

The three were moving dangerously close to an encounter. Caveat's speed was such that in less than two milicons she would reach Zontam. The crowd sensed a showdown.

Suddenly, Zontam changed both speed and direction, and moved away from Caveat and toward Kelahya. He darted to the right as Kelahya made a left. The ensuing collision sent both combatants sprawling.

With the speed of light, Kelahya fired her weapon. One shot found its mark.

As the wounded Zontam scrambled to evade defeat, he projected his boomerang vacator toward Kelahya, then lifted his arm and released his shield.

Kelahya, also shielded, disappeared around the corner at full speed. The boomerang followed. As she made the turn, she dropped to the ground, and released the shield. She fired her speeder, not only to leave her mark on the sand, but to deflect the vacator. It worked. Zontam's boomerang sailed by her and returned without finding its target.

Kelahya darted away en route to what she hoped would be victory.

Shielded and limping, Zontam picked up the pursuit. Kelahya's new heading was now on a direct path toward Caveat.

Wounded, Zontam followed at a reduced speed. Krat also headed toward the center of the maze.

Kelahya and Caveat turned a corner and collided head on and pivoted instinctively to face opposing directions, their weapons ready.

"It has flaws," Kelahya snapped.

"What flaws?"

"For one, the multiple choice of weapons cuts down on their response ti—"

Simultaneously, both Zontam and Krat appeared from opposite directions, each facing one of the women. Without hesitation, the Argols discharged their weapons.

Both women dropped to the ground, fired their speeders, released their shields, and rolled out toward opposite sides.

The explosion, created by the impact of the laser blasters, formed an enormous cloud of dust and smoke that the women used to cover their escape.

Once again, Zontam released his boomerang toward Kelahya.

"Boomerang right," Caveat yelled out, as Krat released his boomerang vacator at her.

As Kelahya turned, she spotted the vacator coming toward her, and beyond it, the one meant for Caveat. Her back was against a wall. Whichever direction she moved to avoid the boomerang, Zontam would follow with a discharge from either his blaster or nullifier. Krat had Caveat pinned in an equally threatening predicament.

A grin flashed across Kelahya's face. She aimed at the boomerang that pursued Caveat and destroyed it, much to her opponents' chagrin and Caveat's surprise. Then, in lightning speed, she leaped to the top of the wall, and discharged her speeder at full force, as the boomerang heading for her aligned with the direction of its sender.

The boomerang and Zontam's head exploded.

She released the final full charge of her speeder at Krat, her beam mixing with Caveat's.

Krat disintegrated. The crowd roared.

Caveat stood in awe as Kelahya jumped down by her side.

"Your exercise program definitely has flaws," Kelahya announced, as she wiped the perspiration from her forehead and face.

"That was brilliant. I never imagined that move. How did you—"

"Stop the virtuoscope, please. The noise of your audience is hurting my ears," Kelahya shouted.

"I will in a moment. Let me catch my breath. I must tell you something." Caveat dropped to the ground and leaned against the wall.

Kelahya joined her, disconnecting her shield disc and tossing it aside.

"I brought you here to deliver a message from Nestor regar—"

"You brought me here to exercise."

"Well, that too. I've been developing this virtuofile for some time. Great fun, isn't it?"

Kelahya smiled and nodded. "I did enjoy myself. It made the workout far more stimulating. Now, the message."

"We are landing tomorrow and Ne—"

"Landing? Where?"

"Airela, a rather distant planet in the northwest quadrant. Have you heard of it?" She rose and walked into the maze.

"No." Kelahya followed her as the crowd began to shout with anticipation. "Caveat," she yelled, "turn the virtuoscope off, please."

Caveat stopped and signaled for Kelahya to come closer. "After I give you Nestor's message. The virtuoscope signals interfere with any communication devices on the ship, and with the crowd roaring, there's no chance that anyone could hear us."

"The message then," Kelahya insisted.

"On the morrow, Nestor and I will come to your quarters and escort you off the ship. Talk to no one, and don't become alarmed if Nestor or I behave somewhat differently toward you than you're now accustomed to."

"Why would you do that?"

"Appearances one must maintain." She winked and smiled. "Virtuofile Caveat/Gladiators discontinue," she commanded. The maze, the arena and the crowd disappeared. The virtuoscope fell silent.

"Ah." Kelahya sighed with deep relief, collapsed to the virtuoscope floor, stretched out, and closed her eyes.

Caveat followed suit. "Nothing like a good stretch after an intense workout."

Kelahya smiled. *I did it! Mind and body stayed together. Whatever is in store, Nestor is the key. If we remain associated as we did for this exercise...perhaps we can survive.*

* * * * * *

The silence, not the landscape, prompted the impression of tranquility. But, the desolate and wicked granite canyons of Surina were anything but tranquil. They teemed with rage and violence. Every jagged ravine, every inhospitable corner crawled with renegades, rebels and insurrectionists, avowed enemies of the Alliance, and experts on surviving the harshest environments. Their expertise was tested hourly on the dismal planet of Surina.

Kelahya, with four battalions, had tracked the largest band of insurrectionists for the past three cycles. At the head of her troops in a methodical march of extermination, over the last cycle, she'd destroyed the smaller bands one by one. The last band, with their legendary and ever evasive leader, Nestor Hathan, remained.

Because of Nestor's suspected presence, Kronos insisted on accompanying Kelahya for this final assault. He harbored a particular dislike for the vermin that populated this planet and wanted to be present at their inevitable capitulation.

The occasional gust of wind was the only sound to be heard as it whistled through the canyons and caves of the rocky desert. It never rained on Surina, and the only temperature change came with an evening freeze, caused by a cold and violent wind that condensed moisture even from exhaled breath on contact. A land of impossible peaks and underground streams, endless labyrinths of natural caves, with no surface vegetation and almost no flat terrain, produced the perfect refuge for the rebels. Surina offered sanctuary for hundreds, even thousands, of insurgents.

Kronos could've disintegrated the entire planet, yet he preferred to capture the rebels, and use them as decoys once they'd been reprogrammed, dropping them as bait wherever other potential rebels might surface. But, most of all, he enjoyed hunting for Nestor.

Alliance intelligence had established that Nestor was on Surina leading this last group of rebels into a dark, narrow gorge. He'd made a tactical mistake, and if indeed that turned out to be true, Kelahya would be ready. Her troops were now deployed at all possible exits. Nestor and his insurgents were trapped.

Surina was Kelahya's commission and therefore was in command. Kronos participation in this last incursion was only as an observer, yet his presence added an element of fear—on both sides.

In her capacity as commanding officer, she'd carried out innumerable such searches, assaults, and exterminations on other planets, always with flawless success. Although, in the eyes of her troops and captives she'd carried out these attacks alone, Kronos had always been within her, present in her mind while physically secure in the safety of his ship. As he observed and sensed her every move and decision, she found his existence within her reassuring and comforting.

This assault, however, was quite different—he stood with her in body, but outside her mind. The reversal of experiencing his physical presence and his mental absence both frightened and excited her.

As she scanned her surroundings, a movement caught her attention.

"There, on the right," she whispered.

Only Kronos, and those battalion leaders with an open channel of communication to her caught a glimpse of the shadow as it disappeared behind a boulder.

"I cannot read the mind of what this shadow is," she said.

"Neither can I," Kronos answered.

"Could be non-humanoid, or… Lieutenant Mathiah," she barked into her comm, "dispatch your scouts. Seal the exit. Direct the release of fire orbs in the direction of the shadow as well."

"Done," came the terse response.

No time to lose. It was imperative they take advantage of the opportunity. The scouts were deployed, and the remaining troops created a wall of granite boulders with systematic laser blasts, closing that exit from the gorge. Within moments every trooper knew what the topography had to offer.

"Close all other exits and release the orbs. Stand by for my signal," she commanded.

The plan, simple and direct, was to flush the rebels from the caves and into the open where they could be dazed and captured with ease. Fire orbs would be detonated in the nearby caves, in all the visible openings in the area, and also where the shadow had been tracked.

Kelahya's troops moved with precision and speed.

When everyone was in place, Kelahya signaled the battalion leaders, who, in turn, ordered their troops to launch the fire orbs.

A chill of anticipation gripped Kelahya as she sensed Kronos' physical proximity, and his own excitement at finally trapping the legendary Dionysian rebel leader.

Kelahya gave the signal and, weapons drawn, they advanced as one toward the caves while the troopers sealed the exits and released the fire orbs.

In an instant, Surina ceased to be a place of stark, serene silence. Instead, the shrieks and cries of the rebels, as they spilled from their hideouts in burning pain, echoed off the granite walls of the canyons.

Kelahya tensed. She wasn't leading this assault with her usual self-assurance and aplomb. Kronos worried her. His presence created an uncomfortable edge, an increased anxiety. What if he were injured or killed? She'd be responsible for his death. She was in command and his safety was her responsibility. Kronos was indispensable, and not only did she need to protect him, but also win this assault and capture Nestor.

The rebels gushed from the caves, discharging their speeders and blasters indiscriminately in all directions, often killing their own.

Leaving Kronos behind, Kelahya broke free from her protective unit of troopers and lurched forward at full speed. She sensed Nestor's presence nearby and it was vital that she find this leader and capture him before he, or any of his rebels, had a chance to flee, or worse, harm Kronos.

A huge Dionysian male emerged from the cave on Kelahya's immediate left. She discharged her laser, hitting him on the side of his chest.

She noted that the injury was not fatal, but he bled profusely. He looked at his wound and grabbed his side, the pain sparking his rage and a sudden burst of strength. He lunged forward and reached for her as she aimed her laser for another shot. This time the shot struck home, and her assailant dropped dead at the very moment a second Dionysian sprung up behind her and yanked away her weapon, throwing it across the rocky canyon.

She twisted free of his grip and raced toward a boulder. Her foot slipped as she tried to climb. She scrambled behind it as her attacker slammed into the boulder with all his force, cracking it in two and pushing it back. The impact propelled Kelahya several feet back against the escarpment, knocking the wind out of her.

He moved toward her, screaming in fury, "Why? Why?"

Her mind however, heard far more than those two simple questions.

As she focused on his words, a quick barrage of lasers hit him, and he crumbled in a dead heap next to her.

Moments later she heard a voice above her.

"Are you all right?" Kronos said, helping her to her feet.

"Yes. Glad you were near."

"I wasn't."

Kelahya glanced around. The troopers had obviously arrived just as Kronos had. Inert bodies lay strewn about her.

"We are victorious. The assault is over."

"Who killed the Dionysian?"

Kronos looked surprised. He'd watched her discharge her weapon and kill the rebel as he lunged at her. Her puzzled look told him she had no memory of the kill. He turned to the troopers, "stand back."

They obeyed.

He leaned close to her and whispered, "What's wrong?"

"Kronos, answer me."

"As he attacked, you discharged your weapon and he dropped dead."

She shook her head and searched for the recollection of what had happened.

"Kelahya, what was he screaming?"

"You didn't hear him?"

"I wasn't close enough."

"He asked why I attacked his people. He couldn't understand. I was his oppressor and he was the victim. He was dying and wondered why I did what I did. It made no sense to him that I am a Commander in your service. He believed my actions could not be mine and that I'm not true to myself. My true self couldn't have killed him." She paused. "But I didn't kill him. He took my weapon when he first came at me. Someone else must have killed him."

Kronos lifted her arm and showed her the weapon firmly clenched in her hand.

"You didn't lose your weapon. You killed him with it. I saw you."

"I killed Nestor Hathan and have no recollection of it?"

Kronos' brow furrowed. With his right foot, he kicked the inert body onto its side to reveal the face. "No, not Nestor. This man is strong, and certainly powerful, but a mere Dionysian youth of no more than three and twenty. What made you reason he was Nestor?"

"I felt Nestor's presence. It had to be him. It was an overpowering sensation inside me. It was Nestor who was questioning me, my motives, my reasons for killing. My devotion to you."

Kelahya fell into silence, reaching to recall what had happened. A bewildered look crept onto her face.

Kronos embraced her and signaled for transport, both dematerializing immediately.

They materialized in his quarters, and he carried her to his bed. Gently, he laid her on it. He removed her weapon and unclasped the collar of her uniform. "Close your eyes and rest. I'll have the Medical Officer take a look at you."

"No need. I'm all right. Just puzzled. I can't—"

"Do as I say."

Kelahya closed her eyes. She dove into the recesses of her mind in search of answers as she relived the assault on Surina.

He left her on the bed and walked to the communications console. "Send Roellus to my quarters, immediately." He then pressed a series of codes on the console. "Maccabeus, status," he commanded.

"The offensive is a success," Maccabeus reported. "Prisoners are in transport modules per your command. Nestor evaded us once again."

"Pulverize the planet."

"As you wish, my Lord."

The chimes announced the Medic's arrival.

"Enter," Kronos ordered.

The Medic entered the Director's private chamber. Kronos nodded and signaled for him to approach the bed.

"My Lady, may I examine you?" he asked.

Kelahya nodded.

Kronos stood nearby as the healer made his examination.

"Aside from minor abrasions, there's no evidence of physical damage, my Lord. Her mind…" he paused as he measured his words, "…she's a much higher-level Minder than I am, and I lack the skills to retrieve her memories. Perhaps, your Lord—"

"Leave us," Kronos said flatly.

When the healer left, Kronos sat by Kelahya, her hands held firmly in his. He closed his eyes and cautiously entered her mind.

She saw Kronos coming toward her, arms extended, with a reassuring smile. She tried to go to him, but something pulled at her, telling her to run away, to escape. The force that rejected Kronos was so powerful she couldn't resist it. So, in spite of herself, she fled from him, only to wander aimlessly through the dark caverns of her own mind.

She could feel Kronos' presence, calling her to return to him, to come to the safety of his embrace. But the force hiding outside her reach said that safety resided away from Kronos. She ran down a dark passage that stretched to infinity, a faint, distant light her only point of reference. Whatever or whoever it was that beckoned, was there. She ran as fast as she could, but the light grew no closer, instead it faded away.

The figure of a Dionysian giant appeared in the corridor ahead of her, his arms open wide, his smile a loving, caring glow.

"*Come, my child,*" he said. It was a voice she'd heard before, a voice from her dreams, a voice she somehow knew well. "*It was I who protected you today. It was I who questioned your motives. It is I who beckons you.*" He opened his arms to her.

"*Father! Da!*" she heard herself scream with delight.

As she ran to him, Kronos stepped between them, his arms outstretched to her, imploring her to come to him. The figures diverged in opposing directions, each calling for her. She stopped, unable to move either way, unable to yield to either man.

"*So be it,*" Modyor said, as his image faded.

"*Father, wait. Da…*" An overwhelming despair enveloped her as she stood in the middle of the emptiness.

Kronos approached and embraced her. *"It's all right now,"* she heard him whisper.

Moments later she felt herself back in his chamber. She could feel every inch of her aching body and the bed beneath her, but most importantly, she could feel Kronos' arms tightly wrapped around her and his voice, gentle, and reassuring.

"It's all right now," he repeated.

She stirred in his arms and he eased his embrace.

"Welcome back, my darling."

"What happened?"

He was solemn. "I'm not sure. I believe your mind tried to dissociate. Your experience on Surina was obviously different than mine. You suffered a very strong assault by the young Dionysian, and it's possible your mind fused with his as he died. If so, he must've implanted images that aren't real. You sensed it, and your mind decided to dissociate and ascertain the real from the unreal as a means of protecting its integrity."

"I saw my father."

Kronos nodded and smiled. "He'll always be with you, protecting you." Then he added with determined emphasis, "And so will I." He smiled and caressed her face. "Kelahya, my darling, please be aware that what you saw could only be an implanted image, it wasn't real."

She sensed a touch of uneasiness in him, and was about to question it, but the wizardry of his gaze told her he was not to be interrogated. His eyes, as blue as the rain drops of Krandelia, filled her with irresistible sensual ecstasy. She understood they needed each other with a desire born out of the dread of loss. She reached out for him, hungering for his kiss.

Chapter 17

Gambit

————◆————

*Excerpt from the **Corpus Galacticum**, 137th Edition*

Gambit, *a League of One war stratagem created by Commodore Zenubus Priaminian, is known as a cleverly contrived scheme designed to gain advantage over the enemy.*

It is initiated by a series of maneuvers whereby opponents are misled by the outcome of their own recognizance into an unnecessary mobilization that weakens its main forces.

The fundamental success of the gambit depends on false information that leaves the opponent unable to respond adequately.

These schemes vary widely in character and execution, from quiet positional operations, to active tactical engagement. The application of such strategies encompasses a sequence of deceptions that limits the opponent's options and results in tangible dominance. The objective, of course, is to consolidate military or political supremacy before the enemy does.

The fundamental building blocks of tactics are move sequences in which the opponent is unable to respond, and the gambit therefore succeeds.

The familiar tone announced the presence of someone outside her chambers.

"Yes?" she asked.

"I have come to escort you back to civilization," Nestor answered.

"It's about time. You've had me locked up all morning."

Kelahya went to the door and pressed the release. The door slid open.

Dressed in his off-duty uniform, Nestor appeared taller, stronger, and more impressive. The aqua and gold with its tiny smatterings of red, accentuated his pearl complexion.

"How are you, Nestor Hathan?"

"Delighted to be back on firm ground, General." His smile was warm and honest and, for an instant, she wondered if she was weakening.

"Firm ground? I didn't feel the shifts."

Caveat appeared, also dressed in off-duty uniform, a broad smile across her face. "We have great skills. May I help you with your belongings, General?"

"Hah, my 'belongings' fit in the palm of my hand, Captain."

"Shall we go?" Nestor stepped aside, offering Kelahya clear passage to the corridor.

She nodded and exited the room.

Jofan, his android, and a handful of battledroids, all in off-duty uniforms, waited. Nestor's hand gently seized her arm as he nudged her forward.

In silence, they traveled the corridor to the ship's gangplank—except it never materialized. Instead, they went through a sliding a door into a vast corridor where a variety of galactic creatures traveled in both directions.

Nestor released her arm but remained so close that she could feel his breath with every step, sending the all too familiar sensation through her body.

"Smile," he whispered. "And relax."

She did as he said. She noticed the occasional hostile glance, almost lost in the flow of faces, but conspicuous, nonetheless. As they neared what appeared to be overcrowded exit ramps, their pace slowed to a virtual crawl.

"Make way." The android's voice was like a clap of thunder. The crowd's reaction was so instantaneous that they appeared to melt into the walls to allow them passage.

Nestor pressed Kelahya forward, she proceeded with renewed determination, and they quickly made their way down the ramp.

As they reached the end, Nestor's hand clamped around her arm again, and as soon as the doors slid open, he propelled her at a faster pace, pushing her close to a wall that fed into another long corridor. Jofan and the android led the small contingent, with Caveat and the battledroids close behind.

In this corridor, males and females of various species, along with androids and replicants, flowed in both directions forming a shimmering rainbow of uniforms.

Is this their army?

As Jofan and the android came to an abrupt stop, Nestor pressed against a panel imbedded into the wall. A door popped open, and in a milicon they went through it, closing it briskly behind them. They had entered a deserted corridor that curved to the right.

"This is a longer route. But safer," Jofan explained. "Only top clearance officers can use these corridors."

"If anyone wanted to kill me, why not do it on the ship? At least there they knew where to find me."

"And we could find them," was the curt response from Jofan. "General Devona, you disappoint me."

"It appears, Jofan, that your expectations of me are far superior to the reality. Perhaps you should revise them. Anyway, I'm tired of your constant disappointment, so keep it to yourself." Kelahya's retort was devoid of humor. No sense, at this point, in pretending she liked him.

They came to a fork in the corridor.

"Stay right. About fifty paces after the split is a door with a blue light above. I'll go first," Jofan ordered.

As they turned, she glimpsed the bluish glow down the hall on her side of the corridor. Nestor placed his palm on a decoder and the door slid open. Kelahya noticed that Nestor was the one the sensors recognized while Jofan continued the pretense of his command.

Why the charade?

Before the door had opened halfway, the android slid through. Jofan followed an instant later, his hand on his weapon. After glancing around, he signaled for the rest of the party to follow.

Nestor guided Kelahya through.

As soon as she stepped through the door her entire body tensed with amazement. They entered an underground transport and conveyer station of such complexity that only a handful of planets could build. This one, as far as she could tell, was exclusively for military use. Nestor ran his index finger down the length of a station call box and a conveyer jitney appeared. Its door slid open as it came to a stop.

"Get in," Jofan barked, and Kelahya obeyed.

The door closed behind them and the panel at the front lit up in an array of colors. A button flickered. Nestor hit the button and typed a series of symbols and numbers into a miniature keyboard. Immediately, the jitney eased out into the flow of unmanned conveyers and raced off.

Nestor kept glancing out the rear of the jitney. "So far, so good," he said.

This vehicle moved faster than most and was more sophisticated. Tunnels branched off every thousand meters, or so, and the conveyer cabs moved from lane to lane with no diminution in speed.

"Is the entire system underground?" she asked.

"The entire city is underground," Nestor answered.

"What city?"

He chuckled and flashed that winning smile. "It is called Bysu. Have you heard of it?"

"Yes, I have. It is the mythical city where Nestor, the 'real' Nestor, is supposed to live."

Jofan's startled reaction gave her a small feeling of victory, which she enjoyed. She liked toying with the old prune.

"Real Nestor?" Jofan's head tilted enough to induce an impression of honest intrigue. "Every Nestor I've met is real."

"Caveat mentioned we were going to a planet called Airela. Is Bysu on Airela?"

No answer. Not even a significant glare.

The conveyer slowed noticeably and pulled into a low tunnel. Kelahya spotted a debarkation ramp ahead.

"We've arrived," Nestor announced.

The jitney stopped and the door slid open. Kelahya rose to exit but the android shoved her back down and moved out ahead of her. Once outside he stood there in silence for several milicons. Then, he stepped away from the door.

"You may exit now."

Kelahya and her entourage emerged. She could feel the familiar tingling of self-preservation crawling along her skin and up her spine. She appreciated how safe she'd felt on board the ship. Now she was back in the real world, whatever that concept entailed, and survival needed to move to the forefront of her consciousness.

"Stay close," Nestor said. "Just in case."

She fell into step with him as soon as he moved up the ramp. There was a buzz behind them as the conveyer jitney sped off. A plain gray door stood at the top of the ramp. Nestor approached the door and placed his hand on the scanner. A tiny panel opened and a bluish beam probed Nestor's face and centered on his eyes.

Epidermal and retinal identification. This underground city shows more sophistication with each passing moment.

The light went out and the door hissed as it opened, then hissed again as it closed behind them.

Only her self-control kept her from issuing an audible reaction to the surprising contrast of the dwelling's drab exterior to the sumptuous, overdone interior. The walls were covered with translucent Saline crystal, the floors were of blue granite, and the ceilings, domes of amber. The echo of their steps reverberated in diminishing tones as they moved down the vast hallway. The opulence astonished her.

"Stop," Nestor whispered. He pointed at the Saline crystal wall. A second later, the wall split, opening into a shining lift. Nestor noticed her hesitation. "Go ahead. It's safe."

Once inside the lift, an almost imperceptible movement indicated the lift was on its way. Its subtlety made it impossible to determine in what direction it traveled.

Nestor leaned back with an audible exhalation. "You're safe, now."

Relieved to find herself alone in the lift with Nestor, she asked, "Where's our entourage?"

"Jofan is off on another mission. Caveat will join us later."

The lift stopped and the door opened onto a vestibule that led to a large chamber adorned with the same crystal, amber, and granite, and with an enormous translucent cylindrical structure at the center of the room. The opulence was overwhelming.

Nestor opened the collar of his uniform. "Now you can relax, General. For the time being, you're utterly safe."

"From whom?"

"I told you. There are those who are convinced that keeping you alive is a mistake. Others simply covet to control you for their own purposes."

"Which faction are you?"

Nestor smiled as he unbuttoned his coat. "Your quarters are down that hallway. You'll find clothing and all the necessary amenities to make your stay here satisfactory. I suggest you retire, rest a bit, and freshen up before dinner."

"Dinner?"

"The time here is late afternoon. Follow me," he said as he headed toward a hallway to one side of the opulent room.

Even the hallway radiated exuberance. The outer wall, a waterfall that changed colors as someone passed by, emitted a fresh cool scent and played a variety of bird songs.

Nestor opened the door to her quarters and signaled for her to go in.

"Will you lock me up like you did on the ship overnight?"

He smiled. "No need. That was for your protection only. As I've said, you're safe here." He nodded and walked down the hallway, presumably to his room.

Kelahya's quarters were elegant and simple, somehow familiar, and comforting. As if designed by combining the elements between her chamber in Uxiel, where she'd grown up, with her quarters on the *Olympus.* The room reminded her of both, yet it had its own touch of class. All the colors were expertly blended—the brown, yellow and orange of Dionysus with the Terrian tones of green, blue, and white—all of which came alive with a spattering of vibrant flowers in bloom. Spacious, yet cozy, it invited her to be at ease.

She dropped back on the bed, allowing the softness of the feathers in the bedclothes to embrace her.

It's odd to feel so at ease. Where has the pain in my head gone? What do they have in store for me? Entrap me with kindness...

"Perhaps," she whispered.

* * * * * *

"There will be time later," Kelahya said with a playful grin. But Kronos didn't respond in the same soft mood as hers. Instead, he kissed her fiercely, crushing her against him until she feared her ribs would crack.

Ever since the attack by the Dionysian in the canyons of Surina, the love he offered had shifted. Not simply becoming stronger and more passionate, it had grown insistent, demanding, as though he feared he'd lose that which he'd finally won.

He fumbled inside her vest, groped for her breasts, ripping her uniform, pulling furiously at the obstacles that denied him access to her.

He knew her body well and had always thrived on this knowledge and skill. Yet lately, there were cravings within him that were stronger than his will and more overwhelming than his love.

Kelahya had learned to recognize this desperate behavior even though she didn't understand what drove it. Willingly, she gave herself completely to him whenever this powerful new expression of love manifested. Or was it need?

In tearing her uniform, most of her body was now exposed to him. Panting with desire, he peeled off his own uniform, and pressed her onto the cold, hard floor of the Command Center. He was on her, his mouth hard against hers, his tongue desperately searching the confirmation of her love for him, of her total submission to him.

She opened to him as he surged into her. She heard his fierce, strangled moan, as he repeatedly stabbed deep inside her. He plunged again and again, until, with a violent shudder, he cried out her name.

He trembled with ever diminishing spasms, then, with a groan, buried his face in her neck and laid immobile, his passion and desperation spent. When his breathing slowed, he raised himself and looked down at her, his forehead knotted with concern.

"I'm sorry," he said.

"About what?"

"My behavior. You didn't feel the moment as I did."

She smiled and kissed his lips. "I didn't need to. I experienced other sensations."

He kissed her and let his lips linger. "Come. You must be cold." He helped her up. "I… your uniform…I—"

"I'll call for Chantall. Don't worry."

"It's unforgivable," he said, with controlled embarrassment. His melancholy touched a place deep inside her that resonated with warmth and love.

"Darling," she whispered, "don't—"

"No. It's over and I'll make it up to you." He cupped her face in his hands and kissed her. "I fear I'm losing you. I can't explain it. I—"

His despair shot through her body. Her eyes flooded with tears.

"Kronos, what's the matter? I'm here. You're not losing me. I love you."

"You're right. It's nothing of importance. It'll pass." He turned to dress. Motionless, she watched him snatch his clothes from the floor and slap them onto his body.

"I'll return," he mumbled as he exited without looking at her.

Kelahya moved to the communications console and entered Chantall's code.

Chantall responded. "May I be of help?"

"I need a uniform." Kelahya didn't have to explain. This wasn't the first time, and she knew it wouldn't be the last.

As she waited for Chantall, Kelahya snuggled into the lounger, disentangling the web of her lover's unsettling behavior.

Chantall arrived with utmost speed, and without a word they went into the cleaning chamber adjacent to the Command Center. Kelahya removed what was left of her torn uniform and stepped into the cleaning unit.

Once bathed and dressed, Kelahya returned to the Command Center, and without a word, Chantall left. She was grateful for Chantall's consideration. Questions were unwanted, especially since she had no answers.

For some time now, Kelahya had distanced herself from Chantall. Her presence reminded her of times past—times of innocence, times of simple love, before Kronos absorbed every fiber of her being. She didn't wish for Chantall's eyes to tell her to be cautious and not give so much of herself to him. Chantall would counsel to care for her own heart and spirit instead. She was right, but for the time being separating herself from the only person who loved her unconditionally, enabled her to ignore her own conscience.

"Am I intruding, General?" Maccabeus' unmistakable voice resounded through the Command Center.

Although startled by the intrusion, Kelahya masked any sign of it. "How did you get in?"

"With my password."

"Didn't his Excellency change it?"

"Apparently not. Shall I return later?"

"No need. Is it time?"

"Indeed." His eyes searched the room for Kronos.

"The Director will be here shortly. Let's get ready," she commanded.

Maccabeus smiled and took his place next to one of the command consoles, entering a series of codes. One of the monitors came to life.

"Aurora is the site of the Rainbow experiment." The monotone voice flowed from the audios as the monitor displayed images of the planet Aurora and its neighboring moons and sister planets. "Members of the same species are not permitted to intermarry or couple. All procreation must be carried out with members of a different species. The Aurora experiment is implemented by confidential instructions of the Scribe of the Legislature, Kronos Deucarrion, to analyze the effects of intra-species procreation. To date, most species have proven incompatible, which—"

Maccabeus switched off the monitor.

"I am truly sorry, my Lady. I—" he dropped to his knees. "Such intelligence is not meant for you, by strict orders of my Lord Kronos. I beg you not to inform him of my unforgivable mistake. Please, my Lady."

Kelahya's face paled. "What was that—"

The doors slid opened and Kronos entered. He froze at the sight of Maccabeus kneeling before an ashen Kelahya. "What's the meaning of this?"

Maccabeus jumped to his feet as his eyes continued pleading with Kelahya. He then turned to Kronos and bowed his head.

"If you please, my Lord, it's an impressive occurrence. One that will please you as much as it has overwhelmed me. General Devona has devised how to trap the traitors from planet Anduhar Slavan. It's a plan of such exquisite perfection that it stirred my utmost admiration. So much so, that I dropped to my knees to thank her, and I regret to say that, in doing so, I startled her. I beg your forgiveness, Lord Kronos."

Kelahya was bewildered. Before her very eyes, and for reasons she couldn't begin to fathom, Maccabeus had lied.

Kronos couldn't read his Minister's mind, but the lie had been delivered directly and without hesitation. He'd also trapped her into being his accomplice, and she felt helpless to unmask his duplicity.

"Well, General, what is this plan?" Kronos asked.

Kelahya blinked as she evaded her lover's eyes. Minute droplets of moisture formed on her upper lip. Kronos would read her mind if she faltered, and it would be a simple matter to determine that Maccabeus had lied.

However, it soon became clear that Maccabeus had prepared for that and, with nonchalance, he stepped between them, effectively distracting Kronos.

"With your permission, my Lady. I would cherish the opportunity to relate this majestic plan to Lord Kronos myself. My enthusiasm is so complete that I'm unable to contain it. It will also help me verify that its subtleties haven't been lost on me. May I?"

"Very well, Maccabeus. Go ahead. But control yourself. You are as annoying as a child." Kronos crossed toward Kelahya and slid into the command chair. "Hurry, we must make ready for the Commissioners Conference."

Maccabeus bowed his head and took his command post. "As you ordered, my Lord, the Anduhar Slavan problem in the Xendrexia Cluster, has been my commission for many cycles."

Kelahya watched in dismay as Maccabeus moved his fingers over the controls, and the monitors and vidscanners flickered with a relentless succession of images from Xendrexia. His words faded into distant echoes as she veiled her mind from Kronos and wondered what had just occurred, and why.

Chapter **18**

Talderon Ideals

—— ◆ ——

*Excerpt from the **Corpus Galacticum**, 137th Edition*

The Talderon Ideals *are a universal experience that touches all creatures in the cosmos in the quest for oneness with divinity.*

They provide a spiritual experience that generates a deep sense of aliveness and interconnectedness.

The Scriptures of the Fellowship recount, how, from within the confines of the Fellowship the Talderon Ideals were birthed during what the Fellowship subsequently termed, the 1st Century TE (Talderon Era).

During their inception the Talderon Ideals provided a grounded philosophy when concrete goals were essential amongst all humanoids trying to survive in chaotic environments. The Ideals built a bridge between the secular and the spiritual and offered a variety of conceptual paths to achieve cosmic peace.

These concepts are understandably impossible to be fully expressed in language, words, or sounds. They can, however, as the Scriptures clearly state, be known or experienced, and their principles can be discerned

*through the teachings of the Clerics under the direction of
the Supreme Pontiff of the Galactic Sanctuary and Scribe
for the Incorporeal Fellowship.*

"Where are we? Why the extravagance?" Kelahya asked as she entered the ample comfortlounge.

"We're in Bysu. This is your home for now. Hope you'll like it," Nestor answered.

"You surround all your prisoners in such luxury?"

"No. Let's be frank, you're an elite captive, so a bit of gratification for us is well deserved. I trust you're rested. That large alcove in the center contains the food and drink storage cabinets. To one side is the temperature alterator. Choose what you prefer."

Kelahya disappeared into the cylinder. She opened one of the cabinets and selected a few vegetables.

"How do you get these things? Who are you people?" She didn't expect an answer since Nestor had remained in the other room—the questions were a simple expression of her amazement.

"We are your enemies, as you so aptly refer to us," Nestor answered to her surprise. "But we enjoy the good life as much as you and your tyrant Kronos do."

"Here we go again. Will you stop the insults?"

"You're right. No need for that at this juncture."

What does he mean by that? She placed the vegetables in the alterator. She opened another cabinet divided into two inner storage areas. The upper unit stored containers that had to be various types of meat, while the lower compartment was full of breads and a variety of appetizing foods. She placed them on a large tray and deftly displayed her choices. When she added the vegetables, she returned to Nestor.

He held a pitcher filled with a green liquid that he poured into two glasses. "Ah, this is living," he said.

His heart-felt satisfaction made Kelahya smile. She often expressed the same satisfaction when returning home after being deprived of such niceties while on long missions. He held a glass up for her. Kelahya hesitated.

"Take it. I promise you'll enjoy it. And before you ask, it doesn't contain altering substances."

She placed the tray on the table and took the drink.

"Nice choices," Nestor commented as he helped himself to a morsel.

"Tell me about Nestor," she said bluntly.

"Direct and to the point." He took his own glass and relaxed into the softness of a lounger. "Where should I start?" He patted the seat next to him, inviting Kelahya to join him.

"Try the beginning," she said as she sat across from him.

"The beginning of Nestor. That…is difficult to define." He sipped the drink and stared into the liquid as if reading a crystal ball. "His story is more complex than you can imagine. And yet, in a curious way, it's quite simple. I suppose the Nestor you speak of, is the man of legend and not me."

He gave her a look of mock innocence that she countered with a smirk of mock approval.

"You do mean the mythical being who seems to be everywhere, and nowhere? The man who has caused entire star systems to revolt against the almighty Kronos, and his surrogates throughout the League of One and the Alliance of Stars?" His eyebrows rose slightly, seeking a confirmation.

Kelahya glared at him with impatience.

"Well, everyone now living under the tyranny of Kronos and the League of One, accepts that Nestor represents liberation. That concept, identified as the ideal of one man, became the battle cry of entire sectors of the galaxies. The Talderon Ideals—"

"Talderon Ideals?"

"Surely, you've heard of the Talderon Ideals?"

"Of course, but what do the Talderon Ideals have to do with the legendary Nestor?"

"They are one and the same. Talderon is Nestor. The ideals were his creation, his dream, his vision. His prophecy."

Kelahya leaned back.

Nestor leaned forward and placed his elbows on his knees. "What's the matter? Do you doubt my words?"

When she didn't respond, Nestor allowed her the time to put her memories in order.

After a few moments, she blinked and moved forward on the edge of the lounger. "The Talderon Ideals can be summed up as…a path for universal peace, am I right?" Kelahya asked.

"Yes."

"And, you say the Talderon Ideals are Nestor's?"

"Yes."

Kelahya chuckled and shook her head. "That's ridiculous. Talderon is the name given by the Incorporeal Fellowship to the set of ideals formulated by Kronos. They serve as the primary mandate for the Galactic Sanctuary of which he is the Master Scribe."

Intrigued, Nestor said, "Please, continue."

"Universal peace," Kelahya went on, "is the prime ideal behind the formation of the League of One and the Alliance of Stars. Kronos' vision was therefore named 'The Talderon Ideals' by the Incorporeal Fellowship."

Nestor stared into Kelahya's eyes. He had no doubt that she was absolutely sincere.

"Kronos told you this?"

"Yes. And I've studied it in the logs of the Alliance. It is written."

"How do you explain then, that the rebel forces have always fought against Kronos on the basis of the Talderon Ideals?"

"Simple, the rebel leaders, including your precious Nestor, have used the Ideals as a decoy and as an affront to the Incorporeal Fellowship. It doesn't require a genius to understand that their real objective, and therefore yours," she said pointedly, "is misinformation to create chaos in the universe, and the elimination of peace."

He leaned back into the lounger. "For what purpose?"

"Isn't it obvious? Power. Individual, tyrannical power. That's why they're rebelling against Kronos' mandate for universal peace."

"You believe this?"

"Yes."

"Individual tyrannical power, you say…interesting. Who in the universe, as you recognize it right now, exercises that type of power?" Nestor chided.

Kelahya's eyes narrowed with fury.

Smiling, Nestor pushed on, "Isn't it your beloved Kronos? Isn't he the most powerful man in the universe?"

"You agreed to curtail your criticisms."

"It's not a criticism. It's a statement of fact. Don't you agree?"

"No. His power is not his or for his individual use. It's used solely in the service of the Alliance of Stars. But never mind that now. Let's get back to Nestor."

He took their glasses and crossed the room to the pitcher, then returned to the lounger handing her a full glass. He sipped his drink before continuing. "There isn't much more to tell. When you consider the origin of the lineages of Nestor and Poliate, there's nothing more to add."

"Lineages? What lineages?"

Nestor smiled in disbelief. "Well, well. You're not acquainted with origins of Nestor and Poliate."

"Do not get into my head."

"I didn't. Your eyes told me that you are truly uninformed. Kronos failed to share this with you. I find that extremely interesting."

"Enough of the melodrama. Just go on."

"May I ask if you're familiar with the different levels of Minders and their anointed tasks?"

Disgusted, Kelahya placed her glass down and stomped away from Nestor, to disguise the embarrassment of her ignorance. She roamed the room pretending to admire the art pieces strewn about and hanging on the walls. "Minders are either weak or strong. So what? What anointed tasks? Your riddles and mysteries are testing my patience."

Nestor leaned back on the lounger with a satisfied grin. "Obviously, he decided not to acquaint you with your own lineage. I find that worthy of note."

"Note it and go on."

"I wonder if you'll realize where you stand once I acquaint you with your lineage."

She spun about and glared at him. "Get to the point."

He nodded. "As you wish. There are four levels of Minders. I'm sure that at least you understand how come you are a Minder."

He paused for effect, but Kelahya didn't take the bait. She remained indifferent, her back to him.

"Ah, apparently, I must start with the beginning. I trust the logs of the Alliance taught you that many of the current species in the universe are the result of countless mutations?"

Kelahya didn't answer.

Nestor continued, "Did they teach you that as humanoids expanded to every corner of the universe the mutations advanced?"

"No need to question me every two sentences."

"I'm curious as to how much you were told and how much you were kept in the dark."

"Don't be. It's not material." She turned to face him. "Continue."

"As you command, General. Where was I? Ah, yes, the mutations. Curious phenomena, mutations. The results are unpredictable. They can be good or bad. Most are bad. The majority resulted in diseases that wiped out entire civilizations, some produced an endless variety of physical transformations, which resulted in the emergence of new species throughout the galaxies, but most ended in death."

He sipped his drink and studied her reaction. He saw none. "Anyway," he continued, "for a select few, the outcome was the evolution of superior mental development. That, Commander, is when Minders first arose. You're aware that Minders can penetrate the minds of various species in the universe..." he paused.

Kelahya rolled her eyes.

He chuckled. "At least you've experienced that, so you know you're one of them."

"Focus, please."

"With the advent of Minders, a power struggle ensued. It became apparent that, as some sought to use their power for evil, a definitive form of constraint was necessary. As time went by, the Incorporeal Fellowship...wait, you do know how the Incorporeal Fellowship came into being?"

"Of course."

"Because if you don't, I can't go on with this lesson."

"Is that what this is, a lesson?"

"Of course, I'm telling you what you should've learned as a child. After all, this is about your lineage."

"Here you go again with my lineage. What do I have in common with Nestor? Isn't all this about Nestor?"

"Yes."

"Then get to it."

"Please come back and join me." Nestor smiled and winked. "I'd rather not have to yell across the room."

Reluctantly she returned to the lounger with a defiant look.

Nestor proffered her drink before continuing. "Now, where were we?"

"The Incorporeal Fellowship! Nestor! Lineage!" she snapped.

"That's right. The telepathic strength of Minders is what determines their level of power, along with their anointed tasks in life."

Kelahya frowned.

"Ah, hah! You didn't know that either, did you? Kronos told you nothing about your heritage."

"You're enjoying this entirely too much. Enough about what he did or didn't do. Go on."

"So be it. The Fellowship established patterns and disciplines for the mental mutations to maintain stability. Each mutation was categorized into the varying levels of proficiency, and specific universal tasks were ordained for each level. As such, Level One Minders are limited in the amount of influence they can exert on other species. Therefore, their tasks are at the lowest level of telepathic mental proficiency in the overall universal order. They're usually soldiers, technicians, or basic scientists. You've come in contact with these Minders, I assume.

Kelahya nodded.

"Level Two Minders are usually assigned the tasks of organizers, officers, or medics. You've interacted with some of them, correct?"

"Get to the point."

"Level Three Minders can exercise a much deeper influence; therefore, their tasks are more sophisticated. They serve as healers of the mind and spirit, or scribes of our sanctuaries. Are you with me so far?"

"You do enjoy toying with me, don't you?"

"In all honesty, yes, I do," he said with a wide grin.

"Well, at least this time you didn't lie. Go on."

"And then, there are the Level Four Minders. They're extremely rare. Born only every two to five generations. For reasons we still don't understand, there are always two born at the same time. Level fours can access the minds of most species in the universe."

Nestor smiled and closed his eyes.

Kelahya took a sip from her glass and stared at Nestor who appeared to have fallen asleep. "Are you awake?"

Nestor opened his eyes with deliberate slowness. "Simply waiting to find out if you'd figured out your level."

"I don't care about my level! This entire story began with you mentioning the lineages of Nestor and Poliate. You haven't said a word about that. I'm waiting."

"No interest…well, well." He sighed with obvious disappointment before he went on. "As you wish. The reason Level Four Minders are so rare, is because they are born exclusively into one of two lineages. Those born into the lineage of Nestor become spiritual leaders, charged with spreading the sacred teachings of The Talderon Ideals throughout the universe. Contrary to your indoctrination, the original Nestor is the one who created the Ideals; thus, the heritage passes to all his descendants. Those born into the lineage of the original Poliate, the creator of the Alliance of Stars, are secular leaders, as he was, and his descendants are those charged with governing the masses through the creation of policies and political alliances intended to maintain peace in the universe."

Kelahya's eyes widened. "Are you telling me that Nestor, the real Nestor, is a Level Four Minder and descendant of the creator of the Ideals?"

Nestor nodded with satisfaction. "Yes, well done. Who then, is the other Level Four Minder, the descendant of Poliate's lineage?"

"Kronos," Kelahya whispered.

Nestor allowed a few moments of silence so she could digest the information.

"But," she asked, "shouldn't Kronos and Nestor be allies and not enemies?"

Nestor nodded slowly and smiled. "Indeed."

"What happened?"

"It's not for me to tell, but for you to uncover. As you may have surmised, by forced necessity, and not by ordained design, ours is now a secret society. The mysterious is more unsettling than the obvious, thus the creation of Nestor's legend and name, and the myth of our elusive leader. The Talderon Ideals travel the universe, and Nestor leaves his mark wherever unrest surges, but never a trail. I, myself, couldn't tell you where the 'real' Nestor is at any given moment. Since I was dubbed Nestor, I receive orders from him or, at times, on his behalf."

"Have you ever met him?"

"What difference does that make?"

"A huge difference. If he is concealed from you, what is to keep whoever is really pulling your strings, from controlling this entire situation, in order to destroy the peace and prosperity that Kronos has created?"

"No one is pulling my strings. Our chain of command is impossible to manipulate."

"You could only say that if you'd met him and knew him to be real. Have you?"

"No."

He lied. Why? "How do you confirm that the orders are his? Or, that he even exists? Anyone could be manipulating you."

"The way you were manipulated by Kronos?" Nestor savored a large swallow of his drink.

Kelahya swirled her untouched drink with a circular motion of her hand. She smiled at him, a piercing defiance in her attitude. "Where do I fit in?"

"Exactly where Nestor said you would."

Kelahya waited for him to continue. When he remained silent, she prodded him on, "Care to elaborate?"

"I have orders not to...for now. I was told to bring you here alive, and I have. Beyond that, I can tell you nothing. We will both remain here until I am told otherwise."

This is an unexpected dead end. Something went wrong. She tried a different approach. "What's your purpose?"

"My purpose?"

"Your level and your task. Why were you dubbed Nestor?"

"My level is high and, as you are now aware, there are many Nestors. However, I, and three of his namesakes, have a special mission—a mission within a mission, if you will. We're more than decoys for the real Nestor. We do, in fact, run operations, plan distractions, anything required to keep the enemy guessing and give us the upper hand. For example, saving your life has been the mission for all four of us."

A chuckle of sarcastic disbelief escaped her lips. "Oh?"

"Reflect on it a bit," he continued. "What happened when you were last on the planet called Surina?"

She gasped at the name. "Surina?"

Nestor nodded.

"You?"

Another nod.

"You killed the Dionysian? You killed your own man to protect me?"

"Yes."

"You implanted his words in my mind?"

"Yes."

"My father's image? You implanted that as well."

Nestor hesitated a moment, gulping down his drink, then answered, "Yes."

Another lie. She stared at him for a moment then shook her head. "I find that beyond belief."

"Consider this, you're here, you're alive, and you're ours."

Kelahya didn't like the sound of it, but she forced a smile. "I admit Surina had me very puzzled. How did you escape?"

"Secrets of the trade. Sorry."

Kelahya shrugged. "All right, where do we go from here?"

Nestor's demeanor changed. He finished his drink, then crossed the room and poured himself another. He seemed worried.

"I have no idea."

His answer conveyed such absence of emotion, such emptiness, that Kelahya was convinced it was the truth.

"I didn't request this mission." A childish smile came to his lips, which he tried to conceal. "In fact, except for feeling the way

I do now, I despise it. Frankly, I'm in a state of confusion." He grabbed the pitcher then made his way back and sat beside her. He placed the pitcher on the table in front of them.

"You, Kelahya, what you represent, your life, your goals, your mission, have been directed at destroying all that I represent, my goals, my mission, my very existence. And you've come dangerously close to succeeding more times than you can imagine. In an ironic sort of way, maybe you finally have."

"Who gave you this unsavory mission?"

"Nestor. The 'real' Nestor, as you call him. He said, 'Make sure not a hair on her head is harmed,' or words to that effect."

She shook her head. "I refuse to believe there is such a person. This whole setup is too convenient, too trite."

Nestor laughed out loud. "Yet you did go to Dionysus in search of Nestor. But, absent that fact, I couldn't agree with you more. That in itself should convince you that it's true. No amateur would use a setup as foolish as this."

"Why have you brought me here? Really." She relaxed into the embrace of the lounger.

"I'm hiding you. You're in far more danger than you know"

It was Kelahya's turn to laugh. "And, of course, no one realizes that we're here. You're one of the most visible men in this city—I did notice how you were gawked at during our travels to this place, and I'm one of the most visible people in the galaxies. But somehow, you are under the delusion that we're safe here."

"In point of fact, this is the only place where we are safe."

Kelahya rolled her eyes.

"It's the truth."

Kelahya smiled in honest amusement. "Let's pretend that I believe you, for the sake of…entertainment. What happens next?"

He leaned close to her and glanced in all directions in mock secrecy. "Can you keep this to yourself?"

"I'll do my best."

"I have no clue."

"Well, I do."

He leaned back, smiling. "Is that so?"

"It's quite transparent. We spend a few days hiding here, 'lying low', as Caveat would say. You do your best to…win my confidence. Especially you, if my guess is correct. But Caveat, or whatever her real name is, plays the part of buffer, or peacemaker, perhaps—you get too aggressive, she steps between us. When the time is right, she tells me how you have certain…feelings for me. Jofan, in the meantime, angers me and fights with me every chance he gets, so that you can play the hero by taking my side against him. And I, at long last, succumb to your irresistible charm. How am I doing?"

A carefree grin formed on his lips. "Please, go on. I beg you."

"You try, each of you according to your agreed upon roles, to make me trust you. Caveat is supposed to protect me or commiserate with my ordeal, or some such nonsense. You, on the other hand, will be playing to my…more basic instincts. You're an attractive man, your charm will make me trust you, maybe even like you, or—dare I say it—love you, perhaps." She leaned her head against the lounger with dramatic flair as she uttered her last words, then looked at him and fluttered her eyelids. "Any corrections to my scenario so far?"

"No, no, no. I like your…scenario far better than my reality." He turned to her, hanging his arm over the back of the lounger. "It is unbearably cliché, however. But I'm pleased that you credit us with such theatrical imagination."

"Oh?" She dropped to her knees in front of him. "Then, please, keep me in suspense no longer, fearless warrior. Tell me my fate, I implore you."

He laughed with honest amusement. "I like that. Until now, I wasn't sure you even had a sense of humor. I'm relieved."

"Sir, I beg you, do not toy with my fragile emotions. Reveal my fate, that I may begin to prepare myself for the inevitable." She finished her display with a deep sigh as she settled back into the lounger. "Torture by boredom is a favorite among you people." Kelahya's voice was loaded with sarcasm.

Nestor nibbled another tidbit. "Very well, General." He poured a drink and lifted his eyebrows as if to ask, 'more'?

She shook her head.

His eyes looked into hers and she felt his sensual appeal. "Shall we start to play out your scenario?"

"You can do whatever you wish. I'm done. The tedium of this imprisonment can only be tolerated in short bursts." She stood, and without another word, exited the comfortlounge, turned down the hallway, and calmly walked toward her chamber.

Nestor smiled as he savored his drink.

CHAPTER **19**

Humanoid Experimentation

---◆---

*Excerpt from the **Corpus Galacticum**, 137th Edition*

The **Declaration of Runtei**, *issued shortly after the end of the 73rd cycle (TE) and currently in its 29th adjustment, governs Humanoid Experimentation throughout the known universe.*

Established and maintained by the Galactic Ethical Conclave, the Declaration limits humanoid experimentation to one and only one purpose—curative exploration.

The Conclave has created strict guidelines and codes for all scientists, medics, Minders, and species' specialists to adhere to in the conduct of humanoid experimentation.

Each and every experiment must be reviewed and receive approval by the Conclave, and subsequently must adhere to the proposed methodologies. All experiments are consistently scrutinized.

Voluntary consent by the subject who participates in any experiment is required and all participants must be informed of the risk-benefit outcomes of the experiment.

Any violation of the Declaration brings with it termination of life for the perpetrator.

Kelahya had no choice but to investigate Maccabeus' so-called slip-up and journey to Aurora. To unmask his duplicity, she had to bear witness to the truth that lay behind his elaborate ruse to cover up the alleged inadvertent mistake.

The masterful plan that Maccabeus had described to Kronos—and attributed to her—required the extermination of Anduhar Slavan by turning his son, Ronhteu Slavan, against his own father. Kelahya—as explained by Maccabeus—had agreed to infiltrate Slavan's ranks, implant suspicion in the mind of his eldest offspring, and sway him to betray his father. A serious threat to Kronos and the Alliance had emerged when three planets, under the guidance of Anduhar Slavan, had developed a new offensive capability that could be exported, almost undetected, to other planets in similarly distant clusters like Xendrexia's. Maccabeus' plan, solely dependent on Kelahya's ability to influence and control Ronhteu's mind, rested on the fact that, he'd reached maturity, had opened all his pores for mating, and therefore was susceptible to suggestion. Her influence would result in his defection to the League of One, the annihilation of his father's armies, and the turnover of the new offensive technology to the Alliance of Stars.

Subsequently, Kelahya used Maccabeus' infiltration strategy to dissect his lies. She convinced Kronos of the need to conduct a survey of the Xendrexia cluster before carrying out the master plan, and after intense discussions on the subject, she left with Kronos' blessing.

A detour to Aurora would go unnoticed.

She completed the survey of the Xendrexia cluster with her select entourage. The return route required that the surveyors evade enemy detection by circumnavigating in the direction opposite the *Olympus*. The route conveniently took them through the Dorian system—home of Planet Aurora. As they entered the system, Kelahya directed her team to head for the *Olympus*, and took off in the opposite direction. This action did not surprise her squad. She often broke ranks to investigate tips or suspicions. They followed her orders and traveled home, while she headed toward Aurora.

Finding Aurora proved no easy task. The planet didn't appear on any of the official galactic maps of the Alliance. To find it she scrutinized the planets, moons, and stars in the quadrants within the cluster. She subsequently matched Aurora's mass with her recollection of the scientific data scrolling on the vidscreen that Maccabeus had accidentally activated. She found two bodies fit, and only one that made sense after the basic surface scan. It was listed as a dead and nameless planetoid, but the scan data indicated something entirely different.

It surprised her to find that it sustained an abundance of life. Analysis of the atmosphere and the composition of the planet indicated it had more than adequate amounts of oxygen, and vidscope scans showed clusters of dwellings scattered about the surface. The probe showed that Aurora was an arid planet with reddish soil, where precipitation occurred only at the poles from where it trickled into underground streams and lakes at lower latitudes.

Dead planet, indeed.

She completed the analysis of the planet and decided to land in an area where the dwellings would be reachable on foot.

Kronos would never authorize an experiment as abhorrent as the vidlog attributed to him. Does Maccabeus covet Kronos' power? What's he up to?

The sensors confirmed that she had landed unseen. She engaged the camouflage array, donned the chameleon insulator suit with internal oxygen and temperature controls, and clamped on the clear moldable facial mask.

No one will ever find out that I've been there.

She added a shield disc and attached a nullifier to her forearm. *Better safe than sorry.*

Cautiously, she stepped onto the surface of Aurora.

The suit quickly self-adjusted to the environment and indicated that her life support systems would last eight hours.

Plenty of time to dispel the lie.

She made her way toward what the sensors identified as a cluster of dwellings. Step by cautious step, she moved forward. Peering over the crest of a dune, she encountered a circle of huge stones placed, as far as she could tell, to deter the sand from encroaching on a tiny village huddled around a few clumps of vegetation. Such oases were common on desert planets.

The dwellings were primitive huts that leaned precariously against one another, and the irregular alleyways were dark and inhospitable. Sensors indicated that the inhabitants were presently concentrated in a small area on the other side of the village.

As she scurried between the huts, she heard occasional groans, but the sensors detected nothing that could be a threat to her. Having successfully traversed the village, she heard loud humanoid noises coming from the largest of the huts. She turned off her night goggles and allowed her own eyes to guide her through the dark shadows as she approached the structure.

She edged around a corner. Physical shock spread through her body, and a fierce clump of anxiety knotted her stomach. She turned away to keep from vomiting and waited until she regained control.

Inside the structure, which amounted to little more than a primitive dome, the Aurorans were crowded in a rough circle, around two creatures that appeared to be attempting to mate, making loud noises that resembled no language Kelahya had ever heard.

The Aurorans were abominations of nature and no two were exactly alike—males and females with mixed organs, some with tails, deformed body parts, misplaced eyes or noses, half one species and half another, or several species intertwined. Monstrosities all, as if a demented wizard had taken parts from every creature in the galaxy and assembled them with diabolical whimsy.

The two creatures in the center were of indistinguishable species and gender. They circled each other and rolled about, sniffing, licking, and examining one another as if trying to ascertain the manner of mating.

Finally, one jumped the other and attempted to insert a protuberance growing from its chest into the ear of the potential mate. The ear clearly was not the mating organ, so the creature roared and threw its attacker to the ground with bone-crushing force. The sickening grunts and screams of the observers became louder, reflecting the excitement of the encounter.

Repulsed by the spectacle, Kelahya looked away when something caught her eye. She saw a platform, high inside the large hut, from where two sneering League of One Troopers in standard uniforms delighted in the spectacle.

Troopers in Aurora? How dare they enjoy this atrocity?

In a reflex action, she aimed the nullifier at the two men, and was about to activate the detonator, when a repressed scream of fury formed in her throat. She realized she shouldn't fire.

She bolted back to her ship like a terrified animal.

She collapsed into the comfort and sanity of her command seat and yanked the mask off as tears gushed down her face and screams of anguish ricocheted about the cabin. After a while, she regained control over her emotions, punched the controls, and shot off the surface of Aurora at breakneck speed.

Her mind whirled as she switched from thrusters to hyper speed.

Get me out of this cluster, away from this disgrace of a planet.

She struggled for air between irrepressible sobs, the images of Aurora playing in her head.

Her conscience kept resisting the reality of what she'd seen, while at the same time, it kept reviewing the inference in the vidreport of Kronos' involvement.

He couldn't possibly have designed this experiment. How could anyone purposely do such a thing?

"Why?" she heard a deep voice say, somewhere in the recesses of her mind.

"Search your mind and heart. Why? Why?" the deep voice insisted.

It was the voice of the Dionysian youth that Kronos said she'd killed in the canyons of Surina, but it was more than that. It came to her not as a memory, but as an emotion, a sensation of connectedness. As if the question emanated from deep within her, at this moment and in this location. A direct question posed to her, here and now.

The Dionysian's intrusion into her consciousness came as a shock. His presence in her mind was beyond comprehension.

"What do you seek from me?" she asked him.

But his presence had vanished.

What possible connection could he have with Aurora? Why would he surface in my awareness? And why does he continue to ask why?

The navigational alert beeped and Kelahya disengaged the hyper speed and reduced to impulse power. Kronos' battleship was within sight. A flight of several hours had felt like only milicons.

Gather yourself before we dock.

But try as she may, she found it impossible to regain full composure. Fearful of discovery, she fled to her quarters as soon as she docked.

The door to her quarters hadn't yet closed when Kronos appeared, a concerned look upon his face. "What happened? Why did you ignore the debriefing?"

"I wish I could have some privacy once in a while," she snapped as she walked away from him. She could not have him inside her head. She had to fight for distance.

"You have privacy. I'm not within you as you can plainly sense. What has agitated you so?"

Afraid and demoralized, Kelahya dropped her head.

Kronos moved closer and put his arm around her. "We're one, you and I," he whispered. "I don't need to enter your mind to feel your anguish."

He was right. She could also sense his moods. She turned to him. Unable to restrain the flood of tears, she ought the comfort of his embrace with hope for his innocence.

"I've been to Aurora," she whispered.

"Aurora?" There was a hint of tightness in the disciplined voice.

"Can you tell me about it?" Her tone carried a plea for a negative reply.

Dragging out the silence between them, he moved away from her. She could sense him withdrawing, building the all too familiar impenetrable barrier around his mind.

He responded with a question of his own. "What about Aurora?"

"Don't evade my inquiry. Answer me!"

Never had she taken such a tone with him. No one ever took that tone with him.

Kelahya felt the fire in his eyes boring through her.

He opened his mouth but decided not to speak.

She held firm demanding an answer.

With his anger under control, Kronos moved close to her again, and spoke. "It's a misbegotten planet. I should've destroyed it long ago."

"How did it become what it is?"

"I'm not sure."

Although he was looking right at her, and appeared not to be hiding anything, she sensed he was not himself. There was a rapid movement in his eyes and an almost imperceptible twitching of his mouth.

"Why have you not destroyed it? Why—"

The fingers of his right hand came to rest on her lips. "Kelahya, my darling. You're not to concern yourself ever again with planets like Aurora. They are for me to worry about and deal with. You are too young for me to allow you to suffer such pain. If I'd wanted you to become acquainted with such a place, I would've told you. Understood?"

His tone had been gentle and almost fatherly, yet the message was direct and inarguable. Kelahya lowered her eyes and nodded.

"Now, tell me how you found out about Aurora."

"I found it accidentally."

"Accidentally?"

She broke his embrace and walked toward her cleaning chamber. "Yes," she responded almost casually, "I was on my way back from the Xendrexia cluster when I passed it. I was testing my sensors by charting any possible pursuers. I scanned the planets and was surprised to find a dead planet with inhabitants. So, I went to take a look." She turned to face him and smiled. "Now, if you'll excuse me, Aurora left me tired and very dirty."

Without waiting for a response, she disappeared into the cleaning chamber.

* * * * * *

Wake up, a voice cried out.

"What? Who?" She bolted up ready to fight the assailants. Yet none were there.

She plopped down on the bed, her hands cradling her head, her elbows resting on her legs.

Why do I have to relive all this? Let me be.

Wishing to escape her memories, she got up and rushed out of her bedchamber. "There must be a training lounge somewhere in this golden cage."

She surveyed the corridors of her new prison, all the while attempting to dislodge the uninvited memories, but in each and every hallway all she found were locked doors.

One of the hallways led down a steep incline so she followed it. There was warm moisture in the air. It piqued her curiosity and, even though it looked like another dead end with yet another locked door, she went on. As she approached the door, it opened.

A breathtaking garden of stalactite and stalagmite crystal formations stretched before Kelahya like the teeth of a dragon. Rose-colored crystal peaks rose from a multicolored lagoon that emanated a soft mist, and a tenuous light radiated from an undetectable source, which together with the mist softened the landscape endowing it with an ethereal beauty.

This garden of her prison, like everything else connected with it, was magnificent.

"The best mineral water in the galaxy," Nestor announced with pride as he walked past her. "Once you bathe in these waters, you'll never dream of bathing in any others, I assure you."

He disrobed and dove in.

Kelahya hesitated.

"Come," he yelled, his voice echoing about. "If you're worried about your nudity, rest assured I've already seen you."

"Nudity is not a concern," she snapped back. She disrobed with deliberate slowness and descended into the waters, allowing enough time for him to savor her body. "It's your self-control that concerns me."

The effect she sought was evident in his eyes.

"It's one thing," she continued, "to observe the nude body of an unconscious person, and quite another to admire that same body in its full living splendor."

His hearty laugh sounded so sincere that Kelahya couldn't resist it and laughed as she swam toward him.

"How much longer are we to remain here?"

"Are you that unhappy?"

"I…" she paused, interrupted by the tingling sensation of the mineral waters penetrating her skin. She closed her eyes and surrendered to the sensation.

Nestor allowed his gaze to feast on her.

"I'm not unhappy," she said at last. "Actually, I'm rather content. But, this peace, this calm, and your full attention, are quite unsettling. As strange as it may sound, I miss sparring with Jofan, and Caveat's presence is sparse. It's unnerving."

"I can imagine it is. It's disconcerting for me as well. I've rarely been stranded like this, without a weapon, without an action-packed commission, without the strain of survival. We're …cradled."

"Cradled? That's a rather interesting choice of words." She closed her eyes once again, as the waters carried her in their embrace.

He watched her intently, then swam close to her. "What compelled you to do all the things you did for Kronos?"

Kelahya's frowned as images of her past flashed before her. She swam away from him. "I prefer not to talk about that. If you wish to interrogate me, let's do it in a more formal manner."

"It's not an interrogation." He followed her. "I seek to find out if we're wrong about you. That you never willingly did the things you're accused of. You wish that as well."

She shot him a glare filled with rage. "Don't presume to know me. You detect only what I wish you to perceive. As you do with me, throwing bits and pieces of your mind into mine."

Nestor was unperturbed. "We're on guard you and I, that's true. But there have been times when—"

"Don't flatter yourself," she snapped. "I'm not even sure anymore of what's real and what's not. I'm not sure if my dreams are true or are part of your elaborate infusion. If I'm not, how could you be?"

She swam to a small island that had several crystalline stalagmite formations in the center. She emerged from the water and sat on the soft sand.

Nestor made his way to the island and sat beside her. "I'm stronger. If you allow me, I can guide you out of the labyrinth of your mind."

Kelahya stared into the depths of his eyes. He meant what he said. He wasn't invading her mind, even though he could easily do so. He was asking permission. "How can you be stronger? You're Terrian. By nature, you're weaker than me."

"I'm…more than Terrian. I'm…" he hesitated, deciding whether to continue. After a lengthy pause, he said, "I'm a Transmutant."

Kelahya's eyes widened. Instinctively she glanced at his naked body, searching.

"Yes, I possess the body of a Terrian, yet I'm a Transmutant. In the universe, or the dimensional fields known to us at this time, there is no higher form than a Transmutant." He paused, allowing her to absorb the meaning of his words. "I'm sure you've noticed that your mind has ceased to ache since your capture. It's not healed yet, but the excruciating pain is gone. It does continue to reminisce. It searches for the truth and believes it lies in your past."

"You woke me up? You brought me here?"

"I can help you associate, if you let me."

She squeezed her eyes shut and covered her face with her hands. Then, she moaned and shook her head.

"Whatever you wish," he said. Disappointed, he lay on his back, and stared at the crystals above them.

She lowered herself down and they rested in silence for a very long time, each aware of the other's proximity, looking deep within themselves, searching for the path that would enable them to trust one another. Their rhythmic breathing and the bubbling of the waters were the only perceptible sounds around them.

When, at last, Kelahya slid back into the water, she stole a glimpse of Nestor. He was the picture of perfection, tall, strong, with vibrant masculinity. She remained motionless in the water, studying every detail of him, aware of his gaze, and thankful for his patience and understanding. After all, Transmutants supposedly understood everything.

No one knew much about Transmutants, really. No one had ever encountered them, but no one denied their existence either, at least, not openly. They were, for all intents and purposes, mythical gods shrouded in mystery. Legend had it that they offered spiritual guidance to civilizations seeking universal peace. To the best of her understanding, there were six Transmutants currently in existence, and they formed the spiritual brotherhood of the Incorporeal Fellowship.

Their Scriptures were handed down to the Clerics and Scribes of the Sanctuaries who, in turn, used them to guide the masses. Nothing was known about them beyond what they permitted to be revealed through the Scriptures, but they were believed to be omnipotent.

Legend had it that the only living being to ever meet them was Kronos Deucarrion, Master Scribe of the Galactic Sanctuary of The Incorporeal Fellowship. A privilege he boasted of, accorded him a status near sainthood, and became the cornerstone of his power.

Kronos never shared the existence of Transmutants with Kelahya, but he conferred with them regularly. She had accepted it as one more element of his life to which she had no access.

All this made it the more impossible to believe that the man who lay before her, with undeniable Terrian characteristics, could be a Transmutant.

A god.

Nestor opened his eyes and gave her a reassuring smile as he entered the water.

"There are more than six in the cosmos. In fact, we are currently ten in number, and one more is to be born in the near future. We can penetrate the minds of all species in the universe. Not all we do is spiritual, although our mental abilities are, for the most part, best used in that pursuit."

He glided through the shimmering waters as if they were parting before him. Kelahya was transfixed, seeing him in an entirely different light.

"Our service is determined according to characteristics of species lineage. Of the ten, there are currently seven at the highest level. This level of Transmutant development is what permits us to have absolute control of our mental abilities. It also imposes on us the obligation to serve in a multitude of commissions throughout the universe. Three Reclusians have less ability to control their powers and therefore remain within the confines of the Incorporeal Fellowship."

"Reclusians?"

"Transmutants whose mutation evolved into a new species of concentrated energy."

"Energy? How?"

"It's complex and not easy to grasp."

"Try me."

"Visualize quantum electromagnetic radiation with elementary particles that are also their own anti-particles. Reclusians exist in a constant polarized state of energy, therefore their mental powers must be contained."

"By whom?"

"By the Clerics of the Fellowship. Those who stay with them, control and direct their power away from chaos and war, and toward peace. It is, in fact, the only mind control we are permitted to exercise."

"You mean domination of your own?"

"Yes. This control generates the spiritual power that we then channel throughout the universe."

"Are you saying that the Fellowship embodies good *and* evil?"

"Yes." He paused as he came very close to her. "Kelahya, only two beings, outside of the Fellowship, are aware of my true nature. You're the third. I trust I will not regret my honesty."

Kelahya shuddered. Whether as a result of his revelation or the aura he emanated, she couldn't tell. "Why all this charade? If you're indeed a Transmutant, you need not ask anything of me. You can simply take it."

"You have nothing to fear from me. I can't harm you. My sacred mandate forbids me to take what is not offered." He caressed her cheek with a gentle, caring stroke. "Because I am a Transmutant," he said at last. "I'm familiar with the delicate balance of the mind. Not only do I understand that nothing can be taken from the spirit unless it is released freely, but I sincerely believe that to be true."

She felt his honesty. His words were true. But she feared their meaning. Transmutant or not, he was holding her against her will. She turned away from him and swam to the shore of the underground lagoon. She wrapped herself in her bedclothes and stood there, motionless.

Moments later, Nestor joined her. He slipped on his robe and placed his hands on her shoulders. The familiar electrical current traveled through their bodies. He stared into her eyes and whispered, "Let's return to our chambers."

"What's your name?"

"I cannot tell you yet. The time will come."

"You've shared much with me already. Why not your name?"

"You've learned of my true nature. That's enough for now."

CHAPTER **20**

Inexorable Attraction

———◆———

*Excerpt from the **Corpus Galacticum**, 137th Edition*

Master Scientist Xiubantes *Treo is credited with pinpointing the multi-dimensional effects of attraction, as outlined in the Compendium* Inexorable Dimensional Magnetism, *issued in 235 TE. He showed how certain beings distributed throughout the universe gravitationally attract and move toward each other even when unwilling to do so. Inborn light elements emanate from within and travel through the dimensional strings towards the subconsciously identified target. This energy release, at the atomic level, yields surges equal to those seen in the stars, or depending on the species, as seen in novae.*

Master Xiubantes demonstrated how electrons and ions attached to spatial field lines travel through dimensional strings like beads on a wire.

The inexorable magnetic attraction between these beings undergoes cosmic wave motions, spreading at times faster than the speed of light.

Once the attraction emanates, it is impossible to control.

256

With the eradication of the insurrectionists of the Yuk-Thar system accomplished, General Kelahya Devona returned to home base with her ship and a fleet of thirty carriers. They had only lost ten fighters during the assault, which by any standard equated to a complete success.

As soon as the fleet crossed the Yuk-Thar border Kelahya retired to her quarters. The battle cruiser *Athena*, the newest and most advanced in the League, had recently been assigned to Kelahya. It provided the comforts and technology that enabled her to carry out military assignments with ease and efficiency. The Yuk-Thar confrontation had been more difficult and complicated than expected, and she was exhausted.

After emerging from the cleaning unit, she dressed in her evening off-duty robe. Without prompting, the vidlog came on.

"Biahn Dah," the unfamiliar voice said, "is governed entirely by the laws prescribed in the Sahatjan, written thirty-four centuries ago by the mystic Atnaid Biahn. Anyone—"

"Vidlog off," Kelahya snapped.

With complete disregard to the command, it continued, "—breaking a single commandment is sentenced to be sacrificed to appease Atnaid's anger. A council—"

"Vidlog off," Kelahya commanded.

The vidlog continued, "—of high priests determines the gravity of…"

Kelahya marched to the communications console to manually stop the vidlog. It didn't respond to manual commands either.

"…the offense and interprets the specificity of the law. There are…"

Kelahya entered the codes hailing the ship's engineer. The codes were rejected. A message appeared on the status screen indicating that there existed an overall malfunction in the communications system. She gave up and walked toward the exit doors of her quarters.

"... three degrees of sacrifice to which the guilty may be sentenced. It's this portion of their belief system that Supreme Commander Kronos Deucarrion tests. The first sacrifice..."

Kelahya froze at the mention of Kronos' name. She returned to the vidlog to observe the images of Biahn Dah as the words flowed.

"...is death by removal of the heart. The heart is then fed to the family and offspring of the offender, thus bringing eternal shame to the family line that they will carry forever."

She sat in front of the vidlog.

"The second is removal of the limbs, which in this case are fed to the offender himself, and the third sacrifice is the removal of the tongue, eyes and reproductive organs. The sacrifices are considered the holy wish of the Atnaid and can be handed down only by the High Council. The Council is considered a sacred part of the body of Atnaid himself and any attack, verbal or physical on the Council or one of its members is heresy. In case of heresy, indefinite torture, without the benefit of a final sacrifice, is the prescribed punishment. The duration of the torture required to accomplish a return to the faith is determined by Atnaid himself and revealed through the High Priests."

Intrigued, she leaned forward as if her proximity to the vidlog would reveal the culprit who was transmitting these messages.

"Supreme Commander Kronos Deucarrion theorized, in recreating this society with primitive beliefs, that fear of punishment from a terrifying god would keep the citizenry under control while the High Priests grew in power. The theory further assumed that, in time, the Priests would abuse their power, fall prey to the stimulation of the sacrifices, causing the citizenry to rebel, even if to do so meant suffering the wrath of a god. The theory proved correct. The uprising occurred, and Biahn Dah was exterminated by Commander Devona's Confinement Brigade."

The emblem of the League of One and the Alliance of Stars appeared on the screen along with the serial code typical of a confidential transmission.

The display flickered again, and another transmission began.

"Indach Dubliay allows any criminal to be punished by the victims or their family in any way they deem satisfactory. No official legal entity exists on the planet. Each citizen carries the law with him or herself and, as a result, every citizen is armed at all times. An interesting result of this experiment has been the tendency of some individuals to live as isolated as possible. Some communities have formed by establishing their own rules for peaceful cohabitation, but many of these have succumbed to outside violence. The most successful social groups are those formed by nomadic bands dedicated to pillage and murder. Life expectancy on Indach Dubliay is twenty-three cycles."

Kelahya stood before the vidlog wanting to leave but unable to move.

"Supreme Commander Kronos Deucarrion maintains that violence and chaos offer the best opportunities for perpetual rule by force and has extended the experiment by creating similar societies on several planets and clusters within each quadrant of this galaxy. With interplanetary travel, it is expected that the mentality of violence and chaos will be exported, at which time the Alliance would intervene and restore peace. As in the case of Emperor Cuetzalan, one of the first tyrants to carry out the experiments on behalf of Director Kronos Deucarrion, the Alliance stepped in to contain the violence and re-establish control, thus acquiring the gratitude of the rescued civilization by enforcing the Principles of the League of One. The capture and execution of Emperor Cuetzalan by Commander Kelahya Devona is a prime example of the success of this experiment."

Once again, the emblem of the League of One and the Alliance appeared on the screen along with the serial code for confidential transmission. The vidlog flickered and a new transmission began.

"The Encasement Project is now in place in over half the planets and thirty of the moons of the Eruit cluster of galaxies. Initially instituted as a survival tactic during the 5th Century TE, Director Kronos Deucarrion has now successfully adapted the idea into a profit-making enterprise for the Alliance."

As Kelahya observed the vidlog, a faint recollection began to form in her mind. She remembered hearing of the Encasement Project and Kronos' dismissal of its veracity.

"The original concept," the transmission went on, "determined that it was safer for the law-abiding citizens on the planets where crime was rampant, to be encased behind impregnable steel walls, and for the criminals to be banished to the outside of the walls to fend for themselves. Director Kronos improved on the original experimental concept by creating, within each Encasement, separate enclaves, segregated by race, and race only. To reach the expected goal, races were expressly forbidden to mix. A natural competitive urge was therefore created between races, resulting in each race seeing itself as superior to the others. Enslaving competing races, though illegal, was encouraged, along with other types of underground criminal activity. The purpose was to increase racial tension and bring profit by monopolizing illicit trade, promoting unlawful competition, and stimulating genocide between the races. It also proved to be a very effective means of population control, requiring minimal involvement by the League to maintain a suitable balance. Profits from underground activities have quadrupled in the last five cycles. Expansion of the project is planned for the Bladarian and Thanathanah systems."

Once more, the emblem of the League of One and the Alliance appeared on the screen along with the serial code of a confidential transmission. This time the screen flicked off and remained dark.

Kelahya stared at the empty screen. She couldn't move.

The communication console came to life with a repetitive buzz. "Yes," she barked.

"Excuse me, General, but there's an urgent transmission for you. Should I send it through to your quarters?"

"Who sent the vidlog transmissions I just received?"

There was a pause.

"We show no record of receiving any transmissions through the vidlogs."

"What about the communications systems. Any malfunction?"

"We experienced an overall ship malfunction as we went through a magnetic distortion, but all systems were back online in a matter of hexicons."

"Put the communication through," she commanded.

The monitor flickered and Maccabeus' face came into focus.

"General, I trust everything is all right?"

"Why do you ask?" was her curt response.

"My ship is rather close to yours and we experienced some anomalies as we passed through the magnetic storm."

"What are you doing out here?"

"I'm returning from a commission, not unlike yours. Might we join your fleet?"

Kelahya searched his face for anything unusual, a gesture, a flinch. As usual, there were none. She wished she could read what lay behind those eyes and that enigmatic crisscrossed face. "Maccabeus, did you 'accidentally' transmit a few vidreports to my quarters?"

"My Lady?" He expressed genuine confusion.

"Never mind. Thank you. You are, of course, welcome to join us."

She studied Maccabeus' response and ended the transmission. She paced about her quarters scrutinizing and unscrambling the information she'd received. At length, exhaustion overcame her. Yet, weary as she was, sleep proved a restless and elusive companion.

* * * * * *

To pass the time, Kelahya had opted to wander through the vacant chambers of her gilded prison in Bysu City. She'd lost track of the time spent in her palatial surroundings. Under normal circumstances, that in itself would have been enough to set off her internal alarms. Yet she'd seldomly enjoyed such peace, so for now, she allowed herself to relish this time, rest her mind, and ignore why she was here, whom she was searching for, and why.

But ignore she could not. On this night, unwanted memories of her unsavory past kept rattling in her head. Although free of pain, her brain kept reminding her over and over, of a past she now wished to deny. It brought forth images of deceit, images of Kronos, of unfathomable actions. Images jumbled, yet vivid, impossible, but true. Above all, the questions came incessantly.

What have I done? Am I a pawn, a puppet? Her melancholy reached deep within her and a couple of desolate tears trickled down her cheeks.

A gentle hand on her shoulder, followed by the now familiar spark, yanked her back from her musings. A deep sensation of inner peace penetrated every cell of her being. Aside from a soft shudder of joy, she remained motionless. She closed her eyes and yielded to the sensation.

Nestor guided her in silence through the hallways toward his apartments. She offered no resistance. Not a word was uttered.

He eased her out of her clothes and onto his bed, then disrobed and crawled in beside her. Sliding his arm around her he caressed and kissed her, his lips resting on hers with such softness that they hardly touched.

As the energy between them intensified, tiny sparks formed where their lips brushed, and the tantalizing effect caused them both to shudder.

With the same soft, almost imperceptible touch, he kissed her face, his lips roving along her cheeks, her eyelids, her nose, her forehead. He cradled her neck in his hand and, with a gentle lift, kissed her ears, the soft sounds of his breath sending shivers down her body. His lips traveled down her neck and remained in the hollow of her throat.

Warmth began to rise within her, and she surrendered fully to his tenderness. A flow of exquisite elation stirred within her, dissolving her melancholy.

His fingertips traced the curve of her shoulder and brushed the length of her arm. Then, slowly, with a whisper of a touch, he caressed and kissed the inside of her arm. With the same lightness, his fingers journeyed along the outline of her entire body.

He kissed her again and again, then ran his tongue down her neck to the valley between her breasts. He cupped them with both hands, brought his lips to her nipples, and suckled them until they were firm.

She gasped.

He made his way down the center of her groin.

She moaned softly as waves of irresistible pleasure washed through her.

As her breathing intensified, his lips coursed up her body finally resting on hers this time with a lingering kiss.

Her fingers combed through his hair, clutching him to her. With joyous abandon, she thrust up to welcome him.

They moved as one, their bodies creating a choreography of ecstasy with its own crescendo of rhythm and poetry. Their dance, fused by an invisible aura of energy, seized them as they journeyed through eternity and back, an indissoluble bond uniting them as one.

They erupted in harmony with an overwhelming explosion of pleasure and release.

As their breathing slowed, they relaxed into each other and lay intertwined, enjoying the intimacy and peace.

At length Nestor rolled onto his side, with a sigh of deep fulfillment.

She turned to him and stroked his handsome face with the back of her hand. "I know so little about you," she whispered.

"You already know more about me than you should." He paused. A fleeting look of concern wrinkled his brow. "What happened between us… just now, was… inevitable."

"I could feel it, but why?"

He smiled and caressed her.

Struggling to understand, Kelahya intruded in his mind. To her astonishment, he didn't recoil. Instead, he welcomed her and led her to the center of his being. She found overwhelming love and desire for her, along with his worries, concerns, and desperate need to save her.

His mind was nothing like that of Kronos. In Nestor there was light. The surroundings were soothing with no distortions. And everywhere, his concern for her, wrapped in passion and desire.

But she couldn't accept his emotions without a reason for their existence. She found them too strong and frightening. How could he feel those things? She was his enemy after all, as he was hers. She felt unworthy of the affection he showed her. The things she'd done in the name of Kronos…she couldn't permit herself to feel these emotions. She snapped out of him. But he reached out inviting her to remain. Despite her fear and wish to retreat, she could sense the purity of Nestor's being.

There is no need to flee. He whispered. *In time you will understand this bond between us and learn to love yourself as I love you.*

A warmth, like a mother's womb, embraced her in peace and safety. The fear of their emotions vanished. She felt transported out of Nestor and, somehow, sleep embraced her.

Chapter 21

Lies

———◆———

*Excerpt from the **Corpus Galacticum**, 137th Edition*

It is written in the Scriptures that, "A truth that is told to injure is worse than a lie told to appease."

Lies, however, are not usually accessed for higher purposes. Instead, in their various categories, lies are accessed according to their fundamental intent. Some categories are disparaged, while others are generally accepted.

Abridgment lies are used to mislead, whether by volunteering false information or by deliberately holding back relevant facts. This type of lie employs the careful use of facts and omits critical information.

Embroidery lies occur when the essential features of a situation are true, but only to a certain degree. These lies twist the truth by embellishing the layers of its meaning.

Protective lies are told when the truth may harm someone. Alternatively, a protective lie could be used when avoiding the truth in the presence of the one it might harm.

Trickery lies are not usually seen as lies when utilized as an act of deception in war tactics. In these situations, lying is acceptable and is commonly expected.

"My Lord, they've lied." Zenubus was passionate on this point. "Their attack on Uxiel is a direct violation of the agreement between the Alliance and the Abherg-Yurian Cluster."

Kronos had evacuated the Command Center permitting only Zenubus, Maccabeus, and Kelahya to remain. In silence, he sat in the command chair listening to his officers.

"General Devona, your opinion?" he said dryly.

"I'm not sure they attacked. I have a feeling this could be a diversionary tactic. I don't—"

"A feeling?" Zenubus snapped with contempt, "My Lady, feelings are not facts, the attack is a fact." His exoskeletal motors buzzed with activity.

"Commodore Zenubus, if you please," Kelahya continued in a calming voice, "hear me out. If you consider the military strength of the Zontirius, you must agree that their attack on Uxiel is little more than a kick in the rear." She turned to Kronos. "My Lord, what they did was meant to catch our attention, not Uxiel's. Something else is behind this half-hearted attack."

Zenubus whirred about in silent acceptance of Kelahya's premise.

"Maccabeus?" Kronos asked.

Maccabeus was slow to respond. "To be honest, I am not sure. We have not been to this sector, or so close to the Abherg-Yurian Cluster, in many cycles." He paused. "It may be a ruse, or it may not. Either way, it should be investigated."

Kronos stared at Maccabeus for a moment, as he decided. "General Devona," he stood and moved toward the exit, "on the morrow take a platoon of battle pods and go to the periphery of the Cluster. Examine Uxiel and make a determination as to—"

"With your permission, My Lord," Zenubus interrupted, "My Lady is too valuable to be sent so far with such a small force. It'll take too long to—"

"Hold your tongue, Commodore," Kronos thundered from the doorway. "I haven't sought your counsel on this," he yelled.

"General, you have your orders." And without a glance he left the room.

The three top ranking officers of the League stood frozen in awkward silence.

After a few moments, Maccabeus mumbled something inaudible and left.

Zenubus approached Kelahya. "I'm sorry, my Lady, Uxiel is—"

"You must stop protecting me, Zenubus," Kelahya interrupted. "You're going to get your head chopped off one of these days."

"I'll obtain a new one. I have a collection of them in my quarters," Zenubus teased, as he placed his metallic hand on Kelahya's.

She grasped his hand with both of hers and looked into his lustful eyes.

"I'm his, old friend. You must stop all your reveries about me."

"Why? Hope dies only when the spirit does, and spirit is all I have left."

She smiled and kissed him softly on the cheek.

His face became flushed. "You see? Not long ago, you wouldn't have dared to even hold my hand. Now you do it regularly. And today, you've kissed me. Things are improving for me."

Kelahya gave him a brief smile then became somber. "Zenubus, tell me about the Aurora experiment."

As all color drained from his face, he stiffened and withdrew from her. "Aurora? What do you mean? Why do you ask?"

"Don't answer my questions with questions. Get a hold of yourself, old man, and answer."

"That subject is forbidden." He moved closer and whispered, "My Lady, if you elect to stay alive, you'll not speak of it again."

"Are you familiar with Anduhar Slavan? Or the Encased cities? How about Biahn Dah? Was I sent to exterminate Biahn Dah because it housed a rebel base, or because the experiment had reached its expected conclusion? What about the capture of

Emperor Cuetzalan? Was it to silence him about the experiments he carried out for Kronos?"

Zenubus' heart rate started to rise, so the whirring increased. "Hush, my Lady. Never speak of that. You'll get us both killed." His eyes fluttered about as he searched for more compelling words, sweat trickled down his cheek. Shocked and confused, he turned and quickly left the room.

Zenubus and Maccabeus are aware of the experiments and both are terrified. Kronos acknowledged Aurora only as a fortuitous accident, not an experiment. And all three refuse to discuss those subjects at all. Why the secrecy? Why the lies?

Kelahya left the Command Center perplexed. She needed to prepare for the mission to Uxiel, but the specter of the experiments made it impossible to concentrate.

Over time, the relationship between Zenubus and Kelahya had evolved into a genuine partnership of trust, mutual admiration, and care for each other. He never evaded her inquiries. He never closed his mind to her. So, his hasty departure meant he needed to escape her probing mind to protect something, or someone.

Why couldn't Zenubus confide in me? The fear that overtook him is perplexing. Are he and Maccabeus working together to undermine Kronos and overthrow him? The only way to accomplish that is by turning me against him. In Kronos' absence we three are the only ones with the power to maintain control of the League and the Alliance. We are dependent on one another. And yet... what if they could find a way to do it without me? Maccabeus is an enigma... anything is possible with him...but Zenubus is loyal to Kronos... that is clear. On the other hand, if Kronos' involvement in the experiments is true, what would Zenubus do then?

"My Lady." Maccabeus appeared, as usual, from nowhere.

"What is it?" she snapped.

He signaled her not to speak and beckoned her to follow him. In silence, they traversed half the ship until they reached one of the engine compartments. Maccabeus opened the hatch and she followed. He secured the hatch behind them.

"We can speak here without fear of being overheard. The ship's listening devices are useless in this chamber."

"What is it?"

"Your mission has changed. Orders of Lord Kronos. Listen carefully because you cannot refer to any established plan. You are to proceed solo and undetected to the city of Bistayde, on the planet Za, which is a few tarsecs from our present location." He paused. When she showed no reaction, he continued, "My Lord Kronos has lost trust in Commodore Zenubus. For this reason, he was unable to dictate this mission to you personally, and I will—"

"He doesn't trust Zenubus? Why not? What has happened?"

Maccabeus lowered his head and looked away. "I have no idea, my Lady, but I am sure he has his reasons. My orders are that I am to convey to you the nature of your new mission without the possibility of it being monitored by anyone. That is all."

"I can't believe this. He trusts Zenubus. What could possibly change that? I didn't sense—"

"Unfortunately, my Lord Kronos did not see fit to confide his motives to me, and I certainly would not ask him. Like you, my Lady, I do as I am told."

"I have orders from Kronos. Prove to me that this machination is really coming from him."

"My Lord Kronos feared that you might not trust me and the message I carry. He told me to say, 'remember Surina.' I assume your Ladyship understands what he meant."

"Proceed, then."

"We have reason to believe that Governor Hu is orchestrating a revolt out of Bistayde City. Specifically, we believe she's organizing a galaxy-wide insurrection designed to commence there, or somewhere within the Abherg-Yurian Cluster. Your orders are to infiltrate and uncover the specifics of her plan. And, if our suspicions are correct, capture Governor Hu and bring her before My Lord Kronos."

"I understand."

"Your official mission to Uxiel remains on the logs of this vessel. Not even with Master Kronos himself are you to discuss your true mission. You can speak of this mission to no one. It is clear there are spies on this—"

"I understand. Get on with it."

"An untapped fighter has been prepared for you. I will board your standard command vessel, the *Athena*, fly at the head of your brigade, and lead them to Uxiel. You will leave in the fighter as a part of the brigade. When we cross the Daltoeen asteroid belt, you'll detach from us—discretely, of course—then go to Bistayde. Here," he handed her a portable viewscape, "these are the details of your mission. Guard this with your life. If it were to—"

"Maccabeus, I understand."

"Good luck, General." Maccabeus turned on his heels and left the engine compartment.

"I don't like this man, or trust him," Kelahya mumbled to herself.

✶ ✶ ✶ ✶ ✶ ✶

Kelahya smiled with the tingling sensations the mineral waters provoked, as she swam beneath the surface to the farthest corner of the crystalline garden of her quarters in Bysu. When her face broke the surface, she exhaled with a loud, satisfied explosion. She floated, head back, arms extended, marveling at the beauty of the translucent formations.

As her eyes scanned the large beautiful cavern, she saw a formation that had escaped her notice before. It appeared to conceal an opening at the far corner. With slow, calm indifference, she emerged from the water and lay down on the sand between two stalagmites. Caution was essential—after all, she remained imprisoned. Although at this moment she enjoyed the garden alone, she was certain she was being watched.

She stretched nonchalantly then headed toward the opening, without looking at it, but rather ambling by while feigning fascination with all the crystal formations. She noticed an appreciable difference in temperature around the area.

With the same casual nonchalance as before, she returned to the water's edge and began scrutinizing the crystalline garden with less artistic fascination and more with a soldier's eye.

As she surveyed her surroundings, Nestor had appeared at the garden entrance. He dove into the water and swam toward her.

She couldn't allow him to sense her discovery, in case it should later prove useful, so, she quickly swam out to join him.

Using it as a diversion, she kissed him.

When their lips parted, he leveled an inquisitive stare at her. "What was that all about?"

"What, the kiss?"

"Yes, the type of kiss."

"Is it so unusual?"

"For you, it is."

"You shouldn't be surprised." She chuckled. "It was a kiss. You kissed me back, didn't you?"

"There is a vast difference. You initiated it, albeit it with a bit of violence I may add. I simply responded. With pleasure."

Kelahya shook her head as she forced a chuckle. She swam away avoiding eye contact. She had to keep him entertained and away from her thoughts and recent discovery. He'd exercised considerable restraint, respecting her wishes and remaining out her head. She had to bank on that notion and prevent herself from thrusting her thoughts into his.

"You fulfilled your part in the scenario and have performed magnificently," she said nonchalantly.

He watched the water trickle down her skin as she strolled onto the sand and put on her robe.

"You know better than that."

She sat down smiling at him, her feet splashing in the water. "Do I?"

Slowly he swam to the shore and sat next to her. "Yes." His smile was gone.

The next instant, his arms were around her and his mouth was on hers. She opened her lips slightly and his response was immediate. As he kissed her, his expert hands caressed every part of her body. The familiar shocks of excitement ran through her, and he pressed her to him.

She inhaled his pleasant, masculine smell. She had never noticed any type of scent on Kronos. But Nestor's aroma was like an irresistible aphrodisiac.

She wanted not to feel, to not weaken under his spell. And yet, resistance was pointless.

"Kelahya," he whispered as he entered her. At that moment nothing mattered but their union. Once again, they moved in harmony, the world around them disappeared, and time stopped as they culminated their bond.

They lay motionless in a tight embrace, savoring the perfection and full satisfaction of their union.

"Thank you for taking the initiative," Nestor whispered.

"Don't make more of this than it is."

"What is it?"

"Whatever it is, don't make it out to be special or exceptional."

"Why not?"

"Please, don't. I need time to understand what's happening to me." She sat up. "What I feel for you, and from you, is…too illusory. I can't and won't trust it."

He closed his eyes and sighed.

She watched him. His disappointment was clear. Finally, she said, "Nestor, would you ever lie to me?"

He opened his eyes and turned his head toward her. "If necessary, I would."

Chapter **22**

Dissociative Trauma

———◆———

*Excerpt from the **Corpus Galacticum**, 137th Edition*

Traumatic dissociation occurs when a relationship perceived as needed for survival is severed.

***The Annals of Inquiry** of 322 (TE), established how the depth of the relationship influences the degree of dissociation, and how events are subsequently processed and remembered.*

Unawareness and forgetfulness of the event that caused the dissociation is substantially higher when the relationship between wrongdoer and victim involved trust, love, or dependency for existence.

Return to equilibrium requires the redefinition of the self and the formation of new biological, psychological, sociological, and spiritual subsystems.

General Kelahya's mission to put down the revolt and capture Governor Hu had been orchestrated to perfection. The Governor's palace was located in Bistayde, the largest city on the planet Za, and the encasement prototype for the cities on all other planets in the galaxy. Usually, Kelahya planned and orchestrated her own missions, finalizing the details with Zenubus, Maccabeus, and Kronos. This time however, she had been given a flawlessly designed plan, the parts of which she discovered one step at a time. This plan included a watertight identity and disguise. It reminded her of the enigma games she'd learned to unravel in her youth. Except this wasn't a game. It was the actual execution of a strategy aimed at eliminating a despot, the undisputed mistress of cruelty, corruption, and slavery.

The one flaw in the mission, however, was the missing likeness of Governor Hu, which Kelahya had been unable to access in any of the ship's systems. An unwelcomed complication, in an otherwise perfect plan.

As instructed, she landed in the Wastelands of Za and made her way toward the encampment of a band of slavers that operated under the leadership of one Alenore Wadiruse, a Terrian of prodigious strength and height.

Alenore's band survived on the slave trade and the transportation of illegal goods from one encasement to another, sometimes moving them over vast deserts and mountains.

The only group whose members came from a variety of races, his band included Dionysians, Terrians, Monsoans, and Zarrians among the most prominent ones. The latter, recognized for their great strength and minute intelligence, were commonly used in missions where danger had a deterrent effect on more discerning beings.

Far more important to Kelahya however, was Alenore's ability to con even the most skeptical humanoid into seeing things his way. As a result, he was recognized as the absolute master of the Wastelands, the open regions of planet Za that surrounded the encasements, and the only Wastelander with access to the encasement of Bistayde and to Governor Hu herself.

Kelahya entered the encampment with a clear understanding of what would come next. Four Zarrians attacked her in unison. Their size alone could intimidate even the largest Dionysian, but they lacked the subtleties of shrewd combat. They approached her in a straight frontal line, in unison, weapons drawn, beating their chests and roaring. They probably had frightened many away by their defiance and horrid appearance. But Kelahya simply shot the first, took his weapon, and shot the second with it. While the other two looked at each other in dismay, she cast a wirelance around their necks and strangled them. Her effortless victory left her wanting more.

She was rewarded when a couple of Dionysian males, who promised to be a greater challenge, ambushed her. They approached from different angles and with no boasting cries, their weapons discharging at measurable intervals in her direction. She evaded their line of fire, timed the intervals of their discharge, and predicted the direction of their beams. She rolled on the ground between them brandishing a lazergun in each arm and killed them. Her intellect and ability to utilize highly stylized combat maneuvers, coupled with her skills in hand-to-hand combat, perfected against the best warriors in the League, made her virtually invincible in this type of warfare.

She collected the weapons from her victims, lopped the heads off a Zarrian and a Dionysian, and marched with them into the center of the encampment.

She burst into the largest structure. "I seek Alenore."

When they recovered from their stunned silence, several creatures took a step in her direction as they reached for their weapons.

"Stay!" came the command from a man sitting on a dais at the back of the room.

With deliberate calmness, Kelahya strutted up to the man, and tossed the weapons and heads upon the ground before him.

"Are you Alenore?" she asked with contempt.

"State your name and purpose," Alenore commanded.

"I am Garta Nalveran and I seek Alenore," Kelahya answered nonchalantly as she aimed her weapons at him.

"I am Alenore. What do you want with me, wench?"

"Fortune."

"You fight well. League training. Why trust you?"

"Indeed, I am trained by the best in the League. I now seek my own fortune. Don't wish to be a pawn in someone else's wars."

Kelahya perceived that Alenore was intrigued by her and, above all, quite taken with her looks. She'd eliminated six of his men, and she sensed he wanted to learn from her. Taking her to his bed would make the arrangement quite enjoyable for him. She represented, in his estimation, a good risk.

"You can join me in my quarters." He motioned for her to follow.

"I'll not bed you."

"Well, then I'll bed you."

"Alenore, you are no match for me. I'll join you in your quarters, but I will not bed you… 'til I choose to. Understood?"

He smiled. "So be it, wench. We shall find out at the end of the day. I'm one who is favored and it'll be hard for you to resist me. Sit by me."

Kelahya joined him as he made the preparations for an audience with Governor Hu. He wished to obtain safe conduct to transport a large number of captive slaves to an encasement on planet Eed, halfway across the system from Za.

As the day went by, Kelahya found herself admiring Alenore's skills as he organized his band of ragtag misfits into a cohesive, well-functioning unit. His self-assurance and charisma served him well, and she could understand how females would be hard pressed to resist him.

Alenore's band was looking forward to this audience with Governor Hu, and what promised to be a good time at the palace while their leader palavered with her. Kelahya watched the band pack a handful of necessities, organize their weapons, and don what looked like their best garments.

Alenore kept Kelahya nearby all day long, flirting, caressing her arms now and then, disrobing before her, and flaunting his alluring body. She played the part of partially softening to his attentions and agreed to be at his side as his "new wench" while they made their way into Bistayde.

Upon their arrival, they were shown into the Great Reception Hall in Governor's palace—an ostentatious room designed to impress her subjects. It boasted enormous white marble pillars holding up a translucent rose stone ceiling that reflected a strange hue from the black marble floor. Coherent radiation signobanners lined the periphery of the room, and huge windows of multicolored crystal surrounded the vast chamber.

At one end of the chamber, majestic gilded doors provided access to the commoners, and at the opposite end, bejeweled doors led to the Governor's private apartments, in front of which stood the solid gold throne of the Governor.

Numerous delegations from the encasements seeking audience with Hu filled the hall. As Alenore and his band entered the room, the hatred and fear toward them was palpable. Kelahya also perceived a strong sense of envy. Governor Hu showed a special partiality toward the leader of the ragtag band. Customarily, after these types of audiences, she extended invitations to him and his tribe to join her for private pleasures. It was this manner of 'closeness' that Kelahya was expected to capitalize on to infiltrate Hu's private chambers. So far, everything was progressing according to plan.

Governor Hu, however, was nowhere to be seen. Time passed, and still no sign of her. Clearly, she knew how to manipulate her guests and petitioners into a hunger for her presence.

After much waiting, the edgy, eager audience was rewarded. A musical fanfare erupted, and the doors to the Governor's apartments flung open. A double line of soldiers filed out to either side as the fanfare hit a crescendo that ended abruptly, leaving a penetrating silence hanging over the congregation.

Governor Hu emerged from a cloud of red smoke that hovered about a meter over the black marble floor. Having accomplished the desired effect, she made her way to the throne. The tactic endowed her with a majestic and ethereal quality. The red smoke cleared and, with a deliberate theatrical gesture, the Governor turned to face her subjects.

At that moment, Kelahya saw her face.

Tzalina!

An overwhelming dread engulfed Kelahya as she glared at Tzalina's red eyes, her crisscrossed gray skin, her long green hair, thick eyebrows, and pale blue lips.

A series of uncontrollable images flashed through Kelahya's mind, screaming the horror of what she had lived as a child when her parents had been murdered.

Impossible! Tzalina can't be alive! Kronos killed her. He told me so. Who is this creature? This can't be real.

Kelahya perceived, somewhere in the depths of her consciousness, that words were being uttered and the proceedings had begun.

How could she have escaped Kronos and be thriving as Governor Hu on an Alliance planet without his knowledge?

Kelahya's thoughts careened through the circuits of her brain. A flash exploded in her head as if someone had fired an eliminator deep within her. A deafening buzz in her ears intensified with each beat of her heart. Nausea overcame her as her eyes refused to focus. The veins in her throat pulsed with increasing ferocity. Her breathing raced until she feared her chest might explode.

Calm down…calm down…I must pull myself together.

One heartbeat at a time, she regained control, her senses returned, her mind cleared. Only the pain in her head refused to subside.

Time became a blur as she watched the hated woman deal with one delegation after another. She noted the insinuating glances Tzalina shot with increasing frequency toward Alenore, and the smug grin they elicited from him. To no one's surprise, Governor Hu saved Alenore's requests until the end, savoring what she hoped would be an exquisite dessert.

When, at last, Alenore's band stood before the Governor's throne, she granted the slave exportation safe conduct as expected, and invited him and his band to enjoy her hospitality in her guest quarters.

They traversed a series of ostentatious corridors, and eventually entered a room lavishly supplied with food and drink, and humanoids available for all possible tastes. Governor Hu winked at Alenore, signaling him to follow her into her private chambers. "Bring a few of your favorites," Tzalina ordered.

Alenore whistled and three of his brigands joined him. He turned to Kelahya with a smirk. "Even the Governor can't resist me." With a smack to her rear, he strutted off in pursuit of the Governor.

Kelahya waited for a moment before following them. A glimpse of a plan to avenge her parents took shape in her mind.

In keeping with the flamboyance of her palace, Tzalina's private quarters were lined with silk draperies of all colors, separating the central nave from the surrounding alcoves, allowing Kelahya ample opportunity for concealment. She followed the voices looking to get close enough to lunge at her enemy. She decided to wait until Alenore and his companions left before carrying out her revenge. She wanted Tzalina to see at whose hands she was dying and for what reason. But first, in honor of her parents, she had to uncover how Tzalina escaped Kronos.

Alenore began disrobing the Governor, and Kelahya's repulsion increased at the sight of the revolting crisscrossing marks that covered her entire body.

A high-pitched whine emerged from an indiscernible source, followed by a frantic voice. "Governor, your—"

"I am not to be interrupted!" Tzalina yelled.

"Governor, My Lord Kronos is arriving."

"Very well." Tzalina dismissed Alenore and his men with a flick of her hand, then slid her garments back on.

Alenore scurried past Kelahya without noticing her.

Kronos? He must've discovered that Tzalina is alive and has come to kill her. But why am I here? As a witness? Constellations! I mustn't let Kronos perceive my presence. I can't distract him.

Kelahya blocked her thoughts.

Moments later a smiling Kronos entered the room from the opposite side.

Tzalina fell to her knees and bowed her head. "Welcome to Bistayde, my Lord Kronos."

Kronos held out his hand and pulled her to her feet.

"Thank you, Governor. It's good to be back here again." Kronos placed his hands on her shoulders, drew her to him, and planted a lingering kiss on her mouth.

A silent wail formed somewhere deep in Kelahya's heart.

The excruciating clamor inside Kelahya's mind blurred her vision, her body shook uncontrollably, beads of perspiration erupted throughout, her muscles refused to move, the room spun in all directions. Her breath remained locked inside her lungs, afraid to be released into the foulness that surrounded her.

Her soul screamed in silence.

She spiraled into nothingness. Then, from within the abyss, an explosion erupted throughout her head as if some invisible hand had reached into her brain and ripped it to shreds.

Time stood still. Darkness engulfed her, emptiness, and void.

"Take charge!" she heard a voice scream. *"End the agony! Kelahya, you must stop this putrid liaison! Take out your knife. Clutch it in your hand. Cut her throat! Cut his throat! Cut! Cut! Kill!"*

The command emanated, not from her own mind, but from someone outside of her, someone in control, someone who compelled her step by step.

"Now, look at what you have done," the voice ordered.

"Kronos looks surprised, lying there in the pool of his own blood," Kelahya muttered.

"He betrayed you! What else could you do? He deserved your wrath. Relish the sight of him dead at your hands. Look at the laser knife you used to kill him. Feel it clutched in your hand. Enjoy its power. You did what needed to be done. You killed the vermin called Kronos Deucarrion. He no longer rules the universe."

She heard laughter, dark, distant laughter.

"No, I didn't kill him," Kelahya said. "You did."

"I am you. You and I are one."

"No."

"Now, now…Kelahya, revel in your deeds. Look at Tzalina."

"She's dead. I killed her. But…no…she was already dead. Kronos killed her."

"Kelahya, you killed her. Enjoy your revenge. Embrace the experience, the cold deliberateness with which you slipped the cord around Tzalina's neck. Relish how you tightened the cord. Pay homage to your triumph. Her terror when she stared back at you, and how you savored watching her witness her own death. Let your body enjoy how you tightened your grip until you had extracted every last breath from her, and how your hands strained with the effort, unwilling to relent."

"Yes, I see that…I enjoyed that…"

"You killed them both."

"No, I—"

"You killed them both."

"Not Kronos, I didn't—"

"You killed them both."

An unfamiliar surge of energy penetrated her soul. She felt soiled, hideous, and unclean. The sense of repugnance deepened, and with blinding pain, something snapped inside her.

The canvas of her mind tore and slipped into darkness.

Awareness returned when she stepped over the inert body of Kronos and activated the hygiene array to eliminate all biosigns of her presence in Hu's chambers.

After a moment, with a coldness that surprised even her own mind, she tossed Tzalina's corpse over her shoulder. She glared at Kronos for one last time, then activated the particle transporter and materialized inside her vessel.

She dumped Tzalina's body into the turbine of the vessel. Upon ignition, it disintegrated her body and, as she took off from planet Za, eradicated every last atom of the viper Tzalina.

She traveled through space, her mind locked in an incessant repetitive loop, projecting images beyond reason. Her unraveling psyche had taken over and now controlled her. Her will was not her own. Her mind had revealed what she'd suspected all along but had chosen to ignore. Everyone in Kronos' inner circle knew the Director enjoyed slipping away to secret destinations, supposedly in an effort to thwart the endless threats against his life. But more likely, he'd disappeared to seek pleasures of the flesh with Tzalina and perhaps with many others.

He had betrayed her all along.

But part of her refused to believe it was true, as if someone had invaded her, implanting visions of filth. Someone had shattered her beliefs, her emotions, and her trust.

Who?

"Someone who knew he'd visit Tzalina."

Kronos had created a security environment so convoluted that even those closest to him never had the exact location of his movements. These precautions were necessary for the sake of all. Covering his trail with false ones ensured that he could only be found if he wished to. Only Zenubus, Maccabeus, and Kelahya had the intelligence of his whereabouts, but never all three at the same time, only two.

Clever, very clever, her mind laughed with a sarcastic slant. *So, what did he plan this time?*

"Kronos probably sent Zenubus halfway across the galaxy on some useless mission while he believes me to be on Uxiel. Maccabeus remains on the Olympus."

But why order Maccabeus to change my mission and send me to Za?

"Unless…he didn't."

Maccabeus did it all on his own?

"Yes, he wanted me to discover Kronos' treachery."

But why? Is he trying to turn me against Kronos? Is this all a ploy?

"Yes. It makes perfect sense."

Before you gave yourself to Kronos, he bragged about his escapades, how he would disappear to enjoy the pleasures of the flesh.

"But he told me all of that resided in the past and that he needed no one but me."

And you believed him.

"I didn't sense he was lying to me. I believed him faithful."

What a fool. He's been visiting Tzalina all along, even while you risked your life for him. He betrayed you. That's why you killed him.

"Impossible!" she screamed. "He loves me. I didn't do what you say I did. I didn't kill him. I didn't. He couldn't betray me. Tzalina was executed long ago. This is all a trick. Someone went inside my mind and planted all these images."

I am your mind. Murderer!

"No! Get out!"

She attempted to seal her mind, but it refused. In a desperate effort to distance herself from it all, she changed from thrusters to hyper speed, leaving the planet Za far, far behind.

She leaned back, closed her eyes, and attempted to sooth her true mind.

* * * * * *

Kelahya bolted up, a cold sweat covering her body, her breathing coming in rapid bursts. A glance about the chamber told her she remained in the golden cage. Nestor's prisoner.

Lies! All of it is a lie! Nestor is a lie! Kronos death is a lie!

She clamped her hands over her ears in an attempt to silence her inner voice, but to no avail. The words echoed through her, each repetition a knife to her soul.

"Stop! Stop, stop!"

Get a hold of yourself! Master your emotions. Fill yourself with the thought of escape. If you stay here, you will die. We will dissociate and we will die.

As she had countless time in her recent past, she slowed her heartbeat and her breathing until, at long last she regained control. She wiped the sweat away with the sheet and regained her determination.

The time to flee is now.

She obeyed and quickly got dressed. She hoped that the impression of emptiness in her senses meant that Nestor was at rest. He would not expect her to escape, and the reason was simple, she had not permitted her mind to entertain such a plan… until now.

In complete silence, she traversed the hallways and made her way to the stalactite garden. As she approached the cavern garden of mineral waters, she formulated an escape plan. With cat-like stealth she moved around the periphery of the garden until she reached the opening she had spotted earlier. Once again, she felt the slight difference in temperature. Carefully, she stepped between the stalagmites toward the aperture, and slithered through, chasing the slight draft that swept through the narrow space. It was tight for someone her size, but she persisted and managed to squeeze through. With expert efficiency and avoiding injury from the rough crystals, other than snags and scratches, she advanced.

The blackness gradually gave way to increasing light. Her heart began to beat in anticipation, and she pushed on faster. At last, she came to the end, and with one last thrust, exited the crevice.

It took her a moment to adjust to the light and take in the surroundings. She found herself in a small anteroom illuminated by a bright light in the ceiling. It had one door to Kelahya's left, and directly in front of her, a ramp leading to another narrower door. The closest door led to a storage unit filled with equipment and materials she surmised were used for the maintenance of the crystalline garden.

"Don't tell me my big escape dead ends with the service crew… no…I don't believe so. I don't detect personnel anywhere. "

Determined to push forward, she followed the ramp toward the other door, tapped the control sensor, and pushed against it. It didn't budge. She studied the sensors and activated the control board. An instant later, a beam shot out scanning her face for identification. Realizing her escape had failed, she froze waiting for the alarms to blare and security personnel to descend upon her. To her astonishment, a moment later, the door opened.

"The scanner must've malfunctioned. Or this is another trap? What if they knew I'd try to escape, and this is all an elaborate ploy to show me I can't? I may end up locked up in here for days. So, what? Either way, I'm not going back."

She peered around the corner of the open door and into a long empty corridor. She stepped in, and immediately, the door shut behind her.

"No sensors on this side. It must be an emergency exit. Like it or not, there's no return."

The corridor slanted up. Except for her steps and her increasingly heavy breathing, the silence was absolute.

Moments later, she arrived at another door, which automatically opened as she approached.

A bright orange light momentarily blinded her, and a suffocating heat made her recoil. As her eyes adjusted, she took a deep breath and stepped through the door into the orange heat. The door closed behind her, and she instinctively turned back toward it. She stopped with the realization of her location. She pivoted toward the brightness and the heat.

"Dionysus! I'm on Dionysus…I never left. They kept me underground all this time. Nestor tricked me."

She staggered back against the wall and stood there, unable to move. The sharp pang of betrayal quickly mutated into boiling fury.

Chapter 23

The Zontirius

*Excerpt from the **Corpus Galacticum**, 137th Edition*

The **Zontirius** are descendants of the ancient **TuhtiouDenan** species of mystical healers. Their makeup is unique to all other inhabitants of the cosmos in that they possess subatomic access to the Remembrances of their ancestors. Over the millennia the Zontirius have mutated to elevated levels of mental development. Their anointed tasks are exclusively dedicated to the healing of the body and mind of all Minders in the known universe.

Their healing practices are steeped in ageless traditions that enable them to reach altered states of consciousness. Therefore, they operate within the spiritual realm to affect the physical world and restore holistic balance in their delicate patients.

The Zontirius are the only species of Level Three Minders and healers capable of entering the numerous layers of existence throughout all known dimensions to obtain solutions to problems afflicting their patients. As such, the Zontirius are revered throughout the cosmos, and their service is highly valued.

In a sudden burst, the heat from the burning Dionysian night overcame her.

Find shelter!

She scanned the horizon and rushed off at full speed toward the nearest dome in the hope of finding a city within it.

I see it clearly now, she surmised as she rushed through the burning dessert. *Maccabeus crafted the perfect plan to eliminate us both in one fell swoop. With Kronos dead and me on the run, he could take over the control of the universe. That's the memory I needed to find.*

The image of a dead Kronos flashed in front of her, and she relived how she stepped over his inert body.

Drops of perspiration trickled into her eyes, causing her to blink.

"Stop! No more images! Stay present!"

But try as she might, the open wounds in her mind and heart ran so deep that she couldn't contain the flow of images.

At every level of consciousness, Kelahya felt the sting of deceit. With Kronos it had slashed her soul. But with Nestor, it brought humiliation.

Her heart admitted no other emotion beyond anguish, and her logic recognized nothing outside of duplicity.

How could Nestor perpetrate this elaborate ruse? What prevented me from seeing through Caveat, Jofan, or any of the other humanoid crewmembers? Is my mind so polluted that it barred me from perceiving this cruel trickery?

Her internal rage intensified. She had ignored the first rule of survival—never, ever trust the enemy—distrust provides protection. Kronos had made sure she learned that right from the start. Under his orders, Zenubus had made her face deception time and time again, until distrust had become second nature to her. But that was a different time, a different place, and a different Kelahya.

"Stop this chatter! Find a safe haven!"

The sand crackled beneath her as she pushed harder. Time was of the essence. She must reach a dome before she succumbed to the deadly heat of the night.

Kronos' words seeped into her consciousness, "Breathe, Kelahya, control your breathing. The longer the distance, the more control you need."

Kronos…always Kronos.

His image kept infesting her mind, forcing her to summon all her strength to shake it free.

Kronos isn't dead. The statement reverberated through her mind. *It's all illusion. A ruse. He never betrayed me. I could never have killed him. He is my lover, my mentor, my…*

The image of Tzalina flashed into focus for an instant. The wound of betrayal bled more profusely. *How could he have lied to me?*

"Stop! If I give into this confusion, I'll die."

The void is pulling me in. Dissociation is overtaking me.

Yes, her mind agreed. *They've infected us with memories that cannot be ours. They've poisoned our thoughts to where we can't recognize the truth.*

She shook her head violently to force her thoughts to fall into place.

"I refuse to die till I uncover the truth!"

She reached the outer shell of a dome. She scanned for the nearest of the caisson entrance cylinders and headed toward it. Aware that the cylinders had multiple sets of compartments designed for controlled access, all she had to do was find the one that would fit her size and volume. After a few failed attempts, she discovered an entrance.

Moments later, she stepped safely into the dome. Within it she found a relatively minor city. Her eyes darted in all directions seeking an inviting route. Unable to decide, she chose a course on impulse and summoned enough resolve to plunge into the stream of humanoids.

She pushed on aimlessly, unaware of time, direction or purpose, her thoughts a kaleidoscope of pandemonium in search of a safe port, slowly dissociating, plunging into the inevitable void.

Her condition produced a fierce pain that increased as time went by. During her captivity she'd been free of the sting of her broken mind. Now, far from Nestor's control the excruciating throbbing had returned, and its intensity threatened her ability to remain lucid.

She had to maintain coherence between her private deliberations, and the barrage of memories and emotions that threatened to invade her weakened mind from every humanoid in close proximity. The strain on the neurons in her brain, as they fought to create a barrier from invaders, while at the same time crafting paths of understanding and logic was, on its own, an exhausting endeavor. Now, coupled with the stress of dissociation, it threatened to tear apart the very fabric of rational thinking.

The agonizing pain signified an internal alarm system designed to push a Minder into retreat in order to heal the mental wound. If unable to do so, uncontrollable fear would eventually surface. Paranoia was the classic symptom of the first stages of final dissociation. The injured mind created the most improbable scenarios and identified enemies that didn't even exist. Knowing all of this didn't make it any easier, though, and Kelahya understood that to maintain whatever coherence she possessed, she needed to retreat and find safety.

But, where to go?

Her rationale dictated that as long as she could keep track of what the symptoms were, she maintained some semblance of control.

But what is this emptiness I feel? What symptom is that?

Kronos' betrayal had caused a deep sense of rage, a desire to lash out, to harm, a need for revenge. All those emotions she could grasp. But with Nestor, it felt different—a hollow she couldn't readily understand. His deceit had created a huge cavity somewhere deep within her chest, a heavy emptiness that constrained her breathing and oppressed her heart.

This emotion, unlike any she had ever experienced, screamed out for her to evade him, to shun his treachery, but at the same time tugged at her to return to him, and damn the consequences. The incongruity bedeviled her resolve and conviction.

Nestor's essence encroached upon her mind. She felt him searching.

Nestor! Get out!

She closed her eyes and slammed her mind as tightly shut as she could.

At length, she sensed him releasing her.

To her surprise, his invasion hadn't been repugnant in any way. His presence had felt like the warm sun breaking through dark clouds on a cold, wintry day. And that was the most dangerous thing about him. His rapport with her had been gentle and all encompassing. He'd shared his entire being, and she'd cherished it. It confused her to find that, in spite of his deceit and betrayal, she felt safer with his inner company than being alone.

He's here!

In a flash, she spun about, her eyes darting in all directions, every fiber of her being tensed for action. Nestor's presence loomed with such abrupt definition that she was certain he must be close enough for her to see him.

No. He's not here. You're confused.

As her eyes searched for him, she noticed a group of Dionysians that looked very familiar. When she spotted them, they turned away. She'd seen them before, but her muddled mind could offer no help in recollecting time or place.

The familiar Dionysian faces forced her to concentrate on her surroundings. She stood in the middle of a crowded conveyer station. She had no memory of how she'd reached the station but would now make good use of it.

With increased speed, she moved at random through the crowd with unpredictable changes of pace and direction. Her actions confirmed that the Dionysian group was following her.

As discretely as she could, she searched for an exit from the conveyer station. She found one. She rushed toward it, but Caveat appeared and clamped her hand around Kelahya's arm.

"Quickly, turn right!" she barked.

"How di—"

"No time. Turn right," Caveat commanded, as she pressed her weapon into Kelahya's ribs.

With no choice but to obey, Kelahya did as she was told. Caveat pushed her into a corridor as she glanced over her shoulder.

"How did you find me?" Kelahya tried again.

"Nestor. Keep quiet and walk faster. We're being followed."

As they traveled down the corridor, Kelahya noticed the eyes of passersby pretending not to glance in her direction. Only the androids reflected true indifference to her presence. She realized that she'd missed all these signs of danger.

The corridor emptied into the passenger egression zone. The exit doors were open, and Caveat steered her toward them.

As they were about to go through, a regulator android blocked their way. His hard, metallic hand clamped onto Kelahya's arm. As she twisted to free herself from his grasp, she saw the group of Dionysians rushing toward them. She sensed, rather than saw, a humanoid presence behind her, but it was too late. As she instinctively turned her head, she felt a stab on the left side of her back.

A knife...how appropriate.

She heard herself grunt with pain. To free her arm from the android's control, she spun right, away from the blade, and in one fluid motion brought up her left foot, then slammed it down, delivering a splintering blow to her assailant's knee.

The last thing she heard was Nestor's voice screaming, "No!"

Then everything went dark.

With concern etched upon their brows, Nestor and Caveat peered at the unconscious Kelahya through the window in the observation lounge of the medical unit.

"Thank you for permitting me to be here," Caveat said, "I'm aware that in normal circumstances I wouldn't be allowed inside this type of facility."

"She likes you and trusted you. She needs those who care about her nearby."

The familiar sound of doors opening behind them permeated the anteroom, and they turned in unison. Jofan entered, accompanied by Halvorian Lembrock, the healer who had treated Kelahya's wound.

Lembrock, a Zontirius, was celebrated for her distinctive use of the Remembrances of her ancestors, all of whom were healers. Her medicinal powers, although unorthodox, were highly effective, and she was renowned for her curative miracles throughout the galaxies. Jofan had specifically requested her assistance, and she had agreed to travel to this highly classified and secure medical unit.

"I have asked Halvorian Lembrock to brief you on her patient's condition," Jofan announced.

Lembrock came to a halt next to Caveat and peered through the window. "Her physical wound is sealed, yet her mental wound, however, is wide and deep. Her mind has dissociated completely, yet somehow, she has not fallen into the void. She hovers on the verge. I don't understand how that is possible. No Remembrances exist of someone surviving in a condition like this. All have succumbed." Lembrock sounded apologetic. "That is her current status."

Caveat's forehead furrowed with concern and lack of understanding.

"Kelahya is a Minder, Officer Caveat," Lembrock clarified. "An extremely powerful one."

"I am aware that she is a Minder," Caveat said, "And as such, she should…Excuse me, I don't mean to question—"

"No need to apologize. What information do you seek?"

"Why can't she regain consciousness? What's happened to her?"

"She's displaying a hysteria not unlike Combat Syndrome in ordinary humanoids. Her mind plays, in a repetitive cycle, an adaptation of some incident, or even a series of them, over and over. For most Minders the common denominator is that the victim sees herself being unavoidably trapped, or killed, within whatever situation it is that terrorizes her. Most lose the battle when they come to believe that they are dead. A rare few, win." Lembrock's voice was not dramatic, but her concern and experience with the terror of mind dissociation had made its way into her tone.

"The physical wound," Lembrock continued, "could have been the catalyst. It set off a shock, and her body prepared to die. The simple fact is that, medically speaking, the physical wound no longer poses any danger. But her mind has yet to realize she has won the physical battle. She now needs to win the spiritual and emotional ones."

Caveat's breath made tiny circles of steam on the window as she spoke. "How long will she stay this way?"

"Impossible to say."

"But it has been so long already," Caveat complained.

The healer turned to face the three officers, resting her back against the window. "Minders are a breed apart. We understand each other, but precious little about the workings of our minds and our particular gifts and tasks. Personally, I have treated numerous Minders in dissociation, and my ancestors an equal or greater number. At the level of dissociation that she is in now, each and every time, we have asked for the assistance of another Zuntirius healer. I not only have used the Remembrances but have also utilized the guidance of my elders. All, to no avail. Officer Caveat, Minders dissociate when reality and fantasy merge and they no longer discern truth from illusion, or their own thoughts from those of others. Misperception sets in, and there is little hope that clarity can be regained."

She turned back toward her patient. "In my experience, if she could win the battle with my help and that of my ancestors alone, she would have done so by now. On the other hand, her vital signs are too stable for her to be losing. That is the dilemma. So, we are at a standstill. We must face, however, the very real possibility that her current condition is likely to be permanent."

"Termination?" Caveat gasped as she glanced at Nestor and back at the healer.

Lembrock crossed her arms and shrugged. "It could come to that. Jofan will wait until we confirm there is no possibility of recovery before he makes a decision. And I concur. There is one thing that might help."

Nestor moved around Caveat and stood so close to the healer that for an instant she feared that he might make physical contact. "What? Try anything," he said.

"Can we find someone who is…close to her, someone she trusts without question?"

Nestor glanced at Jofan.

"How about Chantall, her surrogate mother?" Caveat asked.

"She's out of reach on the *Olympus*," Jofan said.

"She needs a Minder with a highly developed Endow to help her through this," Lembrock added, "and it must be someone she trusts. Physical and verbal stimulation by someone she cares for might also help. You must find someone who could fulfill that role." Lembrock turned to glance at her patient one more time. "I'll return, later."

"Wait," Jofan took her arm and glanced at Nestor as he spoke. "Maybe there is someone."

Nestor shook his head in silent refusal.

"You are such a Minder?" Caveat asked in dismay.

Nestor nodded.

"Then do it! Help her!" Caveat exclaimed.

"She believes I've betrayed her. She hates me," Nestor answered.

"So what? We have nothing to lose. Try it. You must try it," Caveat pleaded with restrained urgency.

Nestor glanced at Kelahya then back at Jofan and Caveat. "She sees me as her enemy and a very negative element within the wound in her mind." He feared he could do more harm than good. He drew close to the glass, as if pulled by a magnet, and rested his forehead against it.

Caveat could see the flame inside him stir. If she was right—and she had no doubts—Nestor was dying to get into that room, if only to touch Kelahya.

Caveat placed a gentle hand on his arm.

The doors behind them slid open and a Dionysian appeared, the likes of which neither Caveat nor Lembrock had ever seen before.

Ducking the doorframe, the colossus crouched into the small observation chamber like a huge cloud descending on a valley before a storm. His eyes focused instantly on the window that looked into Kelahya's room. His voice, little more than a whisper, sounded like distant thunder.

"I am aware of her status. I'm angry." The statement vibrated through the air and permeated all.

Caveat started a move to intercept the giant when she caught a glimpse of Nestor raising a hand in a signal of reassurance.

The healer struggled to find her voice, "I—" Her eyes darted from the giant, to Nestor, then to Jofan seeking an explanation.

"You're free to leave, Healer," the Dionysian said. "I'm thankful for what you have done."

Lembrock was happy to oblige and quickly rushed out the door.

The giant moved closer to the window, bending down to see in, his face almost touching the glass.

A silence hung in the room as the giant gazed with sadness upon Kelahya in a battle with her demons to the death.

Jofan broke the tension by initiating introductions, "Sir, this is Captain Lyndsor Caveat," he said, nodding toward the petite officer. Then, nodding toward the giant, he looked at Caveat and said with grand formality, "This is his Excellency, Supreme Commander Nestor, Spiritual Leader, Scribe of the Incorporeal Fellowship, Warden of the Talderon Ideals."

The giant nodded as Caveat's mouth open and her eyes widened. She dropped to one knee, her head bowed.

"Please stand. No need for ceremony," the Spiritual Leader whispered.

His demeanor changed as he turned to Nestor. "Namesake, grave disappointing of me. How do you permit?" he said in Eniat.

As Nestor was about to respond, Caveat took a tiny, but decisive step in the giant's direction.

"It was my fault, your Eminence," she managed to say through a dry mouth. "It was my watch. Nestor had departed the dwell to attend to…well…I…well, I didn't expect her to escape. She'd given no signs of wanting to run away. The emergency door sensors somehow recognized her epidermal imprint." She dropped her head, attempting to hide the tears that started trickling down her cheeks. "Nestor is not to blame. It was he who finally located her."

She glanced at Jofan for support. He had none to offer.

"I was closest and tried to bring her back." Caveat ran her dry tongue across her even drier lips. "The attack came from the rear while I was covering the front."

"I understand."

Even though he listened calmly, Caveat felt as if the thunder of his voice grew louder. She felt obliged to earn the culpability of her actions.

"There were five assailants," she went on. "Three Dionysians and two Terrians. Once they hit their mark, they attempted to disperse. Kelahya eliminated her own assailant before she fainted. The rest have been detained."

The giant nodded as his eyes shifted from Caveat to Nestor.

"There are no excuses," Nestor whispered. "I should've anticipated—"

"I understand," the Dionysian interrupted. "Wait here." They moved aside as he stepped between them. He touched the entrance panel and the door to Kelahya's room slid open. He squeezed through, and the door closed behind him.

Jofan, Nestor, and Caveat watched as the huge figure crossed to the bed and sat next to Kelahya. He reached for her hand and cradled it in his.

"Why is he here?" Caveat managed to ask. "What—"

Jofan raised his hand to stop the questions. "His universal name is Nestor, but his birth name is Modyor Devon. He is Kelahya's father."

Chapter 24

Prophecy

———◆———

*Excerpt from the **Corpus Galacticum**, 137th Edition*

*The Scriptures assert the existence of an imperishable **Creator** of all things in the cosmos, eternal, omniscient, and omnipresent.*

The Creator's divine message is conveyed through the Clerics of the Incorporeal Fellowship who are anointed with divine vision and are the prophetic predictors.

The Scriptures manifest that the Clerics rely upon an underlying divine order whereby they can predict sensitive dependence between simple systems and complex organisms.

It is written that the relationship between astronomical phenomena and the events that affect the cosmos consists of celestial cycles of divine communication.

Due to its transcendental origin, prophecy is founded on absolute veracity, is eternal, and is regarded as sacred and holy.

Kelahya traveled on a cruiser, the likes of which she'd never experienced. The open halls were shrouded in fog and converged on a command bridge where only a black mist was visible. A familiar presence hid in the mist.

"Da!" she cried out. Her voice was childlike even though her body was her own. "Da!" she heard herself call out again.

The only response was an almost inaudible laugh, like a frightening whisper, that echoed along an endless labyrinth of corridors.

The mist stirred and a cloud floated into the control room, which had now taken on the character of a habitat dwell. As the mist dispersed, a boy stood before her. It was he who laughed.

The control panels that should be at the child's right had metamorphosed into a bed, a setting complete with evening lighting and drinks in long-stem glasses. The child sat upon the bed and beckoned with his little hand for Kelahya to join him.

She fought to resist him. She had to escape. She turned to run, but somehow, her feet were far too heavy to do more than drag an inch at a time. She reached for the command chair at her right and pulled herself along with agonizing slowness. Escape was not an option.

She heard the chilling laughter and spun around. A naked Kronos stood before her, laughing in a cruel tone. He beckoned to her.

"Release me!" she yelled with all her might, yet her words floated away, soft and unimportant.

Kronos patted the bed beside him, a lascivious grin across his face. He laughed, but now his laughter came with the usual seductive tenor. It beckoned her. Unable to maintain her grip on the chair, she felt herself sucked along the floor and into his arms.

With tears erupting from her eyes, she feared his loathsome embrace. When it came, it felt far different than expected.

"I love you, Kelahya," he whispered.

And her heart melted.

The boy stood at her side and whispered, "He's lying. It's a trick. Kronos will lie, as he always has. He'll stop at nothing to get what he wants. And he wants you."

In a flash of rage, she pushed the child away.

Nestor's gentle face appeared before her.

She gasped.

He smiled and kissed her forehead. "Smile for me," he said. And she did. And he chuckled with that alluring contagious joy that was uniquely his. Reassuringly, he pulled her to him. As she relaxed into his embrace, a knife stabbed her back and she screamed. She struggled to break loose, but there was no escape from his powerful grip. He'd tricked her into trusting him, and then stabbed her.

Nestor laughed, and as he did, he became Kronos, then Nestor, then Kronos again.

Then, there was only the black mist.

An instant later, the dream started again—the command bridge, the halls, the mist. The laugh. The fear. The void.

Kelahya clawed at the command chair in an attempt to escape the child, and in a distant corner of her psyche, she realized that it would all start again.

But something changed. She felt arms around her, a gentle voice, and an unfamiliar stabbing pain on her back. A voice reached out to her from one of the mist-filled corridors, like a storm in the distance.

"Kelahya." The voice was soft and deep.

Something touched her arm. She spun around, ready to fight, but there was only mist.

"Kelahya." The safe voice called again. "Come to me." The voice spoke in Eniat, the language of her birthplace. Familiar. She could trust it. She dashed blindly down one of the corridors into a mist that led to nowhere.

"Is Mody, my little one…I am come so to take you home."

In a burst of light, she found herself outside her childhood home. It stood in ruins, smoke pouring through the door and windows.

Someone dressed all in black and wearing a helmet with a visor shield took her by the shoulders. Behind the shield she could make out a face, and upon the face, a smile. It was Kronos.

She struggled in a fruitless effort to escape from this deceit. Kronos had mocked her again pretending to be her father.

She screamed with all her might, "Release me!"

Without releasing her, the figure began to shift away, its arms stretching to keep her in his grasp. Darkness swallowed the image, and through a black mist she saw Kronos holding her tightly against him, his naked body intertwined with hers, his kisses, and his caresses possessively drawing her to him. She felt herself lulled into the full enjoyment of the moment.

Then, in an instant of searing pain, all sensations of pleasure stopped, and she felt the ache of recognition penetrate her heart—Kronos was not making love to her, he was making love to Tzalina.

She fled through the corridors of her mind, screaming to exorcise the agony of betrayal.

"Come to me, Kelahya. Home of us is here," the calming voice called out.

"Where comes it from? How I to find?" she heard herself ask in Eniat.

Kelahya, in her chamber on the *Olympus,* calmly paced back and forth. Kronos, in full splendor, approached her, his arms beckoning. He bent to kiss her lips, as he had bent to kiss Tzalina. She could sense the lust in his eyes and felt the knot in her throat. His lips came closer and closer to her, but before they could touch hers, a mouthful of vipers spewed out.

The boy appeared at her side. "He lusts for Tzalina, not you," he whispered. "Take your laser knife and use it."

Her right hand darted up, and the laser knife slashed Kronos' throat. His body dropped to the floor, eyes wide with surprise.

"Murderer," he said, his voice a deathly rattle.

Kelahya, the knife clutched in her hand, stood immobile, watching him. "No, not me," she whispered.

Kronos locked his eyes on hers as he twitched his way toward death. The black mist rolled in and swallowed his body, then wrapped around her, and lifted her upward.

As the mist dissipated and with cold deliberateness, Kelahya slipped a cord around Tzalina's neck. She tightened the cord, savoring the moment as Tzalina died. Smiling, Kelahya watched her until every last breath had been extracted.

"Kelahya," said the gentle familiar voice that called out to her, "time for calming now. Is Mody, my little one. Come to me."

She was back in the command center. She looked for the source of the voice in all directions, and the room began to spin, only to be stopped by the arrival of the black mist. Then, the black mist gave way to a dazzling light, making it impossible to see with any clarity.

"Come to me, my little one," the voice called out again.

"I cannot find you," she screamed, as she ran into the empty corridor.

The black mist enveloped her. It was thicker this time, but she rushed into the darkness with an abandon fed by panic and self-preservation. Once again, she traveled on a cruiser, and the corridors, which converged on the command bridge, all opened into the black mist. This familiarity of sorts offered an odd comfort. This was a dream and soon she would emerge from the foggy corridors.

Tzalina and Kronos appeared, hand in hand. They walked toward her, laughing, kissing, and toying with each other.

Then, Nestor emerged from another corridor also laughing, his arms outstretched to her.

Jofan and his androids followed him. Then Caveat with the two gladiators appeared.

This time Kelahya couldn't move. Her feet had melted into the floor of the ship. "Help!" she screamed.

"Kelahya. Not to fear. All well. Come, my child," the gentle voice called to her.

A flash of light blinded her. When it subsided, she stood alone, trembling, crying.

"Kelahya. It is Mody, my little one. It is Da. Is time for calming. This dream to end now. Come. I am here, little one. Come to Da."

Her eyes flashed open.

The bright light of the medical unit blinded her for an instant then he saw a kind and familiar face.

She screamed, "Da!"

"Yes, it is I," her father answered as he held her in his arms.

Her uncontrollable sobs came in rapid succession, her throat throbbed, and her back was on fire.

"The dream to no longer have. The fear to have no more. Calm is now to have."

A profound sense of relief flowed through her body infused with comforting warmth.

Modyor kissed his daughter's forehead and lowered her back onto the bed. "To sleep now it is time." He placed his hands around her temples, and eased her into a dreamless, natural, curative sleep.

Kelahya slept undisturbed for three days, her body healing her physical wounds with surprising efficiency. When at last she opened her eyes, they met her father's loving gaze.

Wrapped in each other's arms and without a word, they both allowed the stream of tears to flow uninterrupted for several minutes.

The giant's shoulders heaved as he enveloped her in his protection. "Kelahya, my child," Modyor whispered, then leaned to kiss her forehead and wet cheeks. He eased her back and wrapped his huge hands around hers with reassuring comfort.

Kelahya, unable to find words, let her tears speak. As smiles gradually replaced the tears, Kelahya found her voice at last.

"Da…you alive, I knew," she said in Eniat.

Modyor nodded.

"Ma?"

Modyor's eyes saddened as he shook his head.

She sighed, before asking, "How to find me? Where this place?"

Modyor smiled and nodded toward Nestor, Caveat, and Jofan, standing a prudent distance away.

Kelahya recoiled instinctively and looked at Modyor, uncomprehending.

"Worry not, my child. One we are." Modyor patted her hands, wishing to ease her apprehension.

"One?" she questioned.

Modyor called for Nestor. As he approached her bedside, her resentment was palpable. He stopped and gave Modyor an inquisitive glance. When the old man nodded reassuringly, Nestor pressed on.

"Kelahya," Nestor ventured, "it's my honor to introduce the one you refer to as the legendary Nestor, most appropriately addressed as is His Excellency Nestor Hathan, Supreme Spiritual Leader and Scribe of the Incorporeal Fellowship. He is celebrated by the seekers of freedom as the Warden of the Talderon Ideals, and is known to you as Modyor Devon, husband of Tenecia Loran, and father of Kelahya Devona."

Kelahya's eyes widened in disbelief. Modyor shrugged.

"I don't understand. Why the deception? Why—"

Modyor's huge fingers gently touched his daughter's lips. "Explain we give. No deception. Protection, caution. Worry you bait in trap." He turned to the others.

"Namesake remain. Others all go." He kissed her on the forehead one more time and started to leave the room with Caveat and Jofan.

"Da," she called out to him.

Modyor smiled at his daughter, and speaking in Eniat said, "Namesake for explain. I later return." He ushered everyone out of the room.

Kelahya turned to him with a cross and baffled look upon her face.

He shrugged. "Your father feels that, since I am the one who seeks your forgiveness, it's my duty to offer the explanations. A duty I am only too glad to perform." He waited for a sign to continue. When she gave none, he pressed on. "Please allow me to introduce myself properly. My birth name is Artyrus Druidiam. I am not permitted to tell you my titles or anointed tasks as of yet, but in time they will become clear to you. Please believe that we never intended to put you through all this. We didn't anticipate what—"

"We? Anticipate? Intend? Start from the beginning. I'm not grasping all of this, I'm—"

Artyrus placed his hand lightly on hers, and the familiar tremor overtook them both. She didn't pull away, and with her hand cradled in his, he began.

"I will do my best to explain," he said in a gentle tone. "As I mentioned earlier, we've been protecting you. Your father has been watching over you and he—"

"Watching over me?" Kelahya interrupted.

"He shielded you as much as he could. Sometimes directly, but mainly through us."

"Us?"

"The Incorporeal Fellowship."

Kelahya's expression became more perplexed with each new revelation.

"Let me try it this way. The attack on your parents we…didn't anticipate. To our dismay, Kronos somehow mastered the ability to close his mind to the universe—a feat not ordained nor prescribed by his lineage. With that faculty under control, he then selected the perfect killer, Tzalina. The use of Tzalina was flawless, given that she was ignorant of whom she was attacking or why. With Kronos shielded, we didn't foretell her actions—"

"We?" Kelahya looked perplexed

"The Fellowship. It's our charge to ensure that the continuum remains as predicted. We felt responsible for the alteration in the continuum, and our inability to prevent it."

"Kronos was predicted?"

"Yes, just as your father was. But Kronos' actions were not. Therefore, we needed to do what we could, within the spiritual mandate under which we operate, to restore order. Throughout your life, your father has maintained a subtle presence in your mind. In part, to protect you, and in part to prevent you from sensing his existence."

"Why?"

"Kronos has been very thorough. He began manipulating your mind long before you met him. Your father couldn't make direct contact with you, mentally or physically, without risking your life, and his own. It was critical for your survival as a child, and while your mind was untrained, that you believed that both your parents were dead. Kronos had to be convinced of their extermination, so your indoctrination couldn't be interfered with or halted."

At the word *indoctrination*, Kelahya turned away from Artyrus, hoping to hide the pain it caused.

Artyrus continued, "But little by little, through your father's subtle intervention you began to perceive his existence, at least in your subconscious. You even searched for him during some of your missions. Somehow you understood the truth at some very deep level of your mind, and you managed to conceal that from Kronos. After the Surina incident occurred, Kronos sensed that you knew more. He realized that you were keeping something from him, and that he no longer controlled your entire mind. He stepped up his mind-control over you and everything became blurred for us, making it much more complicated to reach you."

"That's when he changed," she whispered.

"It also made it difficult for us to ascertain your true intentions when you arrived on Dionysus. Those secret corners of your mind were unreachable, even for us. We knew you only as a very astute and tenacious soldier, and the most powerful weapon of Kronos Deucarrion." He paused for a moment.

His pull was strong. She turned to him and the magic of his eyes tugged at her heart. She made no attempt to control it, opting instead to let the sensation flow.

Artyrus remained motionless, allowing the current of her emotions to permeate him. He tightened his grip on her hand in gentle acknowledgement.

"Thank you," he whispered.

A smile was her response.

They remained silent for a while, permitting themselves, for the first time, to freely experience the luxury of trust.

She urged him to continue. "Why the deception?"

"We had no choice. You surprised us in the cave. When we probed your mind, it shocked us to find that you believed you had killed Kronos. We weren't prepared for that. Our only recourse was to isolate you. If it turned out to be true, our main course of action would've been your protection. But if, on the other hand, you were a deliberate plant, and Kronos was manipulating you, the ramifications and significance were terrifying. The fact that you were experiencing mind dissociation, made that determination impossible. In effect, your capture presented us with an insolvable dilemma."

He paused for a moment, allowing Kelahya to analyze the situation they had been faced with.

"But why pretend we were elsewhere?"

"If you believed you were succeeding in your quest, it's reasonable that your mind would become more accessible, as in fact it did. It also provided us with extra time to sift through your memories. We didn't know with certainty how much control Kronos had over your mind. Was he guiding every step you took, or was it your need of him that kept him so much alive in your thoughts?"

"You're a Transmutant, certainly you could've—"

"No. I couldn't. You were already dissociating when you came to us. You didn't trust me—with good reason, I may add—and without your permission I cannot alter your being. And there were…some additional factors…less destructive, yet nonetheless, troublesome."

"What factors?"

He searched for the right words fearing that what he said might result in her withdrawing from him. But there was only one way to say it. "You may find it hard to accept, in view of our short acquaintance, but I have feelings for you," he said at last.

Kelahya smiled.

"That fact," Artyrus continued, "made my relationship with you even more precarious and vulnerable."

Kelahya took a deep breath, then nodded and closed her eyes. "Have you confirmed Kronos' death? Did I really kill him?"

Artyrus' eyes rested on her lovely face. He shook his head as he spoke, "We have no official confirmation. He hasn't been seen in public since you left the command vessel and his brain patterns are inaccessible."

Kelahya glanced up at him through weary eyes.

"This phenomenon is normal," Artyrus said. "Attempts to penetrate his mind have been fruitless for decades, so we have no way of making telepathic confirmation. Kronos has appointed himself Scribe for the Incorporeal Fellowship and, has mastered the ability to close his mind to us. In part, this is required of his position when conducting the matters of the Fellowship, but he has expanded it to all aspects of his life. His mental development has surpassed Level Four. He's not a Transmutant, but he has evolved far beyond his anointed status."

Artyrus remained silent for a few moments, Kelahya's hand in his.

"Was it Kronos' men that attacked me? I recognized them from somewhere."

Artyrus shook his head with embarrassment. "They were our men. A random assault, simple bad luck, actually. They recognized you as Kronos' right hand and wanted you dead. They followed you for hours. That may be why you recognized them. You saw them often enough as they tracked you. Once, when I entered your mind to locate you, I saw them in your subconscious. I attempted to warn you, but you refused to listen. Understandably, you didn't trust me. I'm sorry for what has happened."

"I'm not. Not now. At least I am here, with my father. And you."

Artyrus smiled, his deep gray eyes alive with affection.

Kelahya returned the smile and closed her eyes. Within moments, he felt her hand relax into the warmth of peaceful sleep. Quietly, he bent over her, and softly placed his lips on hers.

Chapter **25**

Mind Fusion Techniques

———◆———

*Excerpt from the **Corpus Galacticum**, 137th Edition*

*While the precise origins of **Mind Fusion** techniques are not known with certainty, historian **Lorenus** writes of evidence that the ancient Tuhtiou Denan were familiar with rudimentary techniques. The earliest Mind Fusion techniques recorded in the **Annals of Inquiry** predate the second millennia, yet the descriptions are far from illustrative.*

As of the 4th Century TE, the Zontirius have codified and recorded Mind Fusion events, resulting in a multiplicity of methodologies. By their nature, Mind Fusing techniques vary according to the species and level of the afflicted Minder.

When two minds fuse, unless each possesses concordant elements of diffusion, they might shatter. Incongruity can cause them to traverse at differing rates resulting in stress fractures where the minds deviate.

However, it is recorded that the Zontirius healers have applied a technique—termed Mind Fusion Spectrum— where minds with certain discordant elements can be

311

fused without fear of destruction. Although in Spectrum the minds will experience differing rates of expansion, the Zontirius have ensured fortification by utilizing a higher-level Minder as the guide within the Fusion. In doing so, the two polarizing healers can observe any potential stressors. As a result, the problematic areas of tension can therefore be addressed before the minds shatter.

If a majority is to be found amongst the recorded Mind Fusing techniques, it is the Stacking methodology, consisting on layering thin sheets of memories, one on top of the other with simple images. The stack is then manipulated until the separate pieces begin to bond together and eventually the afflicted Minder is capable of reliving the traumatic moment when the fissure of the mind took place.

Once the moment of fissure is relived, the wound begins to heal, the event horizon is averted, and mental balance can be achieved.

Although Kelahya had recovered from the injury to her body, her mind was still unhealed. She remained uncertain as to what had actually occurred—her psyche unable to accept Kronos' betrayal and murder.

The one remaining hope to heal her mind depended on the application of the highly perilous Mind Fusion Spectrum. Lembrock felt uneasy about this uncommon practice and knew from experience that searching for truth in a Minder's dissociating mind could be a dangerous proposition at best, and possibly fatal to both patient and healer. Yet, having exhausted all other alternatives, Lembrock reluctantly gave her consent.

She had, in the earliest days of her novitiate, witnessed the death of a Minder who, halfway through the Mind Fusion, had plunged into the void, his mind destroyed beyond any possible recovery. An agonizing and violent spiral of living decay followed, as synapse by synapse, his brain disconnected itself from every organ and tissue over a period of weeks. The Zontirius healer who Lembrock had assisted had come dangerously close to meeting his own doom. Lembrock had avoided similar results with other Minders in full dissociation, but her curative Remembrances told her of others who had suffered the same fate.

Healing the dissociated mind through Mind Fusion was a highly delicate process, requiring the Minder to face the truth, and relive the traumatic moment that had caused the fissure. Given Kelahya's powerful mind, and its degree of dissociation, Lembrock feared a violent reaction to the moment of truth. Most of all, she feared causing the death of the Warden's daughter.

Furthermore, and to add to Lembrock's reticence, was the matter of who would assist her during the procedures. Artyrus had been chosen for the task, and since she could not be told of his true nature, she felt decidedly insecure. She sensed that Artyrus was a powerful Minder but felt uncertain of his inner strength and ability to withstand the pressure of performing the technique, especially given his young age. She would've preferred for an elder Zontirius healer to join her, or better yet, for Modyor to lead the fusion—after all he was the Scribe of the Incorporeal Fellowship and the young woman's father. But to her surprise, Modyor had refused the presence of another healer, and instead, had designated Artyrus. The young man was overjoyed with the assignment, and when Kelahya accepted his presence, Lembrock finally acquiesced. Only when all the players were in agreement, did Modyor offered his assistance.

The event itself was steeped in tradition and ritual. Over the millennia, the Zontirius had found it more effective and comforting to carry out their proceedings wrapped in the trappings of a spiritual ceremony. After all, spiritual wholeness was central to their existence. Mind Fusions were conducted in the Mindheal temples, which were sparse by design, and adorned with firebrush wreaths around their periphery and on the altar in the center.

Modyor would not allow his daughter to travel, so her presence in a Mindheal temple was out of the question. Therefore, on the day of Kelahya's Mind Fusion, one of the largest rooms in the medical unit had been transformed into a Mindheal sanctuary, and resourcefully furnished as such.

Modyor and Artyrus wore the crimson robes of the Mindheal ceremony and took their places at each side of the altar, while Lembrock stood solemnly at the head.

Upon Lembrock's signal, the firebrush wreaths were lit and a heavy silence descended over the proceedings. Moments later, the large doors opened and four Zontirius disciples entered with metered step, carrying a starlit frond stretcher upon which lay the motionless Kelahya.

Modyor felt a shudder of apprehension at the sight of his daughter veiled from head to toe. His dread was quelled almost instantly by Artyrus' gentle reassurance in his mind.

The disciples placed Kelahya on the altar and stood to one side of the large room.

Lembrock ran her hands over the thin white veil that covered Kelahya's body. Then, she signaled Artyrus and Modyor to each place their hands on the woman's arms. Lembrock herself placed her hands upon Kelahya's brow and hummed the ancient chant.

And so, it began.

With expert softness, Artyrus' mind fused with Kelahya's. She offered no resistance. He painted her mind with the colors of love and reassurance. When he felt that Kelahya was ready, he brought Modyor inside his daughter's mind. Modyor calmly entered the bond.

As Lembrock eased into the Fusion, the vast mental power emanating from the two men stunned her. Their dominance represented a new experience for her, and she instinctively pulled back. However, Artyrus' temperate coaxing helped her understand the necessity for her presence.

For his part, Artyrus' admiration for Modyor increased as he felt his mental supremacy. Never had he experienced the force of Modyor's mind to the degree the giant now allowed. Clearly Modyor's abilities transcended all other Level Four Minders that had ever lived in the universe and came extremely close to those of a Transmutant.

Their minds melded with ease and comfort, as though the universe itself had embraced them. Lembrock found her presence reduced to that of an observer, her Minding abilities too limited to match the subtleties of the other two.

Once Artyrus ascertained that Kelahya felt comfortable with their presence, he initiated the journey.

Artyrus' dominant authority permeated her being, and Kelahya awed at his power. His serenity and spiritual peace flowed through her, emanating a brilliant hue—brightness unlike any she'd ever experienced, and clearly the source of his Endow.

The presence of her father added to her sense of security and comfort, allowing her to move forward with confidence, and confront her demons without fear.

At that moment, she knew she would return from this journey.

Kelahya allowed herself to be guided without resistance. She delved into the exploration of her mind, sifting effortlessly through her memories and emotions, retaining those that were real, and dismissing all implanted or false images, with the ease of a child discarding unwanted toys.

She soon realized that the sensations caused by pleasant memories lingered far longer than unpleasant ones. Thus, armed with the comfort of absolute safety, she confronted Kronos. She saw his manipulation of her soul, the indoctrination of her mind, and domination of her senses. She understood how he had gained total mastery of her being and grasped the subtlety of his strategy to web his control over her. The gentleness of his initial approach, the first invasion of her mind where he introduced desire, the constant images he'd projected into her until her entire being was under his control. She saw, understood, and accepted.

Her mind sighed with relief.

Time came to confront the final truth. Without resistance, she relived her visit to the planet Za. She saw herself concealed in the shadows behind the silk curtains of Tzalina's quarters, watching Kronos kiss the villain she'd hated, and believed dead for so long.

Fear pulled her back, and she tried to close her mind to the memory, unwilling to witness the betrayal and live through the agony again. But the reassuring presence of her father and Artyrus, their hands gently touching hers, held her firm.

With new resolve, she faced the truth, and allowed the past to replay itself.

"I'm here, Tzalina." She heard Kronos' impatient tone. "Why did you summon me? I have little time to waste."

Kelahya noted her own surprise at his cold attitude—she had forgotten that.

Then, Kronos walked away from Tzalina, wiping his lips in disgust. She'd also forgotten his repulsion.

Kelahya observed her own puzzled look and remembered the confusion she'd experienced wondering why he'd kissed the viper, if he despised her so.

"No longer interested, my Lord? You used to like when I—"

"Let's not go through that again," Kronos snapped.

"Your kiss, I—"

"A confirmation of my distaste. Nothing more."

"That child who shares your bed has softened you. Have you lost your taste for—"

"Enough! What do you require of me?"

Kelahya saw Tzalina strut toward him and caress his chest. "You were in the vicinity…so I sought to introduce you to your son."

The shock wave that had run through Kelahya at that moment emerged with renewed vigor, causing her to shake uncontrollably. Artyrus and Modyor spread their reassurance all around her like a cocoon, transferring warmth and a sense of calm. Lembrock's gentle hand resting on her forehead, appeased her body, soothing her fear. The convulsions subsided, and the memories continued.

She observed Kronos clench Tzalina's arm and twist it back forcing her to drop to the floor. "What?" he shouted.

"We have a son. His name is Sutekh. Sutekh Deucarrion."

"Impossible." Kronos threw Tzalina to one corner of the room. "I am not in the mood for your schemes."

"Not a scheme, my Lord. A fact." Tzalina shook her head letting her green hair fall freely about her. She smiled coquettishly, and slowly rose to face him. "Yes, we have a son."

"You and I cannot procreate. Have you kept alive an abomination?" Kronos yelled.

"Abomination? No, my Lord, far from it." She moved toward Kronos, her blue lips stretched into a foul smile. "Our failed experiments in crossbreeding species did produce hideous creatures. But, then again, there's no one like you in the universe, so…imagine my surprise when I bore you a perfect son who has grown into a glorious specimen, whose powers may even surpass your own."

Kronos' hands locked around Tzalina's neck. "What have you done?"

"Bore you a son you'll be proud of. A son that will—"

"Release her, Father." The voice came from directly behind Kronos. He spun around, Tzalina dangling under his grip.

Before him stood a strapping Kayroan male boasting a strong Dionysian body. He had brown crisscrossed skin, deep blue eyes, hair as black as charcoal, and a caustic smile.

He calmly placed one hand on Kronos and, with a look of pure disdain, uttered a threat veiled as a suggestion. "You should release my mother."

Kronos dropped Tzalina.

Without releasing Kronos, Sutekh added, "Before you deny me as your own, let me share my birth with you, Father."

For a moment Kronos' eyes glazed over, and his body slackened.

Kelahya realized that Sutekh had marched into his mind.

A moment later, Kronos snapped the link and struck Sutekh with the back of his hand. "I may have contributed to your birth, but you are no son of mine!"

Kelahya caught a mere glimpse of the laser knife before it sliced Kronos' throat. Blood erupted from the open wound and his knees buckled. Perplexed, his eyes sought the source of the strike.

"Sutekh!" Tzalina screamed. "What have you done?"

Kelahya sprung from her hiding place and, in one swift action, lunged at Sutekh and discharged her weapon.

Sutekh's chest burst open, and his body crashed against the wall with the impact of Kelahya's blast.

Tzalina pounced on Kelahya, bit her hand, wrenched the weapon from her, and sent it flying.

With Artyrus and Modyor at her side, Kelahya witnessed her own dexterity as she pinned Tzalina down to the floor, yanked the cord that held garment together, and wrapped it around her throat. With deep satisfaction, she relived the moment when she tightened the cord and watched Tzalina struggle for breath.

"Can you see me, Tzalina? It is I, Kelahya. You die at my hands. I have killed your son. Your monstrous offspring is no more. Feel the agony of loss. The agony I felt as a child."

She watched Tzalina's eyes bulge, both from the pressure around her neck and the rage that erupted from within.

Kelahya relived the pleasure of squeezing the cord tighter and tighter, until Tzalina's last breath escaped her body. Even then, her grip did not relent, a lifetime of repressed hatred refusing to let go.

The intensity of her emotions had masked her senses, and she now understood why she hadn't noticed Sutekh approach her from behind.

He'd smacked her head and flung her off his mother's corpse.

As she saw her own stunned body trying to pull itself together, she felt the need to step in and save Kelahya, save herself from Sutekh.

Artyrus' voice held her back. *You cannot alter the past. You can only relive it, witness it, and accept it.*

A thick, black, putrid liquid oozed between Sutekh's fingers as he gripped the wound on his chest closed. The smirk on his face reemerged slowly as he stood over Tzalina. He kicked her body several times to confirm his mother's death, then turned to Kelahya with a smile that emanated from the depths of hell itself. "Well done, Kelahya. You've been a great help."

She bolted to her feet and reached for Sutekh's wound, but he averted her lunge and pounded the back of her head with his fist. She landed face down on the floor.

Sutekh straddled her into immobility, his free hand pinning down her head, the smirk even more pronounced. "Now, Kelahya let's become acquainted with one another."

She shivered as she witnessed how he reached into her mind and gnarled its insides, the piercing pain debilitating her into submission.

With unrelenting horror, she watched Sutekh relish in ecstasy, as time and again, he violated her mind.

Protected by her father and Artyrus, Kelahya relived how she'd plummeted toward the event horizon, the void devouring every fiber of her being.

She recognized her determination not to die, and with a burst of energy, discharged from the depths of her soul, forced Sutekh to release his hold.

As she writhed in agony between life and death, Sutekh proceeded to systematically obliterate her mind, implant false images of the murder, and erase all memories of his own existence.

When he was done, she watched Sutekh stumble away and vanish.

She saw her depleted body, and like a thick fog that ravages the horizon, everything faded away as she fainted.

The convulsions returned, and as before, Lembrock's hands on her forehead soothed her body.

You are safe, Artyrus and her father said in unison. *You must go on. Embrace the truth.*

She obeyed and watched herself regain consciousness after Sutekh's assault. She witnessed how her injured body came back to life and understood why her mind had not.

Dishonored and corrupted, it dissociated.

Modyor and Artyrus stood at her side, helpless witnesses to her torment, but also active guides to her eventual understanding and acceptance. They helped recognize her own strength and resolve, her ability to fight Sutekh, and most importantly, her refusal to die.

At length, she accepted at whose hands Kronos had perished, how her mind had fought Sutekh's implanted memories, and how she had vanquished his intent to end her life.

As the process was repeated at a painstaking pace over the next several thexicons, Artyrus encouraged her to continue experiencing the truth.

Without resistance she probed the full impact of her memories, sensed the depths of her emotions, touched the pain and anger, and at last, accepted it all without reservations.

Only then, did they leave the past, and slowly, step by precarious step, brought her back to the present.

The fusion was complete. All that remained of the firebrush wreaths was a subtle scent in the air.

All that remained of Kronos was his ghost.

All that remained of Sutekh was his ominous absence.

CHAPTER **26**

Spiritual Teachings

———•———

*Excerpt from the **Corpus Galacticum**, 137th Edition*

During the 1st Century TE, when the Incorporeal Fellowship arose to put an end to the age of Anarchic Disarray, it established criterions for spiritual balance throughout the cosmos.

Nestor, the creator of the Talderon Ideals, wrote that spirituality is an inner path that enables a being to discover its core essence whereby a harmonious inner life can reside.

Spirituality, he wrote, unites us to a larger reality, yielding a more comprehensive self that is able to generate a nexus with the cosmic laws of balance and order. As such, beings can then perceive the immanent transcendent nature of the universe.

The Talderon Ideals profess, that through spirituality, and not through the material world we experience, can the path to universal peace be achieved.

Observance of spiritual teachings yields thoughts, emotions, words and actions that are in harmony with the divine laws of universal interdependency that enlighten the path to achieve oneness.

After the painstaking recovery of Kelahya's memories, the days that followed the Mind Fusion passed fleetingly by. Time didn't manifest as usual. Kelahya found herself in some sort of time warp, disoriented at times, unable to distinguish where or what she was doing, as if she'd been absent from herself for a while. One moment she felt exhilarated, only to feel despondent the next.

Then, impatience set in. She wanted to be done with all the recovery protocols her father and Artyrus insisted upon. She yearned to put it all behind her, purge it from her mind, and move forward. But they wouldn't permit it.

Though fully aware of what had transpired, her mind needed time to come to terms with the damage it had sustained and gather its shattered pieces. It was during those moments, when her mind searched for the links Sutekh had crushed, that time stood still. As with the aftermath of devastation, when survivors search for their possessions strewn through the rubble, her mind searched for its belongings and, once retrieved, bonded them together piece by piece. The trauma she'd sustained had left scars that needed to be expunged. If left untreated they could spread the venom Sutekh had infused, and eventually consume her.

So, despite her impatience, little by little she found all the wounds within her mind, searched for the true memories, and one by one brought them in, recognized them, repaired them, embraced them, and placed them where they belonged. At length, the mosaic of her mind emerged, resilient, buoyant, and poised.

"What's this luminous aura I sense inside me?" Kelahya asked Artyrus as they strolled the gardens of the healing facility.

"You have found your core," he answered with a smile.

"My core…another new one for me. I'm sure you're going to let me discover what that means on my own."

"Yes. It's better that way. You'll own the discovery."

"All right, but does it mean that I'm healed? Is it over at last?" she pleaded.

He laughed. "You're anxious to move on, but it's best to be methodical and make sure all is in place."

"Can't you answer my question?" She was clearly exasperated.

"All right, all right. How's your sense of time? Do you continue losing moments?"

"Not for a while now. I'm aware of every moment. Actually, I'm aware of a lot more than I'm accustomed to. It's as if…I sense what's going to happen next. Not big universal events, but small, near me, near us, type of occurrences."

"Good. I imagined as much." Artyrus smiled and reached for her hand. "You are healed."

"You can feel what I'm experiencing? My mind, these sensations—"

"Yes. It's your new Endow."

"New?"

"You've absorbed your father's Minder abilities and some of mine."

"Absorbed? How?"

"Through the Mind Fusion. Our gift to you."

"Gift? This is too much. How could you do that to me?" She dropped Artyrus' hand and turned her back to him.

Artyrus burst out laughing, his handsome face radiant with joy. "Most Minders would covet such a gift, and you're angry about it. How befitting."

Kelahya spun around, her eyes filled with anger. "Befitting is it? I'm no longer playing games with you, so, don't patronize me. I didn't ask for this gift. It's invasive. Can't you understand that? I've finally dealt with Sutekh's violation, and it's intolerable that you and Da have done the same, and—"

"Stop." Artyrus placed a finger across her lips. "I understand your anger." His hand caressed her cheek, and a sense of calm and honesty transpired between them. "Please hear me out." He waited until her eyes reflected her agreement to listen. "The gift you received from me and your father is not an invasion. Far from it. It's a transference that occurs at a subconscious level only when the Minders are instinctively in accord. Neither your father nor I placed it within you. You sought it, and we granted it."

"I'm not aware of seeking anything. If it happened subconsciously, then somewhere within me I should sense that I asked for it."

"In time you'll sense it, though not as you described it. Your Endow did not ask to receive our abilities. It reached a level in the continuum whereby it deserved them. So, we opened ourselves to you and allowed your Endow to absorb what it merited."

Kelahya stood silent for a few moments, peering deep into his eyes, then nodded. "I understand."

"Your Endow will become more and more accustomed to these new abilities, and in time you'll understand them at a subconscious level, and subsequently, at a conscious level."

She opened her mouth to speak, but just as quickly she closed it. She tried again, but once more she retracted.

"It's all right to ask about what you fear," he said.

"I wish you didn't anticipate what I'm about to say before I'm ready to say it."

"Well, then don't think so loudly," he teased. "And the answer is yes, it is it likely that you also captured some of Sutekh's abilities."

"You sense him?"

"No. He's closed his mind to the Fellowship. A skill his father learned early on. Coupled with the fact he's a Kayroan, it's not surprising."

"You were aware of his existence?"

"We knew of his birth and Tzalina's desire to keep him alive. But around the age of two we lost the ability to sense him. We tried to physically locate him, but with no success. We assumed that he'd perished. After all, inbreeding between Kayroans and Dionysians, even with Terrian blood such as Kronos had, results in the inevitable death of the offspring. At about the same time we also discovered that Tzalina's mind had been shielded."

"Shielded?"

"A skill only Level Four Minders and Transmutants have. So, we assumed Kronos had placed the shield around her mind, principally to hide her from us."

"Did he do that when he ordered the execution of my parents?"

"That's what we assumed. Subsequently we located her on the planet Za, and tracked her actions, but her spirit and mind were unattainable."

"How did you sense Sutekh's birth?"

"The Fellowship perceives all Level Four Minders when they're born. Kronos, however, appeared oblivious to his birth."

"It makes sense. Tzalina didn't tell Kronos she'd bore him a son, and he couldn't sense it because we can't enter Kayroan minds."

"Indeed. As for Tzalina's shield, we were mistaken. Sutekh placed the shield."

"He's a Level Four Minder?"

"Yes. As you are."

The realization made Kelahya's knees buckle. Artyrus took her arm and guided her to a nearby bench.

"Sutekh and I…Kronos and my father…" she whispered.

"All Level Four Minders born in consecutive generations. An unprecedented irregularity in the continuum."

"He'll inherit the Poliate anointed tasks from Kronos?"

"That remains a question. You might've killed him."

"We have no confirmation of that, or of Kronos' death either. Why is that?"

"We have no insight into why the Alliance is concealing Kronos' death…if he is dead. The Fellowship has not perceived the termination of his life, so we must assume that he hasn't perished. As far as Sutekh is concerned, he has vanished. Tell me what you sense."

"I sense rage, but I'm not sure if it's my own fury or his."

"Describe it to me."

"I sense wrath. And throbbing pain. It doesn't feel like it's my anger or my pain, but I can't be certain It's as if I'm aware that he's hurting and furious, but something blocks me from the certainty of what I sense."

"Does it frighten you? Do you feel soreness in your own body when you sense the pain?"

"No. I feel no aches of my own, and the sensations don't frighten me. They're too distant."

"You might indeed be sensing him."

"If, that's the case, and if I did absorb some of his power, I will use it to destroy him." Kelahya sighed, wishing the air she breathed could cleanse the filth of Sutekh's memory.

"Come." He took her hand and led her toward a secluded corner of the gardens. "Let's cleanse that filth with our own iridescence."

"Iridescence?"

He turned to her, his eyes dancing with joy. "The sparks between us." He paused. "Have you wondered why?"

"Attraction?"

"At a profound level. The result of the fusion of our essence. We generate pure energy."

She cocked her head. "How?"

"The electric field between us exceeds our individual dielectric strength."

She frowned.

"Think of our bodies as the material that contains our energy, insulating it. When we touch, that insulation breaks down, and we...spark."

"But not when I touch others, not even my father. Why only between us?"

He smiled. "The thread that binds us is unique."

She shook her head. "What thread? Or do I have to discover it on my own?

"Let's discover it together."

He disrobed and arranged his garments on the grass. Desire permeated his entire being, and his body reacted.

"You're glowing," she whispered. "What—"

As his lips caressed hers, his radiance embraced them, and tiny sparks scattered.

An overwhelming warmth engulfed her.

His tongue waltzed around her lips as he eased her out of her clothes.

She held her breath.

He cradled her, knelt down, and placed her on top of his robes. He lay beside her, then caressed and kissed her entire body, his lips traversing with such softness that she shivered with desire.

When his skin brushed against hers, the energy between them intensified. Sparks flew, and the tantalizing effect caused them both to shudder.

He explored her body with an almost imperceptible touch that flickered as he savored every surface, tasted every corner, and consumed her scent.

She closed her eyes, and the shimmer of her body magnified.

He teased her ears, the soft sounds of his breath generating an electric tremor through her.

She arched her back. *I understand.*

He smiled. *Good.*

How can so much energy emanate from such softness?

Stardust transference.

As he made his way down the length of her body, an overwhelming desire intensified. He slid inside her, his manhood pulsating with unrestrained energy bursts.

She responded with equal throbs.

They moved in unison, creating a rhythm of euphoria with an apex of fluorescence.

With a burst of electrical fusion, they climaxed.

Their breathing slowed and they relaxed, bodies intertwined, savoring intimacy.

"Love without restraints is electrifying," she whispered.

He laughed and rolled onto his back. "Are you implying you love me?"

She turned, placed her leg over him, and caressed his chest. "Not as effectively as you just did."

"Are you going to say it?"

She peered deep into his eyes. "Artyrus Druidiam, yes, I love you."

He kissed her. "It's about time you accepted it."

She sighed. "Hard to recognize. It's so different...so unlike Kronos—"

"Hush." He placed his lips on hers. "I'm aware."

"This is...intimate, graceful. Not tense, uneasy, or anxious."

"Not that I want to brag." He winked. "But I am much more than a mere mortal."

"Yes, yes, I get it. I'll stop comparing."

"By all means, compare. I'm way ahead of you."

She combed her fingers through his hair. "Will it always be like this?"

"No."

She pulled back. "What?"

"It will grow."

Her eyes widened. "How often can we do it...safely?"

He laughed. "There's no danger. As often as we desire. However, we'll have to hold back for now."

"Why?"

"When we return, we'll inhabit our formal personae. Our obligations will take precedence. Intimacy can weaken our resolve."

She frowned. "I don't like it, but I accept it."

He kissed her, rose to his feet, and helped her stand. "Let's get the all clear from Lembrock and leave."

"To go where?"

"To your father's home."

She smiled, filled with optimism for her new life.

The return to Modyor's stable dwell under the surface of Dionysus proved to be a pleasant experience. The transport from the medical facility to her new home, surrounded by her father, Artyrus, Jofan, and Caveat, offered her a unique opportunity to observe the underground city of Bysu.

"You created this city?" she asked her father.

"No," Modyor answered in between laughs. "It's been here for many a cycle, crafted over time by my ancestors."

"You've optimized its original configuration and brought in many updated structures, technologies, and systems, Mody," Jofan added. "Without Bysu, the Rebellion would've failed." Jofan's loyalty and admiration to Modyor were palpable.

He smiled and winked at Kelahya, who was unaccustomed to the feelings of friendship Jofan offered. His devotion to her father—and to her—was undeniable, and she loved the new sense of complete trust that his comradeship afforded.

"How did you do that?" Kelahya asked her father. "Look at this conveyer station, it's one of the most sophisticated I've ever been in. I noted that when I first set eyes on it."

"All I did was give the go ahead to those whose brilliant minds conceived what you observe all around you."

"Modesty has no place here, my friend, "Jofan cut in, and then turned to Kelahya. "Your father designed the entire modernization of Bysu. He then launched a methodical search for those brilliant minds he mentioned to bring it all about. He conceived and built this city, whether he admits it or not."

Kelahya brimmed with pride. Her father was not only an extraordinary Minder and revered Warden of the Scriptures, but a true genius.

The transport unit arrived at Modyor's dwell.

She glanced at her father in dismay. "My golden cage is your home?"

Modyor chuckled as he stepped from the transport unit. The familiar plain gray door stood at the top of the ramp. This time it was Modyor who approached the door and placed his hand on the scanner. The tiny panel opened, and a bluish beam probed her father's face and centered on his eyes. The beam went out and the door hissed as it opened.

"Epidermal imprint and iris scan?" Kelahya asked.

Modyor nodded. "It does have one flaw. It mistook your epidermal composition for mine and allowed you to escape."

She winked at Artyrus. "You didn't prepare for that? Shame on you."

Artyrus shrugged.

They entered, and the door hissed again as it closed behind them. Kelahya had indeed returned, but it no longer felt like a prison—after all it was her father's home, and her new home. She sighed with delight as her eyes feasted on the sumptuous interior. "Did you design this dwell also?" she asked.

Artyrus interrupted, before Modyor could deny his involvement. "Mody, we'll retire to our chambers and leave you two alone. Kelahya, make sure your father tells you every detail of how and why he built this opulence." And, with that bit of advice, he ushered everyone down the hall toward their own chambers.

Once they were alone, she turned to Modyor. "Well?" Kelahya insisted.

He shrugged. "Looks much like what I imagined Kronos would build."

"What does Kronos have to do with this dwell?"

He sauntered toward the large alcove in the center that contained the food and drink storage cabinets. "I'll prepare us something to eat and drink."

"Da, stop. To return to me now. Evasive tricks not to accept." Kelahya said in Eniat. "Time is now for telling."

"Eniat is for Modyor comfort. Daughter use to soften Da heart."

"It is. Now for Da to tell daughter."

"My child used to best in life with Kronos. Modyor to wish Kelahya find this to be home when return to me."

"Certain be I return to you?"

"Yes. Always."

She walked to him, and snuggled into his arms, touched by his life-long certainty that she would one day return to him.

She experienced an inner peace and solace like never before. Her father's unconditional love provided a desperately needed sense of security and tranquility. Life had denied her the ease of such emotions, and she marveled with childlike glee in the delight of Modyor's affection. The entire dwell encompassed far more than opulent chambers and underground gardens. It also housed her father's command center, with fully equipped tactical transport and communication systems. A self-contained environment, which Kelahya now accepted as her home, in her native land, with her father.

To Modyor fell the honor of acquainting his long-lost daughter with the highly complex underground structure and introducing her to the deeper meanings of the ideology of his ancestral line, the Talderon Ideals. An honor he bore with deep personal satisfaction. Step by step, he led her through the intricacies of his organizational infrastructures, his sophisticated intergalactic communications systems, the complicated societal structures within each command nucleus, and the web of manifold approaches designed for one specific purpose—the downfall of Kronos without the collapse of the Alliance of Stars.

Kronos' machinations had prevented her from glimpsing the level of discontent that existed throughout the Alliance of Stars. Now that the truth was at her fingertips,

it amazed her to discover the vast number of civilizations throughout the galaxies that had secretly joined the Rebellion.

Her only discomfort was an increasing restlessness. Inactivity had never been part of her life.

"Patience, to have, Kelahya," Modyor said one day, as they made their way toward the Operations Center. Their conversations in both Terrian and Eniat had become second nature, and they flowed between the two with ease.

"I feel useless here. Societies all over the cosmos suffer the tyranny of vicious leaders, while I remain here, doing nothing. If Kronos remains absent, chaos will reign, and the few restraints imposed on his handpicked tyrants will vanish. We must do something. I must do something."

"You've already done much. You have provided us with invaluable information on the *Olympus*, Kronos' operational channels, his control structure, tactical strategies, and more."

"Nothing compared to the havoc I created. I need to do something to reverse all the damage I have inflicted."

Modyor placed his arm about Kelahya's shoulders, a wry smile upon his lips. "All in good time. The most important thing now is your recovery. It is never an easy return from dissociation. Give yourself time. We must be certain your mind is completely healed."

"Da, I've fulfilled all the tests you and Artyrus have laid before me. My physical strength has returned. You've done so much for me. It's my turn now."

The giant turned Kelahya toward him and stared into her eyes. "Other perils are there yet. Even here. Resentment to you in Rebellion members. Harm to you some wish. Many trust you not."

"Can you blame them? How many times did I come close to killing you? To killing your namesake Nestors? My armies slaughtered your followers by the thousands. I can never make amends for that, but I must try. Somehow." She turned away, the shame and self-recrimination increasing each day as she learned of the endless destruction she had rained upon the Rebellion.

"Of this we spoke, daughter and I, yes?"

"Help did not," she whispered. "In guilt I lay each night in dreams that haunt."

"Kelahya, I'm as guilty as you, perhaps more. But the Augurs—"

"Da, I find no comfort in your spiritual world."

"I understand. Kronos kept it from you, but eventually you will open yourself to it and accept the anointed spiritual tasks of your lineage."

"But—Augurs? I am unable to wrap my mind around that. I never heard of them. No one has. I've been on innumerable planets and not a word about Augurs. Nothing is written about them."

"I've told you, they are available only to direct descendants of the Nestor lineage. Not even Kronos could reach them. He knew of their existence, but not matter how hard he tried, they never revealed their presence to him."

"How could they prevent it?"

"They descend from an ancient civilization that dates back to prehistoric times. Always in a group of seven, they are born with the gift to transcend time and place. A gift which—I believe—is granted by the universal laws of order. They must be together, all seven, to experience the oracles. Individually, they cannot. The Nestor lineage originated within that civilization, and our spiritual essence cannot be expressed in words—it must be sensed. It creates an energy that lives within our genetic makeup—perpetually still, yet in constant motion, greater than the greatest of vibrations, yet smaller than the smallest, and forever in unity. Before the universe—as we understand it now—was born, the explosion of stars created the primordial substance from which we come."

"But we all come from this star matter. It's everywhere, with no danger of being exhausted. That's what keeps the universe growing."

"Indeed, but in our case, and the case of the Augurs, the chemical composition of the substance within us, is unique. It formed distinctively from all others and is the source of our essential core. It enables us to perceive what others can't. Not even the mighty Kronos."

"You really communicate with these seven beings?"

"I do, and you shall as well when you are spiritually ready."

"When will that be?"

"When you reveal your essence."

"Da, you speak in abstractions that are difficult to grasp."

Modyor smiled and embraced his daughter. "Imagine your essence as matter possessing the predominant properties from which it is extracted—your ancestors, Nestor's lineage—the nucleus of you and me. In other words, the individual being has many names, the most ancient being *ousía* or core substance. We each have our own *ousía* within our own genetic heritage. This substance is your essence, the real and physical aspect of your *ousía*—meaning the supreme moral entity that holds the core self."

"So, if I have inherited this essence, why can't I sense the Augurs?"

"Your essence hasn't evolved as it should have. Kronos prevented it and kept you far from it. In time it will emerge and soon enough you'll sense their presence."

"And you find solace in their presence?"

"I do. The Augurs were clear. Kronos was prophesied to die at the hands of a traitor. And it has been so."

"They foretold his own son would kill him?"

"The Augurs prophesized he would die, but they didn't name the traitor."

"I find it difficult to believe such prophecies."

"And yet, here we are."

Kelahya paced as she searched for ways to argue against her father's convictions. The Augurs always proved right, according to Modyor and the Fellowship. But to Kelahya, the idea that in a distant corner of space, in some obscure temple, seven semi-conscious beings read the future, defied all logic, regardless of their powerful souls.

"What if they're wrong?" she managed to say at last.

"You ask me this, yet again?"

"It makes no sense. If they have such great ability, why didn't they mention Sutekh? After all, it's his son. Why not say that the traitor was his son?"

"That, I cannot answer."

"Why don't they point a way to avoid all this suffering and war?"

"Destiny is not theirs to write, only to foresee. How Modyor make daughter see this?"

She approached him, a subtle plea in her eyes. "I'll tell you how. Ask them if Sutekh is alive or dead. Ask them what his future holds. Ask them who will take control of the Alliance."

Modyor shook his head ever so slightly. "I have told you that the Augurs do not respond to questions. They give form to oracles. Even I can't change that. What they have prophesized is the fear of chaos that will befall the universe upon Kronos' death, and the eventual rise of a new leader who will rule in the name of peace."

"More intangibles." She shook her head.

"In time, you'll accept them." He nudged Kelahya through the entrance to the Operations Center.

Artyrus, Caveat, and Jofan were conferring at the far end of the Center. They grew silent and Kelahya could tell that the discussion involved her.

"Greetings, all," Modyor said.

"Greetings," the three responded as one.

"Why the long faces?" Kelahya asked.

Caveat and Jofan glanced at Artyrus. He nodded and stepped forward. "We've been discussing the matter of your safety." His words were directed at Kelahya, but he also acknowledged Modyor.

Jofan stepped forward. "We must focus on Kelahya's future." He turned to Modyor. "Many harbor deep antipathy toward your daughter, and when she leaves the safety of these facilities, they might make another attempt on her life."

"Until we learn why Kronos' death is being kept secret, we're at a loss as to what to do," Caveat interjected. "If Kelahya moves about in our world, it will only increase the danger to her. On the other hand, sending her back to the *Olympus* could be worse."

Kelahya sighed. "They're right, Da."

"The future of our civilization," Modyor said calmly. "For better or worse, depends on the steps we take now to define the roll that Kelahya will play. We need time to develop a strategy."

"Da, Kronos is dead. The issue is who will take control of the Alliance. If I am to take control, I'll need the support of Kronos' followers, and I need to act now. We can't wait. We must assume that Sutekh, if he is alive, has the same goal. He could be dead or planning an uprising. I am uneasy."

"Do you sense him?" Artyrus asked Kelahya.

"Not exactly. I sense a commotion, like a torrent descending upon the cosmos. Do you?"

"Yes, I perceive an indistinct disturbance," Artyrus answered.

"A wave of evil is upon us," Modyor added.

Unaware of the conversation between the Minders, Jofan went on. "One vital thing is missing—Kronos has not been declared dead. Why? Who's controlling that? And we have received no word from—"

"Do not speak Jofan," Modyor interrupted. "All will soon be revealed." Modyor's private emergency communicator announced an incoming confidential message. He acknowledged receipt and entered the appropriate codes in response. "The mystery of Kronos is about to be solved. Come."

They traversed through several corridors, until they reached a hermetic particle transport unit.

"Stand aside," Modyor ordered, as he entered a series of operational codes. Within moments, a familiar figure materialized.

Kelahya's heart skipped, and a cold fear swept through her. Instinctively, she reached for her weapon. She had none.

"Maccabeus," she muttered.

CHAPTER **27**

Subversion

———◆———

*Excerpt from the **Corpus Galacticum**, 137th Edition*

Virtuosity in Subversion *issued sometime during the 3rd millennia, is attributed to **Wortiaron,** the conqueror of the Aleusian Cluster. It describes his philosophy of subversion, which he utilized to weaken the enemy and conquer its domains. This philosophy is frequently cited and referred to by high ranking officers in the League of One and theorists of the Alliance of Stars.*

In his writings, Wortiaron states that of the most effective manner to gather data and information about an enemy is by infiltrating the enemy's ranks.

Virtuosity in Subversion *outlines a myriad of tactics utilizing subversive agents, for the collection of key information concerning the size and strength of the enemy, or identification of dissidents within the enemy's forces. Subversive agents can influence enemy officers to defect, steal key technologies, or incapacitate the enemy's capabilities. Infiltrators can feed false information, prevent counteraction, or create mayhem with the enemy's plans. Only lack of ingenuity can limit their use.*

*"Secrecy is at the heart of any successful infiltration,"
the ancient writings state. "And the ability to hide
information from the target while sharing it with others,
requires extreme proficiency."*

*Wortiaron is credited with having penned that, "an
infiltrator must be serene, inscrutable, and capable of
executing impermeable plans".*

Maccabeus rushed to Modyor, who welcomed him with open arms.

"Modyor, you are well," Maccabeus uttered in relief as he hugged the giant. "I was so concerned. Too much time with no news, dear friend."

"Well indeed, my friend, and at long last united with my daughter," Modyor responded as he released Maccabeus.

Maccabeus turned toward Kelahya and smiled. This was the very first time Kelahya had ever seen him smile with such pleasure. His presence so astonished her that she found herself unable to react to him.

"My Lady," said Maccabeus as he approached her, his hands amicably stretched to greet her, "I'm relieved to find you safe. We have been extremely concerned for your wellbeing."

Kelahya remained frozen as Maccabeus reached for her hands and held them tightly in his.

"Are you all right, my Lady?"

Kelahya nodded. Then, finding her voice, finally uttered, "Don't call me, my Lady please."

Maccabeus smiled. "I'm not sure I'll be able to do otherwise. Please indulge me."

Maccabeus turned to Jofan and Artyrus and embraced each in turn. He then looked at Caveat, eyeing her with considerable interest.

"Captain Lyndsor Caveat," Jofan offered, "this is Maccabeus Zunsirias, Commandant of the Galactic Triad and Director of the Political Parliament."

Maccabeus took Caveat's hand and gently kissed it. "Enchanted."

"Likewise," she said dryly.

"Maccabeus, old friend," Modyor said. "I am sorry to worry you, but I had to break off all communications. Kelahya's mind needed to be closed to me. I had to exercise caution toward Minders loyal to the Alliance and the League of One."

"I understand, Mody."

"Please tell us the news," Modyor requested.

"You must forgive me, Mody. I have so few opportunities to be with you that I cherish every moment. And this new acquaintance," he nodded toward Caveat, "takes my breath away. Please accept my apology for delaying the news."

Caveat blushed so visibly that everyone laughed, easing the tension that Maccabeus' sudden appearance had created.

"You must be prepared for a shock." Maccabeus glanced at Kelahya. "Can you take it, My Lady?"

"Proceed, Maccabeus, I'm fine," Kelahya snapped.

"I'm overjoyed to hear it," he continued. "I'll be brief. Kronos lives."

"What?" Kelahya gasped and her body trembled.

Immediately, Artyrus and her father's reassuring hands were on her.

"Explain," Modyor said.

Maccabeus nodded. "More precisely, his body lives. His mind and spirit do not." Maccabeus approached Modyor. "I made the decision to keep him alive."

"That's not possible," Kelahya uttered.

Maccabeus raised his hand in a pleading gesture. "I shall explain as fully as I can, in the short time I am able to be here. Please allow me." He cleared his throat before proceeding. "I never went to Uxiel as I told you," he said to Kelahya. He then turned to Modyor. "I knew of My Lady's strength and power of spirit and feared for her wellbeing. She would have a strong reaction to the discovery of Kronos' deception, and to seeing Tzalina alive. I assumed, and hoped, that she would kill Tzalina."

"You sent me to Za to kill Tzalina? You designed the plan and mission?" Kelahya cut in.

"My Lady, we were attempting to open your eyes to the real Kronos, we—"

"You are the one who sent me the transmissions on the experiments."

Maccabeus nodded and lowered his head.

"You knew that Kronos was Tzalina's lover all this time?"

"They had been lovers, and I saw a good opportunity to show you his character. I didn't know why he was going to visit her this time, and I certainly didn't expect you to kill him. That was my mistake Modyor my friend, and for that I am sincerely sorry." Maccabeus closed his eyes.

Modyor placed a comforting hand on his friends' shoulder. "She is not the one who attacked Kronos. His son did."

Maccabeus gasped audibly.

"May I enter your mind to describe what happened?" asked Modyor.

Maccabeus smiled and nodded.

With the ease born of close friendship, Modyor projected a quick explanation of events, and the shock on Maccabeus' face gave way to clear understanding.

"I am relieved the attempt on his life did not come from you, my Lady." Maccabeus smiled.

"What does the League know of Kronos' son?" Modyor asked.

"Nothing. There has never been mention of a son."

"When you arrived on Za, he was already gone?" Kelahya asked.

"Not a trace of him or Tzalina. If this…Sutekh is alive, he hasn't revealed his presence."

"How did you find Kronos?" Modyor asked.

"When I managed to gain access to Tzalina's chambers, I found Kronos' inert body in a pool of blood, with but a faint whisper of life. My Lady had disappeared. She'd acted with her legendary efficiency and, as usual, had outwitted me and everyone else. But it was clear I had to protect her. I used the particle transporter and took Kronos with me. I then, called Zenubus. Together we took Kronos to his medical unit."

"Zenubus?" Kelahya asked.

Maccabeus nodded. He glanced at Kelahya and found her glaring at him, mouth agape. "Thanks to the remarkable talents of Commodore Zenubus, Kronos Deucarrion has now joined the ranks of the cybernetics."

Everyone in the room gasped, with the exception of Modyor, who laughed.

"What have you done?" Kelahya's outrage brought her within a hair of Maccabeus.

The normally cool Commandant had a difficult time keeping his tension from showing.

"Dear friend," Modyor said. "I can see that the last few months have increased the stress level in you. It makes you highly irritable. In such a state, admittedly a rarity for you, you are not as effective as usual."

Maccabeus nodded and attempted to calm himself before continuing. "My Lady, as I mentioned, I wasn't certain where you were—or, if you were even alive. But Kronos' murder, if discovered, could spell your own doom. I couldn't risk your life. I needed time, and an accomplished strategist to join me in protecting you—Zenubus. As expected, he proposed an outrageous and, in my opinion, brilliant idea."

He noted that Kelahya's anger had been replaced by curiosity. With a deep sigh of relief, he continued. "Kronos, though not entirely dead, had been shocked beyond even his remarkable capacity to fight back. We assumed that your actions, my Lady, were so unexpected, that his mind dissociated beyond repair. He was…well… is, to quote Zenubus, 'at our mercy'. If he comes back from dissociation, we might wield the power to control him."

Kelahya smiled. "Zenubus never ceases to amaze me."

"Yet, in view of Sutekh's mental powers, maybe the Director's mind is beyond repair, and our plans are no longer viable."

"Tell us of those plans," Modyor said.

"Keeping him alive offered the opportunity to control the entire Alliance without bloodshed, or even major uprisings. We could, in effect, use Kronos himself to bring about the very changes we have all been fighting for."

A heavy silence descended upon the room.

Maccabeus turned to Kelahya. "While we remained with Kronos, I was, by necessity, unable to personally search for you or attempt to reach you. I did place a priority request for My Lady to return, but with little expectation of a response. I couldn't call attention to our situation, and I couldn't search openly for you."

Modyor approached his old friend and placed a hand on his shoulder.

"Once Kronos' situation stabilized," Maccabeus went on, "I was able to leave. I tried, dear friend, to reach you on hyper distance frequency, but didn't receive confirmation. I then worried about your safety as well as hers."

"You worry too much, my friend," Modyor said. "Not good for your health."

Maccabeus smiled. "You're right, my temperature has been rather high of late."

"No wonder you responded so favorably to our Captain," Artyrus chided.

Again, everyone laughed, easing the tension.

"I'm indeed quite taken by the Captain and would certainly enjoy meeting with her more intimately." Seductively, he kissed Caveat's hand once more.

This was a Maccabeus Kelahya had never experienced, and the sight of this dreadful man flirting with Caveat was repulsive to her. Yet, Caveat was enchanted by him, and actually responded coquettishly to his advances.

Irritated, Kelahya interrupted their exchange. "Enough of this flirtation, Maccabeus. Let's get back to Kronos. How is he now? What does he remember?"

"I notice that My Lady hasn't lost her touch. So be it. As I mentioned, his mind is completely dissociated. He's not in this world, and we don't believe he's likely to return on his own. We believe that only you, My Lady, can bring him back, if at all. At least, that's what we've promoted."

Again, silence permeated the chamber.

"Can't we keep him as is, and assume leadership of the Alliance?" Kelahya asked.

"Risky…I'm not sure it would last. Eventually someone would challenge it." Maccabeus shook his head.

"Maccabeus, my friend. You decided well. We must deliberate this more thoroughly and design the best strategy. If Kelahya returns, will she be safe?" Modyor's question was offered with measured fatherly apprehension.

"Yes, Mody. Zenubus and I are of one mind regarding the wellbeing of your daughter. Most Minders in the universe can't penetrate our minds. The secret is safe." He turned toward Kelahya. "My Lady, as you probably are aware, Commodore Zenubus is in love with you, and understands full well the hopelessness of his love, but without hesitation he would give his own life for yours."

Kelahya smiled.

"But there's more, my Lady. The Commodore has harbored a deep hatred toward Kronos for much of his life."

"I never sensed that from him," Kelahya said.

"He trained himself to not dwell on those thoughts or feelings in order to survive. That's why neither you, nor even Kronos himself, could read his mind. He's a remarkable human. The machines that keep the Commodore alive can also inflict upon him unbearable pain. Kronos made sure of that when he installed him into the unit."

Kelahya's face went pale. "What?"

"It was Kronos' way of controlling him. I believe he was afraid that Zenubus would outwit him and take over the leadership of the Alliance. Unlikely, given that it is not ordained, or that Zenubus never harbored such desires, but nevertheless, Kronos made sure it couldn't happen. He encased him and thus controlled him."

"How could I not have sensed that? I knew him so well. I knew his mind and his heart."

"You sensed what he permitted you to. After he was installed in the unit, he understood that his survival depended on his ability to close his mind to his torturer. Zenubus created his own survival strategy, an 'alter ego'. His real persona lives within, as his body lives within his exoskeleton. His external persona is what we all see. Though he told me he's shown you glimpses of his true self."

"Through his eyes," Kelahya whispered.

Jofan stepped in. "Who's with Kronos now? Can Zenubus handle him by himself?"

"Kronos is in the hands of his medical team and the handful of officers closest to him. You're familiar with this group, my Lady."

Kelahya nodded.

Maccabeus went on. "They accept without question that Tzalina inflicted his injuries, and you then killed her upon discovery of her treachery. They also acknowledge that only you can rescue his mind. As for your absence, it's been made clear to all that Tzalina didn't act alone. You set out to personally avenge Kronos and would return when that was accomplished. Everyone hopes you will. This ruse bought us time while we searched for you."

"Exemplary, my friend," Modyor said. "You should return and continue with the scenario you've designed. My daughter most likely will follow, but first we must devise a well-crafted plan. Communications are now open between us."

Maccabeus nodded and affectionately embraced his friend.

"I'll see you soon, I trust."

"Soon it will be." Modyor smiled.

"Maccabeus, please convey my appreciation to Zenubus," Kelahya added. "As for you…it's difficult to…well, I'm not used to you—"

"To embrace old friend, accept." Modyor coaxed in Eniat as he nudged Kelahya toward Maccabeus.

"Modyor, it's not appropriate. She must continue to communicate with me in her customary way. I understand, my Lady. I understand your discomfort and—"

Kelahya stepped forward and embraced Maccabeus, whose temperature rose almost to the boiling point.

"Maccabeus, thank you. It must've been quite difficult for you to cope with my hatred toward you. I'll keep my distance when we're in view of others. When alone, I'd like to—"

"Thank you, my Lady. I'm honored. I look forward to having you back on the *Olympus*." He turned to Caveat and kissed her hand. "Hope to see you soon as well, my dear." He turned to the others and bowed. "To a better future."

Maccabeus entered the transport unit and, moments later, disappeared.

"We must create an airtight strategy. For now, I need time to myself," Modyor commanded.

The next morning, Kelahya accompanied her father on his daily stroll through the Talothia Hage in the early dawn. She relished the fresh air. "I never imagined this desert to be so… appealing," she whispered.

"Early morn is for appeal. Night is for death."

"What is this place you wish to show me today?"

"Patience, we'll be there in no time." Her father placed his arm around her shoulder. "Da, tell me about your friendship with Maccabeus so I can understand how it all came about."

"Oh, it's a long story."

"What better time than as we witness the new day emerge?"

Modyor tightened his hold around his daughter's shoulder and took a deep breath. "We became friends during our training in military academy. Kronos and I were sent there as young men. Maccabeus was already there."

"You and Kronos? Sent by whom?"

"We were born during the same cycle, both Level Four Minders. As befitting our birthrights and anointed tasks, we were both schooled by the Incorporeal Fellowship from an early age."

"When did you meet Kronos?"

"As children. We were both born on Dionysius, unusual for Level Four Minders to be born within the same race and on the same planet, but that's what happened."

"How did you become enemies?"

Modyor laughed and hugged his daughter. "That's what makes it a long story, but I will attempt to shorten it. Kronos found his Endow at the age of three. Both his parents perished when he'd barely turned five. Betrayal by his mother is what I sensed."

"You're not sure?"

"Kronos kept an iron grip on his mind and soul. He felt his own actions were responsible for his father's anger that led to his mother's death. Then, he killed his father."

"He's responsible for the death of both his parents?"

"I sense only bits of Kronos' early life. I'm not sure it's the truth or even if it represents the facts. The Fellowship removed Kronos from Dionysus when he was five. He was cared for by the Fellowship, all by himself, for two cycles. He learned much during that time."

"And you?"

"I came to the Fellowship at the age of seven, as required by the Scriptures. Kronos didn't like sharing the attention of our elders with me. That's when his envy began. We remained with the Fellowship until we turned fifteen, then we were sent to military academy."

"That's when you and Kronos met Maccabeus."

"Yes. Maccabeus and I became very good friends. Kronos wasn't the kind to make friends. It's not in his nature. He truly believes he has supremacy over anyone and everyone."

"I believed that."

"He became a mighty military schemer. His anointed task and lineage dictated his tendencies as Secular Leader, so his conviction of secular supremacy was not surprising. But what shouldn't have happened is the fact that he also craved to be the Spiritual Leader instead of me. He desired complete dominance."

"Maybe the fact that he lived with the Fellowship alone for those two cycles shifted the balance in the continuum," Kelahya suggested.

"Perhaps. It's clear that he didn't wish to share the power as ordained. He wished to be the one—the only one."

"So, what did he do?"

"You lived through it. He ordered my execution. He murdered my Tenecia. If it hadn't been for Maccabeus, you and I would be dead." Tears flowed freely down Modyor's cheeks. He felt his daughter's embrace and smiled. "Come. We're almost there."

Hand in hand they walked till they reached the peak of an escarpment that overlooked the Talothia Hage. A stele obelisk of multi-colored desert stones reached toward the sky. As they approached it, Kelahya noticed a series of inscriptions that ran across the four-sided monument. The top of the obelisk showed figures carved into the stone. One side displayed the carved sculpture of Tenecia, another side exhibited a sculpture of Modyor. The third side branded the sculpture of Kelahya as a little girl of four hand-in-hand with her father and mother, and the last side, showed the sculpture of Kelahya as a grown woman.

"Da, beautiful this to be."

But Modyor had no words, only tears rolled down his cheeks. All he could do was nod and embrace his daughter.

Under the relative coolness of the Dionysian desert's dawn, they mourned together the loss of Tenecia, beloved mother and wife.

Chapter 28

Good and Evil

*Excerpt from the **Corpus Galacticum**, 137th Edition*

*In the ancient times of Terra, a large compilation of Scriptures termed "**The Bible**" was considered sacred. Many Terrians heavily relied upon these Scriptures in all aspects of their spiritual evolution.*

Its influence has extended over the millennia and although only fragments of certain texts remain, many have been incorporated into current Scriptures.

When Nestor, the creator of the Talderon Ideals, discusses good and evil, he does so in reference to these ancient Scriptures. Good, he wrote, emanates from the acceptance the universal truth, while evil is an aberration resulting from the purposeful denial of such truth.

Mathew, an originator of several of the Scripture texts found in The Bible is quoted in script 15.11-20, "How can activity be good or wicked? That which is performed with good intention is good; and that which is performed with evil intention is wicked."

"The simplicity of the return plan is what will enable it to succeed," Jofan stated.

"I'm not sure. It's too easy. We're forgetting something," Caveat responded as she paced around the loungeroom.

"It is a simple and ingenuous plan," Modyor stood and reached for Caveat's hands, "with little room for error. You must trust that you can do this."

She blushed and smiled. "I am certain you are right, sir."

Kelahya walked toward her father. "Da—"

Modyor smiled. "Let us stop overthinking the strategy and execute the plan. We must depart, time is of the essence."

"All is in place," Jofan said to Kelahya. "Please, make sure you stay close to me and Caveat as we traverse the conveyor station toward our destination, there are—"

"I know, I know. There are many on Dionysus who would love to kill me."

Modyor reached for his daughter and warmly embraced her.

To see you soon it will be.

Da, I wish—

To wish no more my presence near you. Your mind must close to mine.

I understand, but—

No more hesitation. You must commit to this endeavor heart and soul. Not only your survival is at stake, but also the wellbeing of everyone in the universe.

I understand.

She tightened the embrace as a couple of tears ran down her cheeks.

He kissed her forehead, broke the embrace, and disappeared down a corridor.

With a pang of apprehension, she heard the doors that led to the hermetic particle transport unit open and close. Her father had left to an undisclosed location. Although uncomfortable with the secrecy, she understood the necessity for safety on all fronts, physical and mental.

Artyrus placed his hand on her shoulder and the familiar energy transference brought her attention back to group behind her.

"Are you ready, General?" Jofan asked.

"I am. Let's go."

"We should have used the particle transporter ourselves," Caveat interjected.

"Not an option when we have no one on the receiving end," Jofan answered with an impatient tone.

"I could've gone ahead and—"

"Enough Caveat!" Jofan commanded. "It is done. We are traversing Dionysus with Kelahya. Focus."

They exited her paternal home, Kelahya flanked by Jofan and Caveat, with Artyrus bringing up the rear.

They climbed into a transport unit and Jofan nodded to Kelahya, who inserted a travel card into the slot.

"Dwell 1543, Caledonian Complex, arrival to conveyer station for appropriate transfer in four hexicons. Transport in progress," said the lifeless voice. The card popped out and a soft melody of crystalline chimes began to play in the background. Kelahya retrieved the card and took a deep breath.

"Good," Jofan sighed with relief, "if the card is active, your dwell should be as well, Quaytra Playaar."

The transport unit stopped. "Conveyer station," said the monotone voice. "Board transfer unit 47A2 through gate 3650 in seven hexicons. Disembark now."

The doors slid open and the small contingent quickly exited, merging into a sea of creatures, transport units, jitneys, and trams traveling in all directions. Commercial establishments and eateries filled with patrons crowded the edges of the bustling station.

"Stay close," Jofan ordered, and they tightened around Kelahya.

"Don't exaggerate," she protested. "We look ridiculous. This bubble will certainly attract attention."

Artyrus laughed and they relaxed their hold on the daughter of the Warden of the Talderon Ideals.

"That's better," she said, "thank you."

They rushed through the station, and toward gate 3650. As they entered, they found their transfer unit at the ready. Once on board, Kelahya inserted her travel card.

"Dwell 1543, Caledonian Complex, arrival in six hexicons. Transport in progress," said the lifeless voice. The card popped out and the familiar melody of crystalline chimes played.

"All is well," Artyrus sighed.

"I did not notice anyone eying Kelahya," Caveat said with a nervous ring in her voice.

They traveled in silence.

"Dwell 1543, Caledonian Complex. Six journals will be charged to your central account. Disembark now," the monotone voice informed.

The door opened onto an enclosed walkway. They exited and the jitney sped away behind them. The entrance nave shot up to a dizzying height.

"Boy, you sure got the best of the best," Caveat said, admiring the housing complex.

"Security is quite good," observed Jofan, "with access to the lift limited to each entry card. I like how the other lifts are cut off by these translucent barriers informing intruders of their limits."

Kelahya placed the magcard against a small screen and the lift doors open. They entered, the doors closed behind them, and the lift began its ascent.

The lift cylinder slowed and rotated forty-five degrees as it came to a stop. Kelahya slipped her card into an access groove and the doors to her dwell slid open. The lights glowed into life as she stepped in.

"Welcome home, Quaytra Playaar," the soothing male voice announced in perfect Terrian.

They stepped into the spacious entry hall.

"Terrian and Dionysian furnishings," Caveat exclaimed. "How much did this alter ego cost you?"

"Five thousand stipends," Kelahya answered.

"The view is spectacular," Jofan said.

"What a good use of the floor-to-ceiling windows," added Caveat. "Esroal looks astonishing."

"The sleep room is to your right," Kelahya told them. "It has an effective communications console and an agreeable hygiene unit."

"I like your dwell, Quaytra," Artyrus chuckled.

"Enough of all this fluff," Jofan faced them. "It's time for Caveat and I to depart. We'll rendezvous in the Entrian Cluster where you will board Tzalina's vessel."

A knot formed in Kelahya's stomach. "I wish you both a safe journey. Jofan, I—"

Jofan reassuringly placed his hand on Kelahya's arm. "Not to worry. We've infiltrated and utilized decoy tactics many times. Stealing Tzalina's' vessel will not present a problem. Plus, don't forget, Maccabeus has made it quite easy for us."

Kelahya embraced Jofan, who turned crimson.

"Kelahya." Caveat stepped forward. "You must call the transport unit that will take you to your vessel from this location, it is imperative that you board it from here, and do not allow anyone to notice you and—"

"Don't worry about me," Kelahya said as she embraced Caveat. "I have Artyrus at my side," she winked. "Safe journey, Caveat."

Without further ado, they crossed the threshold onto the lift as the doors to Quaytra Playaar's dwell hissed shut behind them.

Kelahya sighed. "This is the last night I will spend on Dionysus," she said with deep melancholy as she approached Artyrus.

"Let's enjoy a good meal before we leave. It'll make you feel better. Where can I find—"

"There," she smiled and nodded to her left.

Artyrus moseyed to the serving chamber, entered a series of codes in the beverage replicator, and placed a large pitcher in the center. He opened several drawers and selected a variety of foods, which he quickly infused and set on a warm tray. He took the pitcher and tray into the loungeroom and placed them on the table, then selected a couple of classes and some dinekits, and brought them over. He poured the beverage into two tall glasses.

"What is this purple fizzing drink?" she asked.

"I don't have a name for it yet. It's made with the Crystals of Salandria, with a sprinkle of stardust here and there. I'm lucky that it came out right on the first try. Normally I have to do it a couple of times. It does produce a nice effect upon drinking it."

"Are you trying to get me drunk?"

"No, just in a good mood."

"And this meal?"

"Nothing much, I used whatever was here." He sipped his drink. "Okay, ask away. What troubles you about Maccabeus?"

Kelahya took a sip and smiled. "Delicious…I'm puzzled about how could he have survived as Kronos' right hand? Kronos knew about his friendship with my father. Wouldn't he have been suspicious?"

"Maccabeus and your father did become very close in military academy, and everyone was aware of their friendship, it wasn't a secret. But, when Maccabeus entered manhood at the age of eighteen, his father ordered him to be placed in the service of the League of One. His lineage is that of soldiers and his father did not approve of Modyor's pacifist influence."

"How could he oppose his friendship with the spiritual leader?"

Artyrus took a bite of the food. "At that time, his father didn't know that Modyor was the Warden of the Talderon Ideals. No one knew the true nature of either Kronos or Modyor. They hadn't been anointed as of yet."

"Did my father try to stop Maccabeus departure?"

"He couldn't intervene. The intent of the separation was not only to detach the youths, but to train Maccabeus in the ways of the warriors he descended from. Your father respected the latter. However, the plan backfired. Maccabeus and your father not only remained close, but their friendship was strengthened with the split. As an act of defiance toward his father, he remained in contact with Modyor, and celebrated his philosophy, spirituality, and credo. So, as time went by, they learned to communicate with each other via a multitude of original devices of their own invention."

Kelahya stood up and walked toward the wall-to-wall windows overlooking the metropolis. "Kronos must've taken the separation as a sign that Modyor might be weak if he'd failed to keep his best friend nearby."

"That's a strong possibility," Artyrus answered as he savored some food. "Come you need to eat."

She approached the table and took a bite. "So, how did they stay connected under the radar?"

"At first, their communication techniques were a game, a challenge of ingenuity that they improved upon with each successive attempt." He sipped his drink. "In a matter of cycles, they'd become expert at hyperspace, subspace, and message attachment techniques. As the tyranny of Kronos' rule evolved, they joined forces to fight him—one from the inside, the other from the outside. The Rebellion uses many of their protocols."

Kelahya sighed. "I wish I'd known they were friends."

"You couldn't. The universal continuum would've shattered if Tzalina had succeeded to exterminate your family, as Kronos had ordered. Your father's survival and your safety became the prime dictate. The connection between Maccabeus and your father had to remain in place, but undetected."

"How did Maccabeus discover what Tzalina would do?"

Artyrus ambled to the table where he had displayed the food and brought with him a few morsels. "Tzalina boasted about it. You can well imagine how he felt when he heard it." He handed some to Kelahya and ate a few himself.

"Why didn't he alert my father?"

"He tried to, but your father declined all comms. He wished to enjoy undisturbed time with you and your mother. Maccabeus couldn't reach him. By the time he was able to get away, Tzalina was in the process of executing Kronos' orders. Your mother was dead, but he managed to intervene in time to save you and your father. Tzalina reported to Kronos that she'd killed both of your parents and taken you prisoner."

"She didn't tell Kronos that it was Maccabeus who ordered her not to kill me?"

"Nor that he had ordered her to take you away and keep you safe. She also didn't mention that Maccabeus had been on Dionysus and had remained there. She sought Kronos' admiration and favor, so she owned it all. Her selfishness served Maccabeus well."

"Obviously, it worked on Kronos too." She savored the morsels of food Artyrus had picked for her. "What happened next?"

"The instant your father witnessed your mother's death, the Fellowship felt his pain and we knew what had happened. We transported Modyor to a secure medical facility. We healed his wound and collectively shielded him from Kronos."

"Now, I understand how he's been safe all this time. You've protected him."

"Yes. Once we ensured his safety, we allowed Kronos' despotic plan to evolve."

"You allowed it? Why?"

"To avoid chaos. If Kronos wanted supremacy of power, why not let him have it? In time, he would fail. His failure would then demonstrate the divine veracity of the ordained natural order of the universe."

"What do you mean?"

"The universal order had decreed that two leaders of equal rank must share the balance of power. It is this balance that brought about spiritual, social, and political stability in the Talderon Era for centuries."

She faced Artyrus, anger etched across her face. "You allowed Kronos to reign alone to set an example?"

"And to avoid any future such coups."

"What about all the lives that have been lost, and the many that have suffered at the hands of Kronos? What about them?"

"An inevitable side effect."

"Inevitable?" Rage constricted her throat. "How about unacceptable? How could you?"

"With great difficulty and pain. You have felt it." He reached to touch her shoulder.

Kelahya closed her eyes and sighed. She had, indeed, felt his agony, and only now did she understand its source. Her anger tempered down, and profound sorrow replaced it.

"That is how and when, we—the members of the Incorporeal Fellowship—agreed to expand our duties beyond our spiritual mandate. Under your father's leadership, we joined the underground Rebellion to bring about Kronos' demise and restore the natural order. That is also when, and how, Maccabeus became a key player in the campaign."

"I comprehend," she said pensively. In silence, she paced aimlessly around the room.

Artyrus understood she needed time to reflect and returned to the lounge chair.

"Why did Kronos agree to keep the child of his nemesis?" she asked walking toward him.

"Maccabeus persuaded him with a simple argument." He paused as he swallowed.

"I'm sorry about all these questions. I haven't given you any time to enjoy your meal."

He took a sip of his drink and cleared his throat. "I've enjoyed it all right, and I don't mind the questions. Where were we?"

"Maccabeus convincing Kronos to keep me."

"Maccabeus told Kronos that you were the only available woman in the universe of his same race, a fact that could prove helpful to him in his quest to procreate. Plus, if you were also born with the Endow and at Level Four, given that you are a descendant of the Nestor lineage, a child from this union would ensure the continuation of his supremacy. His heir would be next in line and there would be no need to split the leadership. He could use you and your abilities to his advantage. As you can well imagine, Kronos recognized the possibilities instantly."

"Thus, began my indoctrination."

"Indeed, but something didn't go exactly to plan." He sipped his drink.

"What do you mean?" She joined him on the lounge chair.

"I believe that Kronos didn't expect the emotions you produced in him. He wanted to use you as he uses all who surround him. But in the end, you did capture his mind and soul. He was in awe of your military prowess, your formidable mind, and your beauty. He was enamored."

She sighed, stood up, and drained her glass. "Thank you. This was very helpful. But now I'm going to enjoy a quick cleaning treatment. The unit in this dwell is an older one. It's quite invigorating, you'll like it." She ambled into the bedchamber.

"I'm sure I will. I'll prepare another pitcher and step in after you're done." Artyrus strolled to the serving chamber, entered a series of codes in the duplicator, but the liquid that poured out was bright orange. He tossed it and started again. His second attempt resulted a thick greenish substance, which he immediately discarded. After two more unsuccessful attempts, the correct purple drink filled the vase.

Kelahya sauntered back into the loungeroom tugging at her League of One uniform. "It doesn't fit right," she complained.

"The molding units we use are not as exact when duplicating the League's uniforms, but it will do. You appear the same as you have in our various encounters." He handed her a glass.

"What other talents do you have?" she asked as he walked toward the bedchamber.

"Well," he winked, "you'll have to discover them, won't you. At least your mood is more upbeat."

She smiled. "Yes. The cleaning treatment was refreshing. Your drink is delicious and very soothing."

"Relax for a bit while I enjoy the cleaning treatment," he said as he disrobed and entered the hygiene unit.

This business about you anticipating what I'm about to say is…unsettling.

I have no idea what you're about say. I do sense what worries you. You can now sense my concerns and fears as well.

I understand what it is, but I'm not sure I like it. Hey, stop that! What?

Don't think of me like that! It's distracting! We agreed not to be intimate!

Did we?

Yes, we did. Oh…please don't touch me like that…

I'm not touching you. We're apart.

Stop it! We mustn't…stop that!

But he didn't obey. *How about a bit of intimacy one last time?*

How are we going to do that? I'm in the loungeroom and you're in the hygiene unit.

We're not tied by time and space. Give into the sensations while you sip your drink and enjoy.

She sensed that her legs had moved apart, although she sat cross-legged in the lounge chair.

It'll take time for you to discover the capacity of your enhanced Endow. For now, trust it. Release it.

Willingly, she surrendered to him.

Good. Feel the warmth of the water caressing my body… and yours.

She sighed. *I do.*

You're intoxicating, my beautiful Kelahya.

Your hands…their touch is arousing. And the warm water…it—

Hush… Come to me. I'm ready for you.

She closed her eyes, and sensed how he lifted her to him, the water fondling every pore. She wrapped her legs around his waist and arched her back to receive him.

With the gentlest of care, he entered, then pressed a bit more.

Free yourself, Artyrus. She tightened her legs around his waist.

He drew back and plunged deeply into her with a thrust that brought a cry of pleasure. *Kelahya!* With complete abandon, he ceded to his own desire, and moved with incremental pulsating thrusts.

The glimmer of her body increased as she rose up to him with each surge, reveling in the sheer sensual pleasure of their rhythmic union.

Their spasmodic release came simultaneously. Every fiber of their beings having shared the experience.

Kelahya opened her eyes, yanked her uniform off, and rushed to the hygiene unit.

Artyrus embraced her. "Not bad."

She kissed him. "I need another cleaning after that."

He laughed. "You loved it."

"I did. Lovemaking in the ether. Not bad at all."

She washed, and with a peck on his nose, stepped into the drying chamber.

I need more of that fancy drink. She winked and blew him a kiss. *Don't take too long or I might drink the entire pitcher.*

You'll get a bad headache.

Laughing, she sauntered back to the loungeroom, put her uniform back on, and gulped down her drink.

"That was amazing."

Moments later, Artyrus emerged from the bedchamber, vested in the white translucent robes of the Incorporeal Fellowship.

"Wow," whispered Kelahya. "You're quite…imposing."

He smiled. "Alas, it's only me underneath these vestments. However, clothed in them, I could never have done what I just did to you, nor could I ever make love to you while you wear that hideous uniform. Consider what happened, our farewell to intimacy."

"A marvelous farewell, I might add," she said as she handed him a drink.

"One that should last a while. You're ready?"

"How could he have turned me into a weapon?"

"It's his lineage. He is, after all, Kronos."

"Yes, he's Kronos." Kelahya took a sip of her drink to wash down the bitter memories. "The one I am now expected to manipulate."

"Indeed."

"You trust me capable of mind fusing with him?"

"If I didn't, I wouldn't have agreed to the plan, or to your return."

"It all depends on whether we can bring him back or not."

"We? It is you who will. If there's anything left of his mind, you'll recover it."

"You'll be the one to—"

"I'll be with you," Artyrus interrupted, "but it is you he has to come to. We rely on his love for you, on his trust, on his conviction that he controls you. That's the place where you must find him so that you can bring him back."

"Are you worried?"

"I'd be a fool if I wasn't."

"What—" she looked startled.

Artyrus smiled. "You sensed Jofan. He has landed Tzalina's spaceship in the Entrian Cluster."

"Is that what it is…this sensation of comfort? It's like a distant memory of a spacecraft landing in a familiar place. How can I ever interpret these new feelings?"

"Give them time."

"We must go, then."

"Indeed," he said as he emptied his glass.

Kelahya rushed to the communications console and placed a request for a transport unit.

"Done," she said as she grabbed her belongings and headed for the door. She stopped and turned toward Artyrus. "I sense that Jofan and Caveat will safely return to Dionysus with our vessel, and somehow I also see us heading toward the *Olympus* in Tzalina's ship. All unharmed."

"I don't sense any disturbances around them or us."

"These sensations that perceive distance, trouble me. I fear I'll misinterpret them, or falsely rely on them."

"With time, you'll learn to differentiate between what is true and what is hope."

"I'm glad you're coming with me Artyrus—no wait." Kelahya chuckled. "Your Excellency. To address you in public with the respect due to a Healer from the Incorporeal Fellowship will be a rather difficult task for me to master."

"I'm sure you'll manage quite well…my Lady."

"What an ironic role reversal. I return to a cybernetic Kronos, whose childlike mind will be mine. Only this time, I'll be the one conducting the indoctrination."

"An action that places the future of the universe in your hands."

Chapter **29**

Revenge

———◆———

*Excerpt from the **Corpus Galacticum**, 137th Edition*

Master Scientist Xiubantes Treo discovered the collective link that spawns vengefulness across all races residing within the known universe.

After numerous approved experiments he pinpointed the cause to an intrinsic tear of a union. He writes that youngsters bond with those who care for them and who remain at their side providing a continuous and secure base to explore from and return to. The bond with the caretaker leads to the development of patterns of dependency, which in turn, generate the youngster's internal models that guide their perceptions, emotions, thoughts and expectations.

The loss of a caregiver after this bond has been established leads to inexorable grief that becomes soldered within the *ousía* also known as our core substance. As the child grows, the psychic perceives that only revenge will heal the wound, and therefore conceives all actions emanating from this perception as altruistic justice. This form of justice considers punishment the best response for the injury to the *ousía*, and as such all vengeful actions are justified.

Tzalina's spaceship was as ostentatious and insufferable as her palace, but Kelahya's return to the *Olympus* in Tzalina's spacecraft would contribute to the subterfuge Zenubus and Maccabeus had created.

The journey to the Olympus had proceeded without incident, and as she approached the home of her youth, every muscle in her body tightened.

Nothing to fear, Artyrus told her.

It's anger, not fear.

You must control both. You are now in command. Announce your arrival.

"This is General Kelahya Devona. Command 3476 Altudion 539 Trentario, open hatch Inverticum. Acknowledge."

"General…the craft that you approach in…we—"

"I have captured Governor Hu's vessel. Notify all senior officers, Commandant Maccabeus, and Commodore Zenubus, of my arrival. Utilize standard landing protocols. You have my command. Obey."

"Acknowledged."

The blockade shields around the *Olympus* disengaged and Kelahya headed forward. Less than a thexicon later, she maneuvered the spacecraft through the hatch and expertly landed.

Moments later, General Kelahya Devona stepped out of Tzalina's craft to a roar of cheers and applause by the League of One Troopers, all gathered in official formation on the *Olympus'* largest landing dock. She saluted and smiled, welcoming their enthusiasm for her safe return.

"Welcome back, Commander." Maccabeus stepped forward and dropped to one knee. His formal greeting created the expected military decorum as the soldiers came to full attention and, in unison, also dropped to one knee. Silence engulfed the dock.

"Thank you, Commandant. You may rise."

She walked past him, as she had many times in the past when returning from her missions. "Please, friends and companions, rise." The soldiers jumped to attention.

She'd always searched for Kronos when returning to the *Olympus*, only this time she searched for Zenubus, whom she saw coming toward her. She rushed to meet him.

"Commodore Zenubus, I'm glad to see you." She reached to shake his hand.

As if holding a delicate flower, he cradled her hand in his and kissed it. "My Lady, we've missed you. Are you well?"

"Quite well. Better than ever now that Tzalina's murderous accomplices are all dead."

"All hail General Devona!" Maccabeus yelled.

The crowd erupted in cheers and applause. Kelahya smiled and joined them in the celebration of her victory.

After a while, the cheers diminished and Artyrus emerged from Tzalina's ship. A hum of inquiries filled the dock. The effect of his delayed appearance created the planned reaction of awe, surmounted only by the fact that he donned the ethereal white robes of the Incorporeal Fellowship. Everyone knew that only those who had been granted the privilege by the Fellowship, or through Kronos himself as their Scribe, were permitted to wear such robes. The seal of the Fellowship that hung from the crystal chain around his neck, accentuated the importance of his persona.

"Commandant Maccabeus, Master Zenubus, League of One warriors, I bring with me Prime Healer and Delegate of the Incorporeal Fellowship, his Excellency, Artyrus Druidiam," Kelahya announced.

Maccabeus dropped to his right knee, his hand on his chest, his head bowed. Every single soldier on the deck followed suit. Zenubus somberly saluted.

"We're honored to have you amongst us, your Excellency," Maccabeus said.

"Please rise Maccabeus, old friend." Artyrus reached for him and warmly embraced him, then turned to Zenubus. "Commodore Zenubus, last we spoke, you were ailing. How are you now?"

Artyrus followed his warm welcome with an affectionate embrace, and healing warmth immediately traveled through Zenubus whisking any and all pain away. For a moment, Zenubus looked startled. Then, he smiled, cleared his throat and said, "My dear Artyrus, your healing touch helped me. I am free of pain. The cause of such pain is dormant."

"That is good news. But let us not stand on ceremony. Please take us to the Supreme Commander."

The soldiers remained at attention as the Healer and their beloved General Devona were escorted from the deck, and toward the Director's medical unit.

This first step turned out as planned, she told Artyrus.

Zenubus was a bit taken aback by my embrace, but he recovered quite nicely. I understand why you've enjoyed his company and how much he loves you. He looked at her and smiled.

Kronos' guard lined the entire corridor that led to the medical unit.

Artyrus, we now must use care when sharing our thoughts. Kronos' medic, Roellus, is a Minder, and several of the healers on the Olympus have the Endow.

He lightly brushed the back of her hand with his. *We are conversing with one another at a level that is completely imperceptible to anyone other than a Transmutant. I assure you no one can sense that this conversation is taking place.*

She smiled. *The effects of the mind fusion continue to disconcert me, to say the least.*

In time, they'll come naturally to you.

"My Lady, do you wish to enter alone?" Maccabeus asked.

"No, please join us. Ask Roellus to briefs us. Afterward, please dismiss everyone. You and Commodore Zenubus shall remain. His Excellency will examine the Director in our presence only."

"As you wish, my Lady."

The doors slid open and they stepped into the antechamber of the medical unit. A white mist bathed them, disinfecting every inch of their bodies. Then, the door to the medical unit slid open.

Kronos lay unconscious, inside an exoskeleton, and cybernetically suspended in midair, an array of tubes connecting him to innumerable machines and equipment spread around the room. His imposing body had been reduced to one-third his previous size. The absence of muscle made his skin stick to his bones, and to the tubes that connected his organs to the cybernetic machinery that kept him alive.

Kelahya gasped, all color drained from her face.

Inhale, Artyrus prodded, his hand gently resting on her shoulder.

"Are you all right, my Lady?" Zenubus asked.

"It's the shock," Maccabeus jumped in, "of seeing the Director in this manner. As you can observe my Lady, Tzalina executed an expert attack on his life. His throat was lacerated, his spinal cord severed, his arteries and veins slashed."

Kelahya stood in silence confronting the hideous consequence of Sutekh's assault.

"Roellus, please inform the General and His Excellency as to the Director's status," Maccabeus ordered.

Roellus stepped forward, and bowed his head before speaking, "Your Excellency, my, Lady, Director Kronos is now physically viable as long as he remains encased within his exoskeleton shell which regulates all of his vital signs and enables him to move. His spinal cord was so completely severed that it is unlikely it would ever regenerate, so his ability to move is completely dependent on the machinery and connections of his exoskeleton. As long as he remains encased, he can survive and safely leave the medical unit. His mind, however, has been unreachable so far." He bowed his head again then stepped back.

Artyrus approached Kronos and rested his right hand on his forehead. After a while, he stepped away from Kronos. "We can proceed with the Mind Fusion, but it must take place in familiar surroundings to both him and General Devona."

"Your Excellency," Zenubus timidly approached. "Presuming that you would give us such orders, we took the liberty to ready the Director's chambers. They await only you and your patient. The crimson robes of the Mindheal have also been prepared for you."

Clever man. Artyrus laughed.

He is that, and more, Kelahya responded.

"Very well. Let us begin. Time is of the essence. Transport him there," Artyrus commanded.

They exited the medical unit and made their way to Kronos' chambers. Kelahya and Artyrus entered the room first. Two of Kronos' medics bowed, respectfully approached them, and donned them with the Mindheal robes.

Kronos' chamber had been transformed into a makeshift Mindheal sanctuary with firebrush wreaths around its periphery. His bed remained untouched and would be used as the altar—a good mixture of the required ceremonial elements and familiar surroundings.

Artyrus stood solemnly at the head of the altar and Kelahya to one side.

Upon Artyrus' signal, the firebrush wreaths were lit, and a heavy silence descended over the proceedings. Moments later, the large doors opened, and four medics entered with metered step, transporting Supreme Commander Kronos, encased in his exoskeleton shell and carried on a suspended platform. The medics carefully lowered him onto his bed.

"Roellus," Artyrus said, "no one but those closest to the Director shall remain in this chamber. Please exit the room with the medics and remain at the door with them. Instruct them to close their minds tightly as to not affect transference of mind matter during the ceremony. You shall do the same while they are in your presence. When it is done, I will sense their obedience and yours. I will then summon you, and only you, back into the chamber. You shall assist us during the Mind Fusion. There shall be no mental interference by the medics of any kind if the procedure is to succeed. Do I make myself clear?"

"Yes, your Excellency." he bowed his head and left the room.

As soon as the doors closed behind them, Maccabeus faced Kelahya and Artyrus, the temperature rising in his body. "Are you sure this will work? Do you realize what will happen to us if he dies in our hands?"

"Quiet!" Zenubus ordered, the whirring in his suit increasing as he floated about the room.

"There are no guarantees." Artyrus' tone was calm. "The mind is a wonder, and there is no telling what we will encounter. But it is worth finding out, and it is the best strategy before us right now. Am I not correct, Master Zenubus?"

"As an intellectual strategy, yes. Operationally, it remains to be seen."

"Maccabeus," Kelahya said, "we must proceed. If we don't, he'll perish. All that you and Zenubus have done will be in vain."

"Are you sure that Roellus should accompany you inside Kronos mind?" Maccabeus asked.

Artyrus nodded. "It is important that he bear witness."

"But it's dangerous. He might perceive your intentions."

"Maccabeus, please don't worry yourself. Roellus' Minder abilities are not sufficient for him to sense what Kelahya and I will be doing, I assure you."

"Will either he or Kronos absorb your abilities or Kelahya's?" Zenubus asked. "The Scriptures tell of mind fusions whereby the Minder being healed then absorbed the abilities of the healers. It is said that the most powerful Transmutants gained their abilities in such a manner."

"I believe the Scriptures state," Artyrus said calmly, "that the transference happens only when the healers freely offer their abilities. Healers in mind fusions have full control of the gift they bestow, and only do so when the Minder who receives it will use it as the healer would. Therefore, it can only happen when a perfect match of body and soul exists."

"Can we proceed, please?" Kelahya urged.

Maccabeus and Zenubus nodded

"Very well," Artyrus said. "Maccabeus, summon Roellus."

Maccabeus approached the doors and ordered, "Roellus, enter."

Nervously, Roellus approached the altar and stood opposite Kelahya.

"Roellus, when it is time, I will use your Endow to ease you into the Director's mind. May I have your permission to do so?"

Roellus nodded. "Of course, Your Excellency."

Let's enter, Kelahya, and find what's left of him. All I sensed when I entered his mind earlier was darkness. Unlike you, his mind's been fully engulfed by the black hole. There's nothing left behind, nothing remains that fights for survival. If there's any mental life left, you must retrieve it.

I'm ready.

With ease she entered Kronos' mind and observed how Artyrus brought Roellus in, allowing him to witness the void of the Director's mind. She sensed Roellus couldn't clearly distinguish her or Artyrus but was aware of their presence. He would remain in the void only sensing that the healing that was taking place.

Kelahya, call his name, bring him to you, Artyrus told her.

It's so dark and cold, she observed, *not a whisper of light.*

Let him sense you're here and wish to help him. Give yourself to the emotion that you're here to save him and bring him to you.

"Kronos, it is I, Kelahya. Come to me. Kronos, can you hear me? Come to me."

Kelahya, use the terms of endearment he's used to hearing from you.

I can't, she protested.

Yes, you can. You can surmount your feelings of betrayal and anger. Use your abilities.

But what about you? How will you feel hearing me speak such words to him?

This is our duty. Our affection for each other remains intact. Nothing can, or will, affect it. Call to him with words of love.

Artyrus was right. She must get past the pain and hurt of Kronos manipulation, and transform her anger into hope for the future. "Kronos, darling," she said with confidence, "come to me. Let me help you, my love. Don't hide from me. Where are you? Let me have a glimpse of you. I beg you, my love, let me help you. I understand that you are hurt, that you're in shock, but I can help you. We can find the way out together. Come to me darling."

A minute spark of light appeared in the darkness of oblivion.

"Kronos, my love, I'm here. I'm within you. I've come to help you. Trust me, dearest. All is well. Come. It's me, your Kelahya. I am here."

He's coming to you Kelahya, slowly but he's coming. As he approaches you will not recognize him. The Kronos you remember is not the one that exists within him any longer. Regardless of his appearance, continue as if you recognize him, Artyrus advised.

"Kronos set your fears aside. I am here to bring you back. Come to me darling."

With Artyrus at her side she continued to call to Kronos over and over again.

At long last, a little boy of no more than five tentatively approached her.

"Who are you?" he asked shyly.

"Hello, my love. I'm Kelahya. You remember me, Kronos," she answered with an assurance that surprised even her.

"Yes. I remember you, Kelahya. I'm lost. Are you here to take me home?"

"I am, my love, if you wish to come with me."

"I do." He took her hand. "How did you find me?"

"I knew you were here, and I called out to you. You came to me of your own accord. I can only take you home if you wish it."

"I do wish it, as long as you're with me. I was afraid. I was very frightened. Something awful happened to me."

"Yes, darling."

"I don't recall what happened, only that it hurt."

"Soon you will," she said and kissed his little hand.

"Now, with you holding my hand I'm no longer fearful. Will you always be at my side?"

"I will always be at your side." And she spoke the truth.

They walked in silence, hand in hand through the darkness, for what seemed to be time without end.

"Who's that man next to you?" Kronos asked.

"I'm Artyrus Druidiam, your healer. You've been injured and I'm here to help you heal."

"I recognize you as well," Kronos pronounced.

He can see you. I didn't expect that he could see you, Kelahya whispered.

His mind is quite resilient.

"You're Artyrus, who sits on of the thrones with your brothers and sisters. Are they here, too? I can't see them. Will they take care of me, as well?" Kronos asked.

He remembers the Incorporeal Fellowship! Artyrus, this isn't safe!

Remain calm, Kelahya. Let me explore with him.

"Yes, my brothers and sisters will also take care of you, and you are right, in noticing that they are not here at the moment. How did you meet us?"

Kronos considered it for a moment. "Not sure, but you cared for me. You are my teachers."

"You are correct. We are healers and teachers. Search your emotions now. Tell me how you feel."

"I am calm. I am no longer afraid. I am not alone, lost in the dark."

"Do you trust Kelahya and me?"

"Trust?"

"Yes. Trust."

"I don't know what that means. I can't answer."

"Do you believe we are here to help you?"

"Yes."

"That means you trust us."

"I am not sure I like the word trust. It makes me quake from within. But I wish to be with you. I can't be here alone any longer."

"Then hold my hand, and together we will show you the way out. Trust us," Artyrus said.

Artyrus, this child is Kronos, the Kronos that doesn't trust. The Kronos that killed his parents. The Kronos we fear.

Yes, you're correct.

He has memories and emotions of his own.

Yes, and he also wishes to be saved. That's what he wants.

Hand in hand they walked as the pitch black began to dissipate, and a thick fog engulfed them.

We shouldn't bring him back, Artyrus. It's too dangerous.

He's not completely gone, that's true. But his mind is open to us.

What if he rebels, what if he remembers who he was?

It's a remote possibility Kelahya. But we are bringing back a very young Kronos. His mind is as young as the boy who holds our hands. It's true that at this early age is when he experienced treachery, and that's when his instinctive fear of trust emerged, but—"

Artyrus, if we don't succeed, we may bring damnation to us all. Can you sense what will happen if we do so?

No, our senses don't permit us to predict a path that has not yet begun. That's why neither you nor I can foresee what will ensue when he returns. It is, however, your choice to bring him back or leave him behind to die. You'll be the one to indoctrinate him, to mold him, and control him.

It's my choice…But it represents a high risk…A very high risk.

Yes, it does.

They walked through the dense fog of Kronos' mind, making little progress of recovery. At times they spotted Roellus through the fog, blindly staring, only sensing that progress had been made, but not enough to enter the Director's mind.

At length, Kelahya said, *All right. So be it. I'm sure I was a risk for him when he took me in as a child. He'll now be my child, a risk I'm willing to take.*

Kelahya tightened her grip on the boy, and the three resolutely marched out of the fog and into the light of Kronos' chambers, bringing Roellus with them.

Kronos, the man, opened his eyes and blinked reflecting the fear of the child within him. "Kelahya, Artyrus, where are you?" Kronos pleaded.

Every person in the room gasped at the artificial sound that emanated from the Director's exoskeleton voice box. Tears rolled down Kelahya's face.

"Here I am, darling. You must rest now," Kelahya answered.

Artyrus put his hand on Kronos' forehead and whispered, "Welcome back, Kronos Deucarrion. Now you must sleep, a restful, peaceful sleep without dreams or darkness."

Holding on to Kelahya's hand, Kronos smiled and obeyed.

No sooner had Kronos' eyes closed than Kelahya freed her hand and turned to the Medic, "Roellus thank you for your assistance. You may leave now along with your medics. Your presence near the Director is no longer necessary. His Excellency is now in charge of both his physical and mental wellbeing. Your mind and those of your medics should remain tightly closed whenever you find yourselves in the presence of our Supreme Commander. We cannot have any mind probing while his mind is recovering. Understood?"

Roellus, nodded, and swiftly existed the chamber.

"Commandant Maccabeus," Kelahya continued, "and Commodore Zenubus, please remain with his Excellency and the Director."

Well done, Kelahya. Your quick response to the Roellus' desire to enter Kronos' mind was excellent.

My response? I saw the shield you placed around Kronos first, and then I sensed his intent. It's you who acted swiftly.

It wasn't I who placed the shield. It was you. Congratulations, your abilities have entered your subconscious now. It'll be easier for you to use them in the future.

No one, other than Artyrus, noticed her look of surprise, and he smiled.

As soon as the doors slid closed behind the medic, Kelahya signaled for them to follow her behind a set of doors to the left of the bedchamber.

They entered a sizeable compartment that held the Director's personal belongings.

Immediately, Maccabeus whispered, "Is it safe to speak here? I've never entered this chamber."

"No need to worry," Kelahya said. "Dear friends, Kronos is back, as you've observed. But he brings with him old memories and instincts."

"Is it safe to have him back like that?" Zenubus asked Artyrus.

"Only time will tell. His mind is young, very young, he is but a child of no more than five, I'd say. It's up to Kelahya to mold him."

"My Lady, can you do it?"

"Maccabeus," Zenubus interrupted, "that's an offensive question. Please observe whom you are addressing. She not only can do it, she will. Apologize immediately."

"Dear Zenubus, thank you for your trust in my abilities," Kelahya said as she placed her hand on his. The whirring intensified, and she smiled.

"I am sorry, my Lady," Maccabeus bowed.

"No need for an apology, I'm not offended by your question." For the first time, Kelahya placed a hand on Maccabeus shoulder, a gesture that visibly softened him.

"Dear friends," she went on, "to succeed in our future endeavor we must not only trust each other, but also feel free to challenge one another. Our survival depends on that. We'll be united, and not stand on ceremony or false hierarchical order. Before the rest of the world we must keep up the façade, but in private we shall not. Agreed?"

They nodded.

"I will proceed with Kronos' indoctrination, and hopefully improve upon what he did to me. It's a challenge that I look forward to. But now, let's deal with more immediate practical matters. Maccabeus, we need to replace Roellus and the entire medical unit. Not a single Minder is to come close to Kronos until his mind is under my control."

"They're devoted to him, they will reject any such efforts."

"Promote them and send them away. I'm sure you and Zenubus can come up with something clever. You always do."

They smiled. "You flatter us, my Lady," Zenubus said.

"Well, it never failed before, so I don't expect it will now."

"How do you propose to go about his indoctrination?" Maccabeus asked.

"To begin with, I will live in these chambers, so that I can be near him at all times. I will ask Chantall to make all the necessary arrangements. Maccabeus, please provide her any assistance she requires."

Maccabeus nodded.

"Then, as he did when he maneuvered me into submission, bit by bit, I'll mold him into the shape we wish him to have. It's a matter of implanting the images we choose in his mind so that he conceives them as his own. It will take time, and patience— that will be a challenge for me—but I'm prepared to conquer my shortcomings."

"What should we communicate to the Alliance?" Zenubus asked.

"By now," Maccabeus answered, "our soldiers and the Alliance emissaries have dispersed the news of my Lady's return, and the annihilation of Tzalina and her accomplices. We'll announce that the Director is recovering nicely, with my Lady and his Excellency at his side, and of course, that he's performing all his duties from his chambers."

"I'm not sure that will be enough. The population, and especially the troops, need to see that he's alive," Zenubus cut in. "They are tired of rumors and communiqués. Is there any chance, My Lady, that you can get him to appear in public and address the masses?"

Kelahya glanced at Artyrus. "That's a tall order."

"It is," Artyrus said, "but Zenubus is right. They need to see for themselves that he's alive and able. I believe we can do it." *I will help, Kelahya. Agree to do it.*

Kelahya turned to Maccabeus. "Announce that Kronos will address the assembly in person and that his message will be broadcast throughout the galaxies in…" she glanced at Artyrus and smiled, "…one third cycle?"

Artyrus nodded. "One third cycle."

Maccabeus shrugged. "So be it."

"Now, let us prepare for what is to come," she said. "Artyrus, I will show you to your quarters. Please follow me. Dear friends, efficiency of speed in arranging all aspects of Kronos enlightenment is of the utmost importance. We shall begin at the morrow."

And with that, Kelahya assumed control.

CHAPTER **30**

Superstitions

———◆———

*Excerpt from the **Corpus Galacticum**, 137th Edition:*

Formeitian Rondias, *self-proclaimed prophet of the Lorhian cluster of galaxies, has predicted a cataclysmic transformative event that will occur on the cusp of the 7th Century TE. He has identified various astronomical alignments and numerological formulae pertaining to a set of precise cycles that support his prophecy. Although he has not described what this event will entail, many civilizations throughout the cosmos have reached their own elucidations.*

Interpretations of this revelation have emerged claiming that this occurrence marks the end of the universe, as it is currently known. These versions explain that the end will come when the black holes that reside at the center of our galaxies will absorb and destroy all matter, or when systems of planets where black holes are absent, will collide with one another annihilating all.

Other interpretations predict the end of the known cosmos but describe the beginning of a new universe where planets and inhabitants will undergo physical and

377

spiritual transformations, marking the beginning of a new era.

Supreme Pontiff Deucarrion has stated that predictions of impending doom are not founded in veracity and are mere superstitions.

The time that followed, sped by in a frenzied blur. Kelahya, with Artyrus at her side, spent endless hours molding Kronos' mind. With the use of her still unfamiliar abilities, she led him into the belief that the thoughts and words that now inhabited his mind were, indeed, his own.

Are you sure that's what it means? she asked Kronos.

"Why are you in my head, Kelahya?" he asked, his eyes searching for the truth in hers.

"When Sutekh cut your throat," Kelahya's eyes filled with sorrow as she reached for his hand, cradling it in hers, "he damaged not only your body, but your thought processes as well."

"How? I don't feel like my mind was damaged."

"That's because the neurons that transmit the information to your brain are damaged."

"Explain." His eyes narrowed into slits while his mind ascertained the veracity of Kelahya's tale.

"Of course, darling. Don't worry, there's no need to furrow your brow." Tenderly, she kissed his forehead before continuing, "I'm sure you remember what a neuron is." She raised an eyebrow and tilted her head toward him.

"I do. I'm no longer that child you brought back from the dark."

"I'm aware of that, my beloved, you've come a long way. You're almost back to your old self. However—", she paused and closed her eyes.

"What? Go on. What's wrong?" Kronos demanded impatiently.

"I'm sorry, it pains me to remember what was done to you, and how it has affected you. I must make certain, every step of the way, that your thoughts are your own, and not something that Sutekh might have implanted in you."

Kronos nodded. "I understand. Do what you must." His eyes softened as he brought Kelahya's hand to his lips and kissed it. "He did the same to you…worse…you've told me so. You've shown me in my mind what—"

"But don't forget, although he attacked my brain, he didn't harm me physically. Most importantly, he failed to destroy my mind. I too, had to return from the abyss." Tears formed in Kelahya's eyes. "That's why I'm here to guide you. Many of the connections in your brain were shattered, and we need to rebuild them."

"How?"

"Continue what we're doing. With my guidance, little by little you'll put it all together. We must restore a great number of neuron pathways. There are sensory neurons, which respond to touch, others to sound, others to light. Stimuli affect the cells of the sensory organs, which, in turn, send signals to the spinal cord and brain. Motor neurons then receive signals from the brain through the spinal cord and cause—"

"Yes, yes, Zenubus already explained how our exoskeletons work. Go on about my brain."

"It's simple. Your mind, as your body, needs similar assistance, and I'm the one providing it for you."

"How did you learn what to do? You're not a medic. Isn't Artyrus the one who knows what to do?"

"He does help me, at times. He's the one that healed me. But most of what I do, I learned from you."

"Me?"

"You don't remember, but when I was a child you taught me everything, you made me who I am today. I trusted you and followed your guidance. Now, you must trust me, and follow my guidance. Search your memories. It'll help."

Slowly Kelahya entered Kronos' mind, projecting the images of her indoctrination, his influence on her, the creation of the woman he loved and admired.

He didn't react, nor did he cower or shut his mind. He remained silent for a moment then smiled. "I like having you in my head, it feels warm and comforting."

"As did I, when you used to enter my mind."

"But don't do it all the time. I do need a bit of privacy."

She smiled and kissed his forehead. "As you wish. You must sleep now. You need your rest. Tomorrow is a big day for you."

"I'm not fearful of tomorrow, but I am tired." Kronos shut his eyes, and Kelahya felt restful sleep enter his mind.

She left his chambers, rushed to Artyrus quarters, and entered without announcing her presence. *He resists me at every turn,* she told him with exasperation. *It's not going to work. Tomorrow will end in disaster.* The door to his chambers closed behind her.

Artyrus calmly approached her and turned her toward him. "It will only fail if you let it," he said. "Each day he shows less resistance to your suggestions, each day he trusts you more. Now, you must trust yourself."

"If it doesn't work, it means the end of us all, the end of everything."

"That isn't going to happen. Your concern is overshadowing your senses. Tomorrow Kronos will address the Assembly and, through the vidscreens, virtuoscopes, vidscanners and viewscapes, civilization as a whole. He will set forth his policies of renewed peace throughout the galaxies. He will say and do exactly what you have inspired him to say."

"Inspired?" she asked with a heavy dose of sarcasm in her voice. "It does sound less invasive than 'manipulate', I suppose." She shook her head and turned away. "It would be far safer if you did the 'inspiring' instead of me."

"I can't do that."

"Yes, the Fellowship and all that."

"As far as Kronos is concerned, your power is every bit as strong as mine. And, you have something I don't have—an insight into the real man. You know him better than anyone alive. In this short time, you've brought him from an insecure child to a confident man. No one will be able to tell that it isn't the same Kronos."

Kelahya uttered a sardonic chuckle. "This new Kronos is far cleverer than we give him credit for. I can feel it. Sometimes I get the sensation that we're the puppets and he's the puppeteer, that he's merely leading us on, and drawing us into some bottomless pit from which there's no escape."

"You're tired. These worries will evaporate by morning, and you'll do what must be done. You have to believe that."

She turned toward him with a look of sadness etched onto her lovely face. "I'm uneasy about it. It's not only my mistrust of Kronos, there's an unfamiliar element that's tugging at me. I sense that something isn't right. I feel a disturbance. Do you?"

"Yes. I do sense something's awry, but I often feel disturbances in the continuum that are unsettling until they come into focus. It could be that you're picking up on my disquiet."

"What do you do about it? What should I do?"

"Nothing, for now. The Fellowship is charged with addressing those disturbances, which frees me, and those of us with assignments throughout the universe, to carry out our tasks without focusing on the instabilities."

"I don't like it."

"Do you sense Sutekh?"

"I can't tell what it is."

"Then, let me worry about it, you should rest. Tomorrow is an important day, and you'll need all your strength for Kronos."

The great hall of the Assembly had been decorated with splendid ornamentation. The signobanners changed constantly in an endless parade of colors and designs, from the green, black and gold, exclusive to Kronos' personal guard and high office, to the endless flags, streamers and garlands, representing every planet, galaxy, and coalition in the Alliance.

The members of the Assembly and special guests, as well as the top officers of the various military branches of the League of One, all wore their ceremonial best. After all, this represented a triumphant return—an unparalleled moment that spelled continued power for some, and continued oppression for others.

Kronos' exoskeleton apparatus had been enhanced to give him a more imposing appearance, while at the same time, minimizing his obvious dependence on the life-sustaining machines. Zenubus had taken personal pride in designing the Director's "new suit", as he called it, making no attempt to conceal his satisfaction.

"I am sure he'll be as happy as I have been," he told Maccabeus on the day the whirring machinery had been fitted onto Kronos. "I can only hope that we'll have occasion for him to experience some of the improvements I made to his design."

Maccabeus felt his blood boil as his temperature shot up, and he glared at Zenubus. "This is not a game."

"To me, it never was," was the terse response.

Now, the moment was near. In a matter of hexicons, Kronos, followed by Kelahya, Maccabeus, Zenubus, and Artyrus, would make their way to the Assembly, and the destiny of all would become clear at last.

If they succeeded, a very different Kronos would announce a new beginning of peace and cooperation throughout the universe. If they failed, the likely chaos that would ensue could require centuries to bring to an end, and even longer to redress.

Remain calm, Kelahya. Whatever happens, stay focused. Artyrus slipped into her mind with a welcome and much needed warmth.

What if I need your help?

*I can provide whatever you need. But I can't dictate Kronos'
actions. Only you can do that.*

I don't like it. The slightest mistake—

*As long as you concentrate, there will be no mistakes. Keep
your wits about you. Stay in control and, above all, stay focused.*

"How do I look?" The question came from a voice box and,
out of habit, Kelahya turned to her old teacher.

Zenubus gave her a half smile and nodded toward Kronos.

Kronos' new reality still hit her like a laser blast. To witness
this powerful man reduced to a whirring piece of machinery was
too cruel. She had observed much of the technical operations
necessary to fit the Director with the variety of devices designed
to keep his heart beating, his lungs breathing, his vital organs
functioning. But most of all, this mechanical voice emanating
from somewhere other than the Director's throat, felt too bizarre.

"Well, Kelahya, how do I look?" the question came again.

Kelahya regained her composure and smiled. "Like a force for
the universe to reckon with."

Good, Artyrus said. *Keep his vanity engaged. It will make
everything else that much easier. Go to him.*

"Are you ready?" she asked.

Kronos gave her a wry smile. "The real question is, are they
ready for me?"

He's got something up his sleeve, Kelahya told Artyrus. *But,
what?*

Stay calm, Artyrus responded. *There's nothing he can do
without you being aware of it first.*

Kelahya forced herself to smile at Kronos. "They will be most
impressed, I'm sure."

She nodded toward Maccabeus who, in turn, relayed the
signal to initiate broadcasting to every corner of the universe. All
vidscreens, virtuoscopes, vidscanners and viewscapes, some as
large as buildings, would carry the image of the Director making
his glorious return after coming so close to death.

It was widely accepted that it was Kelahya's and the Fellowship's intervention that had brought Kronos back from the edge of oblivion. However, the rumors of his demise had been so widely circulated, that conspiracy theorists everywhere, promoted the notion that this, in fact, was not Kronos at all. It was, they assured all who would listen, a mere android designed to sound and look like the Director. Some went as far as to say they had seen Kronos' dead body with their own eyes. Relics, reputed to have been obtained from the very site where he had died, became available in every city within a ten-cycle distance of the planet Za—swatches of cloth, pieces of leather, even fragments of flesh or bone, were for sale everywhere.

The combination of all these elements made his reappearance the most widely anticipated event in the last hundred cycles. No one anywhere, intended to miss it.

"Shall we, my Lord?" Kelahya bowed slightly and motioned toward the Assembly floor.

Kronos allowed his eyes to rest on her beautiful face for a moment, then, in a whirr of activity, his exoskeleton floated ever so slowly toward the Assembly.

The new, reborn Kronos Deucarrion, Director of the League of One, Supreme Commander of the Alliance of Stars, and Scribe of the Incorporeal Fellowship, emerged into the vast room to thunderous applause. A total of six gigantic vidscreens lined the precinct, providing an unmistakable picture of the powerful man.

Images of huge crowds, gathered in streets and city squares, were broadcast as well, in an effort to ensure that all bore witness, and succumbed to the emotion of the event.

As the image of his face filled the screens, Kronos' eyes scanned the throngs, and a satisfied smile crossed his lips. The din of the crowd ebbed toward silence.

Kelahya had been made aware of the preparations, but nevertheless, it took her breath away. This man, reviled and revered, loved and hated, cherished and feared, clearly held the imagination of the masses securely in his grasp.

Kronos made his way to the dais with Kelahya firmly at his side. He gazed around and prepared to speak.

And then, it happened.

The screens went blank for a moment, and the crowd looked about in confusion. The entire Assembly was stunned.

Without warning, Artyrus' knees buckled, and he fell to the ground, supporting his upper body by gripping on to Kelahya's arm.

"Agony!" he blurted out, his eyes focused somewhere away from where he knelt.

Kelahya's head snapped back, victim of an invisible blow. She lost her balance and swayed.

Maccabeus and Zenubus rushed to her.

Kronos remained frozen, uncomprehending, and impotent.

Kelahya dropped to the floor, her hands clenched over her heart.

Artyrus slumped next to her, his face a mask of unbearable anguish.

An intense murmur permeated the cavernous room as the vidscreens flickered again.

Kelahya glanced up in time to see the image of Sutekh replace that of Kronos. A collective gasp ensued.

"What is it?" Maccabeus asked, a look of bewilderment etched upon his face.

"Sutekh!" Kelahya yelled.

Shaking, Artyrus rose to his feet and tried to breathe.

Kelahya stood up and turned to Artyrus. *What has he done?*

A tear. He's ripped the very fabric of the universe.

What does that mean?

He's manipulating bosons and tachyon particles, and the dimensional strings have ruptured.

"You!" Kronos said as he glared at the image on the vids.

"Greetings, Father. You've gathered everyone. How practical."

The crowd's eyes shot from Sutekh to Kronos, and back again.

Kronos shook his head in a futile attempt to free some hidden memory. He turned to Kelahya with a perplexed look on his face.

When she stared into Kronos eyes, she saw confusion turn to understanding. Then, she recognized the familiar look that with inexorable slowness, overcame his countenance—a calm that transitioned into determination, and gradually changed into rage. His eyes shot back toward the vids with a hatred that made his exoskeleton rise to a frenzied whirr as it struggled to keep his vital signs and organs in check. "Tzalina's offspring is no son of mine. You are an abomination."

"Of your own making, Father, and with powers far beyond yours."

"So, you are alive," Kelahya cut in.

"Ah…Kelahya. Yes, I am. No thanks to you."

Artyrus raised his hand to indicate he was taking over. "What do you seek? Where is Demetrian?"

"The Fellowship's senior Cleric is alive—in pain, but alive. For the moment. Like my Father…alive, for now."

"The Director has recovered from your murderous attempt, and has resumed his duties," Artyrus declared.

The crowd roared its approval.

"State your purpose," Artyrus ordered.

"I simply demand what's mine," Sutekh said with a smirk.

"We have nothing of yours here," Artyrus said with an icy tone. "Except, perhaps, your execution chamber."

The Assembly broke into applause and cheers.

Sutekh's laughter thundered over the crowd. "I have a better idea. I'll begin to execute the Fellowship Clerics that I hold prisoner. Cleric Hardatian has already left us, as you've sensed, Artyrus. I'm sure you felt it. Did it hurt? I imagine so."

Artyrus' face contorted in pain. The crowd went silent.

Kelahya leaned toward Maccabeus. "Where is this coming from?"

"The signal comes from the Fellowship."

"That's impossible. No one has access but the—"

"As for the three Fellowship Reclusians," Sutekh went on, "you need not worry. They're alive and well. I've moved them to a safe place. They'll be very helpful as you'll soon find out."

Artyrus gripped the edge of the dais, his head shaking, his face twisted into a grimace of misery, his body trembling.

"Enough!" Kronos yelled.

"Well, Father, I'm glad to notice you haven't lost your valor. I fear it will not serve you. I do have the upper hand."

"Sutekh, what have you done?" Kelahya yelled.

Artyrus shot his hand up, pleading with her not to engage with Sutekh.

"Ah, Kelahya, my darling, nice to hear the fury in your voice. I like your fire. But, beware. I'm no longer injured and will easily overtake you next time. I hold all of you in my grasp."

A collective gasp permeated the room.

Sutekh waited, a theatrical pause asserting his dominion. He took a deep breath, and the grin upon his face repulsed Kelahya.

"Kelahya, in case you or your puppets Maccabeus and Zenubus are unaware, or the rest of those assembled, for that matter, your friend Artyrus can tell you the chaos my captive Reclusians are capable of generating under my control." His hideous laughter filled the room.

"Before you die, Father," Sutekh added with cold indifference, "you need to name me as your successor."

Kronos glared at his son. "I will see you dead first." The voice box gave his threat a hollow, pathetic sound.

"Such a hasty decision. Unworthy of such a powerful man. Let me show you something."

As the image shifted, three humanoids, two females and one male, came into view. The faces of all three reflected unimaginable terror, their eyes darting about as if fending off an army of demons.

He's torturing the Reclusians! Artyrus shut his eyes.

Kelahya sensed dread in Artyrus' painful cry.

The Reclusians' eyes stared straight ahead. Their faces became calm.

Sutekh's voice permeated the Assembly. "Let me show you what I can do, Father, with help from my…friends."

The image changed to some area of deep space where a large planet and its moon floated in the vast darkness.

"Za," Kelahya whispered.

"Watch," Sutekh commanded.

The next image showed the streets of Bistayde City overrun with panic. Its citizens fled from some unseen terror, trampling underfoot any who suffered the misfortune of a fall, or were too weak to withstand the pandemonium of the crowd.

Kelahya watched in horror as the source of the chaos came into view. She recognized, in a flash of repugnance, the misshapen forms of the inhabitants of the Aurora experiment as they ripped the Bistaydians limb from limb and fed on their living bodies.

"I will soon have my pretty army visit other planets and other cities. Thank you, Father, for providing me with these abominations, a most useful weapon," he said with a smile.

As the crowds watched the revolting massacre, a swarm of attack raptors appeared out of nowhere, and laser-strafed the abominations with unerring precision. In an instant, the Auroran horde was eliminated from the face of the planet.

Rebellion raptors. Kelahya turned to Artyrus.

Yes.

How did they know where—?

Nestor.

"My armies will crush you. Have no doubt of that," Kronos managed to utter in a panting rage. "That was but a taste!"

"Your armies?" Sutekh laughed. "One small victory is of no importance. Observe," Sutekh said as the image changed yet again.

In rapid succession, images from planets throughout the galaxies popped into view, each showing entire legions of soldiers, troopers and machinery of war brandishing the red insignia of Tzalina's ancestry.

"Recognize them, Father? It amazed even me to find how many civilizations really do hate you. Mother initiated their assemblage as soon as she realized I could easily overcome you. Interesting that you never guessed. We outsmarted you and your almighty League of One, and, by the way, the entire Alliance. My armies come from the countless societies who seek a new order. They understand that I offer more than you ever did."

Sutekh's face filled the screens once again. "One more trifle before I leave you."

Planet Learmes filled the screen. Kelahya recognized it as the place she had flown to the first time Kronos allowed her to pilot a shuttle. The memory of the pristine waters and the lush vegetation flashed in her mind.

Screams of agony from the Reclusians shot across the Assembly monitors.

Kelahya turned to Artyrus once more.

His hands were clamped around his head. *He's inside their minds, he's torturing them, forcing them. I can't reach them.*

We must stop him! Kelahya yelled.

He's shielded them!

We have to protect Learmes!

A moment later, a translucent shield covered Learmes.

The image shifted back to Sutekh. "Clever, Kelahya."

For an instant, Kelahya noticed exhaustion on Sutekh's face, but he turned away and pointed to the Reclusians who writhed in pain.

"Release them!" Artyrus demanded. "They'll destroy you."

"Not yet." Sutekh sneered. "What say you, Father? Am I your heir?"

"Never!" was Kronos' unflinching reply. "My only heir is Kelahya."

"So be it," Sutekh said. A milicon later, the eyes of the Reclusians focused on Kronos and they screamed.

Kelahya shielded Kronos' mind, only to realize that the attack was not directed at his mind, but at his exoskeleton, which began to shake as its various components malfunctioned, and overheated. A look of horror formed on Kronos' face, and he quivered.

Kelahya turned to Artyrus and yelled, *He's killing Kronos! I've shielded his mind, but he's using the exoskeleton to kill him!*

We can't prevent it, Artyrus said. *The Reclusians wield unbridled power, and Sutekh is giving it focus.*

Abruptly, Kronos' exoskeleton went silent, and the man inside froze into immobility. His eyes became fixed, his mouth went limp, and his entire body shrunk. The exoskeleton dropped to the floor in a clatter of metal alloys.

Kronos was dead.

The Reclusians fell silent, and the look of horror returned to their faces.

Sutekh remained out of sight as he spoke, his voice hollow and distant. "You have three turns to capitulate. One way or another, I now rule where my father once did. Artyrus will tell you what the Reclusians are capable of. Especially, with my guidance."

Sutekh reappeared for an instant, and Kelahya bore into him.

He contorted in agony, his eyes erupting in green tears and disappeared.

The crowd gasped.

What happened? Artyrus asked.

I willed the Reclusians free of his hold and they snapped free. Kelahya answered. *Sutekh's distress was collateral damage.*

Artyrus inhaled deeply his eyes focused on a distant expanse.

Artyrus? Kelahya prodded.

He turned to her but seemed distant. *Astral projection,* he told her. *I am here, but I am also with your father and the Clerics. We're collecting the Reclusians. Thank you.*

How—

Later. Tend to Kronos now.

The vidscreens, once again under the control of the *Olympus*, broadcast the gruesome sight of Kronos' inert body.

Kelahya dropped to her knees and cradled Kronos' head, tears streaming down her cheeks. She caressed his face, fixed his hair, and rocked him in her arms.

Maccabeus placed a hand on her shoulder. "His medics are here, my Lady."

She stood up and stepped out of the way. Kronos' medics placed him on a suspended platform and covered him with the charcoal cloth of death.

A solemn silence descended upon the Assembly.

As Kronos' body was escorted from the hall, Maccabeus dropped to one knee. In one simultaneous action, everyone present kneeled. Zenubus inclined his head, Kelahya placed her hand over her heart and chanted the song of lament.

As soon as the doors closed behind the Director, everyone stood, their eyes focused on the dais.

"Dear friends." Kelahya turned to face them. "I ask your forgiveness."

A confused murmur swept over the crowd.

"My Lady," Maccabeus protested, "there's nothing you could've done. These beings—"

"Yes, there was," she said with conviction. "Fellow citizens, I failed to kill Sutekh. I left him for dead and beyond repair, but somehow, he survived. Honorable members of the Assembly and all inhabitants of the Alliance of Stars, I beg your forgiveness. But more importantly, I ask that you entrust me to go after him and finish what I started."

The members of the Assembly cheered. The crowds everywhere roared their approval.

"Hail, Kronos' heir!" Maccabeus bellowed.

"Hail, the new Director of the League of One. Hail Kelahya Devona!" Zenubus yelled.

The crowd cheered as one, "Hail, Kelahya Devona."

I'm back, Artyrus whispered. *The Reclusians and Clerics are safe. Your father remains with the Fellowship. All is well.*

I'm relieved. You must now give everyone hope.

Artyrus nodded.

Kelahya raised her hands and quieted the Assembly. "Thank you, I am honored. But first and foremost, we must understand what has just happened, and focus on the elimination of Sutekh's threat." She turned to Artyrus. She signaled for him to come forward. "Your Excellency, please."

"My Lady." With a respectful bow of the head, Artyrus stepped forward. His aura had recovered its full luster, and once again he stood tall, strong, and in full command, his ethereal persona permeating the room. "Permit me to enlighten all as to the nature of the Reclusians."

She nodded and gave him the dais.

As he turned to the Assembly, his image filled the vidscreens. "Please understand that I'm limited in what I can share. The Scriptures are clear—the Incorporeal Fellowship is sacred. Few in our entire universe have been granted the honor to serve them, and none have been given the authority to disclose their sacred mandates unless authorized to do so. Only the Scribe has full access to the Fellowship, and Kronos Deucarrion now lies dead."

The members of the Alliance turned to each other in consternation and a hubbub erupted.

Artyrus raised his hands to quiet the crowd. "We all witnessed the clear decree from Director Kronos to name Kelahya Devona as his sole heir. Therefore, by the authority vested in me by the Incorporeal Fellowship, I convey to you that Kelahya Devona will indeed take his place, and carry out his divine duties. In due time, the Clerics will anoint her as the Scribe. As such, rest assured that order is restored."

The Assembly and the crowds broke into uproarious applause.

"Your Excellency, what about the Reclusians?" someone called out.

"There is little information I can share about the Reclusians, but what I can tell you is that the they are of a species so rare in the universe, that only three exist. Incapable of caring for themselves, they're attended by the Clerics of the Incorporeal Fellowship. They may have looked like humanoids, but what you saw was a holographic image. They are capable of creating pure energy which, under the care of the Incorporeal Fellowship, is channeled toward constructive actions. But, as you witnessed moments ago, that energy, in the wrong hands, can be used to create havoc. However," he glanced at Kelahya. *May I describe what you did?*

She nodded. *But don't attribute it to me.*

"As we speak," he faced the audience, "Sutekh's hold on them has been severed. You witnessed the moment when it occurred with the eruption of his tears and distortion of his face. Rest assured that Director Devona will retrieve the Reclusians and peace will be restored."

"Your Excellency," Ambassador Fronsaret called out. The members of the Assembly parted, as he moved forward and respectfully bowed to Artyrus. "Until that time, can Sutekh destroy our planets?"

"Ambassador Fronsaret," Artyrus addressed him solemnly. "I understand your concern. It is in everyone's mind. However, there is no immediate danger. Sutekh will need time to recover from the energy he utilized in manipulating the Reclusians. No matter how much power he claims to have, no single humanoid can control them for long."

The Ambassador saluted and retreated into the crowd. The members of the Assembly stood silent. Artyrus bowed his head and stepped back to take his place between Maccabeus and Zenubus.

Kelahya moved resolutely forward and addressed the Assembly and the members of the Alliance of Stars. "For all his boasting, and purported military strength, it is clear that, above all, Sutekh covets the Directorship of the League of One and the command of the Alliance of Stars. This is to our advantage. As Director of the League of One, I pledge to you that as long as we remain united, as long as the League of One is undivided, we will annihilate this evil. Inhabitants of the Alliance of Stars, are you with me?" She raised both arms, the signal of solidarity throughout the Alliance.

Without a moment's hesitation, every member of the Assembly raised their arms and called out "We are one!" The cheers from crowds filled the room to the chant, "We are one, we are one!"

Kelahya waited a few moments, then the projected image shifted, and Kelahya's face filled the screens—her countenance unyielding. The cheers subsided in anticipation of her next move until silence descended once more upon the Assembly.

Kelahya stared at the masses directly from the vidscreens, her fierce eyes focused on one and all. "Wherever you are Sutekh, I will find you, and I will kill you. On behalf of the League of One and the Alliance of Stars, I declare war on Sutekh and his tyranny!"

The crowds exploded into a frenzied ovation, and angry cries of war erupted throughout the galaxies.

Well done, daughter.

Da, you are with me.

Always.

CHAPTER **31**

IWE

———◆———

*Excerpt from the **Corpus Galacticum**, 137th edition:*

*The Scriptures of the Incorporeal Fellowship, written during the 11th cycle (TE), record the conception of the IWE by Master **Ituh Lingepw**. He noted that at the highest level of mental potency, some Clerics had reached IWE—an altered state of consciousness. Their bodies had transmuted and absorbed a celestial substance that pervades the cosmos capable of forming an alternate body – the astral form. By achieving IWE, these unique Clerics were able to leave the body at will and move through space and time.*

Master Lingepw noted that time is an illusion since it is relative, and it can vary depending on the speed of travel through space. Therefore, to be able to move through space and time, these rare Clerics achieved IWE within the multi-dimensional universe by mentally utilizing the coordinates of the selected location and manifesting in that site.

Astral projection could be realized by their use of self-created wormholes, or by employing the cosmic strings.

For astral projections within short distances, the select few Clerics with this ability, described to Master Lingepw their experience as they mentally produced a wormhole, a tunnel in curved space-time, connecting two separate places, thus being present at both, with full consciousness in both realms.

When reaching IWE for long distances, they described their voyage as speeding through the cosmic strings portrayed as narrow tubes of energy stretched across the entire length of the universe.

Master Lingepw surmised that the strings—left over from the early cosmos—contain enormous amounts of energy and therefore warp the space-time around them. He posits that it is the approach of the strings parallel to each other that bends space-time so dynamically that it enables astral projection.

Astral projection, however, is limited to a select few Clerics and Transmutants, who by divine intervention, have been selected to reach IWE.

Kelahya stared at the myriad of screens in the Command Center on board the Olympus.

"Sutekh is somewhere there…"

"What happened to him?" Zenubus asked.

Kelahya turned. Maccabeus, Zenubus, and Artyrus faced her, eager for a response. "I freed the Reclusians from his hold and the snap injured him."

"You did what?" Maccabeus eyes widened.

"Dear friends," Kelahya smiled, "these new abilities of my Endow are as puzzling to me as they are to you. I'm learning as I go, and soon I'll be able to share with you what I am capable of doing. My Endow has transformed...into what I do not know as of yet. But it appears that at a subconscious level my desire for the

Reclusians to be freed projected to the location where Sutekh held them, and I shattered his hold on them."

"Modyor and the Clerics are now caring for the Reclusians," Artyrus added. "They are all safe, thanks to Kelahya."

"You are a sacred Cleric, Artyrus. Why couldn't you have done that before he caused such havoc?" Zenubus asked.

"Don't be impertinent, Zenubus," Maccabeus admonished.

"I understand his query." Artyrus smiled. "I am joined with the Clerics of the Fellowship and as such, I was also held captive by the energy released by the Reclusians."

"These high-level connections and space teleportation of the mind are a bit too much for me." Zenubus complained.

Maccabeus rolled his eyes. "Then remain quiet." He turned to Artyrus and stepped forward. "What is to come? How can we locate Sutekh?"

"Director Kelahya and I will Mind Fuse and join Modyor in the Chambers of the Fellowship. Once there—"

"You're leaving the Olympus?" asked Zenubus with surprise.

"No," answered Artyrus. "We'll both remain here, with you, in the Command Center…in body, and fully conscious of our surroundings. But our subconscious selves will join Modyor's and the Clerics of the Fellowship."

"How can that be?" asked Zenubus.

"Enough," interrupted Maccabeus, "let him finish."

"For now," Kelahya answered, "all I can say in the form of a logical explanation is what we can do together. When Artyrus and I enter the subconscious levels of our Endows, we're able to move across all dimensions of the known universe. I still require the assistance of Artyrus and my father to do it, but I'm learning fast."

"You always did." Zenubus smiled.

"Do what you must do," Maccabeus said. "Time is of the essence. How long will you be…traveling?"

"In terms of the amount of time it will appear to be a matter of milicons for you. You won't have to wait long for our return." Artyrus held out his hand to Kelahya. "Shall we?"

She took it, and they sat side by side.

Artyrus entered her mind, and she smiled.

"He's joined her Endow," Zenubus whispered.

Maccabeus rolled his eyes.

Kelahya and Artyrus materialized in the central nave of the Incorporeal Fellowship. Kelahya's eyes widened as she witnessed the splendor before her. The Fellowship glistened with celestial star dust, and the whiteness of the entire hall created a sense of suspension, as if erected atop an invisible cloud.

The Clerics were shrouded behind a translucent veil that distorted their images into white shadows.

At once, Artyrus fused with the Clerics and smiled with satisfaction.

Modyor glided forward and embraced his daughter. "Welcome, my child. Quite impressive, aren't they?"

"So are you Da." She melted into his arms. "The Reclusians are well?"

He nodded and turned to face Artyrus. "Welcome, Artyrus. Thank you for caring for my child."

"It's both my privilege and my honor."

Modyor faced the Clerics. "Your Excellencies, may I formally introduce my beloved daughter, Devona Kelahya."

An ethereal whisper filled her soul conveying their gratitude and admiration. Not a word was uttered, but the message was conveyed. She bowed.

"Sutekh, was not present when we retrieved the Reclusians," Modyor explained to his daughter. "He's in hiding while he recovers his strength."

"I sense that, but I cannot find him." Kelahya's frustration was evident.

"As your new abilities develop, clarity will follow." Modyor placed his arm around her shoulders. He turned toward the Clerics. "Your Excellencies, if you permit, and with your assistance, may I guide my daughter into the realm of her IWE?"

She registered an imperceptible nod from the Clerics as she was whisked into a translucent tube traveling at unnerving speed.

Cosmic strings, Modyor offered. *You've reached IWE. Your soul has absorbed celestial stardust. You've transmuted into an altered state of consciousness.*

The speed of travel slowed down, and as if suspended in the ethos, she looked down at the universe at her feet.

Sutekh!

Kelahya blinked. She realized she stood before the Clerics of the Fellowship. "Sutekh is hiding in Gortik cluster. Thank your Excellencies for enabling my ascension." She lowered her head.

As one, the Clerics spoke, "Kelahya Devona it is by divine intervention that your transmutation has occurred. Your destiny is foretold. Care for your abilities, as they are precious gifts."

Kelahya bowed.

Modyor nodded in appreciation. "Excellencies, with your leave, Artyrus, Kelahya, and I will convene on the Olympus."

Kelahya stared at her father.

He smiled and reassured her, "I'm approaching the Olympus at this very moment. Maccabeus has authorized my arrival."

With the Fellowship's encouragement, they departed.

"How were you able to locate him so quickly?" wondered Maccabeus.

"He's far too weak, having used most of his energy controlling the Reclusians," Modyor said. "Therefore, he couldn't shield himself from the combined effort of our Endows."

"How long before we reach the Gortik cluster?" asked Zenubus.

"In hexicons," Maccabeus' calculated. "Once we approach, the Olympus will hover in orbit."

"I'll lead the charge from the Athena. The battlestar cruisers and attack raptors will follow." Kelahya glanced at Zenubus.

He nodded. "Artyrus, you'll lead the other flank."

Artyrus acknowledged the command.

"Jofan and the Rebellion warriors, will cover the rest," Modyor added.

"No longer the Rebellion, Father."

Modyor smiled. "I stand corrected. *The Peace Warriors* will join the Alliance troopers. I do not see us using all of this might, but the Alliance of Stars vidlogs will document your war strategy, daughter. The overwhelming victory will confirm your strength and ability to lead."

The Athena entered the Gortik cluster at hyper speed, followed by her fleet. In a flash, she landed on Fanrahm, the planet where Sutekh had taken shelter. The fleet, and all other military battalions, hovered over the planet, awaiting further orders.

Kelahya spoke into her comm. "Artyrus, no need for you to remain in orbit. Sutekh's forces are nowhere in sight."

In a matter of hexicons, Artyrus' ship landed alongside the Athena. *Sensors confirm we have landed undetected.*

He's underground, in those escarpments to our right, Kelahya said.

Engaging camouflage array. They said in unison.

They donned the insulator suits, activated the internal oxygen and temperature controls, and clamped on the clear moldable facial cover. They converged outside the ships and scurried toward the rocky cliffs. With the cave entrance located, they rushed to opposite sides of the entrance. The race across the arid surface had left them gasping for breath.

He's in there. I am certain.

He is, Artyrus agreed.

Kelahya gave the silent signal to attack, and with stealth and speed, they entered the cave.

The meager light from the distant sun, lit only the entrance to the cave, beyond which, darkness ruled.

Kelahya and Artyrus reached out to sense their prey.

He's close. Kelahya tipped her head to the left.

Artyrus nodded.

Sutekh materialized out of the pitch black, his haggard face betraying his combative stance. "You won't survive!" he growled.

Kelahya's Endow captured his being and he crumbled to his knees. "You're under my control. This time, it is you, abominable filth, who won't survive."

Writhing in pain, Sutekh shook unconsolably. "What is this? How can you do this to me!"

"I have full dominance of your feculent body."

Sutekh contorted, an invisible force pulling and yanking every muscle and bone. "No more! It can't be, your Endow is not… you're not strong enough!"

"I am and it is. What you are experiencing throughout your repulsive body is what Kronos endured as you killed him. Only I am decelerating the process. I want you to suffer moment by moment."

"No! Stop!" Black blood oozed out of his nostrils and ears.

"There is no cessation to your slow demise." She strolled around him, watching him contort and writhe. After a few turns, she stopped and glared at him. "What? No more begging for a reprieve?"

Sutekh tried to respond, but he convulsed and choked on his own rancid blood.

"Well, then… you're ready for more. You're about to bear the agony of what you put me through when you violated my mind."

Sutekh's body jerked and his gurgling screams engulfed the cavern.

"Endure the slow disintegration of your Endow as it reaches its event horizon, and bit by bit disappears into the black hole of your putrid soul."

He squeezed his temples, his eyes bulged, green tears gushed, and his mouth opened, only this time, there was no sound, no screams, no fight. Sutekh could only inhale in short bursts, as the blood dried up.

Undeterred by his torment, Kelahya remained fixed on her prey.

"You will never hurt anyone else. Never!"

But at that very moment, her rage-filled threat fell on deaf ears.

Sutekh is dead, Kelahya.

She blinked and stared at Sutekh's inert body. She stepped towards it and kicked it several times. He didn't respond.

Artyrus approached the body and placed his ungloved hand on Sutekh's forehead. "He's dead. You can sense it."

"I can, but I wanted him to suffer more. Much more."

"You unleashed and enormous amount of energy. He couldn't tolerate it. He was nothing but a paper doll amidst the flames of your anger."

"His death is not enough…"

"You'll get more once you show his body to the members of the Alliance of Stars. You'll get more when you join forces with your father. You'll get more when your rule brings the peace and stability we've all been striving for."

Kelahya glanced at Artyrus, and gradually regained her composure, then tapped her communicator. When she spoke, she did so with unflinching resolve. "Sutekh is dead. Let us crush his armies, then return to the Olympus and celebrate our victory."

The comm erupted with the triumphant cheers of her elated troops.

Artyrus embraced her.

She leaned her head on his shoulder and sighed. *It's gone… the anxiety.*

And? What's left?

Calm. She paused. *I feel free…unbound.*

He tightened his embrace.

The great hall of the Assembly erupted in thunderous applause as Kelahya made her triumphant entrance. The gigantic vidscreens that lined the precinct, projected the image of this beautiful and commanding woman. She carried the inert body of Sutekh slung over her shoulder.

Images of huge crowds, gathered in streets and city squares, were broadcast as well, to ensure that all bore witness to her triumph, and celebrated the elation of having won the war.

As the image of her face filled the screens, she smiled, and the din of the crowd slowly ebbed toward silence.

She tossed Sutekh's body to the floor, with a gesture of utter contempt. "Behold what's become of this parasite." She paused for effect. "He will trouble us no more."

The crowds roared their approval and chanted her name endlessly.

She raised her arms to elicit their silence. "After hearing of his death, his so-called armies, capitulated. Let this be a lesson to all who seek to destroy the Alliance of Stars and the League of One!"

A fanfare exploded throughout the Assembly Hall. The crowd erupted with more cheers and applause.

In due course, Kelahya raised her hand, and the music ceased. "It is my great honor to welcome to the Alliance of Stars and the League of One, our Peace Warriors, without whom, we would have been unable to defeat our enemy, liberate the Clerics of the Incorporeal Fellowship, and recuperate the Reclusians. All hail to them."

Artyrus, clad in his battle uniform, with the seal of the Fellowship hanging around his neck, joined Kelahya.

She turned to him and reached for his hand. Their Endows joined, and their luminous essence permeated one and all.

Murmurs of awe flowed from everyone's lips.

"Welcome, your Excellency, Peace Warrior Artyrus Druidiam." Zenubus bowed.

The crowd cheered but was silenced by the sudden entrance of a large contingent of warriors, led by Jofan, marching in unison into the hall.

"Welcome, Peace Warriors!" yelled Maccabeus.

The crowd echoed his words.

"Hail. Hail. Hail," reverberated through halls and cities everywhere.

Kelahya raised her hand once more, and everyone quieted down.

"Citizens of the Alliance of Stars, it is my pleasure to introduce Modyor Devon, direct descendant of Nestor, Supreme Pontiff of the Galactic Sanctuary, and Scribe of the Incorporeal Fellowship. My beloved father."

Modyor appeared from behind Kelahya, clad in the ethereal vestments of the Incorporeal Fellowship, and donning the medallion of Supreme Pontiff across his chest.

The crowd gasped in wonder at the image of the legendary giant, who, until now, they had only heard of in prophecy. The sight of the man, who many had believed to be no more than myth, caused humanoids in the inhabited universe, to sink as one to their knees, overcome by a spiritual force none had ever experienced before. Prayers and hymns broke out spontaneously. Many wept, others simply froze in stunned silence.

Nestor was real.

"Greetings, all," he said at last. "It is my greatest pleasure to finally stand before you." He smiled broadly.

The crowd cheered.

"I am honored," his thunderous voice silenced the crowd, "to serve alongside my daughter, Kelahya Devona, as she carries out her prophesied duties as Supreme Commander of the Alliance of Stars."

Kelahya shot a surprised glance at her father.

You were meant to unite the anointed tasks. Modyor reassured her.

The Augurs foretold this?

Yes.

"This is what the Scriptures tell us," Modyor addressed the assembly and the throngs that watched from far and near. His voice softened to a silken smoothness, enveloping in mysticism all who heard him. "One shall emerge, after endless years of conflict and suffering, one who will bring finality to war and tyranny, one who shall rule with justice and compassion. One who shall protect and defend the rights and freedoms of all species in our vast universe. One who shall arise from the lineage of Nestor and be known as the Great Liberator. One who shall inherit the mantle of Poliate and assume the title of Divine Ruler and Conciliator. One who shall unite the lineages of Nestor and Poliate. The fulfillment of this prophecy has been confirmed by the venerable Augurs, and sanctioned by the Clerics of the Incorporeal Fellowship. This truth is indisputable."

Modyor paused to allow his words to permeate his audience before continuing. "The Incorporeal Fellowship has decreed that our beloved and esteemed Prime Healer and Peace Warrior, Artyrus Druidiam, shall remain at her side," he paused, "as her anointed mate."

A whirr of curiosity erupted.

Modyor smiled and raised an eyebrow.

The crowd hushed.

He turned to face the couple. "It is prophesized that through their offspring a new species will emerge, with the genetic makeup of stability, harmony, and exceptional mental mastery. Their entry into our world will ensure peace and prosperity throughout the known universe for millennia to come."

Da, do the Augurs have any more surprises?

That is for you to discover, my child.

He turned to the audience with a proud grin on his face. "I give you my daughter, Kelahya Devona, Director of the League of One, Supreme Commander of the Alliance of Stars, Liberator, Conciliator." He stepped aside and ushered her in as the new ruler of the universe.

Kelahya hesitated.

You are their leader, my child. Lead them.

She stepped forward, hand in hand with Artyrus.

Artyrus released her hand and eased back. *This is your moment Kelahya. Own it.*

She nodded and stared out at the Assembly.

The vidscreens showed vast multitudes gathered in cities on planets spread throughout the galaxies, and Kelahya sensed everyone's eyes locked onto to her.

A deafening silence ensued.

She moved toward Modyor and raised his arm, then reached for her mate and drew him to her side. "Together, my father, Artyrus, and I, will create a future where there shall be peace. But we shall not do it alone. Each and every one of you, is vital to the peace and prosperity to come. I pledge my devotion to you and ask that you pledge your devotion to me. I promise you justice and an undying commitment to each and every citizen in the Alliance of Stars. Upon my life, I make this vow to you."

The fanfares that broke out were instantly drowned by cheers and shouts. To a person, there was, for the first time, a true belief that tyranny and aggression were at an end and that peace had finally come to the universe.

Biography

V. & D. Povall are a husband-and-wife team who partner in the creation of tales that capture your imagination and entertain you. With rich international family backgrounds, they bring to the page a wealth of experiences and interesting points of view.

Thanks to their rich international family backgrounds they know different cultures and languages and bring to their writing a broad understanding of human nature.

D. Povall

David is a producer, director, and actor who has been involved in films, television, theater, and commercials. He wrote his first play when he entered the field of Theater Arts, and over the years has written poetry, short stories, and screenplays. For a time, he lived in Mexico, surrounded by historians—his mother being one of them—as well as anthropologists, and archeologists. He traveled to remote areas of the country and even dabbled in Nahuatl, the language spoken by the Aztecs.

V. Povall

Victoria, born in Mexico, grew up in a family of artists and storytellers. Her father was the Director of the Classical Theater of Mexico City, and after returning to his homeland Spain, he was appointed Artistic Director of the Royal Theater. Her French mother was a well-known theatrical costume designer and esthéticienne. From an early age, Victoria participated in the critique process of her father's novels, screenplays, and plays, as well as her mother's designs. She wrote and staged her first play at the age of fourteen. This creative practice propelled her lifelong passion for teaching—or as Victoria calls it, storytelling. Her doctoral dissertation focused on transformation—stimulating one's audience to imagine the future.

Other published books:

The Gift of the Twin Houses: Book One of the Perils of a Reluctant Psychic

Secrets of Innocence: Book Two of the Perils of a Reluctant Psychic

Jackal in Mourning: Book Three of the Perils of a Reluctant Psychic

For more information, please visit their website at www.2authors.com.